A SONG EVERLASTING

A SONG
EVERLASTING

Ha Jin

PANTHEON BOOKS | NEW YORK

Published in the United States by Pantheon Books,
a division of Penguin Random House LLC, New York, and distributed
in Canada by Penguin Random House Canada Limited, Toronto.

Pantheon Books and colophon
are registered trademarks of Penguin Random House LLC.

Library of Congress Cataloging-in-Publication Data
Name: Jin, Ha, [date] author.
Title: A song everlasting: a novel / Ha Jin.
Description: First edition. New York: Pantheon Books, 2021
Identifiers: LCCN 2020047331 (print). LCCN 2020047332 (ebook).
ISBN 9781524748791 (hardcover). ISBN 9781524748807 (ebook).
Classification: LCC PS3560.I6 S66 2021 (print) |
LCC PS3560.I6 (ebook) | DDC 813/.54—dc23
LC record available at lccn.loc.gov/2020047331
LC ebook record available at lccn.loc.gov/2020047332

www.pantheonbooks.com

Jacket images: (birds) Hibrida13 / Getty Images; (background) Roc Canals / Getty Images
Jacket design by Jenny Carrow

Printed in the United States of America
First Edition

9 8 7 6 5 4 3 2 1

For Lisha

PART ONE

THE EVENING'S PERFORMANCE had been a success. After the finale, Yao Tian and his fellow performers from the People's Ensemble gathered onstage and bowed to the six hundred people in the auditorium. As he was making his way down the side stairs, he caught sight of a tall man at the end of the front row. The man stood there, smiling at him, while the crowd filed out the back and side doors. Soon he approached Tian. "Teacher Yao," he said in English, his voice warm. "I'm so delighted to see you in New York. Your voice is as spectacular as it was a decade ago!"

Now Tian recognized him. "Han Yabin, what a miracle!" Without thinking, he cried out in English, which he could speak well.

He paused, hesitant to hug his friend, aware of his colleagues observing them in amazement. Some of them might make a mental note of his warm greetings to this local man and report it to their leaders back home. So, instead, Tian held out his hand. Yabin shook it, then leaned in and whispered, "Can we have a drink nearby, Teacher Yao?"

By rule, Tian could not accept such an invitation without permission from the head of his troupe, so he excused himself and went up to Director Meng. "I just ran into an old friend," Tian began. "Can I spend a little time with him tonight? I'll be back to the hotel soon."

Meng's heavy-lidded eyes fixed on him, alarmed. Obviously he felt uneasy to let anyone in the troupe go out of his control here. Still, he said, "That's fine, but don't be gone too long."

"I'll be back before midnight for sure."

Out in the streets of downtown Flushing, the air smelled of rainwater. It was already nine o'clock. Pedestrians rushed past Tian and Yabin as they walked down Roosevelt Avenue together. Around them, people wove brazenly through traffic to cross the street, heedless of the honking cars. The ground trembled as a semi-trailer rolled past, its side printed with Chinese characters: FRESH VEGETABLES AND FRUITS.

"Heavens, this is like China," Tian said. "It's like in the middle of a provincial town."

"Flushing is like a big county seat, isn't it?" Yabin laughed and got hold of Tian's arm to guide him through the bustling thoroughfare.

The laugh reminded Tian of when they were both young in Beijing. Yabin had been dashing, energetic; he organized private concerts, poetry readings, literary salons, art exhibitions. Before his cultural activities were banned by the police, he had often invited Tian to sing at his events, paying him promptly and generously. He'd been one of the few young Chinese in Beijing who could mingle easily with foreigners. His handsome looks opened many doors, and his two years' studying at Oxford (sponsored by the Ministry of Education) taught him to speak English fluently, with a British flair, like a well-educated gentleman from Hong Kong. Americans and Brits had often assumed his accent was an affectation, and some even mocked him, saying, "Your beautiful English puts me to shame." But Yabin didn't bother to acknowledge their slights, and never changed his way of speaking. Last Tian had heard, his old friend had quit his English lectureship at his university because he was not allowed to keep a relationship with a foreign woman teacher and he had gone abroad again, but Tian hadn't known he had come to New York.

Yabin still looked elegant. He was living here in Flushing now, he told Tian. He'd lost his Beijing residential status—it had been canceled by the police.

He took Tian to a bar called Dreamland at 38th Avenue and Prince Street. The place was crowded and noisy even on a Wednesday night, filled with young professional men and women in suits. Yabin knew the manager of the place, a thin man with brushy hair, who quickly led them to a quiet table in the back room, where a karaoke machine was still on. A tallish waitress turned off the Hong Kong music and pulled an iPad out of the pocket of her orange apron. Yabin ordered Jinmen sorghum baijiu and suggested Tian try it too, saying it was Taiwan's iconic drink, smooth and mellow—it wouldn't go to your head. Yabin loved Jinmen even more than Mao-tai. He ordered it the American way, on the rocks. Tian didn't drink liquor and ordered a Heineken. He had to be careful and avoid hard alcohol that might hurt his vocal cords.

In no time the waitress returned, holding a tray loaded with their orders, a bottle of beer and four fingers of the sorghum baijiu in a squad glass. She closed the door with her hip and then served their drinks. A thin platinum band flashed on her finger as she placed a bowl of mixed nuts on the table.

When she'd left, Yabin said, "Now we can relax and enjoy ourselves."

Although Tian was eager to hear about his friend's life in New York, he was also tired, and nervous about spending too much time with him. He feared that his director might suspect he had an ulterior motive in meeting with a local. Quite often, members of cultural delegations—consisting of artists, musicians, actors, writers, scholars—had stolen away while visiting foreign countries, joining relatives or friends there so as to avoid returning to China. Now their troupe, a group of twenty performers from the People's Ensemble in Beijing, was on the last leg of its five-city tour in the States. Thus far, everything had gone well, so Director Meng seemed anxious, afraid they might fall short of a complete success if someone walked away on their final night. At this very moment Meng was probably fretting about Tian's absence, restless like an ant on a hot pan.

Yabin gave Tian his business card, which stated that he had earned his MBA from Fordham University and was an insurance broker now, with an office on Main Street in Flushing. Tian commended him, saying this was extraordinary, a model of success. "Obviously America is a land of opportunities," he said, though aware how stale those words were.

Yabin shook his head. "That's just a myth, Teacher Yao. Opportunities are mainly for the rich and powerful here, the same as in China. I'm no different from other FOJs—fresh off the jet. We all have to struggle hard to get anywhere."

"Please, just call me Tian," he said. He was thirty-seven, only one or two years older than Yabin, and preferred the American way of addressing someone by their first name.

"All right, Tian. The truth is, I'm just like most people here who have to work their asses off."

"Still, you're free and there's no one lording it over you."

Yabin laughed, as if Tian had said something vacuous. As Tian was wondering what he wanted from him, Yabin revealed his intention, saying, "There'll be a celebration of the National Day on October 10, organized by the Great China Cultural Association. Will you be able to sing a couple of songs for them?"

Tian was surprised, uncertain how to respond—that is Taiwan's National Day, not a holiday in the People's Republic, whose National Day was October 1. Few people on the mainland even know Taiwan's National Day, which is called "Double Tens" (October 10). Tian asked, "Who's sponsoring the celebration? The Taiwanese government?"

"Not at all. Some Chinese immigrant communities in New York and New Jersey are sponsoring it, though a lot of the people are from Taiwan. If you can sing for them, I can negotiate a fee of four thousand dollars for you."

Tian knew that Yabin was good at delivering what he promised. Four grand was almost a quarter of Tian's annual salary, and his daughter Tingting was about to apply for an international prep school in Beijing, which required him to pay twenty thousand yuan as the first installment of the tuition—nearly three thousand dollars. The money Yabin offered was significant, worth the risk. He agreed to sing for them.

"Great, they'll be thrilled to hear this," Yabin said. "They've never had a singer of your caliber before."

Tian knew they'd surely use his name to promote the event, but there was something else that needed arranging. He said, "Look,

Yabin, I can sing for them, but my return flight to Beijing is already booked for tomorrow. I'm not sure I can change it. And also, I'd need a place to stay until the event on Saturday."

"I'll ask my secretary to rebook a flight for you. Rest assured, it will work out. You can stay with me after you check out of your hotel."

"Thank you so much, Yabin. I'm not sure I can get permission from my director, but I'll do my best."

Tian had his flight information on his phone, which he took out and sent to Yabin's phone. They agreed that Yabin would hear from him early the next morning for the final answer. His friend was elated, saying he hoped they could collaborate more often in the future. He told Tian, "Chinese immigrants here are too materialistic and should have more cultural life. Your appearance will make a difference."

What Yabin said pleased Tian. He promised to consider Yabin's future offers.

Stepping out of the bar, they said good night. Tian walked back toward the Sheraton, where he and his colleagues were staying. The neon sign glowed atop the hotel building and made it appear more imposing than it did in daylight. Beyond its domed roof a single star was flashing and glittering against a vast constellation.

Director Meng was taken aback when Tian told him that he'd agreed to sing for the local cultural organization. "You can't do this to me, Yao Tian!" he said. "We're flying back tomorrow. If you stay behind, I'll be the one who gets in trouble. And you might be viewed as a transgressor of our travel rules."

"But I'll stay behind just two or three days," Tian said, his temper flaring.

"You can't control people's tongues, can you?" Meng said.

"Give me a break! The Chinese communities here need me and I'm obligated to sing for them, to promote the cultural life of the immigrants. Please let our ensemble's leaders know I'm going back, just by another flight. I'll show up at work next Monday, like everyone else. Besides, there're more than two hundred employees in our ensemble and nobody will notice my absence. Why make such a big fuss? It's not like I'm going to defect or something."

"Comrade Yao Tian, you don't understand politics." Meng pointed his stubby forefinger at Tian's lean face. "You've been behaving willfully and breaking the rules. How can our leaders trust you in the future? Besides, who can help you if you get mugged or kidnapped here?"

"I'll be responsible for myself. I'm an adult."

"No, I am responsible for you."

"Please let me be in charge of myself for a couple of days."

They went on arguing for a few more minutes. When Meng realized Tian wasn't giving in, he relented some. "All right, you've already started to change your flight, and I might not be able to stop you. But you must promise me you'll show up at work next week as usual, or I might have to let our leaders know."

"You have my word."

"To be honest, Tian, if I were you, I wouldn't run such a risk. People might think less of you if they knew you stayed behind to make money. Nobody is supposed to take a side gig like what you're doing."

"Then please don't let them know."

"I can cover for you only for two days."

They shook on that, though the director's face was still sour. He must have felt he had no choice but to grant Tian permission, because Tian was their premier soloist. Yet seeing Meng so frustrated, Tian added, "Director Meng, don't take this too hard. My wife and daughter are in Beijing, where I have a nice home and a rising career. How could I possibly go elsewhere? I just bumped into an old friend who offered me an opportunity to sing. Doesn't our country encourage more cultural exchanges with Taiwanese people as preparatory work for the national unification?" He offered this as a possible explanation to their leaders if Meng had to answer their inquiry, though Tian knew people could see through him—he was staying behind to make money.

"Fine, I can see your point," Meng said tiredly. "Just don't overstay, and make sure to get back early next week. Keep in mind that I don't approve of what you're doing, but I simply cannot dissuade you."

Tian nodded, realizing that this was the excuse Meng would expect him to make if any trouble cropped up.

To be fair, Meng had never acted like a boss. He respected the members of their troupe and said he felt lucky to work with them— many of the singers and instrumentalists and dancers had national reputations. Tian knew that from Meng's point of view, his change of flights was unlikely to signal a defection. If Tian had truly meant to flee, he wouldn't have bothered to speak to him about staying behind. Meng was already sixty-two; in three or four years he would retire, and there was no reason for him to be strict and rob Tian of this opportunity. He didn't ask Tian how much he was making for the October 10 performance, but Tian understood that he owed Meng a generous gift when he got back.

Before going to bed, he called his wife, Shuna, and told her about his delayed return. She was pleased to hear about his opportunity to pick up some cash, but urged him to be cautious and avoid making any public statements.

2

AFTER HE CHECKED OUT OF THE HOTEL the next morning, Tian walked to Yabin's apartment on 45th Avenue in Flushing. He hadn't expected to find Yabin living with a girlfriend, Barrie, a white woman who worked as a nurse at a hospital in Queens. She was not in when he arrived, but Yabin pointed at a photo of her and said she was his girlfriend and they were living together. Tian had always thought of Yabin as a perpetual bachelor. Now it felt intrusive to be staying in their one-bedroom apartment. Apart from impinging on their privacy, he needed his own peace and quiet, to focus on the performance ahead. Based on the fee they'd pay him, he had proposed a two-song set for the celebration: "At a Faraway Place," a 1930s love song, and "Song of the Plateau," a theme song of the movie *A Visitor from an Ice Mountain,* which originally appeared in the early 1960s. It had an Islamic melody, lively and exotic. Both might be known to some older overseas Chinese who were nostalgic about the fine old songs. Taiwanese immigrants often couldn't stomach the propaganda songs popular on the mainland, and also Tian wanted to avoid the current Hong Kong and Taiwanese hits because they might already be too familiar. Yabin passed Tian's choices on to the event organizers so that, if they approved the songs, they could have an appropriate band arranged for him.

As soon as Tian sat down in Yabin's living room, he told his friend that he didn't want to invade his and Barrie's privacy. He wondered whether Yabin could find a motel for him nearby. Yabin smiled and assured him, "There're a good number of family-run hostels in this area and I know one just a block away."

He made a phone call and then told Tian that it was settled—
the cost for the room was seventy-five dollars a night and he could
check in anytime. Yabin assured him that he could pick up the bill
for him. After lunch at a restaurant called Red Chopsticks on Kis-
sena Boulevard, they set out for the hostel. Tian liked the place,
owned by a Korean-Chinese family. It was a two-story brick building, and his room, clean and quiet, had three beds in it. He seemed
to be the only guest there, the adjacent rooms all vacant. The low
occupancy made the place very peaceful. The hostel even offered
homemade breakfast.

On Saturday evening, Yabin drove him to Chinatown in lower
Manhattan, where the venue was on Eldridge Street. Tian was surprised to see a full-size auditorium instead of a dining hall. Chinese
immigrants often liked to combine entertainment with a banquet,
so usually such a celebration would be held in a place with dozens
of dining tables. Tian was glad that this event would have nothing
to do with eating. The auditorium looked expensive and a little
solemn. Yabin said with a knowing smile, "They moved the event
to this bigger venue because of you. When I said you had agreed to
sing for them, they all went into raptures. Many of them had seen
you sing at the CCTV's Spring Festival's gala, so they feel honored
by your presence here."

Together they got into a greenroom behind the stage, where some
of the performers were already gathered. A pair of flat monitors
was pinned to the walls in the lounge, allowing everyone to watch
the performances as they happened. He was to close the show, so
for now he could relax. He greeted the others in the room, who
were mingling around a table spread with soft drinks, tea and coffee, pastries, cheese, and fruits. Among the performers there were a
few dancers and musicians. A fortyish woman sat alone. She wore a
loose outfit—a peach tunic with long sleeves and beige slacks. Her
seemingly casual clothes belied her well-proportioned figure, which
showed when she stood and went over to the table to pour a cup
of coffee. She had an oval face and shoulder-length hair. As Yabin
introduced Tian to her, her eyes sparkled. She said, "I'm Tan Mai, a
pi-pa player. It's an honor to meet you in person, Mr. Yao." Her crisp
accent indicated that she must be from the Yangtze delta.

Tian had heard of her and knew she had gained some recognition in North America, but he wasn't sure how accomplished she was. He mumbled a few polite words and then sat down in an armchair. He rested his head on the back of the chair and closed his eyes. He tried to doze while the others were chatting. But from time to time he glanced at the monitor on the right—the show was already under way.

A spindly official from the Taipei Economic and Cultural Office in New York, which was somewhat like Taiwan's consulate here because there was no formal relationship between the U.S. and the island state anymore, went onstage and spoke in refined official Mandarin about the significance of the National Day to the Chinese diaspora: Whether one supported unification or Taiwan's independence, they were all Chinese sharing the same language and culture. Indeed, the audience was composed of people from many parts of the world, but mostly from mainland China and Taiwan, and some were American-born. The official then read out a letter from President Ma Ying-jeou, who congratulated the Chinese in America for their love of peace and for their achievements in life and work.

Then the show began. First a children's choir came on the stage, all the boys in navy suits and striped ties and all the girls in red skirts and white shirts. They were from a local church and sang two hymns; their singing was sweet and serene, yet quite passionate. Tian had rarely heard Christian hymns like those, whose swelling melodies he enjoyed. It was refreshing for him to hear the religious songs at such a secular gathering. The next act was a solo piece of traditional Chinese music played on the erhu, a two-stringed violin of sorts; the player was very young, probably under twenty, but clearly he had many years' training and played vigorously, with bravado. But the music was sad, even heart-wrenching. Indeed, Tian couldn't recall having ever heard an uplifting composition for the erhu.

After the erhu player came a pair of young acrobats, a man and a woman, each riding a tall unicycle while the band was playing a brisk tune to urge them on. Having circled a few laps around the stage, they stopped to start tossing bowls onto their heads with their feet. They kicked up the bowls one after another, all landing atop their heads. In spite of the extraordinary skill and cheerful spirit, it was just a standard Chinese acrobatic routine, of which Tian had seen plenty when he was a young boy. It bored him.

Tan Mai appeared onstage next. She sat on a chair and held her pi-pa, a strummed lutelike instrument with four strings. She explained that the piece she was about to play was called "Night Thoughts," an ancient composition by a Buddhist monk in the ninth century. Recently she had stumbled upon fragments of this sheet music in an ancient temple outside Hangzhou, and she was still trying to restore it, or "put it together," as she told the audience. Tian was amazed that she would perform something still in the making. But once she started to play, he felt a gentle force transporting him to a remote tranquil landscape, where there were woods and valleys and babbling streams, a bright moon hanging over a mountain ridge. The music was slow, at ease, but full of texture and small surprises, completely different from anything else he'd ever heard on the pi-pa, which usually produces rapid and crisp notes. As he listened with rapt attention, he realized this was a genuine piece of ancient music, deep and peaceful, infused with passion and memories. Beyond any doubt it was a masterpiece! He was touched, his eyes turning misty and his nose stuffy. But the audience didn't respond warmly when Tan Mai finished, and the applause was sparse.

She seemed to expect the lukewarm response. She said she was going to play another piece, which was livelier and her own composition. "It's called 'Leaves Flying in Autumn,'" she told the audience.

She began to play. It was a lovely and joyful piece, typical of pi-pa music, full of energy and verve, so different from the traditional piece about fallen leaves in autumn, a season that suggests the decline of vitality and the twilight of life. As she was plucking away with all five fingers of her right hand, her body seemed to become part of the instrument and her head swayed with the rhythm. Her face grew more animated and her smile turned radiant and at moments mysterious. Tian could tell that she was a virtuoso, a unique artist. He wished he had seen her perform before so that he could have talked with her and found out more about her. Surely her kind of mastery must have resulted from a great deal of hard work.

The audience went wild when she was done. She stood and bowed. They called for an encore, but she said she was sorry and couldn't stay any longer. After another bow, she hurried off the stage, hugging her pi-pa.

Tian could hardly focus on the act that followed, an umbrella dance, which was rather traditional and performed by a troupe from a local arts school. The dozen dancers were elegant, their limbs supple, and the choreography well done, every movement poised and graceful. The whole stage was transformed into a scene from a rainy day, pedestrians raising umbrellas and walking in misty streets. But Tian's mind was still with the pi-pa player, who he'd heard had lived in America for many years and was probably teaching at a college or contracted with an orchestra.

When his cue came, he went onstage, stood in front of the microphone, and began to sing. He hadn't often sung the old love song "At a Faraway Place," but, good at folk songs, he managed to do this one naturally. While singing, inspired by the lyrics, he imagined a young man on horseback stopping on a mountain ridge and chanting to his beloved far away. He could feel his voice cascading and, at moments, holding the audience under its spell. The next piece, the movie song, was in his regular repertoire, so he sang with more ease. Still, both felt like routine work to him, similar to his performances back in China, though the audience here responded with fervent applause. As he was about to leave the stage, a middle-aged man in a back row stood up and called, "Hey, Yao Tian, sing for us 'A Happy Song Flying from the Green Fields'!"

Tian was rattled—he hadn't sung that song in a decade. It had been one of his hits. It was a piece of sheer propaganda, filled with insipid lines like "Let us work hard to modernize our great country. / There are heroes everywhere." For years Tian was known for this song, which was broadcast every day in schools and factories and even in military barracks. He used to think that song was his lucky charm that had brought him fame and opportunities. Then in the late 1990s the song faded from public life, probably due to the change of people's interest and taste. Tian felt deeply ashamed to be associated with it now. In fact, he'd given much thought to this change of public acceptance, to the vicissitudes of popularity. Isn't it tragic to see your signature song die before you do?

Unsure whether the man standing in a back row was serious or just heckling him, Tian shook his head and waved at him, trying to convey that he couldn't sing that song anymore, and that he begged for his understanding. He hurried back to the greenroom, flustered, his face hot.

But he couldn't stay in there for long. Yabin came and beckoned to him, saying, "Tian, the sponsors, the organizers, and the other performers all would like to take photos with you. Please honor their wish."

Tian got back onstage again for the group photograph. A handful of reporters from the local Chinese-language media were there too, and shot a number of pictures. It looked like one or two of the shots would appear in the Chinese newspapers.

Yabin drove him back to Queens. The immense Manhattan Bridge over the East River looked more striking at night, glowing with torrents of automobiles. When the water was behind them, most of the streetlamps were wrapped in orange halos, some shining against damp foliage and some against the shimmering sky. Remembering Tan Mai's performance, Tian said to Yabin, "That pi-pa player is already a master—how come I had never seen her play before? Are you sure that people didn't come to the show mainly for her?"

"Do you think I was lying when I said the organizers changed the venue for you?" Yabin asked teasingly.

"I'm sure she must be quite famous," Tian said, feeling a twinge of envy as he often did when he met a truly accomplished artist, even though he viewed himself as an artist.

"She does have an excellent reputation and she performs all over the world. But the Chinese here are not familiar with her music yet, and don't know how to appreciate her because she plays differently from the traditional pi-pa players. Many of them came tonight mainly to see you."

"I was very impressed by the way she played."

"Me too. In my opinion she's absolutely an original, but she's not as famous as you."

"I loved her first piece more than her second one. It's a piece of genuine ancient music. It touched me. I respect her more for not catering to the audience by playing it. How long has she lived in America, do you know?"

"About fifteen years, according to her bio."

"It's phenomenal that a Chinese musician like her could thrive here. I'm sure she'll become a star."

"Her reputation is on the rise indeed. She'll grow into a major figure in the music world."

"She's someone to watch."

Yabin didn't want to pay Tian by check, afraid he might not be able to cash it here or deposit it in Beijing. Tian actually had an account at the Bank of America, but he still preferred banknotes. Yabin told Tian that he had the four thousand dollars in cash, which they should stop at his place to pick up. Tian was more than willing to go with him.

Barrie was at home, just having returned from a long shift at the hospital. Her sky-blue poncho was hanging on the top of the closet door in the short hallway. At the sight of Tian, she said, "Welcome! It's an honor to have you here."

He replied in English, "It's very nice to meet you. You have a lovely home." Indeed, the apartment was elegantly furnished, the faux-antique furniture brand-new, and there were two vases of flowers, one of jasmines and the other of striped orchids, the blooms like butterflies.

Seated on the puffy sofas, they chatted idly. Barrie was also an immigrant, from Argentina, a blonde with green eyes. She spoke flawless English—Tian assumed she must have grown up in the States. She said she had listened to one of his albums and was very fond of his songs. He wasn't sure which songs she was referring to. In the U.S., his albums were mostly pirated by Hong Kong poachers. Barrie crossed her long-calved legs, her feet in flip-flops. Her ankles were shapely and muscular, and so were her arms and hands. He wondered how she and Yabin got along. Barrie seemed more like a country girl, while Yabin was urbane. Back in Beijing, he'd been known for having fine taste in women and for changing girlfriends frequently.

Barrie told Tian, "Yabin was over the moon that you were performing tonight. Everyone was thrilled to have you."

Yabin uncorked a bottle of white wine and poured a glass for each of them. Tian touched his with theirs as they said, "Congratulations on a successful performance!"

Tian took a mouthful and then set the glass down. By habit he avoided drinking.

His flight was early the next morning, so after Yabin handed him a thick kraft envelope stuffed with cash, Tian stayed for a few more minutes, then took his leave. It was raining again, and Yabin drove him back to the family hostel. He told the owner's wife to give Tian a wake-up call at five a.m.

"Of course," she promised. "We won't let him miss his plane."

3

AT JFK AIRPORT THE NEXT MORNING, Tian bought a jar of Krönung instant coffee for Director Meng. Meng had grown fond of coffee in recent years and frequented Starbucks in Beijing, but like most Chinese coffee drinkers, he didn't know how to brew it at home. Tian paid almost thirty dollars for the jar, the most expensive kind in the duty-free shop. He'd go and see Meng as soon as he got back, to show that he had kept his word.

But when he arrived at work on Monday, he found Meng disconcerted. The man looked startled as he raised his big head to see Tian stepping into his office, which was deep inside a rehearsal hall. "Well, surprise, surprise!" he said in jest, rubbing his eyebrows. "I thought you'd disappeared on the American continent."

"I'm back without leaving behind a hair," Tian said, and placed the jar of coffee on his desk. "This is for you." He twisted his shoulders, still sore and stiff from the long flight back.

"Thanks, Tian. This must be gourmet stuff."

"It's a genuine German product—you'll like it."

Meng put the present into the bottom drawer of his desk. He said in a low voice, "I have to tell you that you might be in trouble. There'll be a meeting about you this afternoon, in our conference room, and all the leaders will be there."

Tian was surprised, because their ensemble, a state-owned work unit, had more than ten leaders above Meng, who were all Party members and had been put into office as "salary drawers" without the ability to contribute anything. He asked, "Why? Am I supposed to attend? Look, I'm back on time and there's no reason to make such a fuss."

"They don't know you're back yet. I'll call Secretary Niu right away and let her know this was a misunderstanding. For some reason word got around that you wouldn't come back anymore. Of course most people take it as a mere rumor at this moment."

Niu was their Party boss, so Tian was stunned, then begged Meng, "Please tell them I was just trying to pick up some extra cash for my daughter's tuition. Don't make this political. You know me—I've never been political. I'm just a singer."

"Boy, now you're scared—you look like you're about to pee your pants. What did I tell you back in New York? Didn't I say not to run the risk?"

"How did they come to know I was delayed in my return? Did you reveal my plan to somebody?"

"Tian, I'm not that low, not that stupid. If I had squealed on you, that would've amounted to turning myself in. I gave you the approval and would be held accountable if anything happened to you."

"Then how in the world did they know I had another engagement there?"

"It was obvious like a fat louse on a bald head. Everybody in our delegation could see that you were not on the return flight. I'll tell you what, stay put and keep your composure. I'll contact Secretary Niu this minute and let her know you're back—no damage is done. If the meeting is still on this afternoon, you should be there to defend yourself."

"Should I mention you gave me the approval?"

Meng lowered his head; his mind seemed to be churning. He raised his thick-lidded eyes and said, "Why not just tell them the truth? After you changed your flight, you came to tell me about that. In other words, you initiated the whole thing."

"Fine, I can do that."

Tian called his wife, Shuna, and told her about his trouble. She was disturbed but said he must remain as composed as though he'd done nothing wrong—even if they accused him of violating rules,

his offense wouldn't be dealt with too harshly. He was the lead
tenor in the People's Ensemble, a major company of theatrical performances in Beijing, and he should be able to find work elsewhere
easily if they fired him. Over the years he had been approached
time and again by some troupes in other cities that offered him
better-paying jobs, but he wouldn't leave Beijing. Nowadays high-
speed trains and frequent flights were so ubiquitous that he could
work in another city while still living in the capital. His wife was a
history professor at Tsinghua University, specializing in the Ming
Dynasty. Today, a Monday, was her busiest day of the week—she
had to go without further delay to teach her graduate seminar.
Before hanging up, she said to Tian, "People can get jealous. If they
want to confiscate the money you made, just let them have it."

His gut told him this whole thing might not be so simple, but
Shuna was right that for now he should remain calm. So he stayed
in another rehearsal hall in the basement, doing some vocal practice, and waited to hear from his director.

Early in the afternoon, Meng phoned, saying Tian should attend
the meeting at three o'clock. He reminded Tian to be patient and
explain everything clearly, as they had agreed that morning. Tian
felt a tad relieved, hoping that the leaders would be lenient if he
told them the whole story. Since he was already back in person, he
shouldn't be too perturbed. He'd better play innocent with them.
As long as he could escape disciplinary action, he'd swallow any
criticism.

The meeting was in their small conference room, about twenty
people seated around an oblong mahogany table. The atmosphere
struck Tian as ominous. He didn't talk with anyone, even though
he knew some of them well. He just nodded at them. Still some
wouldn't return his nodding. Secretary Niu sat at the head of the
table and motioned for him to sit down three or four people away
from her, near a high window. Then she gave a sheaf of a Xeroxed
handout to the young man who was a flutist and headed the Communist Youth League of their ensemble, and asked him to pass it
around. Tian picked up his sheet and was shocked to see one of
the group photos that had been taken onstage in Manhattan with

himself, Yabin, and his colleagues. What does this mean? he asked himself, but couldn't find an answer. His heart buckled and his head began to spin as he noticed a faint smirk cross Niu's flat face. She was close to fifty and had been assigned to head their ensemble mainly because her husband had transferred to the capital as a vice minister in the State Council, so hers was more like a spousal appointment, considering she didn't even have a college degree and knew little about the performing arts. Usually she had been polite to Tian, and in a way he liked her outspokenness and gusty temper.

When all the attendees were seated, Niu waved the Xeroxed sheet and said in a grating voice, "This was sent over by the Ministry of Culture. Comrade Yao Tian owes us an explanation." She turned to him. "What on earth made you join the ranks of those reactionaries? Didn't you know this would contravene our government's policies?"

"I can't follow you, Secretary Niu," Tian said honestly. "They invited me to sing two songs on their National Day. I knew Taiwan's National Day was different from ours, but they were celebrating China as one nation, and I joined them in that. What's wrong with that? I can't comprehend. Doesn't our government always encourage cultural exchanges with the Taiwanese?"

"The show was mainly organized by Taiwan's Pan-Green Coalition. This means most of the sponsors and organizers belong to the Democratic Progressive Party that advocates Taiwan's secession from China. By rule, we are not allowed to mix with them. Before you left for America, we told you that."

He became more baffled and asked, "How could I tell which party the organizers belonged to? I asked the man who approached me about the organizers of the event, and he told me it was sponsored by the Chinese immigrants in New York and New Jersey. The man was originally from Beijing and said they'd be honored if I could join them in their celebration of China as a nation. That was why I agreed to sing. In fact, President Ma Ying-jeou wrote them an official letter that emphasized one China."

Director Meng joined in, "Tian, I just read the memo sent over from the Ministry. The organizers were mostly members of the Pan-Green Coalition."

"Come on now, I don't even know what that term means," Tian said frankly.

"In essence it means independence from mainland China," Niu told him again.

"Then why did they celebrate the National Day?" He still couldn't make full sense of this.

Niu went on, "Because they want to gain influence over the Chinese community in New York. And you helped them, and for that you got four thousand dollars."

He was startled. Did Yabin rat on me? he wondered. Unlikely. Then how could they know the exact figure? He'd heard there were Chinese spies everywhere in America, but he hadn't thought they would be interested in how much he'd been paid for a small gig. He turned speechless and hung his head.

People at the meeting began to talk about his breach of rules, but most of them sounded sympathetic, especially those he knew well. One even argued that Tian should be forgiven because this was his first violation. An older woman, however, mentioned the four thousand dollars he'd made, wondering if he should surrender it to their company, but no one else picked up the topic.

Finally Niu smirked and said, "I don't want to discipline Yao Tian either. I can see he might have stepped into this mess by accident. But we cannot afford to do nothing. This case was sent down from above, and Comrade Yao Tian should give us a formal explanation and hand in his self-criticism."

The attendees all nodded and agreed. So she announced that she would allow him a week to write his explanation and self-criticism. In the meantime, he should stay home from work and focus on soul-searching and the writing. Once he handed it in, she would dispatch it to the Ministry of Culture and let them decide what to do. He had misgivings about this arrangement, but was not in a position to argue, so he said he'd do his best to produce what she wanted.

·　·　·

Neither Shuna nor Tian took his weeklong paid suspension as a serious punishment. She even joked that now he could cook for her and their daughter, Tingting, which he was glad to do. It wouldn't be difficult to write the explanation and self-criticism, so he could take it easy. They lived in the university's housing and Shuna walked to her office each day. Tingting's middle school, affiliated with Tsinghua University, was nearby; and, already thirteen, she could go there by herself.

He slept in the next morning, and after a late brunch, he practiced his voice for two hours, exercising diaphragmic breathing, blowing his lips, and singing some long phrases slowly. He then listened to the recordings of a few classical songs and also played some snatches on his small piano to find the right notes. After the work, he went to the supermarket nearby to pick up groceries for dinner. He bought a carp, a stout bamboo shoot, and a piece of streaky pork. On his way back, he stopped at a food stand and had a chive calzone and a bowl of jellied tofu spiced with a touch of chili oil and minced toon leaves. Whenever Shuna and Tingting were not home, he'd eat out at a snack bar or food stand. He was a fine cook, but usually didn't spend much time preparing meals.

As Tian was passing a tea stand outside his building, a few old men motioned for him to sit with them and chat, but he waved back, saying he couldn't join them today. Those elders were all retired, had too much time on their hands, and enjoyed gossiping and prattling. Once alone at home, Tian began writing the self-criticism. He wasn't a Party member, nor did he plan to join the Party in the future, so he wouldn't have to talk much about his political position or his ideology. Instead, he focused on his lack of discipline and on his negligence. He wrote: "First, I should have consulted our troupe's director before I changed my return flight. Second, I should have been more careful about the background of the people who invited me, and at least asked more questions. That way and with Director Meng's help, I might be able to figure out the true nature of the event organizers. Third, I shouldn't have been seduced by the hefty fee. I got greedy when I heard that they would pay me four thousand dollars, and I let that sway me. Money is a useful tool for a rational person, but it must not be the other way around: letting money rule oneself. This is a painful lesson for me. Now I am prepared to surrender the whole sum to our company, or donate it to an orphanage or a senior folks' home."

He got stuck there, unable to say anything else of substance, so he put the paper and pen away. It was time to make dinner. Tingting loved the fish Tian cooked, so he braised the carp with his signature method. After cleaning the fish, he rubbed it with rice vinegar so that its skin wouldn't be too slippery, then he did the same with soy sauce and cooking wine and let the carp marinate. Meanwhile, he cut the pork into small cubes, the bamboo shoot to lozenge slivers, and a handful of soaked shiitake mushrooms to slices. Next he heated a wok and deep-fried the fish. With smashed garlic, diced scallion, and ginger, he stir-fried the meat and the bamboo shoot and the mushrooms for a moment, then put in some water to make a stock. Having placed the fish into the wok, he dripped some rice wine onto it to get rid of the fishy smell. He put the glass lid on the wok and let it stew.

In addition to the fish, he made two vegetable dishes, steamed eggplant and sautéed string beans. To go with this, there were a bitter melon soup and boiled rice.

He enjoyed seeing Tingting and Shuna eat heartily. His daughter kept saying she wished he could stay home every day so he could make dinner like this for her. "Daddy, I love this fish," she said, and her eyes gleamed. "Whenever you take over the kitchen, it's my holiday." She licked her thin bottom lip, which glistened with the gravy of the fish.

"Eat quickly," Shuna told her. "You'll have to study with Miss Chen after dinner."

They had engaged a math tutor for their daughter. The young woman, Aili, was a student at Beijing Normal University and would come and teach Tingting math two evenings a week. They paid her eighty yuan an hour, about twelve dollars, so that Tingting could catch up with her classmates in math. Math was her weakest subject, whereas she excelled in English and Chinese. She was doing well in the foreign language partly because Tian often taught her, having majored in English at college. Like most parents who had teenage kids, he and Shuna were already worried about their daughter's college. They had discussed Tingting's education, and both believed she should go abroad for college. The girl liked the plan too, partly because many of her schoolmates were preparing to go to college in Europe and North America without bothering to cram for the national entrance exam. Besides the cutthroat completion for top schools, universities in China merely fed students with platitudes and jargons, manufacturing the sort of minds needed by the governing apparatus.

That night Shuna and Tian talked about his situation and the self-criticism he'd been writing. They were cuddling on their canvas sofa, her head on his chest and her hand on his belly. She urged him never to lose his temper when dealing with his superiors. Even if they put him through a denunciation session, at which he might have to read out his self-criticism, he mustn't lose heart. Whatever they wanted, he should just let them have it. In a matter of weeks the whole thing would fizzle out.

"Don't worry too much about that, sweetie," he said. "Secretary Niu doesn't seem eager to pounce on me. She just has to report back to her superiors in the Ministry of Culture and give them the impression that she has been trying to discipline me."

"I can't trust that woman," Shuna said. "But just give her what she wants. We cannot afford to alienate her now."

"I'll be all right, believe me."

He slipped his hand beneath her shirt, stroking her side, smooth but firm. As his hand was going down into her panties, she batted it away. "I have a ton of work to do tonight," she said. "One of the graduate students is defending her master's thesis tomorrow afternoon, and I haven't read it yet."

That meant they'd sleep separately tonight. This wasn't unusual. Whenever he had a performance, they slept in different beds the night before. Likewise, Shuna often stayed up alone late at night, reading and writing. She was a rising star in her field and had to seize the momentum of her success so that she could be promoted to full professor and supervise PhD students. For now she could direct only master's theses. Still, for a scholar of thirty-eight she had already accomplished a lot.

Five years ago, the Music Center at Tsinghua University had

offered Tian an administrative position: a junior official of music education and events on campus, with opportunities to teach from time to time. His wife urged him to take the job—she thought it would be more comfortable for their family if they worked at the same school. She told him, "A university job is reliable and nurturing, and you can hold it for the rest of your life." But an office job was not what he wanted. He would like to sing every day and experience the thrill of performing in front of an audience. He said to Shuna, "I belong to the stage, not to a cage of office. I won't take a nine-to-five job." She was displeased, saying he was too arrogant, but she passed his refusal on to her school's administration. To date, she still believed he'd lost a precious opportunity.

The next morning, right after breakfast, he got a call from Tong Ran, an air force veteran who was now in charge of security for the People's Ensemble. Ran said he'd been instructed to take possession of Tian's passport—Tian must surrender it as soon as he returned to work. Tian was stunned and asked whether this meant he was going to lose his passport.

"Not necessarily," Ran said. "From now on, the Ministry of Culture will directly control the international travel of senior officials and artists like yourself. You know how many criminals are fleeing abroad with their stolen wealth—our national leaders want to step up border control."

"But I'm a singer and need the papers for performing abroad," Tian said. "Do others in our ensemble have to turn in their passports too?"

"That I can't tell you. I have to do what I'm told. Just bring me your passport when you come in next time."

Tian had heard there was such a passport-control office in every ministry now, but they'd been established mainly to prevent corrupt officials from fleeing China with their money. To his knowledge, few of his colleagues had surrendered their passports. Now he seemed to have been put in a different category of strict control and surveillance.

Shuna hadn't left for work yet, so he told her what had happened. They both saw the immediate outcome of losing free use of his passport—he wouldn't be able to perform outside China anymore. This would damage his career in a way, because he often got invited by cultural associations from other countries. For him, this also meant the loss of the basic freedom he was entitled to. Worse yet, once he was confined within China, the authorities could reduce him little by little until they smothered him altogether. Such suppression had already happened to many disobedient artists. There is even a saying about such cruel measures: "Shut the door and beat the trapped dog."

After Shuna left, he tried getting his mind around the security officer's instructions. On the spur of the moment, he wrote to Yabin and asked him to send him an invitation to perform again in New York. Tian briefly described his trouble and said he'd like to come stay awhile in America to wait for this ridiculous hubbub to die down. He felt he could trust Yabin because the man had been banished by the Chinese government, a kind of dissident. Tian assured him that owing to his frequent traveling abroad, he had an account at the Bank of America and wouldn't compromise him financially. After sending the message, he was still on edge. He wasn't positive that he would actually take the drastic step of fleeing to New York. For the entire day he waited anxiously to hear from Yabin. He was too preoccupied to cook dinner, for which he just went out and bought some pork buns and a box of stir-fried vegetables.

After dinner, Shuna and Tian again talked about the recall of his passport. He told her that he'd written Yabin to request an invitation letter. She was aghast, but then gathered her wits. Her eyebrows, thick and sloping, rose upward, and her slightly deep-set eyes narrowed; her mind seemed to be racing. Her jaw appeared more angular and the silky skin of her neck crinkled with two thin lines. Then she said she could see the logic of his request and believed it would do him good if he could live in America for some time. Considering she'd have to parent their daughter alone if he left home, she wanted to blame him for not talking with her first, but she refrained. She knew that as long as he remained in his leaders' clutches, they could have their way with him. At worst, the People's Ensemble might fire him, but that wouldn't be a big deal. With his reputation he should be able to find employment anywhere in China. The important thing was that he must not remain passive, letting them abuse him at will. He was pleased that Shuna supported him.

They were unsure that Yabin would send him an invitation; all they could do was wait patiently while preparing a backup plan. But early the next morning when Tian flipped on his computer, he saw a message on the stationery of the New York Great China Cultural Association, which stated that he was invited to join a group of artists they had chosen to tour both the East and the West Coasts. The letter sounded very convincing, partly due to the elevated language Yabin used: "a stupendous troupe," "a groundbreaking endeavor," "great virtuosity." In a separate, personal message to Tian, Yabin said he was sorry for the quagmire he had landed in, and hoped he could help: "Whatever you need, I'll do my utmost to assist you."

Tian decided to begin applying for a visa, making good use of the passport still in his hands. Shuna encouraged him to do that, saying, "We're in the twenty-first century now. Your company's leaders ought to know they can't treat you as if they own you." She also remarked with a chuckle that Yabin sounded like "a fabulous liar."

Tian was emboldened by her support, so after breakfast he called Steve Jackson, a friend of his, who headed the Beijing office of the Ford Foundation. Steve was well connected, and after hearing him explain his predicament, agreed to help. He said he'd speak to someone in the U.S. embassy and try to have Tian's visa application expedited. Steve would need a copy of Yabin's letter, which Tian forwarded to him right away.

4

WONDER OF WONDERS: Within two days Tian was granted an interview for a visa. He went to the U.S. embassy, bringing with him his passport and a copy of the paperwork based on what he had prepared just two months earlier. The officer at the visa office, a young handsome American woman, spoke crisp midwestern English and had a divot in her roundish chin. She checked his papers, then lifted her gray eyes to look him in the face. She asked, "You are the singer Yao Tian?"

"Yes, I am," he said.

She flipped to the back of his passport. "You just came back from the States. Why do you want to go again so soon?"

"I received a new invitation. This cultural association invited me to take part in a series of events." He pointed at Yabin's letter attached to his application form.

"I see. In that case, come back in two days."

"Does this mean you will grant me a visa?"

"I cannot assure you of that. All I can say is have a wonderful trip." She winked, then smiled.

"You too!" he blurted out. Then, "Sorry, sorry. You will still be here working. I'm too thrilled to express my gratitude properly."

"I understand. Goodbye now." She waved at him, then motioned for the next person in line.

Shuna was pleased to hear about his interview at the U.S. embassy and said he must keep a low profile from now on. When going out, he had best avoid those retirees who gathered in their neighborhood's miniature park every day, playing chess and doing group dances. Nor should he sit at the tea stand outside their building anymore, which was viewed as a rumor mill. For now even Tingting should remain unaware of their plan. His suspension was already over and he'd have to go to work the next day. But what about surrendering his passport to the security officer?

The next morning Shuna called Director Meng and told him that Tian was bedridden with a sore throat and chills. She insisted that his superiors had been putting too much pressure on him, and as a result, his health had collapsed. Meng sounded anxious on the phone—there was a major tour through the coastal provinces in early November, and if Tian couldn't join them, they'd lose their lead tenor even though they had an understudy. Shuna assured him that Tian had been working on the self-criticism. "You know he isn't a glib writer, Director Meng," his wife said. "This kind of writing has taken a heavy toll on his health. But he'll send you what he has written. Right now he can hardly speak. He's losing his voice."

Tian then spoke with Meng briefly, wearing a thick face mask to muffle his voice. The director sounded very concerned—he told Tian to relax and that his disciplinary troubles would soon pass. Now he had to rest well for a speedy recovery because there was important work ahead. Tian thanked him and promised to email him what he'd written for the self-criticism, which he did send along that night.

Assuming he was to be granted the visa, Shuna and Tian discussed his plans. The next step was to purchase a plane ticket to New York. Normally it would cost around eight hundred dollars, but since he needed to leave as soon as possible, the price was likely triple or quadruple that. They didn't have that kind of money in their bank account—the only way to get the funds was to break their high-yield CD, which carried 150,000 yuan and was invested for them by Shuna's younger brother in a financing project at the bank where he was an accountant. Shuna said she'd get hold of the money as soon as possible and put it into their checking account. They did have some cash in U.S. dollars, about five thousand, but Shuna wanted him to take the whole amount with him, believing he would need it once he landed in the States. Her job was secure and paid a decent salary. A traveler needs more money than those at home and must be amply provided for, so Tian should take the funds they could spare with him now. Shuna had full confidence in his ability to succeed in America. They both knew of other Chinese artists who had made their careers there, and Tian, with his English skills, had even more of an advantage than they had. The potential payoffs were boundless. While China was a big lake, North America was an ocean. He agreed with her totally. More important, without his artistic freedom in China his career would be thwarted and wasted eventually. If the political wind shifted, he might have to sing only propaganda songs again. To survive here, he'd have to learn how to adapt. Look at the older generation of singers and composers in China. They had all been stymied after age forty because they'd had to self-censor, avoid controversy, and meet the requirements placed on them from above. Encouraged by his wife, he imagined his international success and thought of Tan Mai, the pi-pa player. If she could thrive in America, he should be able to do that too.

Two days later he went to the U.S. embassy again and got the visa. Now he had to proceed cautiously. Any misstep might trigger a disaster—the police could intervene and revoke his passport and put him on the list of people under special control. That night Shuna and he lay in bed for hours, talking about what he should do in America, his hand resting between her legs. She had been to the States once and liked the West Coast, especially the Bay Area, where winter was mild and summer wasn't hot, though he preferred New England for its distinct seasons and had been there several times for performing tours. She wasn't sure she'd leave for America in the near future, because she didn't know enough English yet and because she had an excellent job already. But she was confident that she could learn enough English to find work in the States if they ended up as immigrants there. They could see that was a possibility. Since they both believed Tingting should go to college in America, they thought they were very likely to live there with her eventually—she might not be willing to come back after she finished college. Nowadays, it was common among friends to greet each other by "Have you started emigration yet?" instead of "Have you eaten?" Nearly all those who had made enough money had left or begun the process of emigration. This country, it was whispered, was like a sinking ship—the sooner you got off, the better. When Shuna and Tian used to talk about their family's future plan they had agreed that they mustn't just follow the trend, but this time they had been thrust into a new situation, so he might become a trailblazer for their family in America. In Shuna's words, "the Vanguard."

The next day he began to shop for a plane ticket. The flights to New York had all sold out for late October and early November. After searching multiple sites, he found a Delta ticket to Seattle, but it was business class and cost five times more than economy. There was also an economy-class seat on a Hainan Airlines flight to Chicago, but it departed from Shanghai.

When Shuna came back in the late afternoon, he told her the prices. Without a second thought she said, "You must get the Delta ticket and fly from Beijing directly." She waved aside the appalling price, saying it was a miracle that they still could get a ticket at all. That was what he liked most about her—she rarely gave a damn about the cost of things they really needed. Her family had never been rich—her parents had taught middle school before they retired—but Shuna had an air of coming from a wealthy and cultured background. She took pride in herself indeed, teaching at a top university in the capital.

The next morning he set out for the airport with a single suitcase. Neither Shuna nor Tingting went to see him off. He wanted to give their neighbors the impression that this was just a regular trip he was taking. Certainly by now his daughter knew he was leaving for America, and she even asked him to come back soon. He said he didn't plan to live abroad for long. Although aware of the possibility of their family's immigration down the road, both Shuna and he also felt that his stay in New York might turn out to be temporary. It would be foolish to assume that everything would definitely work out as planned. Nowadays nobody could afford to do anything wholeheartedly. Deep down, neither Shuna nor Tian wanted to burn their boats. So in a way this trip felt like a stunt he was pulling, to show the People's Ensemble that he had his choices. When he came back, he might have another job elsewhere. If his company resolved to keep him, they ought to grant him more freedom. Above all, he wanted the freedom of international travel so that he could often perform abroad. The Chinese diaspora had been becoming a fertile ground for arts in recent years, bustling with activities in cinema, theater, book publishing, the fine arts. Any sensible, ambitious artist should explore the opportunities there.

Everything went smoothly at the airport, thanks partly to his business-class ticket. The young woman at the counter looked at his passport and observed his face for a moment. She seemed to have recognized him but said nothing. She must be eager to facilitate his check-in quickly since there was a waiting line. He passed the security checkpoint without a glitch and entered the waiting area. Most seats were vacant at the gate. A group of older passengers were sitting together near a wall of windows that looked onto the runway. Surrounded by their parcels and bags, they looked a little agitated; this might be their first trip to America. Perhaps some of them hadn't even flown before.

There was still an hour before boarding, and it was hard for Tian to keep composed. He knew he had cleared the security checkpoint and the police were unlikely to come and seize him, but still he put on the pair of powerless glasses that he sometimes wore to keep from being recognized by fans and the media. He forced himself not to look around and tried to read a magazine in his lap, but he couldn't register the meaning of the words at all. About half an hour later, the desk at the gate was still unmanned and he felt something might be amiss. He rose and asked a young clerk passing by, but the man told him, "Just wait patiently. If there's any change, it will be announced."

A frequent traveler, Tian knew that international flights usually began boarding at least half an hour before the departing time. Meanwhile those older passengers were still seated there, a couple of them nodding off. Finally Tian caught sight of a row of monitors down the hall and went over to take a look. To his astonishment, the gate had been changed. He hurried back to the older passengers and told them, "This is not the gate for our flight. We have to go elsewhere for boarding."

His words galvanized them. They picked up their bags and parcels and followed him to the new gate. When they arrived, a large crowd was already standing in line for boarding. By leading the group of older passengers, Tian was able to act as if he were one of them, or their guide, so the clerk at the gate just glanced at his passport, scanned his pass, and let him through.

The final line was crossed. Now he could say he was leaving China behind.

PART TWO

5

YABIN HELPED TIAN find a furnished one-bedroom apartment on 34th Avenue in Flushing, which was near a bus stop and within walking distance of the 7 train. He leased it for Tian in his own name, on a monthly basis, because Tian feared being tracked down by someone employed by the Chinese government. Yabin often called him to check whether he needed anything. Tian could navigate the city on his own and had enough money for three or four months, so he told him he was fine and enjoyed the peace and quiet.

He revealed his predicament to Yabin partially, saying that some of his colleagues in Beijing had become jealous and that the Ministry of Culture wanted him to surrender his passport, so he had come to New York and planned to stay here for a few months. He meant to show his superiors that he was not someone they could kick around at will and that he had his own dignity and principles. Ideally, he hoped he could work out an agreement with his leaders in the end and get more freedom for himself, specifically the freedom to travel and perform abroad.

Yabin shook his head sympathetically but didn't speak. They were lounging on armchairs in Tian's living room, which had a wide south-facing window that let in a flood of sunlight in the mornings. Yabin's reticence annoyed Tian, so he asked, "You think I've overreacted?"

"To be frank, Tian, you're being kind of nearsighted. If you love freedom so much, you shouldn't think about going back. How could you get more freedom for yourself while all your colleagues are lackeys or servants of the state? If you go back, you won't be different from them. Either you'll be a slave or an accomplice."

"Don't get too political," Tian said. "I have little interest in politics. I just want to be a free artist."

"Would that be possible while nobody around you is free? Freedom is not just a personal choice—it's also social conditions."

Tian turned tongue-tied. Yabin was a smart man and must be quite active in politics. Tian had heard that he was a member of a democratic association formed by a group of Chinese expats, and that he helped them organize events and apply for grants. Their headquarters were in a suite inside a grungy midrise building, which sat in an alleyway in downtown Flushing. Their conversation ended there, as Yabin had to leave and meet a client for an injury claim.

But what he said made Tian thoughtful. To date, he hadn't communicated with his ensemble directly and meant to keep silent as long as he could. Yet if his superiors caved to him, his colleagues would be emboldened and start putting forward their own demands too. This realization made him more nervous, anxious to hear from his leaders. Nevertheless, in his emails to Shuna, he told her to remain composed and not to hurry to respond to any questions from his ensemble. She should feign ignorance and just say she thought he was on a long tour with his friends in North America. He knew that would make his superiors furious, but he meant to upset them some. He was sick of always being at their beck and call.

Soon both Secretary Niu and Director Meng wrote to him separately, saying he had to return without further delay. Niu was stern and declared that if he didn't come back within a month, he'd lose his job, and no place would hire him with such "a huge stain" in his file. He wasn't troubled by her words. She was a fossil, still thinking in terms of confidential dossiers and permanent jobs in state-owned companies. Even though their ensemble was a public organization that offered secure employment, he might end up working for a private theater or another company, which wouldn't need his file. (Your name is your résumé, he often reminded himself.) Meng was less harsh, but what he revealed sounded more ominous. He wrote:

"Your case was already reported to the Ministry of Culture and the Ministry of State Security, and they might treat it as a defection if you don't come back soon. Think about it—can you afford to have such a criminal name on your head? It would affect your family, especially your daughter. Tian, please don't be so obstinate. Listen to me just this once. Otherwise you will ruin your future and your family's well-being."

Meng's note unsettled him, but he didn't write back at once. Instead, he replied to Secretary Niu first and asked her to let him keep his passport if he returned. She answered immediately: "I cannot promise you that, Comrade Yao Tian. Even if I allowed you to keep your passport, the police can revoke it at any time. This is beyond my power."

What she was saying was true, Tian realized—she was merely a tiny cog in the large ruling machine. Very likely, his departure was already known to the Beijing municipality and its police department, with which Tian and Shuna had never thought to deal. He had assumed that this whole thing was between him and his work unit. Now he couldn't help but question the wisdom of leaving China in a hurry. Even if he went back at once, his return would be viewed by others as his failure to continue in the States, and he could become a joke to many people and would be placed under strict control by the police. Very likely he would lose his freedom of movement. Unsure how to respond to his bosses, he phoned his wife one night and discussed the impasse with her. It was around seven a.m. in Beijing, and she sounded sleepy and for a few moments seemed unable to focus her mind.

Tian repeated his concern, saying, "Look, they might treat me as a defector. If that happens, I would become a semi-criminal and my crime could compromise you and damage Tingting's future."

A long silence followed. Then Shuna said, "Don't be intimidated by them. You're well known all over the country. If they can't get you back, they'll be held responsible and even their careers might be jeopardized. They must be more anxious than we are. Sit tight and just wait and see."

"What if the police cancel my Beijing residential status?" He had been unnerved by this possibility, which might reduce him to an illegal urban resident like a migrant worker if he returned.

"Don't let that bother you. You can find employment in other cities easily if you come back. Some cities in the south have already abolished the system of residential status. It will be obsolete pretty soon. Your bosses know that you're their cash machine."

That must be true, his ability to make money for his ensemble, and he ought to stay put. "Does Tingting know I won't be coming back soon?" he asked.

"Of course, she knows everything now."

"Can I have a word with her?"

"She went to bed at two in the morning and is still sleeping. Do you want me to wake her up?"

"Never mind. Just tell her I love her."

He realized that this was the beginning of a long tussle between him and his superiors—a psychological duel from across the world. He must not allow them to intimidate or dissuade him. Now clearly he might have to live in America for a long time, so he'd better find some way to support himself. He had been here for two months already; fortunately, his visa allowed him to stay for a year. He liked it here and enjoyed the free, uneventful life, even though he had realized that freedom was contingent on the ability to accept solitude and isolation. You can live honestly here, he often said to himself. Perhaps he should learn to view himself like a prospective immigrant from now on.

But, not having sung publicly since his arrival in New York, he was beginning to feel out of sorts, irritable, unable to concentrate. Now that he no longer appeared onstage or went to rehearsals, he even neglected his personal hygiene and sometimes didn't shave or shower for days. He realized he couldn't continue like this, so he spoke with Yabin about singing opportunities. His friend patted his own forehead, then assured him that he could help him. There were all kinds of gigs that Tian could do—celebratory gatherings and school reunions and evening parties. Tian interrupted him, saying he wouldn't do private events. Yabin seemed to have sensed the reason for his objection. He smiled and said, "I wouldn't make a distinction between public events and private ones. If I were you, whoever paid me more would get my service. You are in a capitalist society now."

"At the very least, I won't sing at weddings," Tian insisted.

"All right, I'll keep that in mind."

With Yabin's help, he soon began to receive offers. They were easy jobs—usually he sang two or three songs and was paid between seven and fifteen hundred dollars. Of course, he had to shift his repertoire—his new patrons wanted mostly folk songs and pop songs from Taiwan and Hong Kong. Most immigrants and expats disliked the revolutionary songs, which he had tried to weed out of his repertoire over the years anyhow. He was invited to take part in some celebratory events in local communities, at some churches, even at NYU's Tisch School of the Arts. Two music departments at local colleges also invited him to give lectures as well as sing some songs, but he didn't like talking to an audience. He preferred just to sing. He practiced daily, learning new songs and improving his artistry, using sheet music as well as the rich audio and video collections in the Queens Public Library branch in Flushing.

It was midwinter now and the cold wind often gave him a sore throat; at times his voice got a bit raw, but he could manage. On the whole, he liked the climate of New York, milder than Beijing's, perhaps because it's on the ocean. From time to time someone would demand he sing a red oldie that would bring back their revolutionary memories—"A Little Boat Floating East" or "A Happy Song Flying from the Green Fields." The former had been a movie theme song, his first success, but as a young singer he hadn't been able to see that it was merely propaganda trash. For years he'd sung it at every performance—audiences had been crazy about it. Then it went out of fashion almost overnight, and he couldn't sing it anymore. Now he would wince at the memory of the lines: "My revolutionary spirit is welling up like waves / And driving me to follow the Party without fear. / Let us smash the old evil world / So our rivers and hills will shine with marvels."

His performance at NYU was for an event that celebrated Chinese culture on New Year's Eve, organized by a group of faculty members and graduate students in Asian studies there. They also invited two exiled poets to read. One of them was an older man who recited his poems in spite of his misshapen mouth and wrinkled face. He'd lost some of his memory due to a brain thrombosis, but some in the audience knew his poems by heart. Whenever he got stuck, someone seated in the front would prompt him. Tian was touched by his reciting. When Tian's turn came, he sang his heart out, delivering his three folk songs with everything he had. After his set, a movie was shown—it was a love story set in China's western region, produced by an independent filmmaker but banned on the mainland. The program went over three hours, but the audience remained in their seats from start to finish. The next day several Chinese-language newspapers ran reviews that praised Tian's singing, saying it was "virtuosic and heartfelt."

Soon more news about him appeared in the media. Some said he'd fled China for freedom in America and that his defection spoke of the insufferable conditions for artists. He was disturbed by such reports with an anti-communist slant, though the publicity did bring him more bookings. A host at Radio Free Asia contacted him and offered to interview him on the air, but he declined, knowing the station was viewed as a hostile media agency by the mainland government. He had better appear less political for the time being.

In addition to the rumors about his defection, other stories were also circulating about him, which, false or true, often sounded extraordinary. One went that former President Jiang Zemin had once invited him to share a drink in Zhongnanhai, the compound of the headquarters inhabited by China's top leaders. This was partly true. Tian had indeed eaten a snack with President Jiang one night after a performance, but at a different location. Jiang loved songs and pretty female singers, and every once in a while he himself would sing in front of an audience, even playing along on the piano. Tian had to admit he was a man of culture, knowing several foreign languages, very proud of his calligraphy. On this occasion, President Jiang invited Tian and two women singers to a provincial center in the Great Hall of the People after their performance. With him they ate dumplings stuffed with date paste and sesame seeds and coconut mash. It was plain fare. Jiang was amiable and talked at length about the old songs he loved. He even hummed the Russian wartime song "Katyusha," which none of the singers knew well enough to sing along to. His hair was dyed glossy and jet black, combed back neatly, and he gave off a faint perfume of acacia blossoms and eucalyptus. One of the women complimented him, saying he must have had a wonderful voice when he was a young man. Jiang's thumb and index finger adjusted his square-rimmed glasses. He said, "I once dated a beautiful Russian girl when I worked at an automobile factory in Moscow. From her I learned many Russian songs." The other woman asked him if he had enjoyed his time there. Jiang replied, "I liked Russian girls and Russian culture, but their food was awful, atrocious. Every day it was bread and potatoes and cabbage soup." He sucked his breath as if suffering from indigestion. They all laughed.

As Tian recalled that strange occasion, he couldn't help but feel a tide of nostalgia. Perhaps he cared too much about the public perception of him. To most people, a moment like that—a private snack with the most powerful man in China—embodied the peak of an artist's career. But never had Tian thought much of it until he was reminded of it by a Chinese-language newspaper in Toronto.

He ignored all the clamor about his "defection." But after Christmas he received a formal letter from the leadership of the People's Ensemble. It was mailed to Shuna first, who scanned it for him. The tone of the letter was unequivocal. Evidently his superiors had received orders from above for how to handle his case, probably directly from the Ministry of Culture. The letter informed him that they had fired him and that from now on, he was completely on his own. It concluded:

> Since you have ignored our persuasion and are resolved to stay in the United States, we have no option but to terminate our ties with you. You are a disgrace to us, to your parents, to our country that raised and nourished you. However, please bear in mind that it is still not too late for you to change your dangerous stance and return to the arms of our motherland.

Like everyone else, here you will have freedom enough for you
to grow and thrive.

From Shuna he learned more about how his superiors had
reached the decision. Originally the Party committee of his work
unit had planned on a regular denunciation meeting to criticize and
condemn him. The leaders didn't want to expel him right away, but
they had to do something in case the higher-ups accused them of
negligence. Yet once the meeting started, some attendees, who were
all his colleagues, mostly non-Party persons, couldn't hold themselves back, condemning him roundly. Some even called him a traitor to their country and said he deserved serious punishment. One
insisted, "Yao Tian must do time in jail if he comes back." Another
declared, "We must make an example of him or more people might
betray our motherland." A third, an older woman about to retire,
added, "Yao Tian prefers to be an American dog. Let him. We can
continue without him." In the end they voted to fire him. In their
eyes, he was an egotistical man, thoroughly corrupted by the Western outlook. Tian finally understood that some young men must be
eager to replace him and take over the role of the principal male
vocalist, also the solo singer, and that his position in the ensemble would thwart their development. Now his permanent removal
could give them more room and hope. Never had he thought that
his presence in their ensemble could be an obstacle to so many
people.

The official letter made him feel as if he'd been tried and sentenced in absentia. It became clear that from now on he was a free
man through and through. This was quite scary, because freedom
also meant he was on his own, responsible for himself body and
soul. Such a state of existence felt odd and alien to him. He would
bet that given a choice between freedom and security, most Chinese
would choose the latter. In this regard he could have been similar
to them if he were still in China. Freedom had finally been dropped
on him, and whether he was ready for it or not, it had become his.

6

To tian's surprise, Professor Wu, his former mentor at the Beijing Conservatory of Music, also wrote to urge him to return.
Mr. Wu was retired now and too feeble to leave home. He didn't
know how to use a computer, so his letter was handwritten in wob-
bly script. Tian's leaders may have demanded that Mr. Wu help
them bring him back. Not having his address in America, the old
man sent his letter to Shuna and asked her to pass it on to Tian. She
scanned it and emailed it along.

Mr. Wu wrote: "Tian, you are too willful and self-centered. I
pointed out this defect in your character several times when you
were studying with me. You must have a broader mind and think
more about others. Each of us, no matter how talented and how
accomplished, is no more than a drop of water, which can disappear
easily, but which will not dry or vanish when it joins a river or sea.
Our country is an ocean in which we all must find our destinies.
Only when we serve our motherland can we realize the meanings
of our lives. Tian, as your teacher and friend, I only have your best
interests in mind. Please come back without further delay."

If the letter had been from someone else, Tian would have deleted
it and put it out of mind. But Mr. Wu was his benefactor, to whom
he was still grateful. He printed out the letter in the public library
so he could carry it with him and read it over and over. Whether he
liked Professor Wu's words or not, he felt obliged to reply properly.

Unlike his fellow graduate students at the conservatory who had
either been vocal majors at a university or graduated from a music

school, Tian had had no professional education in music before enrolling in the MFA program. At college he had been a foreign language major and didn't begin to sing until the first semester of his third year. Even that was due to a coincidence. At their annual sports meet in the early spring, they, the juniors, competed with the seniors in a tug-of-war. They had two teams, of men and women, each composed of twelve people. The rest of the students in both classes gathered around them to spectate and cheer them on. At the men's tug-of-war, the juniors lost to the senior team, who ridiculed them as "a bunch of cats" because most of the junior men were scrawny and wore glasses. But the women's contest was different. Their team crushed the seniors, and this was partly thanks to Tian.

Their coach figured that their men's team had lost because of poor synchronization. So he assigned Tian the task of synchronizing their female team, because he knew Tian had a powerful voice. Tian had no idea how to do it, but the coach said, waving a Diamond cigarette, "Just cry out 'Junior Team' so our girls can pull in unison. We'll organize the rest of the juniors to respond to your calls." Compared to the seniors, their team was smaller, especially their anchor, the girl gripping the big knot at the end of the rope. She was chubbier and shorter than her teammates, and her thick hair was unkempt. A couple of women on the senior team pointed at her and laughed, saying she looked like a giant turnip.

The instant the match began, Tian shouted at the top of his lungs, "Junior Team!"

"Pull—pull—pull!" the junior class cheered in one voice while their twelve women pulled—three powerful tugs for every cry from the cheering crowd.

"Junior Team!" he boomed again.

"Pull—pull—pull!"

"Junior Team!"

"Pull—pull—pull!"

The senior team was taken by surprise and fell into disarray, their arms flailing and their feet sliding forward and sideways. One of them fell on her rear end and was dragged along on the grass. They also had a cheerleader, who was wildly brandishing a tiny red triangular flag, but her voice was thin, and Tian easily shouted over her. They simply couldn't resist the Junior Team's explosive bursts of tugs. Within one minute the junior women dragged them over the line, and the anchor girl tied the end of the rope around a poplar trunk as if to make sure that the victory was irreversible.

Despite the seniors' protests that Tian, a man, shouldn't have been involved in the women's event, the victory went to the junior women. Some of them came up to him and thanked him for his help. One said, "What a magical voice you have! You unified us like one person."

Soon Tian became known on campus for his big, magnetic voice. Their college chorus approached him and invited him to try out. They were an active group of students under the supervision of a young teacher of French and often represented their college in competition with other schools in Beijing, but they didn't have a strong tenor. Most times they performed popular songs, but as a chorus from a college of foreign languages, they also attempted to sing some opera snatches to make themselves different from others. Tian liked singing and could sing a few folk and movie songs, but he didn't know how to pronounce Italian words and couldn't possibly sing arias from *Turandot* or *La Traviata*. Yet they convinced him to come to an audition anyhow, saying nobody among them knew Italian and they sometimes performed opera melodies mainly to impress the audience, most of whom were ignorant of foreign operas anyway. Moreover, he wouldn't perform alone, since they'd usually sing a duet or chorus. They could practice together and put on something that sounded Italian. So he agreed to try. At the audition he sang a few popular songs and impressed them enough that they offered him a spot. Thus his performances onstage began. His fellow singers often said that he'd been studying the wrong major and should have attended a conservatory. They joked that their college was too small a puddle for a big frog like him. In his senior year he became their lead tenor and once in a while sang off campus with some of them to pick up a bit of cash.

Toward graduation, many of his classmates were preparing to take the exams for graduate school. A few lucky ones were about to go abroad to study toward MAs and PhDs. As usual, the Beijing Conservatory of Music was admitting MFA students, and Tian's friends urged him to give it a try. He was intrigued and sent in his application and a tape of his singing, including some Italian operatic melodies, such as "The Mountain of the East" and "Let's Drink from the Joyful Cups." But he was halfhearted with his attempt, believing it was a long shot and that his performances, especially of the opera snatches, were awful. To his surprise, in June he was instructed to report to an audition at the conservatory, where Professor Wu Chuan would personally view his performance.

Mr. Wu was a leading expert in vocal education and had been the mentor of numerous successful singers. His specialty was operatic singing, which he had studied in Warsaw in the late '50s and the early '60s. But he hadn't performed much after he came back to China, his career disrupted by one political movement after another. Later during the Cultural Revolution he was banished to the countryside to feed pigs and grow vegetables and grind soybeans at a tofu mill at night. Eventually he was summoned back to the capital and became a professor and a legendary vocal educator. Tian was overwhelmed by the official notice, which he kept looking at incredulously, since he couldn't sing opera in Italian at all and the samples he had sent in were just bad imitations of Luciano Pavarotti. Professionally he was an absolute tyro.

Fearful of failure and humiliation, he didn't tell anyone about the audition, to which he planned to go alone. Above all, he had to keep the news from his parents, who wouldn't want him to become a singer, a mere entertainer. His father was an engineer in a textile plant and his mother a clerk in a tax office. They were intent on him finding a real, stable job, but they were far away in Dalian and he didn't have to obey them. At the audition, he came to know that some of the other applicants would sing operatic arias by Western masters like Puccini, Mozart, Rossini. They made him feel intimidated and inadequate. When his turn came, he just let himself go and belted out two folk songs, one fishing song and the other praising the immense Mongolian prairie. He sang them with gusto and total abandon. When he was done, he had to kick his right leg to stop it from shaking. One of the faculty members, a young woman, tittered and covered her mouth with her bony fingers.

Yet three weeks later he was notified that he had been admitted as one of Professor Wu's four new students. He was flabbergasted and wondered what had made the old man pick him from dozens of more accomplished applicants. There was no way he'd done better than the others. After he enrolled in the graduate program, he came to learn that Mr. Wu had taken a shine to the raw quality of his voice, which the professor felt was full of joie de vivre. In his words, "Yao Tian's singing has an earthiness that brings to mind vast grasslands and tumbling waters." So despite his colleagues' reservations he chose him. What moved Tian even more was that Mr. Wu had taken the extra trouble to admit him—Tian, never believing in Mao Zedong Thought and Marxism, had done poorly in the political exam, on which he had scored only a 58, two points below the passing line. Professor Wu wrote to the graduate admissions, arguing that because Tian knew English well, he had more potential than the others and would be more likely to sing foreign operas successfully. Indeed, among hundreds of applicants to the MFA program he'd scored the highest points—97—in the foreign language test. The old man argued (though his argument could have been considered specious) that over the years most of his students, unfamiliar with Western tongues, hadn't been able to perform in classical operas professionally, and eventually just sang for public gatherings and TV plays. He insisted that Tian was rare, "like a phoenix plume."

His admission to the conservatory finally appeased his parents, who knew the school was a mecca of performing arts in China. They even said they were proud of him. Anji, his little sister, told him on the phone that their mother often bragged about him to their neighbors. Her pride was a relief to him.

In every aspect Mr. Wu was a gentle, generous soul. Later when he found that Tian was not interested in performing foreign operas, he wasn't put out and allowed him to sing whatever he liked as long as he did the graduate work. In his course he always let Tian pass with a grade higher than a B. This was how Tian gradually became an aberrant singer of sorts; he was an operatic tenor by training but mostly sang for concerts and movies. He performed in his own way—ideally, he wanted his whole being to vibrate with the song. Professor Wu often said, "Every genuine artist has a unique path to success. None can be reproduced."

Now as he reread the old man's letter, recalling the time they had spent together in rehearsal spaces and concert halls, his teacher's round face glowing with a gentle smile, Tian's eyes filled. Then he noticed something ambiguous in the last paragraph of Professor Wu's letter: "Of course arts have no national boundary, but every artist has a country. Tian, I know you are a faithful man. You must never do anything against our motherland."

His words seemed to imply that he could accept the fact that Tian had emigrated, as long as he remained loyal to China. Tian realized that Mr. Wu might have shown officials his letter before sending it to him. This also meant that his reply might be under others' scrutiny as well, because Mr. Wu, still holding many honorific positions, would be obligated to convince the Ministry of Culture that he'd done his best to dissuade Tian. So he'd better be careful in his reply. He handwrote his letter, and in two full pages expressed his abiding gratitude and his appreciation for his mentor's thoughts. He assured the old man that he would never let him down, artistically or ethically. Yet Tian also emphasized that he was not a nationalist but an internationalist, "a proletarian altogether" in the Marxist sense. He'd do his best to make his teacher proud.

7

WHEN TIAN HAD FREE TIME, he read a lot of modern poetry, in both Chinese and English. The Flushing branch of the Queens Public Library on Main Street was comprehensive, and he often checked out books and albums there. Long ago he had come to the conclusion that although good songs fundamentally came from unique melodies, fine lyrics were also essential. The words should be poetic in spirit and sensibility. He appreciated the poets who could write musical lines infused with subtle meanings and feelings. He loved Dai Wangshu, Feng Zhi, Dylan Thomas, Jorge Luis Borges. "Do Not Go Gentle into That Good Night," which he'd learned by heart, often brought tears to his eyes. Deep in his soul, he harbored a secret ambition: When he was too old to sing onstage, he hoped to become a songwriter. Even though he might not be talented enough to produce great poems, by writing songs he might have a longer artistic life.

When he wasn't reading poetry, he tried to learn new songs to enlarge his repertoire. His repertoire was rich, even vast, but most of the songs were propaganda rubbish that he'd had to sing back in China. Fortunately the library carried some albums of traditional Chinese folk songs and a substantial collection of performances by singers in Taiwan and Hong Kong. He watched these as much as possible so that he could learn their stage manners, which were friendlier and more engaging than his had been. Most of those singers used a softer voice, and some merely murmured into the microphone while singing, as if they were having an intimate conversation with an individual listener. Almost without exception, they would smile from start to finish. They appeared so natural, so different from his performance back in China, where everything was strictly planned ahead. However, these styles were not what he wanted for his performance. He wanted to lean more on the strength and range of his voice, using stage manners as a supplementary component in his delivery. If he gestured, he must do it naturally, without exaggeration. At times he might sing without a microphone, letting his natural voice carry the show. More essential, he wanted to find the songs that would last. There were so many popular songs that were merely bubbles of the moment.

In mid-January he got a call from a woman named Cindy Wong, who spoke English with a slight Cantonese accent. She represented a troupe named the Divine Grace and invited him to join them in their Spring Festival series. Although the troupe was new, they had already booked a four-city tour in the States. Most tickets had been purchased through preorders, she said, and with Tian added to their cast, their show would become even more popular.

"I'm a big fan of yours, Mr. Yao," Cindy told him.

"Thank you. Your troupe has an interesting name. Do you belong to a denomination?"

"Well, we are religious, but we're not a cult."

Her defensive answer made him skeptical. He managed to say, "I have a very tight schedule, but can I get back to you tomorrow? I'll have to speak with my manager, who knows my schedule better."

"Of course. Take this as a standing invitation. You're welcome to join our troupe anytime before the holiday season starts." By "holiday" she meant the Spring Festival, which would fall on January 27 this year. Even though the Chinese immigrants couldn't have a long holiday season as they did back in their homeland, many of them still carried on the festive tradition, having family dinners, friendly gatherings, communal celebrations.

That night Tian phoned Yabin and asked him about the Divine Grace, which turned out to be sponsored by Falun Gong. The troupe was composed of dancers and musicians from all over the world and was intended to counter Communist China's artistic influence in the West. To date, it had been very successful and was grow-ing more popular each year. Nevertheless, Yabin believed Tian shouldn't become involved.

"Thank you," Tian said. "It would have been hard for me to tell who they were." Then a thought came to him and he asked Yabin, "Why don't you be my manager? I can pay you fifteen percent of my earnings."

"No, no, I can't take money from you."

"Look, you've been helping me all along, already like a manager. I really need you to help me navigate through the hurdles and snares here. Please say yes. This will make my life easier."

So Yabin agreed. By now Tian had complete trust in him and believed there wasn't a better person to represent him. Yabin was savvy about American life and well connected with its Asian com-munities. Best of all, he was prudent and perceptive and would be able to help him develop while shielding him from harm. Yabin seemed pleased to be his manager and said he'd have some busi-ness cards made.

Then he asked Tian whether they could meet to discuss a per-sonal matter, saying it was so complicated that he'd better explain it in person. Tian agreed to see him at the Dreamland bar the next evening.

The following afternoon he called Cindy Wong and told her he was unavailable at the moment. For any future queries, she should contact his manager directly. He gave her Yabin's name and phone number. "Oh, I know the guy," Cindy said. "His insurance office is on Main Street and his English name is Hugo. I will check with him every now and then."

Although he had declined the offer, he wanted to be cordial to Falun Gong—his mother and his sister Anji, back in Dalian City, had been involved with the religious group for years. The north-east of China was actually the birthplace of Falun Gong. Before its practice was outlawed there, Tian's mother and sister would do the breathing exercises in People's Square. Then they both formally dropped out of Falun Gong for fear of punishment, though Anji seemed still passionate about the religion and Tian believed she was an underground practitioner. He often pressed her to sever ties with Falun Gong altogether, but she never bothered to respond to his words. Though she would rarely raise her voice, she had always been bullheaded.

Dreamland was crowded, as it usually was in the evenings. As soon as the two of them had settled into a booth, Yabin began to relate his problem. He wanted to propose to Barrie but had begun to have second thoughts of late. Although he loved her vivacious personality and her shapely figure and her honesty, she was not good with money. He had given her a credit card connected to his account the previous summer, and since then, at the end of every month she had exceeded the three-thousand-dollar line he had specified for her. She bought plenty of stuff for herself: purses, shoes and boots, dresses, an iPhone, a pair of jade bracelets, assorted earrings, CDs, books on the *New York Times* Best Sellers list. Even though some of the things she'd bought could be shared by both of them, like suitcases and wines, he found them unappealing to his taste. Imagine what it would be like if they were married. She might bankrupt him in a year or two. "I've been thinking whether to insist that Barrie and I split our living expenses," he said, as if wondering aloud to himself. "But if I do that, she'll be so upset that she might walk out on me, partly because since day one I have been picking up the bills."

"Maybe you should approve all major purchases from now on?" Tian suggested.

"That might not work. For her, anything under three hundred dollars can't be a major purchase."

"Or get the credit card back?" Tian was also at a loss for a sensible solution. He was amazed that Yabin would pay all the living expenses for both of them.

"If we were married," Yabin went on, "I would want her to be absolutely reliable—an emotional anchor."

"'Or like a haven for a little boat,'" Tian quoted the line from a song.

They both laughed. Yabin resumed, "To tell you the truth, if I can't trust my wife with money, the marriage will be difficult. Barrie is like a safe without a lock."

"She's a beautiful woman, healthy and lovely," Tian said. "Don't you feel lucky to have her?"

"Well, as a girlfriend she's fine, but I'm getting tired of dating one woman after another. I want to settle down and have more security."

"Then why didn't you look for a Chinese woman instead? I'm sure that most Chinese women are more sensible with money, especially those from Shanghai, who know how to manage a household and even how to invest."

"You're generalizing, Tian, and only thinking of women of the older generation, or of our age. Women in their twenties are completely different. Their values and worldviews are different from ours. Their men have to be both a protector and a rice-winner. Most of them don't have marriage in mind and just want to enjoy life while they're still young. I've dated Chinese women before and they all wanted too much from me, so I just avoid them now. One of my ex-girlfriends had more than a hundred pairs of shoes. Imagine, she was from a small city in Hubei province, but she was so enamored of brand names—she wanted to make her life appear expensive in every facet. I called her a brand-name animal. It's so hard to find someone you can love and trust!"

"True, such a person would be your ideal," Tian agreed. "But where can you find her?"

Their conversation didn't really help Yabin. He had yet to figure out what to do about his relationship with Barrie. The only reasonable advice Tian could give him was "Don't rush to pop the question." Yabin agreed to wait. He was an urbane man with refined manners and long fingers and usually seemed carefree, but their conversation revealed another aspect of him.

Tian was also beset with misgivings. He missed his family, especially at night when he felt lonely and wondered how Shuna was spending her time. He was in touch with both her and Tingting, but his daughter didn't write him very often. Sometimes she would just drop him a few words, like "I miss you" or "love you, Dad." She always gave him the impression of being preoccupied with something. She was a quiet child and kept a lot to herself. One night in March she wrote to him, with unusual urgency: "When are you going to come back, Dad? You have been away too long! Have you forgotten us?"

He pressed her, asking, "What's going on? Is your mother all right?"

"She's fine, but she's out more often these days," Tingting returned.

"Where does she go?"

"Out with her friends, I guess."

"Who are her friends?"

"Most times with Uncle Bai."

"I see. Thanks, little dove."

He knew that Shuna was still attractive—she sometimes called herself an old woman in front of her students, but she looked thirtyish. Bai was an old friend of hers, a history professor at Beijing Normal University. They had been schoolmates at college, Shuna two years after him, and she'd told Tian that Bai had once had a crush on her. The more he thought about this, the more wary he got.

As agreed, he would phone his wife every other day. The next night he called to sound her out. To his surprise, she told him that she had been collaborating with Bai on a college textbook on the maritime adventures in the Ming Dynasty. It was a project sponsored by the Ministry of Education and proposed to them by an academic press. They had just signed the contract. Shuna was a little gruff on the phone, saying there was no reason for him to become suspicious or jealous. Then she wanted to know how he spent his days.

"Don't you have many friends there?" she asked.

"I have a few. What do you mean by 'friends'?" he said.

"You know what I mean. You never lack women around you."

"Come on, I'm struggling to survive here. If you don't trust me, I can come back straightaway."

"No, I was just kidding. But promise me, you'll never keep it from me if you meet someone there?"

"All right, you have my word. I want you to treat me the same way, always aboveboard." Despite saying that, he was surprised by their mutual demand. The conversation shouldn't have turned into such a corner.

"I'll always be honest with you. I miss you a lot, Tian."

"I miss you too. But it looks like I might have to live here for a long time. Perhaps I ought to stretch my stay out until Tingting comes to America for college."

"That makes sense."

Shuna also said she'd be up for a promotion to full professor soon. Once that was done, she'd be qualified to supervise PhD dissertations. That was why her textbook was vital for her career. With another book published, her promotion would be assured. In addition to that, she might apply for a research grant from the Ministry of Education so that she could come to the States as a visiting scholar—several of her colleagues had already received such funding and were doing research abroad. Neither Shuna nor Tian ever mentioned immigration on the phone, which was tapped in China, but they knew that it was a possibility. They treated their email communications with the same caution. Whatever they said and wrote, they assumed someone else had access to it. Yet they both understood that Tian might need to stay in America to wait for Tingting and eventually also for Shuna.

Their phone conversation reassured Tian to a certain extent, but he didn't feel completely secure. From April on, he began to wire one thousand dollars to his wife at the end of every month, saying that the money was for Tingting's tuition and to help with their living costs. His income varied, but on average he could make upward of three thousand dollars a month, three times more than he had made in China, though he had no idea where to get his next check. He didn't spend much apart from rent and groceries, so he could spare the money he sent home. It was meant to increase his presence in his family, even though Shuna's salary was enough for her and Tingting to live on.

8

I N LATE MAY, as the twentieth anniversary of the Tiananmen massacre was approaching, the Chinese government prepared by
beefing up security all over the nation. In America, many Chinese
expats and immigrants were organizing memorial observances. A
group of dissidents from the Democracy Party of China asked Tian
to perform in Central Park together with some artists who lived in
New York. Yabin, though active in promoting the event, told Tian
to be careful—he was sure that the Chinese consulate would keep
a record of those involved and that Tian risked getting blacklisted
if he joined them. By disposition Tian abhorred politics, but he had
his principles and believed in justice and personal freedom. He
remembered how he had burst into tears when he heard two boys
in his high school, who had gone to Beijing to demonstrate against
corruption and demand democracy, give their account of the bodies
and bicycles crushed by tanks near Tiananmen Square. The killing
of the peaceful civilians by the standing army was more than he
could stomach. At that time, in the spring of 1989, he was in his
late teens and regretted not having gone to the capital to join the
demonstrators. Now, far from the clutches of the Chinese police,
he had access to the censored information on the tragedy and had
seen many of the horrific photographs and videos and footage that
the CCP kept suppressed. If he didn't protest this atrocity and fight
the official effort to erase the public memory of it, he'd feel like a
spineless coward.

So he agreed to sing at the memorial concert in Central Park without getting paid. Within days he saw ads in community news-papers about the event, which listed him as a performer. There was also a bigger ad in *The Epoch Times,* the English paper of Falun Gong, which announced it was an event free and open to the public. Tian noticed that besides the Chinese performers, some American artists would attend the gathering too. This was heartening, though most Chinese artists in New York seemed to shun it, fearful of the mainland government's retaliation. He wondered whether he was too rash in agreeing to sing, but he dismissed his second-guessing, convinced that he must not remain silent. "I protest, I exist," as a Hong Kong poet had claimed recently.

Two days before the memorial concert, he got a call from a Chi-nese official, Vice Consul Kong. The man spoke in a smooth voice with a trace of a Henan accent. He said he was in charge of cultural affairs at China's consulate in New York and would like to meet Tian in person. Tian was unsure of his motivation and claimed that his schedule was full for the next two weeks. A prolonged pause ensued. He guessed that Kong seldom encountered such a refusal.

Then the vice consul bluntly asked Tian to cancel his commit-ment to the memorial in Central Park. For a moment Tian was too rattled to answer coherently, but he collected himself and said, "I can't back out now. The concert is only two days away. It would be unprofessional for me to withdraw." The truth was that he just wouldn't give up such an opportunity to sing publicly, though he could not explain to the official his artistic yearning and reason. To Kong, everything must be political, and the concert was reaction-ary by nature. Then, everyone with a free mindset and believing in human rights must be a troublemaker to the CCP.

The official replied, "Is it because they pay you well? If that's the case, we can pay you double or triple the amount."

"No, no, I'm not taking a penny for this appearance."

"Mr. Yao Tian, you know our Party's position on the Tiananmen event, which was a riot, and the organizers of this concert intend to vilify our country. We hope you won't help them carry out their vicious plan."

"You know, I know, everyone knows the massacre was a terrible tragedy and the Party made an atrocious blunder. Some people even consider it a crime against humanity. It's about time the Party righted the wrong and apologized openly. Otherwise how can you inspire people's trust and continue to keep peace and order?" Tian was surprised by his own blunt words, which he realized he could voice only because he was here.

"I'm not arguing with you about the nature of the tragedy. We simply advise you not to associate with this group. Some of them are criminals and enemies of China."

"I don't see it that way, Mr. Kong. We ought to let people remember an event like that. I've never been interested in politics, but this is a different case. To my mind, the cause of the tragedy is clear: A bunch of old oligarchs were holding on to power at the cost of young lives. The old killed the young in order to—"

"Yao Tian, you have an attitude problem! Keep in mind that your family is still in China. You must be careful and responsible for what you say and do here. You're a smart man and I don't need to dwell more on this."

Tian was incensed, his temper smoldering, but before he could respond, the official hung up. His mention of Tian's family unnerved him, yet he was not intimidated. He was just a singer, and to sing a couple of songs at the memorial concert couldn't possibly be a crime. Every year on the anniversary of the Tiananmen massacre, more than one hundred thousand people gathered at Victoria Park in Hong Kong, where musicians would perform, and none of those artists had been punished. If what they did was considered a crime, then there'd be too many criminals to prosecute. Yet, while Vice Consul Kong's warning might not be an empty threat, Tian could ignore it partly because his wife was in academia and their livelihood didn't completely depend on the Chinese state, since her school, though a public university, was unlikely to fire her because of his activities abroad. Above all, as an individual he needed to hold on to his integrity.

He planned to sing two songs. One, written collectively by some twenty Taiwanese artists in memory of Tiananmen, was titled "The Wound of History." It was usually performed by a chorus, but Tian would be the lead singer. The other song was "In a Blooming Season," a recent collaborative project between a composer and a poet in Hong Kong to commemorate the tragedy. Tian was unfamiliar with the second song and had to learn it and rehearse it, but it wasn't a difficult piece. The organizers were pleased about the way he delivered the two songs, with both poise and feeling.

It was a little overcast on June 3, and the evening in Central Park was cool and slightly hushed. Yabin, who had helped to publicize the concert, assured Tian there'd be no rain, according to the weather forecast. About six hundred people, mostly Chinese, attended the concert held in Sheep Meadow, a beautiful open field on the west side of the park. Many of the attendees had brought candles for a vigil later that night, but Tian didn't plan to stay for the entire program. His job was to sing; what he had was a voice, which he would contribute as his support. Several exiled men and women who'd been involved in the Tiananmen movement were present. They were all in middle age now but looked spirited. Apparently the banishment from their homeland had not diminished their vitality—the new continent seemed to have given them a new life. At the back of the low platform hung a wide screen, on which footage of the violence and bloodshed was being shown. A bespectacled older man spoke first. His Mandarin had a Shandong accent, but his voice was resonant and a bit metallic. He told how the Chinese government had been mistreating a group of older women, the Tiananmen Mothers, who had lost their children in the massacre; the police would routinely stop them from leaving home on holidays and whenever there was an important event in Beijing. He also testified that Chinese diplomats in America had attempted to sabotage the memorial efforts made by local communities. He raised his voice to declare that the organizers of this memorial night, the Democracy Party of China, had decided to hold such a gathering every June, until the Communist regime redressed the wrong and the criminals were brought to justice.

After him, the dissidents in attendance spoke by turns. Among them was Chai Ling, who'd been the student commander in Tiananmen Square. She had bulked up some now, with raven-black hair and bright eyes. In the 1989 photos, she'd been skinny, haggard, even a little timid. Now she spoke in a quiet but assured voice. As soon as she started, some people booed and a man shouted, "Get off the stage! You too have blood on your hands." Tian knew that some people believed she was partly responsible for the bloodshed, having fled the square before the students in her command had found safety.

Chai Ling straightened up, staring at the man, unintimidated. She then told the audience, "Truth will prevail sooner or later. We are gathering here to commemorate the dead and to condemn the atrocities, not to point fingers at each other." She sounded familiar with this kind of challenge. Calmly she said a few more words and then left the platform to scattered applause.

Tian looked at the printed program, which didn't specify all the individual speakers. He wondered why so many people would go up to give speeches at this concert. Then he realized this must be mainly a memorial gathering, advertised as a concert so as to draw a bigger crowd. Among the speakers, he was especially impressed by a man in a wheelchair. His name was Fang Zheng and he'd lost both legs, crushed by a tank outside Tiananmen Square. Fang said he had been trying to help a girl who had fainted from a gas bomb, then couldn't get out of the way of a tank charging toward them. The girl was saved, but his legs were crushed. His thick shoulders shook and he raised his voice to say, "I saw with my own eyes people shot on the streets. Some officials claim there was no death or bloodshed that night. That's a bald-faced lie. If I were not rushed to a hospital by some goodhearted folks, I would've been among the dead. Now I am a living witness for those who didn't make it."

His voice was even and a touch monotonous, and it was clear he wasn't used to giving speeches, but his mere presence spoke volumes. He was the most eloquent among the speakers.

As the twilight was deepening, people began to light their candles. Yabin was standing in the front row; although not belonging to the Democracy Party of China, he was an enthusiastic promoter of this event and was regarded as an active dissident. His face and upper body were dappled with patches of light from the crowd.

More bloody footage appeared on the screen, demonstrators fleeing soundlessly, gunfire and flames flaring in Beijing's night sky.
Against this silent, violent backdrop, the concert began. Tian was
first to perform. He held the mic and said, "I'm not a political person, but I want to support what is just. That's why I'm here to sing
two songs, to entertain you and hopefully bring you some moments
of peace."

About a dozen or so young people were getting onstage as the
chorus, standing behind him. He started with "The Wound of History." He was touched by the shadowy faces wavering below him
as he sang:

> Eyes closed, you might not see,
> Ears covered, you might not hear,
> But the truth is in your heart,
> The wound in your chest.
> How long can you endure?
> How long will you keep silent?
>
> If hot tears can wash dusts away,
> If warm blood can be exchanged for freedom,
> Let tomorrow remember today's howling,
> Let the whole world see the wound of history!

Together with him, the chorus repeated the lyrics while some in
the audience hummed along. Tian had heard this song a few times
at small underground gatherings back in China, but this was his
first time to sing it publicly. Never had it been so moving and so
meaningful to him. He tried hard to hold back his tears while singing along with the chorus and the audience.

The next song was new to the audience, so they listened quietly
and attentively. The piece was like a mourning lullaby:

> Mama, don't be upset, don't yield to them.
> Together we will look after the children
> And let them sleep in peace.

When the right season comes
They will again bloom everywhere. . . .

The moment he was done, he bowed to the audience and hurried off the stand, even as, behind him, a female voice called for an encore.

An American band got on the stand next. Their lead guitarist, a lanky man with long hair, thanked the audience: "We're honored to be here and to take part in this memorial service. Thank you all for being here." Without further ado, the rock group started their set, which sounded angry and loud and fierce. The audience, mostly unfamiliar with heavy metal, seemed bewildered and less engaged, some shifting their weight from leg to leg and talking to each other in whispers. Tian had never heard of the local band—Trust No More—which might have made itself available free of charge for this gathering. By now all the candles were lit, flickering among the crowd.

Tian saw Yabin emerging from behind a large maple tree. He held a square lantern draped with double tassels. Tian went up to him and said, "I should be going."

Yabin looked puzzled. "Leaving so soon? Don't you want to see the other performances? There'll be a group doing a drum dance, and the former student leader Wang Dan might show up."

"I've done my part. You know I don't like crowds. There's nothing else for me to do here."

"Good night, then."

Yabin waved his lantern. Tian turned and headed for the nearby exit of the park.

9

S EVERAL NEWSPAPERS wrote about the memorial concert. A photograph of Tian was published, showing him singing with his head tossed back and with one arm open. That made him uneasy, but he was used to this kind of publicity, which tended to highlight what he preferred not to be seen. He didn't want to give the impression that he tried his hardest to please an audience. This photo showed that his stage manners were too extravagant, and it reminded him that he ought to sing with more economy of movement onstage. The coverage also circulated online, so Shuna saw it too. She told him on the phone one night that the director of her school's political bureau had summoned her to his office.

"About what?" Tian asked.

"About your involvement in the memorial gathering two weeks ago," Shuna said.

"Thousands of people took part in the memorial activities in America. I am just a singer, one of them."

"But you are better known. In any event, the official who talked with me wanted me to stop you from being so active."

"Did you agree with him?"

"No. I said you were an adult and had your own convictions and should be responsible for your own acts, but I would speak to you. He seemed unhappy that I wouldn't do my best to dissuade you. Forget about him. I told him that you were apolitical, but I know that was just a façade you put on in front of others. Like you often said to me, you're not a slave of the state and don't have to follow their orders. Didn't you used to say you wanted to go somewhere you could live as a real citizen, not like a servant?"

"I did. I don't want to live a life on my knees."

"Do you think you can find such a place in China now?"

"No, I can't."

"Then you mustn't rush back, not before you figure out what to do. Given your new activities there, it might not be safe for you to come back right now."

"Thanks, Shuna. Do you think your school talked to you because they got instructions from above, say, the Ministry of State Security?"

"Absolutely. Who would volunteer to deal with a character like you?"

"What should I do?"

"Nothing. Just live your life and do what you've been doing."

He was glad to have Shuna's support. She really wanted him to put down roots in America so that their daughter could come and join him. Yet he was not entirely happy about this plan, because Shuna might assume that he could make enough money here for their daughter's tuition, which was a task more daunting for him now. He had heard from Yabin that very few schools here gave scholarships to international undergraduates, and that most of the Chinese students were from well-to-do families that could fork over fifty grand a year. Shuna herself had just applied for a fellowship offered by the Ministry of Education, requesting support for a research trip to visit a top Asian studies library, either at Berkeley or at Harvard–Yenching Institute, which were treasure troves of ancient books and rare materials. For their future reunion, then, Tian had to make and save as much as he could. He hoped Shuna would like America enough to immigrate eventually. In spite of the uncertainty he'd gone through in recent months, he had grown to appreciate his life here—the solitude and the freedom, the fresh air and the safe food. Here few people recognized him, and he enjoyed his newfound obscurity.

Yet there was no way he could remain totally obscure. One evening in late summer he got a call from a man who introduced himself as Harry Hong. Hong wanted to meet with him somewhere in Flushing to discuss an important business opportunity. Usually Tian referred people to Yabin, but the man persisted, saying this was something that a manager couldn't handle. He sounded polite and amiable, and kept emphasizing the importance of the opportunity. Tian thought of hanging up, but Hong brought up some singers they both knew personally and then chatted effusively about Tian's hometown, Dalian, its charming beaches and picturesque islands and even its dialect. Tian was so intrigued by his earnestness and his polite tone of voice and his fits of laughter that he agreed to meet with him the next afternoon at Purple Lilacs, a teahouse on Northern Boulevard. Hong said he'd wear reading glasses and carry a copy of *Asiaweek*.

The teahouse was quite small. When Tian had stepped in, he could see all the faces in the room. There were about a dozen customers, all seated. In a corner a squat man in his early fifties in a gray serge suit and a purple tie was reading *Asiaweek*. Tian went up to him and said, "Mr. Hong?"

"Yes, delighted to meet you, Mr. Yao." The man stood and held out his hand.

Tian shook it, its palm meaty. He sat down across from Hong and ordered aster tea. Hong was having espresso, two demitasses standing on the table, one already empty and the other half full. He must have been there for a while.

Harry Hong took off his glasses, revealing his hooded eyes. He said he'd been a longtime fan of Tian's and owned all of his albums. He had an odd accent Tian couldn't place. Probably he was a Korean who had lived in China—there were many Koreans in Flushing who came from Yanbian, the Korean autonomous region in Jilin province. His rugged face indicated that he must be a northerner, probably a businessman, as his expensive suit showed.

"I'm here now, Mr. Hong," Tian said. "I hope we have something interesting to discuss."

"I have a business proposal for you," Mr. Hong said, leaning his lumpy face in. "Actually, the proposal is not from me. I'm representing a client."

"Who is your client?"

"I can't name him—or them. But I can put their terms on the table for you to consider. My clients would like to offer you a sum of money in exchange for your cooperation."

"What do you mean by 'cooperation'?"

"Stop performing outside China altogether." He grinned, revealing a gold crown in the back of his mouth.

"So your clients want to buy my voice, my silence?"

"You can put it that way if you wish."

"Well, I've never heard such a proposal before. Tell me, how much is my silence worth?"

"They can offer four million."

"Yuan or dollars?"

"Certainly U.S. dollars."

Tian shook his head, too dazzled to speak.

"Think about this, Mr. Yao," Harry Hong went on. "This is an extraordinary offer, isn't it? I hope it's acceptable to you."

Finally Tian got his wits back and said, "Let me sleep on it, all right? I can't decide now."

"Of course, take your time. But let me make it clear that once you accept the offer, you will have to abide by our agreement. If you break your word, my clients will ruin you and your family. They have infinite ways to do that." He took a pen out of the inside pocket of his jacket and scribbled a phone number on the back of his business card. His index finger had no nail, its tip merely a tapered stump.

"I understand," Tian said. "I'll let you know my decision soon."

Mr. Hong knocked back the remaining espresso and then handed him the card. "Here's my mobile number, and you can call me anytime."

After exchanging a few pleasantries, Tian decided to leave. Mr. Hong assured him that if he took the offer, the money could be delivered in any way he preferred. Tian told him he appreciated that and would figure out an appropriate way. Then they stood up and said goodbye. Mr. Hong headed to the men's room, his olive-green trench coat still draped over his chair, while Tian turned to the front door.

Four million dollars would be enough for him and his family to live on comfortably for the rest of their lives. He'd better talk with Shuna—they ought to consider it carefully. He emailed her so that he could make everything clear to her. He wrote, "They would like to buy my voice, my total silence, for four million U.S. dollars. We must discuss this before I answer Mr. Hong. I will call tonight."

He thought Shuna would reject the offer immediately, but on the phone she sounded excited. She asked how they'd pay him. "They could deposit the money into our joint account in Beijing," he told her. "The delivery can be arranged according to our preference. Mr. Hong promised me."

"Gosh, I've never thought they would spend so extravagantly."

"It's not their money to begin with, and they wouldn't give a damn about whether I'm worth that much. I've heard that the government is flush with so much cash in recent years that they worry about how to spend it. They even put a huge TV screen in Times Square to show what's going on in Beijing. Someone in power must be uncomfortable about my presence among the dissidents in America and wants to rein me in. My performances here might undermine their Grand Propaganda Plan. What do you think I should do?"

"Logically speaking, if you love Tingting and our family above anything else, you should consider the offer favorably. With four million dollars, our family will be all set. We'll have the funds we need for Tingting's education abroad. We can also consider investment immigration to the U.S. or to Canada—I've heard that if you plunk down half a million dollars, you can get a green card within three months. In short, this is a great opportunity."

He was taken aback by her enthusiasm. He had been tempted by the offer, but was counting on her support to resist the temptation. Yet what she said perplexed and unnerved him. He did love his wife and daughter, and he knew that he had brought them a great deal of stress lately, but this offer was a different matter and he felt it shouldn't be confused with his devotion to his family. Tingting and Shuna had their lives, and he had his own. How could he sell himself all at once only for their comfort and security? He grew quiet on the phone, unable to express these thoughts that might upset his wife.

"Well," she continued, "it will be your call, Tian. No one but yourself should decide what to do."

"What if I were to turn down the offer?" he asked.

"I'll understand and won't blame you. Let me say this: If you love our daughter unconditionally, you should seriously consider the offer. Of course, you have your own ego, your own demons that you have to wrestle with on your own."

He couldn't sleep that night. He was a singer, and without his voice, what would become of him? He'd be nobody—he'd have nothing to work for, nothing to strive for, nothing to believe in. What troubled him more was that Shuna seemed to think mainly about their family's security and comfort. What if he went mad from grief and remorse after he cut this deal with the devil? He could foresee that he'd never be able to live with himself after making this impossible bargain.

He called Harry Hong the next morning and told him that he had decided to decline the offer, its great generosity notwithstanding. "Please thank your clients for me," he said.

For a while Mr. Hong didn't say a word, though Tian could hear him breathing. Then Hong said, "On a personal note, Mr. Yao, I will remain your fan."

"Thanks very much for understanding."

What a relief he felt. He remembered Li Bai's line: "I am equal to any duke and prince when mingling with them."

When he told Yabin about the offer and his refusal two days later, his friend was stunned into silence for half a minute. Then he smiled warmly and said, "You have all my respect, Tian. Truth be told, if I were you, I might have taken the money. It makes one's life so much easier and more secure."

Tian was uncertain about that and felt money could also bring a lot of turmoil into one's life. Yabin then told him about a secret campaign called "Mouth Sealing," which was being carried out both inside and outside China. Some offices in the central government, particularly those in charge of global propaganda and overseas

Chinese affairs, had been making offers of money and real estate to intellectuals and dissidents who were critical about the state's policies. The condition for such an offer was to remain silent about anything the government undertook. Yabin knew that some people had accepted the money and the apartments and had stopped criticizing the Party. In fact, they had all disappeared from the media and the public view. Word had it that a few exiled dissidents in North America had accepted home loans and business deals from the Chinese government. In exchange, they worked as informers to sabotage efforts here to promote human rights and democracy back in China. Some of them took advantage of such an opportunity and just returned home, where they could remain silent and anonymous for good.

Their offer to Tian was, by far, the biggest that Yabin had ever heard of. "You're a man I can trust," Yabin told him. "You're upright and steadfast because you have no desire for material gain. But be careful. They'll make more trouble for you, I'm sure."

E VEN AS SHUNA URGED TIAN to stay in America, she was beginning to feel frustrated about his absence from home. In their
phone calls she often said how much she missed him and that
Tingting kept asking when he'd be back. She told him to be careful about women in New York. Back in China, when he went on
tour, he always traveled with female colleagues and mixed choirs,
and met talented, beautiful women at the performances, though
he managed to stay clear of any emotional entanglements. But it
wasn't like that here. Every once in a while, after a show, women
would approach him and show their interest in getting to know
him better, but they made him uneasy because he was uncertain
about their backgrounds. Some of them were likely covert agents
employed by the Chinese government. So he treated them perfunc-
torily and avoided any involvement. Unlike other men he knew,
Tian couldn't spend time with an attractive woman without becoming emotionally invested. Back in his former ensemble, there'd been
a lead dancer who'd always had a gaggle of young women around
him—he claimed they were all his girlfriends. Tian used to tease
him, saying he must be awfully exhausted. But the dancer said Tian
was too old-fashioned—for him, hopping into bed with a woman
was just a way to have fun and to relax. The amazing thing was that
the less commitment the dancer showed to any of the women, the
more eager they seemed to be with him.

Yabin, however, didn't seem to be so careful with women. In
early August he told Tian that Barrie had moved out and that he

was seeing someone new—a young Chinese woman, and a rare beauty. Her name was Freda Liu; she had just gotten her master's from Hunter College and began to work in foreign trade. When the three of them had brunch together one Sunday morning, she seemed poised and eager to find out more about Tian. She told him that her parents had both been army doctors in Chengdu, where she'd grown up. Tian was impressed by her Mandarin—it was flawless, without a trace of Sichuan accent. She also told him she'd gone to the University of International Relations in Beijing. At the mention of that school, Tian became leery—it was known as a top spy college that produced special graduates, many of whom were dispatched abroad as secret agents. Freda was talkative and laughed freely. When she laughed, she seemed unable to close her prominent eyes. Her egg-shaped face was so pale that Tian was surprised to hear that she traveled a lot and frequented seaside resorts. She loved the beaches in Dubai—they made her feel like she was living in a mirage.

"I enjoy your songs," she told him. "I'm sorry you're having a precarious life here."

"His career will pick up soon," Yabin joined in. "He has more freedom in choosing what to sing in America."

Tian told Freda, "I like it here. At least I have no one bossing me around."

She nodded in appreciation.

As they were eating egg foo yong, she told him he shouldn't be living alone. In this city, most people were too preoccupied with their own lives to pay attention to others. It was possible to grow sick and even die without anyone noticing. Freda had learned this lesson from the case of an old man, an immigrant from Bosnia, who'd lived alone and passed away in his apartment in Brooklyn—no one found him until two weeks later. By then his body already smelled, the odor spoiling the air in the hallway. To share your life with someone was a way of survival, a way to keep yourself balanced and sane. Freda hinted that she might be able to find Tian a girlfriend.

"I'm a married man with a young daughter," he said. "I have to do right by my old wife."

"I know your wife is a history professor, quite young actually," Freda said. "She's a good-looking lady, to say the least."

"That's why I ought to cherish her all the more," he quipped.

Freda and Yabin giggled, as if what he'd said was beside the point. Indeed, neither of them seemed serious about their new relationship. Freda even said she wasn't sure how long she would stay in this country, though she hoped she could immigrate if such an opportunity presented itself. Nowadays it was so difficult to get a green card, she said and sighed.

She was living on Long Island now, where she had just started working part-time at an import-export company. She couldn't keep a full-time job because she was taking courses at Hunter College. Only by remaining a student could she stay in the States legally. She loved to come to Flushing, though, for the shopping and the genuine provincial foods, so she and Yabin managed to spend a lot of time together. Yabin later told Tian that Freda was eager to move in with him, but he felt it was too soon. Whenever Tian saw the two of them, Freda brought up the topic of his single life, even though he kept reminding her that he was a family man. "For many immigrants and expats," she told him, "if your spouse can't join you in six months, you can be considered single and may live with a girlfriend or boyfriend. It's a healthier way of doing things."

But now that Shuna and he spoke every other day, she was on Tian's mind all the time, and he couldn't help but live and act as a family man. Before he'd left for the States, Shuna had told him that she wouldn't mind if he had a girlfriend abroad, believing he might have such a need. In recent weeks she often alluded to this topic in her emails, as though anxious to find out if he was still living alone.

He didn't like the way she had shown her generosity, as if she wouldn't have gotten hurt if he had lived with a woman in America. Shuna tried to play the role of the good, understanding wife, but he didn't need her to force herself like that. He once countered her in his email, asking, "How about you? Aren't you lonely yourself? Sometimes I wonder whether it's worth such a long separation for us to pursue the dream, or the illusion, of freedom. Now I can see why lots of people prefer security to freedom."

She didn't respond to his question directly and instead offered a

suggestion: "Perhaps we should allow each other to choose a temporary partner." It set his head spinning with misgivings. He remembered that Tingting had insinuated that her mother and Professor
Bai had been quite close lately and that Shuna had many friends.
Are there already other men in her life? he wondered.

The more Tian mulled about Shuna, the more agitated he became.
But he kept his unease to himself and always assumed a cheerful
tone in his emails to her. He wanted to maintain their mutual trust.

Freda knew quite a bit about his wife and referred to her as
"the smart lady." He told her, "It won't be easy for any woman to
outshine my wife. Some women have told me they felt intimidated
when they met her."

Yabin laughed and jumped in, "That's why I always say smart
women are sexy."

He sometimes talked about wealthy Chinese businessmen
who were looking for young women—mistresses as well as
child-bearers—who'd graduated from top colleges so that their children would inherit good genes and high intelligence. Tian thought
it preposterous—he felt that the intimacy between a man and a
woman should be based on the feelings they had for each other, not
on procreation. "You still believe in the bullshit of romantic love?"
Yabin challenged, grimacing. "It's an obsolete notion. Love pitches
its tent in excrement—that's from Yeats almost a century ago."

Tian sighed and admitted, "Perhaps I'm behind the times."

On Labor Day weekend, Yabin invited Tian to join him and Freda
and a few other friends at a shooting range in Edison, New Jersey.
Tian knew Yabin was fond of guns, and had once seen an M16 and a
revolver in his car, but Yabin didn't keep his firearms in New York.
He stored them at a club in New Jersey. The group he liked to go
shooting with was composed of other expats and exiled Chinese.
Some of them, having seen the crushed peaceful demonstration
in Tiananmen Square, overtly advocated violence and dreamed of
forming their own force to overthrow the Communist regime. They
argued that ten thousand unarmed civilians couldn't resist a squad
of soldiers who fired at them. One dissident had even tried to solicit

donations from successful businesspeople for raising a regiment of Chinese SEALs a thousand men strong. Yabin, though gentle and peace-loving, also wanted to become a marksman—not to kill but to master the skill. He revealed to Tian that some of the exiles had been taking lessons from a professional sniper. Tian wasn't interested in guns, but Yabin said some well-known dissidents would be at the shooting range, so he agreed to come along to meet those exiles.

The range was behind a knoll south of Edison. It looked like a man-made gulch, its slopes built of sandbags. Standing at the open end of the range, it felt safe and quiet, as the semi-enclosure seemed able to contain the firing. Five men from Yabin's group were already there when they arrived. They stood in wooden stalls, where they had been firing handguns at a pair of targets planted at the deep end of the range. Tian could see that none of them was a particularly capable shooter—they were all somewhat clumsy with guns. He recognized two of the men: Huang Fan, president of the Democratic Party of Chinese Nationals, a new political party composed of more than seven hundred expats, and a political commentator for the New Tang Dynasty Television network in North America, which was owned by Falun Gong. With them was a young American, Michael Pauley, who introduced himself as a professor of global studies at Columbia. Tian liked Huang Fan, who was more like a scholar than a political activist—he was book-smart and idealistic, eloquent with a tongue loose like a waterfall whenever he appeared on TV.

As Tian was shaking hands with them, they all said they were happy to meet him in person. Chang Huan, the political commentator, offered him his pistol. Tian fired three rounds, but none of them hit the target, so he handed the pistol back, saying he shouldn't waste their ammo. Yabin was more capable. He emptied a whole clip of bullets and didn't miss a single shot, though Tian could tell by the jumping puffs of dust behind the target that he had mostly hit the sides of the human figure, not the chest or head.

Freda shook her head. "You're not that good, Yabin. You can't kill an enemy if you shoot like that."

"Show me how well you can do, then," he challenged. "Always easier said than done."

Freda removed her sunglasses and took the pistol from him. She loaded five bullets and stepped aside to face a target on the right that hadn't been used yet. Without hesitation she began to fire. One after another, the shots hit the center of the human form. They were all astounded, and nobody said a word for a good while.

Yabin ran over and verified five bullet holes in the central part of the target. Shaking his head while striding back, he cried, "You've got forty-nine points."

Freda smiled and said almost apologetically, "I was on a shooting team at college."

Still, most of them remained silent. Professor Pauley said, "No wonder you're such a markswoman."

Freda teased Yabin, "You should keep in mind I can shoot. Don't ever be mean to me."

Yabin grimaced. He glanced at Tian, obviously uncertain how to respond, his eyes shifting.

The bespectacled Huang Fan drew Tian aside and whispered, "Who's this woman? Is she from mainland China?"

Tian nodded and said under his breath, "She's from Beijing and graduated from the University of International Relations."

"That explains it," Huang Fen said. "I'm wondering if Yabin really knows enough about her. I've never seen anyone who can shoot that well."

Tian also suspected that Freda might not have been completely honest with them. In a college shooting team, one would learn how to use a rifle or a small-caliber pistol for sports, not a Kimber Micro handgun like the one she had just fired. Who was this woman? A special agent? A former cadet of a military academy? If so, who sent her here? What was her mission? The questions hovered in Tian's mind for the rest of the day. Yabin must have been grappling with them as well.

On their way back, Yabin drove quietly with Freda in the passenger seat, and they hardly made any conversation. Tian pretended to be asleep in the backseat.

11

TIAN'S APARTMENT was in a four-story building. During the day most tenants went to work, so it was a quiet place. Since he lived on the first floor, with no neighbors below him to complain about noise, he began each day with his vocal exercises. These exercises made him feel alive and centered. Some people in the building must have heard him, but few grumbled except for Mrs. Guzzo, his landlady, who was in an adjoining unit. Once in a while she would hit a water pipe with a metallic object, perhaps the bottom of a pan or a hammer, though seldom would she come to complain in person. When he heard the protesting clanks, he'd do breathing exercises quietly instead, inhaling with his diaphragm slowly to keep his sternum elevated and his ribs expanded fully and then releasing the breath. This was to open his lungs smoothly. Whether he performed or not, he practiced diaphragmic breathing every day to keep himself in shape so he could sing with a loosened jaw, like he was cascading his voice. Later he went out to Bowne Park, which was nearby and had a limpid lake in it. Some Canada geese and mallards and small turtles lived on the waterside. Though older people would gather there, some with toddlers or pushing baby carriages, the place was secluded, wooded, and peaceful. After being there several times, Tian gave up singing there because he couldn't hear his own voice outdoors. Fortunately he wasn't far away from Queens College, where Ms. Fong, a librarian, loved his songs and allowed him to use a practice studio. But he had to call her beforehand to make sure a room would be available. He was amazed he could use a studio there for free. He would raise his voice gradually to the maximum, singing a self-made arpeggio. This was to ensure that he could sing high notes without straining his larynx. While singing, he'd keep smiling. In this way he could develop the brightness and clarity of his voice. There was a piano in the studio that he could use to find the right notes. He enjoyed getting around the campus incognito. If he'd practiced his voice somewhere in China, many people might have turned up to watch and greet him.

In late fall Shuna emailed him that his sister Anji was in danger— she'd been arrested in Dalian City for her involvement with Falun Gong. The news threw him into confusion and despair. He had suspected that his mother and sister might still be members of a Falun Gong branch in Liaoning province. Yet by his own observation, he could see that those practitioners were peaceful and posed no threat to anyone. Who had authorized the government to suppress them? The Chinese Constitution allowed free religious belief and expression. Tian couldn't help but view such suppression as another huge blunder by the national leaders, who, it seemed, never hesitated to make enemies. They were human beings who enjoyed making others suffer, and they were truly evil.

Anji's arrest indicated that she had still been a practitioner, and Tian knew his mother hadn't quit either—but why had his sister gone to prison alone? He called home and his mother picked up the phone. She sounded lethargic and a little hoarse.

"You must come back, Tian, to help your sister out of jail," she said.

"Where is she now? Where is she being held?" he asked.

"I don't have any clue. I go to the police station every day, but they won't let me see your sister, or tell me where she is. They said her case was beyond their power and they couldn't interfere with the campaign against Falun Gong started from Beijing."

"But they must know her whereabouts, don't they?"

"They said they had no idea."

"Why did they arrest her and not both of you? Were you not with her when they seized her?"

"I was sick that day and stayed home instead of going to the square for the group exercise. That was where they rounded up the practitioners."

He couldn't promise his mother that he would come back, unsure that his presence would be of any help. He talked about this with Shuna. She urged him to remain in America, saying he should consider returning only once they were clear about the charge against Anji and where she was, and how he could help her. Besides, he might be on the government's blacklist now. Shuna promised to keep in close touch with his mother and notify him of any new developments. She was going to Dalian City, about six hundred miles away, that weekend to see how his mother was managing.

For weeks he was restless, afraid something terrible would happen to Anji. She had just turned twenty-eight, worked as a technician at a veterinary clinic, and had been taking care of their mother. Now her absence would ruin their family. Tian had heard horrible stories of how Falun Gong practitioners suffered and were maimed in prison and labor camps. Some died of disease and malnourishment; and some lost their minds. When Shuna had visited Dalian, she'd offered to take his mother back to Beijing with her, but the old woman refused to leave home. She worried that she'd feel out of place in the capital, without her neighbors and friends and the beach—her apartment faced the ocean with a tiny patch of water view. Moreover, she had to find out what had happened to Anji, and had persisted with the local police every day. Shuna had no choice but to let her be.

A month later, in mid-November, word about Anji finally came. She was in a prison called Deliverance Detention Center outside Yingkou, a coastal city on Liaodong Peninsula. Her mother registered a request to visit her, but it was denied on the grounds that Anji was refusing to renounce her belief in "the pernicious cult." Not until Anji denounced Falun Gong publicly would they allow her to communicate with anyone outside, or allow her mother to visit her in jail. There was no way to make Anji change her mind, but her mother continued to go to the police station every day, saying she wanted to speak to her daughter. Tian knew that he wouldn't be able to bring his sister around either—like most Falun Gong practitioners, she was quite zealous. For many of them this must be their first communal religious experience, so for them apostasy was out of the question. Even his mother, he knew, would refuse to give it up. He had once pressed them to reflect on their devotion and even to question some of Master Li's teachings, but neither his mother nor Anji had heeded his words.

Still, he had to do something. From now on, he would remit an additional thousand dollars to Shuna every month so that she could exchange them for yuan and then pass the money on to his mother. To deal with the officials and the police, she'd need more cash on hand. Even her daily expenses would increase considerably because she wouldn't have time to shop or cook and would have to travel a lot to make inquiries and present petitions at higher offices. On the phone, he told her to find a way to visit Anji and buy her some warm winter clothes.

Then, in early December, his mother was informed that Anji was dying of kidney failure. They had shipped her to a hospital nearby, but they wouldn't say which one—only that she wasn't responding to treatment. When his mother at long last arrived at the detention center, there was only a small wooden urn containing Anji's ashes. She demanded an explanation, but the prison authorities said that Anji's body had begun to decay and couldn't have been kept any longer. That was the end of the story. As desperately as his mother tried, she couldn't get more information. Among the Falun Gong practitioners, it was said that Anji had been drugged, her kidneys chosen for important recipients in Beijing, and that the prison had rushed her execution to synchronize with the transplant operations. But no one could prove anything. Anji was dead, and her ashes were later interred together with their father's in their home village.

According to Yabin, many imprisoned Falun Gong practitioners had indeed been used as organ suppliers in mainland China. Some Party officials even had a hand in this lucrative underground business, which brought foreign customers over to major Chinese cities to receive organ transplants. Tian had seen such news reports, but he couldn't tell how prevalent this kind of organ harvesting was.

Nor was he absolutely positive that his sister had been killed for her kidneys.

His mother still could speak coherently, even though ravaged by grief. She told him not to even think about returning to China. "This country devours its people," she said. "Stay away from it, the farther the better. Settle down in America and then take your wife and child out of China." She spoke with total conviction.

He too was grieving for Anji. She had died so young, and to his knowledge, her boyfriend had broken up with her two years earlier because of her religious zeal. Her life seemed to have been misspent and misused. The loss of such a young life made Tian ponder the nature and meaning of the individual's existence in China. Anji seemed to have lived without a clear purpose of her own. Her religious devotion must have come out of hopelessness, and Falun Gong must have offered her a kind of solace. In spite of his calm appearance, Tian was seething with rage, angry at a society that couldn't provide adequate room for a young life to exist and grow. He felt something constantly clawing at him from within, trying to get out. Often he was on the verge of lashing out at someone, as if he could have grabbed hold of a person responsible for his loss.

12

TIAN HAD TO MAKE MORE MONEY, as he was now responsible for supporting his mother. Fortunately there was enough work in the winter, and he accepted any offer that came his way. From time to time he was contacted by associations in Asian countries—Singapore, Indonesia, the Philippines—with robust Chinese communities that often held cultural events. He had also received invitations from Australia. In spite of the good pay they offered, he couldn't go to any of those places on a Chinese passport—the visas were too hard for Chinese nationals to come by. Even if he got the visas needed for entry to other countries, he might not be able to come back to the States smoothly. In fact, what people in his situation feared most was that they couldn't return to America once they left, so most of them just avoided traveling abroad. Tian spoke about his predicament with Yabin. Yabin suggested he try to acquire a green card, with which he could travel outside the States and return without incident. His friend even recommended an American immigration attorney, saying Tian must avoid Chinese lawyers, especially those originally from China.

According to Yabin, there were two ways for him to get a green card: one was to seek political asylum and the other was to apply as a special professional for an H-1B visa, which would serve as a transitional step toward permanent residency. (After holding such a visa, he would qualify to apply for a green card.) Although he could be classified as a dissident of some sort, Tian would not seek political asylum. To his mind, that was a line that, once crossed, would make him an enemy of the Chinese government and endanger his family back in China. Yabin offered to look for a sponsor for his H-1B. Given that Tian was a reputable singer, there must be some cultural association that needed his service.

Attorney Marge Johnson, a tall middle-aged woman with thick glasses, accepted Tian's case and told him the process might take several months. Even though he still had to use a Chinese passport when traveling abroad, at least with long-term legal status in America, he could have the States as his base to return to, so ultimately he should get a green card. Besides a full folder of his paperwork, he left two albums with her so that she could review them and assess his case fully.

Three days later she called and asked him to meet with her on Monday. She didn't tell him why, and he felt anxious. For the whole weekend he wondered if there might be a problem with his application. When he went to Johnson's office on Monday morning, she was in good spirits and told him, "I listened to your albums and was very impressed. Maybe you should apply for immigration directly instead of an H1-B visa—you certainly qualify as a distinguished talent."

"You mean I should apply for a green card as an artist?" he asked.

"Correct. Obviously you are highly accomplished, a tremendous tenor. Now, I want you to come up with some names of artists who know your work and are already naturalized, or who were born Americans. Ideally they can vouch for your reputation and achievement. We should contact them and request letters of endorsement. Their support will be vital for your application and can expedite the process with USCIS."

"I will think up some names," he said.

They talked briefly about the cost, which would be similar to an H-1B visa, around three thousand dollars if everything went smoothly. He was pleased to hear that.

Later he spoke to Yabin about Johnson's suggestion. His friend believed that the lawyer was right and that he should apply directly for a green card, but Tian didn't know many artists in America. Yabin mentioned Tan Mai, the pi-pa player, and Hao Jiang, based at the Metropolitan Opera. Tian knew of Hao Jiang, who was a wonderful bass, originally from Beijing. In the States, Hao Jiang had overcome tremendous odds—professional competitions, English, poverty, prejudice, a divorce—and gained worldwide recognition during his tenure at the Met. But Tian didn't know him in person. Yabin urged him to write to Hao Jiang nonetheless, saying any decent person should give Tian a hand in a situation like this. Yabin had the contact information for both Tan Mai and Hao Jiang. The opera singer went to work at Lincoln Center, so Tian could send a letter to him care of the Met's office there, but he should print his name in the Chinese characters on the envelope so that Hao Jiang could recognize him as the sender. Following Yabin's advice, Tian wrote to both of them with his request.

To his amazement, they both agreed to write on his behalf and send their letters directly to Attorney Johnson. In total he needed four letters. With the support secured from the accomplished artists, the other two letters were easy to come by. Yabin would write one for him in the name of the community's cultural association, and Tian asked a professor of film studies at NYU, a first-rate poet who had once invited him to sing for an event. He was grateful for the help they gave him readily. He'd heard that such letters could cost a lot of money. In fact, there were people who charged hundreds of dollars for immigration letters, especially for applicants who didn't know English.

His sister's death was always on his mind. It cast dark shadows over his heart even when he was surrounded by cheer. What upset him most was the unclear cause of her death. Who would believe that a healthy young woman suddenly died of kidney failure?

Having nowhere else to turn, he approached Falun Gong's community center in Flushing to see if they might help him discover the truth. Cindy Wong received him in her office. She was all smiles, her heart-shaped face smooth and pale. She said she was elated to meet him in person finally.

"It sounds like your sister was used for organ transplants," Cindy said after he had explained Anji's imprisonment and death. Her curved eyebrows joined and her face fell a little. "I'm terribly sorry to hear this, Mr. Yao. This kind of sudden death happened to many of our fellow practitioners jailed in China. All the violent suppressions have been directed by 610 Office, which was set up in every city and every county there for religious persecution. For years organ harvesting has been some officials' way of generating their personal income. A cornea can sell for fifteen thousand dollars there. Those monsters would do anything to make money." Her bright eyes dimmed, blinking as she spoke.

"If that's what happened to my sister," he said, "I won't let the Chinese government get away with such an atrocity. It was murder!"

"I'm going to speak to my colleagues and we'll look into your sister's case."

"Thanks. That means a lot to me."

They also conversed a bit about themselves. In spite of her slight accent, she had never lived in China. He was amazed that she had grown up in Europe and could speak French, Italian, and Spanish. Her husband was a Serbian immigrant and currently a chemistry professor at Queens College. Tian hadn't expected to meet such an articulate, well-educated woman among the Falun Gong practitioners, most of whom had always seemed to him to be simplehearted hotheads. Cindy had an outgoing personality and even told him that she had worked on Wall Street, hired by a finance firm mainly thanks to her ability to read business transitions in several languages, but she had quit making money that way after she joined Falun Gong. She sincerely believed in the teachings of Master Li and felt she'd found her life's purpose in the religion. This was something Tian couldn't understand—he thought that some of Li's principles verged on bigotry, especially those regarding magic cures and homosexuality, though he admired Falun Gong's fundamental trinary belief: Truthfulness, Compassion, and Tolerance.

Falun Gong's network in China had largely been destroyed, so their investigation of Anji's case couldn't get any conclusive evidence. Still, Cindy contacted Tian from time to time. When the Spring Festival was at hand again, she called and invited him to join the Divine Grace troupe on an East Coast holiday tour. He accepted, partly as a way to mourn his sister's death, which—except for telling Cindy and Yabin—he'd kept to himself. Cindy said the troupe was thrilled that he would be joining them. Soon he saw their posters bearing his name and photo in community newspapers and grocery stores. He was glad that this time Shuna did not object to his new association with Falun Gong, even though it was likely to incite the Chinese government. She even said, "Sometimes you have to dismantle your bridges if you want to move ahead."

This year the troupe was much stronger, joined by several accomplished musicians and a large group of young dancers from an arts school in Taipei. Tian once suggested to Cindy that they invite Tan Mai as well, but Cindy said, "Ms. Tan won't play for us and says she's fully booked. I think she's afraid to make any kind of political statement."

Unlike him, Tan Mai must have drawn a line between her politics and her professional life. He couldn't blame her. But his association with the Divine Grace had personal reasons. He felt insulted and injured by the power that had destroyed his sister, and he resolved to protest its atrocity. In front of such savagery he couldn't simply cower and remain silent.

In mid-January, after joining for a few rehearsals, he began to travel with the troupe. They went to D.C., Boston, Providence, Chicago, Philadelphia. Their show was usually sold out before they'd even arrived. The performances were well received and rave reviews appeared in major newspapers, which gushed about the traditional Chinese choreography, the elegant dancers in long-sleeved costumes, the beautiful sets. Many American critics, who hadn't seen such a show before, even said that they were surprised by its genuine beauty and deep passion, that "every detail was perfect and every movement effortless and marvelous." Some said they would come back to the show next year, since the troupe would perform every winter from now on. Tian's songs were better received by the Chinese in the audience. He always sang two pieces, one composed by Falun Gong to celebrate their beliefs and another of his own choice, usually a folk song. The religious song was clunky, too didactic and flat, but he sang it with zest. Still, he couldn't summon up a lot of emotion for lines like these:

> We came down to look for the Way
> And be cleansed of our sins
> So we can form our divine bodies anew
> And return to Heaven in perfection.

As he sang, he pictured his sister as a young girl, innocent and full of life, with a small, mild voice and a delicate, birdlike frame, as a child who shone in recess games, shuttlecock, and jumping rope. The memories gave a sorrowful edge to his voice, and at moments he even turned tearful.

Chinese-language newspapers published photos of his performances, and one even ran the phrase "the Prince of Songs" in the headline, which gave him mixed feelings. Such publicity made him uneasy, because to perform with a Falun Gong troupe could be viewed as degradation by his brainwashed colleagues back in China, but he wanted to sing for the Divine Grace as a kind of grieving for his sister. From time to time, after a performance someone would come up to him and ask to take a photo, which he usually agreed to. A young man once presented him with a bottle of wine as a token of gratitude. Tian didn't drink but accepted the gift, which he later passed on to Yabin.

His travels with the troupe began to agitate Shuna, however. She saw photos online of the Divine Grace's performances, which showed many pretty young dancers. Again she assumed he was surrounded by women when on tour. At night he would phone her because it was six or seven times cheaper for him to call China than vice versa. One night Shuna even said, "I won't mind if you spend time with someone there as long as you don't catch disease and take good care of yourself."

"Why did you say that?" he asked. "You know I'm not that kind of a man and can't trust any woman here."

"You might feel lonely and need some company." She tittered, somewhat nervously.

"How about you?" he asked, thinking of Professor Bai.

"I'm fine . . . I can manage. I mean, I have so many friends and colleagues here that I don't feel lonely or isolated. I'm worried about you, though. Don't work too hard. You don't need to send us money every month."

He was moved. Deep inside, he could trust Shuna. What he told her about his uneasiness with other women was true. Even when he found a woman attractive, he usually felt too uncomfortable in her presence to act on it. Some women here reminded him of Yabin's girlfriend, Freda, who could easily unnerve a man.

He asked Shuna to keep an eye on his mother. Shuna promised to go see her at least once a month, to give her money and make sure she was managing on her own. His mother still refused to go to Beijing, bent on staying with her fellow Falun Gong practitioners. Shuna said that the local police might simply leave his mother alone, fearing that she might die on their hands if they took her in. It was said that their superiors were instructing them, above all, to prevent people from going to the capital to air their grievances against the local government, so every day a policewoman stopped by his mother's to see if she was in. Other than that, they avoided her, afraid she'd demand a clear answer to the cause of her daughter's death and the names of those who had received Anji's organs. She seemed to have become a dreaded nuisance to the local police, who always claimed they hadn't been involved with Anji's death at all.

13

A FTER THE DIVINE GRACE TOUR ENDED and Tian had returned to New York, a man from the Chinese consulate called him. He introduced himself as Guo Fen, a new vice consul in charge of cultural affairs. He'd been following Tian in the news and was wondering why he had suddenly become so active, performing in various cities with the Divine Grace, which the Chinese government viewed as a subversive association abroad.

"Can we meet in my office tomorrow afternoon?" the vice consul asked.

Aghast, Tian managed to say, "I have another engagement tomorrow afternoon."

"I can be very flexible about time," Guo went on. "How about the day after tomorrow?"

"What's this about?"

"There's been some misunderstanding between us, which has been exploited by people with ulterior motives. We'd better have direct communication to sort things out, don't you think?"

Considering he might have his passport renewed in the near future, Tian agreed to come and see the diplomat in two days, though he was disturbed by the invitation. He called Yabin and shared his concerns with him—he feared that once he entered the consulate at the western end of 42nd Street, he might not be able to come out. Yabin chuckled and said they were unlikely to detain someone like him, because that would make news. Tian was still nervous and uncertain about the visit.

After a pause, Yabin said, "I can accompany you to the consulate and wait for you at the entrance. If they don't let you out, I'll contact the media."

"That's very generous of you. Thank you so much, Yabin. I wouldn't know how to manage without your help."

"That's what friends are for, and I'm glad I'm available."

Two days later, they took the 7 train into Manhattan. To their surprise, the guard at the entrance to the consulate, a middle-aged man with a beardless equine face and a nasal voice, would not allow Yabin to stay in the tiny lobby. Yabin waved at the man dismissively, then told Tian, "I can wait outside. Try to speak as little as possible and just let the official do the talking. Remember, don't lose your temper or make any promises."

"I'll remember," Tian said, and headed toward the elevators.

Vice Consul Guo's office was on the third floor. Tian was led in by a young woman. There was nobody in the spacious room; one of its windows looked out on the Hudson. An opened laptop, swathed in a pool of sunshine, was sitting on a desk beside another window. He sat down on a maroon pleather sofa and took a sip of the tea the woman had poured for him. The tea was Dragon Well but tasted a little bland, no longer fresh and maybe already two or three years old. An acrid smell hung in the room and made him wonder whether someone had been smoking. On the wall was a horizontal scroll of calligraphy, which declared: "Man's Role Is to Try!" Left out was the second half of the ancient motto: "Heaven Decides."

Vice Consul Guo stepped in, stretching out his hand. He was smiling, the ends of his eyes tilted up. The official was in his late forties and looked smooth and intelligent, the hair at his temples graying. Tian shook his hand, which oddly felt callused, like a carpenter's. "Sit down, sit down," he urged Tian.

Tian looked at his watch: 3:15—Guo was a quarter-hour late.

"We have time," the vice consul said. "Sorry about being late."

"My friend is waiting outside. He was not allowed to enter the building."

Guo smiled understandingly. "We won't take long. I was with Ambassador Zhou and couldn't excuse myself sooner." He lifted his tea and drank a mouthful.

He insisted that they simply make friendly conversation and that he meant to help Tian. Indeed, he sounded like an older brother with more experience of life. Tian tried to remain quiet, to listen and not speak.

"To be honest, I question the wisdom of your leaving China," Guo continued. "It was a rash move, to say the least. See how hard your life is here. Back in our motherland you never needed to stoop to random gigs. Wherever you went, you were in the limelight. Look how you have reduced yourself—you must be living from hand to mouth now. Doesn't it feel terrible not to be able to draw a monthly salary anymore? As a longtime admirer of yours, I feel sorry for you."

"True, there's a lot of uncertainty here, but I'm free at least," Tian said, unable to remain silent any longer.

The vice consul tipped back his head and laughed. "Freedom is largely an illusion. At most it's merely a feeling, perhaps not even a healthy feeling. Freedom is always contingent on the agency you have. A beggar might have freedom but no dignity. His freedom is worthless when his stomach rumbles with hunger pangs. In China you're famous and can have all the opportunities others can only dream of. Why abandon everything and start from square one here? If I were you, I wouldn't forfeit all the advantages you've had."

"Well, I know freedom is a different kind of suffering away from tyranny, but I am willing to suffer for it."

Guo didn't seem to understand Tian's words and went on, "Come to think of it: You were already well ahead of the multitudes back in China. Why should you restart your life here and have to compete with Americans?"

"I don't see anyone as a rival here—no competition to speak of."

"Still, you're striving to get ahead of others."

"You ought to think differently from the typical Chinese mindset."

"What do you mean?"

"To put it more candidly, many of our compatriots have this as their goal of life: to live above others. That's a typical Chinese way of thinking, but that's not what I want for my life."

"What would you like to achieve, then?"

"To be an artist following my own heart."

"Do you think you can do that by joining the Falun Gong troupe?"

"I'm not a practitioner of Falun Gong, but my younger sister was a believer, and she died in prison outside Yingkou because she wouldn't renounce her belief. There's no clear explanation of her death. The prison authorities told my mother that my sister had died of kidney failure, but she had no history of kidney problems. So the government owes my family an explanation and an apology."

"This is news to me," Guo said, looking genuinely astonished. After a pause, he resumed, "But if your sister was a Falun Gong practitioner, she broke the law and was incarcerated for that. That is clear."

"China's constitution says clearly that every citizen has the right of free religious expression. The government had no right to imprison my sister in the first place."

Guo lowered his head wordlessly. Tian continued with tears of anger in his voice, "It's also said that my sister was executed so as to supply organs for important recipients in Beijing."

"You can't buy that kind of malicious slander. Our country would never commit such an atrocity."

"Then we need a clear explanation all the more. Can you look into this for me? I simply can't stop mourning my sister. That's why I have been performing with the Divine Grace."

Vice Consul Guo said he would file an inquiry about Anji's case, but he made clear that this might be beyond the power of the Ministry of Foreign Affairs, so he couldn't promise answers. He also emphasized that no hospital in China would engage in harvesting organs, so Falun Gong's report on the use of his sister's kidneys was a downright lie. Tian didn't argue with him. He thanked him, but repeated his position that unless the government gave him a reasonable explanation, he would continue to mourn his sister's death. Their conversation ended on a somewhat agreeable note. Guo Fen appeared concerned and considerate, but he also conveyed the official stand that Tian must come back to China as soon as possible so that he could salvage his career and resume "a more normal life." Guo even showed some pity for Tian's current state, which to him was a terrible waste of his talent. To him the Divine Grace was like a joke, an absolute degradation for Tian. The vice consul assured him that once he returned, he could perform anywhere in China, provided that he cut all ties with Falun Gong. Tian thanked him again but did not accept his offer, knowing that once he was back, he wouldn't be able to leave. Also, in China he'd have to sing more propaganda songs. He wanted to develop a new career here, though he wouldn't say this openly to the official. Nonetheless, he had to confess he liked Guo Fen's mild manner. If Guo hadn't represented the government, Tian might have been willing to get to know him better.

Yabin was sitting on a bench on the other side of the street on the Hudson near the *Intrepid,* the old aircraft carrier on display, whose deck was lined with red-tailed white fighters. He seemed to be skimming a copy of *The New York Times.* The afternoon sun showered patches of light on the sidewalk. A young woman in a navy sweatsuit jogged by, holding the leash of her black schnauzer. Beyond her, a mother was pushing a stroller. At the sight of Tian, Yabin stood up and crossed the street to join him. As they rounded the corner of the gray building, Tian saw a camera flash twice on a pole about three hundred feet away. Apparently visitors to the consulate were recorded visually by the FBI or the CIA, but this didn't bother him. There must be numerous cameras concealed in this area.

Together the two of them headed east toward the subway station. In spite of Tian's composed appearance, his meeting with the vice consul had unsettled him. What the man said about his opportunities and privileges back in China was by no means groundless. To some extent, Guo was correct to point out that his coming to America had reduced him considerably. Now Tian had to take his livelihood into his own hands, responsible for every meal and every bill, though freedom he did have, which he had realized was essentially a willingness to be responsible for himself.

On the train back to Flushing, he remained reticent, his mind heavy with reflections on his situation. When Yabin asked him about his meeting with the vice consul, he answered succinctly, saying the official had tried to persuade him to return to China but he had refused.

That evening Tian took Yabin to dinner at Little Taipei on 39th Avenue. He liked the food there, which wasn't too spicy or greasy. The place usually offered live entertainment, a small band with a guitar and a mandolin, sometimes an oboe, but this evening there was no music. They ordered four dishes: squid cabbage, sautéed watercress, a steamed white fish, and shredded pork with bamboo shoots. They each had a tall bottle of Tsingtao beer.

The tasty dinner loosened them both up, and Yabin became more talkative. He said that these days he was having trouble getting along with Freda. She expected him to do something with her on every holiday, in both the Western and the lunar calendars. He couldn't imagine continuing to live with such a troublesome woman.

Tian hadn't known they were living together now. "Are you not scared of her?" he asked Yabin jokingly. "It must be nerve-racking to have a sniper in bed."

"Not really. She went through firearms training in college. That doesn't bother me. She can be tender and sweet, even caring, but she has a hell of a temper and is always jealous. She might have had some bad experiences with men in the past."

"She seems quite smart." Tian took a swallow of his beer.

"She's capable but obstinate." Yabin picked up a tiny stout squid with his chopsticks and put it into his mouth.

"Don't you want to settle down and start a family soon?"

"I've thought a great deal about that of late," Yabin admitted, "but it's hard to imagine marrying a woman like Freda."

"How old are you now?"

"Thirty-seven."

"So you still want to date around?"

Yabin laughed. "It's just because I haven't met a woman I can love wholeheartedly. I can be very devoted, but I won't compromise on the matter of love."

Tian remembered Yabin quoting the line from Yeats: Love pitches its tent in excrement. Apparently Yabin still believed in love after all. Tian told him, "If you want to break up with Freda, you should do it soon. Otherwise she'll think you've been misleading her and wasting her time."

"That's what I've been thinking too. I have to be careful with her, though. At any moment she can go off like a firecracker."

No one but Yabin would share his innermost thoughts with him like that, so Tian confessed that he missed his family terribly. But Yabin shook his head and said, "If I were you, I'd find a woman here. It must be very lonely to stay single like you."

"I have a daughter," Tian said. "If I lived with someone else, it would be hard for me to face my family when we are together again."

"Can't you live with a woman without any commitment? No strings attached, you know. This can also save a lot of expenses for both sides."

"It would be hard for me. I couldn't help but get entangled emotionally. In a way, I admire a man like you. I cannot relax with a woman I really like. For me, love is like a fever, an illness."

"I'm not who you think I am. If I met the right person, I could be very devoted and loyal too."

Tian wasn't sure Yabin could truly be that serious about a relationship. His friend sighed and said he knew several Chinese exiles who were living as Tian did. That kind of separation from their spouses was entirely man-made. "Unnatural," in his opinion.

"Don't worry about me," Tian told him. "I'm an artist and can use my energy creatively."

"That's a Freudian idea. He believed that a genuine artist must live moderately so as to conserve his creative energy, including sexual energy."

Tian was not familiar with Freud but was impressed by what Yabin said. Compared to him, Yabin was a learned man.

14

S INCE HIS TOUR WITH THE DIVINE GRACE, few offers of work had come to him. When the holiday season was over, opportunities became scarcer. Tian began to worry about how he would earn a regular income. No matter what, he had to send money home every month. Yabin suggested he take on a couple of students, and Tian liked the idea. With Yabin's help, he put out an ad in a small Chinese newspaper and also distributed flyers throughout his neighborhood—in grocery stores, Laundromats, hair salons, the public library.

His fee was reasonable, fifty dollars per lesson, but the students were a disappointment to him. Five people of various ages applied, and he accepted them all regardless of their talent. They came to his apartment individually to take lessons. He didn't have a piano but used a keyboard instead, which was good enough for practice and teaching. One student, a Mr. Chang, was already eighty-one. He was retired and had worked as a hotel shift supervisor, but he loved singing. He admired Tian so much that the instant he'd seen his ad he had called him to schedule a lesson. He introduced himself as a fellow provincial, though his hometown, Harbin, was nowhere near Dalian. Many people from the northeast of China act this way, viewing anyone from one of the three provinces as a fellow provincial. The northeasterners in the diaspora would hold picnics and outings and festive gatherings together, as if the region, formerly Manchuria, were one big province. So Tian acquiesced when Mr. Chang claimed him as a fellow provincial. The old man was scrawny and withered, with a narrow face and a shiny bald head, but he had a strong voice. Tian could imagine him dreaming of singing onstage when he'd been young. But Tian would have rejected him on the spot if they'd been in China. At his age Chang couldn't possibly train his hoarse voice and grow into a decent singer.

The other students were younger: two girls in their late teens, still in high school, and two men in their thirties—one was a custodian at City Hall and the other an accountant in a furniture company. Unlike the four younger students, Mr. Chang didn't seem interested in learning how to sing. He gave Tian the impression that he didn't care about the tuition he'd paid and was only eager to get to know the teacher better. Chang had a low opinion of the earlier immigrants from Guangdong and Fujian who had come to America two generations before, and blamed them for the backward image imposed on the Chinese in American society. "They brought here the worst of our culture," he'd say. Although Tian didn't share his view, he didn't argue with him. Sometimes, when he asked Chang to repeat a phrase or a note after him, the codger would shake his head and claim, "I'm too old to go through this. I'm dog-tired—don't treat me like a child." Tian let him have his way. Mr. Chang once invited Tian to dinner at a Shanghainese restaurant. "They use real crabmeat in their small soup buns," he assured him. Tian declined, saying he had too many other engagements. Chang's odd behavior made him nervous, and Tian suspected he might be an agent hired by someone to spy on him. He told Yabin his suspicion. His friend said this was likely—there were all sorts of agents and informers here under the employ of the Chinese government. Some people were ready to undertake such a mission without pay—college students often viewed it as something that could enrich their credentials for when they returned to China after graduation.

About six weeks after Tian had begun teaching, he got a call from Freda.

"Can you accept me as your student?" she asked blithely. Over the phone she sounded younger than she was.

"Well, I never thought you'd be interested in singing," he said, a little flummoxed.

"I've always enjoyed listening to music. Studying with a great singer like you, at least I can find out if I'm talented." She giggled shyly. "Also, someday I might brag about being your student."

"Does Yabin know this? I mean, was this his idea for you to study with me?" He was still nonplussed.

"He told me you were accepting students. But I don't have to get his permission if I want to learn from you, do I?"

"Of course not."

"Then take me on. Who is to tell I won't bring honor to you one of these days?"

That only made him more baffled. He said, "You mustn't think of success that way. Better start with some sense of failure."

"What do you mean?"

"Ultimately there's no success, but in confronting difficulties we can display our worth as a human being. So in the long run even success might not mean anything."

"Wow, that's philosophical. I knew you were deep, but I didn't expect you had that kind of take on life. This makes me more eager to study with you. Can you accept me or not? I'll pay you three months' fee in advance."

"All right, I can take you, but there's no need to pay for more than one month at a time—four lessons."

"I'm so glad to hear this. You made my day, Teacher Yao."

"Just call me Tian. We've known each other for a long time."

"Sure, thank you, Tian!"

They both laughed. He was amazed that he could relax with Freda, who had so many unanswered questions surrounding her. He hoped she wouldn't disturb the peaceful order of his teaching.

Later, over lunch at a congee house, he told Yabin about Freda's phone call. Yabin shook his head and said, "She's starstruck. To her, you're a big celebrity, you know."

"But I'm like nobody here." Tian tried to sound casual, without any bitterness.

"Freda doesn't have a balanced sense of time and place. Part of her mind seems to still operate with a Chinese compass."

Tian made no comment, but could see there might be some virtue in such a mind uninfluenced by the force of circumstances. If nothing else, it suggested a strong will. He wasn't sure whether Freda was such a willful person that she couldn't see his true condition here: He was already diminished almost to nobody. How come she couldn't see that he had never bothered to teach to make a living back in China?

"If you want me to turn her away," he said to Yabin, "I can tell her my teaching load is full."

"No need to be so serious about her. To be honest, I might wash my hands of her."

"What do you mean?"

"She's a free woman and can do whatever she wants. I won't be involved with her from now on."

Seeing him still bewildered, Yabin added, "I might break up with her."

"Why? She's too much trouble?"

"Not exactly. I'm just tired of her. She's very interested in you, though—she keeps asking about you."

Tian was alarmed, wondering whether her studying with him might be a secret assignment of some sort. As their conversation continued, Yabin talked at length about the difference between dating a Chinese woman and dating a non-Chinese. He mentioned his former girlfriend Barrie, comparing her with Freda. If he had to choose between the two, he would prefer Barrie, because, according to him, foreign women tended to appreciate small kindnesses he showed them and were willing to divide the chores with him. Freda, being a single child in her family, took him for granted and always expected more. More than that, she openly demanded that he love her wholeheartedly, with total commitment. How could he possibly commit himself to a woman he didn't know fully yet?

"But didn't you often go to bed with her?" Tian asked, unconvinced by his reasoning.

Yabin laughed. "That's the question Freda often asks, like I've robbed her of something precious by sleeping with her. Barrie wasn't like that. She viewed sex as something we gave to each other. She appreciated the effort I made."

Tian chuckled but didn't say any more. Yabin's words convinced him that it would be safe to take Freda as a student, but he must be careful when dealing with her.

Mr. Chang stopped showing up for his lessons. At first, Tian thought this was due to his old age and frail health, but Tian overheard at the nearby Laundromat that a bunch of old men, Mr. Chang among them, had gone to the Foxwoods casino in Connecticut last weekend and that they'd lost so much money that some of them were laid up. Tian called him to see if he still wanted his lessons. Chang sounded hoarse over the phone, and said he had a nasty cold. He told his teacher that he couldn't join him anymore.

"How should I refund the remaining fees you've paid me?" Tian asked him.

"I don't need a refund, Mr. Yao. Keep the money as my donation."

"Thank you, Mr. Chang. But I still owe you two lessons. Whenever you feel like coming, just give me a call."

"That might not happen again. At my age, do you really believe I can become a good singer even though I go through all the necessary training?"

"That's still possible."

"I'm not that optimistic. I went to see you only because they assigned me the job."

"Assigned you? What do you mean?"

"An official whose name I'd better not disclose. Let me just say this: They thought me incapable of keeping tabs on you, so they had me replaced."

"With whom?" Tian persisted, surprised that Chang's tongue was so loose. He must be addled by his rotten luck at the casino and by his anger at being dismissed from his spying mission. It had been stupid of the officials to hire such an octogenarian in the first place.

"I'm not sure who my replacement is," he said, and heaved a wheezy sigh. "I hated to rat on you anyway. Just be careful, Mr. Yao. Like I said, I'm a big fan of yours and wish you all the best of luck. Even though we've met only a couple times, I can see you're a kind-hearted man."

"Come on," Tian said, exasperated, "tell me who the spy is. You don't even have to name him or her. Let me mention the students one by one, and you just cough when I reach that name."

"Don't trouble yourself about this. I've already said too much."

In spite of his bafflement, Tian thanked him and wished him a speedy recovery. Chang's revelation unsettled him and forced him to wonder about the man's successor. None of the other students seemed like a spy at all except for Freda, who had enrolled just the previous week. But there was no way Tian could verify his guess. He thought of declining her as a student, but she'd already paid him two hundred dollars, so he decided to keep her and reminded himself to be cautious when he was with her. He believed he had nothing to hide and wouldn't mind if they sent over ten spies, as long as they all paid him his fee.

Freda turned out to be a better student than the others. She didn't have an exceptional voice, but she was serious about bringing out its potential, and it was clear that she was practicing at home. By contrast, most of the other students weren't taking their practicing seriously, and he could see that the two girls had come to him mainly because their parents had paid the fees for them. They took the lessons merely for a lark.

Soon Freda offered to work for Tian, to be his manager. She said she knew a lot of people and was good at business management. These months he'd hardly had any bookings and he was anxious about how to maintain his singing career. At first he was skeptical about Freda's offering, but when he mentioned it to Yabin, his friend said that it was worth trying her out, given her extensive connections.

"But how about you?" Tian asked him. "Are you willing to let Freda take over?"

"Don't worry about me. I'm already too busy with my insurance work. She might do a better job for you. If I were you, I'd give her a try."

Tian also mentioned the possibility that Freda might be a spy, at which Yabin laughed, saying no sane person would employ her for an espionage mission. She was simply too extroverted to hide anything. So Tian decided to hire her.

She began to reach out to cultural organizations and art centers to see if they were interested in Tian. Yet only four places offered to engage him, and they didn't pay much, between five and thirteen hundred dollars per job. Still, he was pleased, believing that when the fall started, business might pick up. There'd be the Moon Festival and the mainland's and Taiwan's national days. Yet Freda seemed disappointed by the meager responses—she must have realized that her work for him would be minor. She had no idea that the Divine Grace toured only in winter, so at best he could have one season's work if they continued to use him. Her frustration also reaffirmed his decision to take on students—there was no way he could make enough by singing. By far teaching these talentless students was easier and steadier work. He offered them basic skills: breathing technique, vocal exercises, singing simple songs. Some of them had learned to read music in China where the notes are transcribed differently, so he also taught them how to read music in the Western way. Obviously none of them was serious enough to aspire to sing onstage someday. This made his work easier, so he wouldn't grumble.

Then in late July the two girls quit, claiming they were going to be away for the rest of the summer. Their leaving at the same time made Tian wonder if this was really coincidental. Two weeks later another student, the custodian at City Hall, dropped out too. Freda told Tian, "Some hands are behind this, I'm sure. They mean to drive you out of business. To show that without the backup of our country, no Chinese artist can survive in the U.S." She sucked her teeth. She had gotten a root canal two days earlier, which cost her almost a thousand dollars. She'd had to pay out of her own pocket, having no dental insurance. She used to have it, but the policy had been canceled due to a missed payment.

He was puzzled but half-joked, "You mean the Chinese government intends to sabotage my business? Aren't you working for them too?"

"Please, I work for you. You're my boss." She pointed her slim finger at his face. "You can trust me."

"So you won't leave me like the others?" he asked.

"Certainly not." She smiled. "You will find me to be a very loyal woman."

15

Later he discovered that a performing arts school had recently opened in Jackson Heights, founded by a group of Chinese expats. They charged very low rates, less than half his fee, and had a small three-story building as their base. Yabin believed that a media company in mainland China was behind them. The school had admitted dozens of students. Freda learned that the two girls who had left Tian were in fact attending that school now. He was upset, though having vaguely expected that the Chinese officials would damage his livelihood one way or another.

Yabin finally broke up with Freda. He claimed she had become a piece of baggage that he couldn't carry anymore, so it was time to drop her. But Freda didn't let him go so easily. She called him a brazen womanizer and claimed she'd make him regret leaving her. That frightened Yabin, who was not as strong-minded as he seemed to be.

"Maybe I should leave New York," Yabin told him one evening.

Tian laughed and said he was silly to consider decamping because of a jilted girlfriend. "Freda should be able to cool down soon," he assured Yabin. "To be fair, she seems to be reasonable and working hard for me. She's just upset that things didn't work out with you."

"She likes you a lot," Yabin said. "Be careful, you might have a groupie on your hands."

Tian held on to his suspicions about her. But when working with Freda, he found her behavior unremarkable and forthcoming. She despised the Chinese government and was outraged by its policies, especially its suppression of the minorities in Tibet and Xinjiang. She used the word "medieval" to describe China's current legal system and its maltreatment of the petitioners from the provinces who went to Beijing to register their grievances and seek justice. In some ways Freda was like an exiled democracy activist, though she didn't like America that much either, saying life was difficult here, especially for someone with yellow skin and black eyes. She did believe, though, that in general Americans worked harder than Chinese because most of them were convinced that you could get rich by working hard. This pointed to a major difference between China and the United States. "Here hard work always gets rewarded, more or less," she once told Tian. "This means that the American social system is basically fair, and supported by most people."

Her way of reasoning impressed him. He too noticed that many Americans believed they could get rich by working hard. As for the issue of fairness, Freda had simplified too much, without considering the immense gap between the haves and the have-nots in America. Yet the more time Tian spent with Freda, the less suspicious he became of her. She was immature at times, willful and fiery, but sympathetic at heart.

To his surprise, Yabin decided to leave New York in the late fall. A cousin of his from Jiangsu province had recently bought a piece of land, twenty-seven acres, in Braintree, Massachusetts, and had asked Yabin to help him set up a new construction business. His cousin was a developer and planned to build more than thirty homes on the land he had just acquired, which was close to the train station. Tian was amazed that a small businessman could be so bold, given that the man hardly knew any English and had never stepped foot in North America. He had clinched the land purchase from his home city, Nantong, through an agent based in Boston's Chinatown. Tian was somewhat demoralized by Yabin's decision to leave and asked him why they'd begin to build houses in the cold weather—it was already early November now. Yabin said he was needed for all the paperwork and the preparations that his cousin had to complete before the construction started in the spring.

Yabin's departure saddened Tian. Yabin had been a good friend, a man-about-town, full of buoyancy and always ready to give him a hand. But he didn't show his feelings in front of Yabin. Yabin assured him that if he found New York too difficult, he could join him in the Boston area. "My cousin is rich, friendly, and generous," he told Tian. "You'll like him."

In his emails to Shuna, Tian couldn't help lamenting the loss of Yabin. She tried to console him, saying he'd surely find new friends and new ways of improving his life in New York. "Friends come and go," she wrote. "If friendship is not based on shared interest, it doesn't always last. You shouldn't be too upset about Yabin leaving."

He didn't tell Shuna about the woman Yabin had left behind— Freda, who was still working for him. By now he had stopped teaching. In December, the Divine Grace embarked on its performing season, so he again traveled with them. He was contracted to sing with them in eight cities in a period of ten weeks. For this seasonal work he'd be paid eight thousand dollars, which he didn't have to share with Freda since his agreement with the troupe had been made long ago. Freda also booked some engagements for him, and his work began to get into full swing again. She worked diligently and seemed to enjoy representing him, probably because, without a boyfriend now, she had more time. She even printed some business cards for herself, as his manager. Though they spoke on the phone almost every day, he rarely saw her in person. While he was on tour, she would call him around eleven p.m., after the show was over and he had returned to his hotel. Little by little he began to expect to hear from her at night. After they'd gone over the business arrangements she was making on his behalf, she often talked about a microeconomics course she was taking at Hunter College (besides a dance class) in order to keep her student status, and about her parents back in Shenyang City. She often asked after his wife and daughter, as if she knew them personally.

Like Shuna, Freda was curious about whether he'd met any women on tour. She also mentioned the elegant young dancers in the Divine Grace and once teased him, saying, "They're so beautiful. Are you not attracted to any of them? If I were a man, I'd do my damnedest to sleep with every one of them."

Annoyed by her crass flippancy, he said, "Then you would be below the average man who thinks of nothing but food and sex all the time. I have to save my energy for work."

Later she explained that nearly all the men she had known regarded sleeping with a pretty woman as an achievement. Even Yabin had told her that whenever he went to bed with a girl, he felt like he'd accomplished something. Tian laughed and told her, "For me, love comes from the mind more than from the body. I'm more attracted to a woman's personality than to her physical beauty."

"Well, that makes you different, above the average man, I guess," she said blandly.

He wasn't sure whether she was mocking him, but he let it pass.

When the Divine Grace tour ended, he returned to Flushing and resumed his everyday life. In April Freda came down with a nasty flu, coughing persistently; her nose was so blocked that she had to blow it hard every few minutes. She was running a fever and claimed she couldn't lie down at night because of her cough, and was forced to nap sitting up on a sofa. As a result, she slept only three or four hours a night. More troublesome, she had no medical insurance (her part-time job didn't provide benefits), and dared not go to the hospital. She asked Tian whether he knew a good doctor of Chinese medicine.

He happened to know an herbal pharmacy on Union Street in downtown Flushing, which had a physician who saw patients for ten dollars per visit. It was called Lasting Health and offered hundreds of medicinal herbs. Tian had been there twice to buy medicines for cold and a sore throat. He had also gotten an herbal ointment for the blisters on his fingers, which would mysteriously appear every two or three years. Freda asked him to accompany her there, afraid they might take advantage of her if she went alone. He agreed, though privately he felt her worries were groundless.

A tall, gaunt woman at the counter greeted them warmly. She remembered Tian, calling him Mr. Yao. He told her that Freda was ill and needed to see Dr. Liang. The woman went into the rear quarters of the pharmacy to see if the old physician was there. Without delay Dr. Liang came out and led them into a back room. He had thin shoulders, one higher than the other, but he looked sturdy given his age, which he claimed was ninety. Tian was impressed by his alert looks, wrinkled eyes, and graying beetle brows, his wide jaw still clearly contoured. In every way he was well preserved.

The doctor placed four fingers on Freda's wrist and closed his eyes to listen. Then he asked her to stick out her tongue. Tian saw her tongue thin and agile, its underside covered with purple veins like filaments. Dr. Liang shook his full head of white hair and told her, "You have too much fire in your liver, and your kidneys lack water."

"You mean I'm sick?" she asked.

"Yes, very sick."

"How serious is it?"

"I'm going to prescribe a set of herbs. They should help. If you don't get better in a week, come back to see me again."

He opened a notebook and wrote on a lined page the names of a dozen or so herbs in the Chinese characters and the amount for each one. He tore off the sheet and told Freda, "Go to the front counter and get the herbs from Mrs. Siu." He handed Freda the prescription.

"Do I need to boil the herbs in a clay pot?" she asked.

"People don't do that anymore. We have the extract of every herb, so you can mix the powders and pour boiled water on them. You drink the concoction like tea. Very easy."

That pleased Freda, who took her leave and went to the front to get the prescription.

"How about you?" the doctor addressed Tian, slitting his eyes.

"I'm well."

"You don't look well. Let me check on you." He lifted his hand, his fingers wiggling.

"How much will you charge me for a diagnosis?" Tian asked.

"Ten dollars, everybody's the same."

"All right." He turned and called, "Freda, I'll join you in a moment."

He let Dr. Liang feel his pulse, which throbbed stronger under the pressure of his fingertips. The old man's face was expressionless, as if he was concentrating his mind.

A moment later he breathed a sigh and shook his head. He said, "Your kidneys are very weak and you must do something to enhance their functions."

"I haven't indulged in alcohol or sex. How could my kidneys have deteriorated so much?"

"In fact, to have sex from time to time can keep your organs functioning normally. There's no need to live like a monk or eunuch, given that you're still young." Liang smiled, his eyes almost disappeared. Then he added, "Don't you often get up to pee at night?"

"I do," Tian admitted.

"How many bathroom trips do you make a night?"

"Three or four."

"Is there froth in your urine like beer?"

"Yes, there is."

"See, you pee protein. You definitely have kidney problems."

"What should I do about them?" Tian suddenly became anxious, though still not fully convinced.

"I can prescribe a set of herbs for you. They should help. If you don't feel stronger, come see me again."

The doctor wrote out the names and the amounts, and Tian took the prescription to the front counter. He didn't read the names carefully, but he noticed schisandra fruit, a kind of wild berry that folks in northern China used as a condiment for cooking meat, while the other herbs were just common items in Chinese medicine—goji, fo-ti, tang kuei. Tian didn't take the whole thing seriously and picked up the prescription just for the heck of it. Those herbs were nothing but natural plants and would do no harm.

Mrs. Siu kept Freda's and Tian's prescriptions for her records. He was surprised they couldn't take their sheets with them. He guessed that must be the pharmacy's way to get patients to return, but he didn't mind. For a week's supply, Freda's herbs had cost about twenty-six dollars, his a few dollars more. Freda was pleased and said the prescription should help her shake off the nasty flu.

16

A s EXPECTED, Freda got well in three days. She called and told Tian about her quick recovery, raving about the magic effect of the medicinal herbs. He'd been taking his herbs too. Although he didn't feel his kidneys getting stronger, his body as a whole seemed to be gaining strength and he got up to pee less often at night. In the early morning, while lying in bed, he'd feel his blood circulating more vigorously around his groin, which made him full of desire. He missed Shuna and imagined caressing and kissing her continuously. Now, physically, he understood why poems spoke about burning love, about aching with desire.

To thank him for recommending the herbal doctor to her, Freda offered to take him out for dinner at Village Fish and Crab. He declined, saying that dining at a seafood restaurant would cost her too much. He'd be happy just to have lunch with her at a noodle joint or a kebab house. Then she mentioned she had been learning tea art lately and could show him what it was like. He was curious, never having seen anyone practice it. It sounded more like a Japanese thing, he pointed out, but Freda said her teacher was from Kaohsiung and it was also an ancient Chinese art, quite popular on the mainland now. So he agreed to have her over on Sunday afternoon to make the tea.

"Should I prepare something?" he asked her.

"No, I'll bring what I need."

Still, he thought it would be nice to have a snack to offer her. He went to the grocery store and picked up a bag of mini-dumplings stuffed with pork and shrimp and chives. By custom, one should avoid drinking too much tea with an empty stomach, so he'd share them with Freda before the ceremony.

Around midafternoon on Sunday she arrived with a stuffed tote bag and a jug of Poland Spring water. He told her to wait. First they should share a bite, then have the tea. She liked the idea and asked if she could help in the kitchen. "Just relax," he said. "I'll get everything ready in a few minutes." The pot was already boiling, so he poured the dumplings into the water. As they were cooking, he opened a jar of spiced bamboo shoots and peeled four preserved eggs so that there would be two cold dishes besides the dumplings. He sliced the eggs and dripped some rice vinegar and a touch of sesame oil over them. He also made a soup with shredded shiitake mushrooms and chicken broth.

Freda went over to the window and plucked a string of Tian's guitar hanging on the wall. It zinged. She said, "You can play the guitar?"

"Yes. But I haven't touched it for a long time," he said, and kept stirring the soup in a pot.

She was impressed when everything was placed on his round dining table within twenty minutes. Together they began eating. The meal was just simple fare, but she enjoyed it so much that she went on about how she wished she could eat like this every evening—she never had any appetite when eating alone after a long day's work. He was pleased to see her relishing the meal. Then she asked if he had wine. He took out a bottle of cabernet and poured her a glass and only two fingers for himself—he told her that he rarely drank. This bottle was a gift from a fan when he had performed in Philadelphia. He used to give to Yabin all the wines and liquors that he'd received from others.

After dinner, when he'd done the dishes, she set about preparing the tea ceremony. First, she went into his bedroom and changed into a white silk gown. Then she took a piece of green fabric out of her tote bag, spread it on the dining table, and placed a whole set of tea things on it: a clay pot, two bowls, a jar, four cups, and a tin of High Mountain oolong from Taiwan. She filled his enamel kettle with spring water, put it on the stove, and waited for it to boil. When the water was ready, she started the ceremony. Her arms and hands moved slowly, with deliberate grace, as if she was appreciating each one of her movements and gestures. Her body and limbs seemed to be following some kind of rhythm. He asked her if this ceremony included music. She answered in a whisper, "There's usually a flute in the background, but we don't have it here. But don't talk. We're supposed to be quiet, like in a Zen meditation."

He wanted to laugh but caught himself. He would rather be pouring boiling water into a teacup or heating a mug of water in the microwave, as he normally did. He saw no need for such elaborateness, transferring the tea from bowl to bowl and from cup to cup, as if each step would increase its fragrance. Yet, as he watched her perform, her eyes half closed and her cheeks shining, he began to grow attentive and enjoy the way she treated the ceremony as a genuine art, like something sacred.

Finally the tea was ready. "Try this," she said softly, and lifted a cup with one hand supporting its bottom.

With both hands, the tea-ceremony style, he held the cup and took a sip. It was indeed delicious, quite different from the tea he always brewed. "This is great," he said.

"See, I told you I was good at it." She jutted her chin and smiled, her eyes glowing. She turned her head, and he noticed she looked much prettier in profile.

"Is this a special kind of tea?" he asked.

"No, it's a fine oolong from Yushan Mountain in Taiwan. You can get it from the gift store on Roosevelt Avenue, near Queens Coffee. Here, we have a whole pot. Enjoy it slowly."

The supper and the tea had made the atmosphere warm and intimate. He put his cup on the table and said, "I really don't know much about you, Freda. You seem quite extraordinary."

"In what way?" she asked.

"Like that day at the shooting range. How come you're so skilled with a gun?"

"I told you—I was on a shooting team at college."

"But for sports you would use small-caliber rifles and pistols, wouldn't you? At the shooting range you fired a handgun like a soldier."

"Oh, I didn't explain everything clearly. In my junior year we were sent to an army barracks in Shandong province to do military drills for a semester. It was awful—"

"You mean that was part of your college education? I went to college a decade before you, but I didn't go through any military drill."

"My school was special. All the students had to go through some military training as a way to make us understand our soldiers better and become more sympathetic to them. In our program they picked five girls to form a shooting team and trained us extensively—they planned on sending us to the national sports meet for college students. We also had a team for throwing grenades, which was also an event at the tournament. Every day they made us aim at targets with bricks hanging from our handguns. We had to practice more than eight hours a day."

He allowed himself to accept her explanation. He asked her, "Did you compete at the sports meet?"

"No. When we got back to Beijing, I smuggled some albums of Teresa Teng's songs and got suspended briefly for selling them to my schoolmates. The university's Party committee believed the music was too decadent and banned it on campus."

"Really! But I always heard her songs everywhere."

"They couldn't keep up with the ban for long, of course."

"So you were a troublemaker!"

"Sort of. In the school leaders' eyes I was a troubled girl."

He boldly decided to change the subject. "Tell me, Freda, why are you working for me? You can hardly make money from being my manager. Have you been keeping tabs on me for someone?"

"What do you mean?" Her eyes widened at him playfully.

He lowered his head and smiled, then looked her in the face. "Didn't some Chinese official hire you to spy on me?"

She tittered and rubbed her thin nose with the knuckle of her forefinger. "Do you think they trust me? Oh, I remember a man at the newspaper funded by the mainland, *The China Dispatch*, who once asked me whether there was a woman living with you."

"What did you tell him?"

"I said, 'No, Yao Tian is living alone. He's very discreet about his private life. He loves his wife.'"

"That was all?"

"Yes. He asked me to report to him if you did something unusual, but I've had no contact with him after that. I wouldn't betray a friend, you know."

She stared at him boldly, as if to challenge him to prove anything untrue in what she'd said. As they were gazing at each other, he felt disturbed. She locked eyes with him, as though she'd been waiting for such a moment. Finally he tore his eyes away.

She leaned in and placed her hands on his shoulders. "I'm very fond of you, Tian," she murmured. "You are a nice man." She rested her head on him while her hand moved down to his belly, caressing him.

The warmth of her voice and her fingers aroused him. He put his arm around her and kissed her. Their mouths turned and stuck together.

She stayed with him that night. Something was roiling inside him—he was so wild that he couldn't stop making love to her. He touched and kissed every part of her, her toes and ears, as if with a woman for the first time. She engaged him with total abandon and at moments cried ecstatically, saying no man had loved her like this before and he'd made her feel like a young girl again. He took her words to be merely her bed ravings. Yet he was surprised he could be so passionate and have such stamina that he didn't let her sleep until midnight.

17

F REDA LEFT FOR WORK early the next morning. Tian's head was woozy with worrisome thoughts. Never had he been so lustful in bed with a woman, not even remotely so when he'd made love to Shuna. He wondered what had happened to him. There was no way he had become that much stronger physically—he was growing older, and the struggle for survival here sapped his energy continuously. How could he have become so passionate about someone he didn't even feel attracted to? Something was wrong.

Then it flashed across him that some of the herbs prescribed by Dr. Liang must have been aphrodisiacs. Why would that old bastard do this to him? Was this a trick he had pulled on him? Tian wondered. As he was making rice porridge mixed with brown sugar for breakfast, his phone chimed and he picked up. It was Freda. She was bubbly and said, "What an unforgettable night we had! I didn't expect you to be so wild in bed. You made me feel like I was hovering between life and death. At moments I thought I was going to pass out—"

"Listen, Freda. It was a mistake. I shouldn't have invited you over to do the tea ceremony to begin with. Also, I was not myself yesterday—"

"I have to go to a meeting now, sweetheart. I'll text or call again when I'm out of the meeting."

Her giddiness unnerved him. He was afraid he wouldn't be able to convince her that their passionate one-night stand was a mistake or an accident. No matter how he looked at it, this was a mess he might not be able to get out of easily. He was at a loss about what to do.

After breakfast he went downtown to Lasting Health to confront Dr. Liang, but the old man was not in. Mrs. Siu, the woman at the front counter, simpered knowingly, then said Dr. Liang was under the weather and wouldn't be able to see patients for some days. Tian asked her for the prescription the doctor had made for him, but she didn't have it because the old man kept all the sheets locked away somewhere. Tian was angry and said the herbs made him sick—it was his patient's right to know what he'd been taking. She assured him that they had a clear record of all the prescriptions, but it was the doctor who kept them. Tian could come later, and Dr. Liang could answer his questions.

"I have an idea," Mrs. Siu said. "Why don't you bring the herbal extracts here so I can tell you what they are?"

"I took the last batch yesterday," he told her. "Is there another way we can find out?"

"Not that I know of." She shook her head of permed hair. "I will tell Dr. Liang that you stopped by for the prescription. You can come back in a few days and speak to him. He has kept track of everything. No worries."

The impasse enraged him. He said he might sue Dr. Liang for malpractice.

"Please don't be so furious, Mr. Yao. Dr. Liang is a poor devil. Even if you take him to court and win the case, you won't get a penny from him. All he has are his old bones and the clothes on him."

He was stumped. Seeing his confusion, she smiled and went on, "Why don't you take this with you, for free?" She placed on the glass counter a bottle of Pei Pa Koa, a traditional cough syrup.

"I'm not coughing, no need for this," he said shortly.

"You're a singer, aren't you? This will help protect your throat. Even if when you're not coughing, just take one teaspoon a day, and you'll see the difference it makes."

She spoke so kindly that he accepted the bottle and left the herbal store. He knew the cough syrup, a classic remedy, which he had taken years before and which might be useful for him indeed. How he wished Yabin were still in town. In a messy situation like this, he could have turned to him for help. Then he realized that he'd just slept with the woman who Yabin would want to avoid at all costs. Talking to him about this would only embarrass them both—he'd better cope with it by himself.

That evening Freda called again and said she had to talk with him. "For a whole day I couldn't think of anything but last night," she confessed, then lowered her voice to a whisper. "I still feel your cock throbbing in me."

He was startled and stammered, "Something was wrong with me. I . . . I wasn't my normal self."

"You're as wonderful in bed as onstage. I love a slim and energetic man. Can I come see you again? Maybe this evening or tomorrow?"

"I'm sorry, Freda. I wasn't myself last night."

She laughed. "Don't you feel lucky to sleep with me?"

"Listen, Freda, I told you it was an accident. I was drugged by the herbs I've been taking and lost self-control."

She laughed again. "That is the craziest thing I've ever heard. Any man can be turned on by drugs, but no man could fuck a woman for six hours if he wasn't crazy about her. Tell me the truth—didn't you have a great time with me last night?"

"I was . . . I was not myself, like I told you."

"Didn't we have a lot of fun?"

"That was not what I intended to do."

"Listen, I dated a man who had to take Viagra. The drug could only help him for thirty minutes at a time. Now you can't say you were wild about me because you took some herbs by mistake. I saw your prescription at the herbal pharmacy and there was nothing special in it."

"I have to admit you did turn me on."

"So you should have come up with a better excuse."

"It was really an accident. I was not myself last night."

"Please, Tian, I can tell that you have lots of feelings for me. You said I was delicious and kissed every part of my body. You can't just walk out on me. I saw the guitar on your wall. Honestly I expect to hear you sing songs to me. I know you can play that instrument too."

"You expect too much," Tian said helplessly.

"Listen, I'm not the kind of woman you can pick up or drop at will. Besides, I know you're better than that. You always treat women with respect and you know how to love a woman. You're a great kisser too, and you don't know how extraordinary a lover you actually are."

She was practically raving. He was tired of this madness, this nonsense, this difficulty in getting his thoughts across to her, but he also felt ashamed. He was sweating a little and his face was hot. Yet, no matter how she raved and ranted, he wouldn't let her come to his place again.

Finally as if tired of her own raging, she said rather calmly, "I will get back at you if you just dump me. You can't treat me like a whore."

"I take you as a friend, a regular friend," he said desperately. "We're also business partners."

"Please, Tian. I love you, I can do anything for you! Just let me come see you tomorrow night."

"You've loved the wrong man. I'm married with a daughter and have a family to take care of. Please leave me alone!"

"I won't. You wait and see."

The more they fought, the harder it was for him to find responses to her demands, so he hung up. Still, he was terribly agitated and couldn't stop imagining what kind of damage she might do to him. For whatever outrageous move she made he might be to blame. In a way, she was right: Any decent man should not drop a woman he'd just slept with. At heart he knew he might have been attracted to her the night before, though he was certain that without the herbs, he couldn't possibly have had sex with her for so long. But if he reflected on the one-night stand objectively, he couldn't pin the blame all on the herbs—he had been horny and lustful. If only he could have been more careful about a crazy woman like Freda. This reminded him of a recent report: A young man in Bangladesh had castrated himself because he believed that most troubles and

miseries in his life came from his genitals. That was quite insight-
ful, wasn't it?

Now Tian felt trapped but was trying to prepare for what Freda
might come up with. She would cause some damage, he was sure.

Two days later he heard from his wife. She emailed to inform him
that a woman named Freda Liu had contacted her, claiming to be
his girlfriend and saying they were having a blazing affair. Shuna
asked him about his true relationship with this woman, who she'd
heard was his manager. He wrote back urging her to ignore Freda
for now. He'd tell her everything later. "It looks like I won't be able
to have her as my manager anymore," he told Shuna.

For several days he was too nervous to broach the matter, and
his wife was quiet about it too. When they spoke on the phone,
she sounded normal and cheerful. She reported that Tingting was
doing well at school and had just came in second in her English
class.

Tian knew what Freda had revealed to his wife might be tanta-
mount to his betrayal of Shuna, so he didn't know how to explain.
Then one night he received a long email from her. Freda had spilled
everything to his wife and even begged her to let her share him
with her, since Shuna was not available for Tian in New York. Freda
promised that she was not a threat to their marriage—she wanted
to be nothing more than his girlfriend while he was here. Freda had
even bragged about the sex they'd had—Shuna pasted the words
Freda had written: "Last Sunday night he kept me busy in bed for
six hours, six hours! He is crazy about me—he said I was sweet and
delicious. I was drunk with love, utterly captivated by him. Elder
Sister Shuna, Tian is still a young man—I've never met a man so
sexually deprived. It's unnatural to make him live in celibacy like a
monk. Please allow me to help you care for him before he returns
to you."

Freda blamed Shuna for being selfish and for letting Tian come
to the States alone. Because of her perverse notion of freedom and
the American dream, Shuna had made her husband suffer alone

here, enduring the drudgery like a menial worker, living from hand to mouth. She simply had no idea what America was really like. In a word, Shuna was ruining him and had better summon him back so that he could resume his illustrious career in China. "He is a celebrity in every sense, not just a rice-winner for you," she'd told his wife.

Reading Freda's words, Tian felt a little upsurge of gratitude—Freda understood his situation better than his wife did. At the same time he wasn't sure of Freda's motive. She appeared mild and more reasonable with Shuna. His wife was smart and wouldn't easily be swayed by a young woman's emotional outbursts. Shuna asked her to give some proof that she had indeed gone to bed with Tian. Freda mentioned a scar near his crotch, about an inch and a half long, from a hernia surgery. "It has six stitches like a crawling insect," she specified. She'd also sent his wife a couple of photos of her and Tian together. The shots were all in public settings, showing nothing intimate, though they contained only the two of them. Freda must have meant to show she was young and pretty, with elegant limbs.

Shuna was furious at Tian and demanded, "What are you going to do? Why didn't you tell me that you were having a woman there? Now you must choose between me and her."

He wrote back, "I was drugged by the damned herbal doctor—his prescription made me lose self-control. He must have been trying to turn me into a regular patient."

Shuna returned, "Don't give me that excuse. The doctor must have sensed something going on between you and that woman. He must have seen on your face that you wanted her."

That made Tian wonder whether Dr. Liang had indeed read something in his looks. If so, that might have emboldened the old codger to prescribe some potent herbs for him. Perhaps Shuna was right—any man who'd gone without touching a woman for more than a year could easily appear lustful. Tian hated himself for having landed in such a mess. He told Shuna he'd break off contact with Freda altogether and stop her from meddling with their marriage.

"I'll fire her straightaway," he promised his wife. At any cost he must keep his family intact.

. . .

Finally he caught Dr. Liang in the herbal pharmacy. The old man was all smiles, showing his blunted teeth, one of which had just fallen out, giving his mouth a new gap. He was happy to see Tian and called him "Mr. Yao" to demonstrate that he remembered his name and was already treating him like a regular patient. This only stoked up Tian's temper even more. Dr. Liang gestured at a leather-encased stool, offering Tian a seat. Tian took it, his eyes fixed on Liang's face, which was pink as though he'd eaten a lot of ginseng.

"Why did you prescribe me those aphrodisiac herbs?" Tian asked.

"Tell me, do you still often get up to pee at night?"

Tian shook his head. "No, not anymore. But the herbs made me act abnormally in bed, like a crazy man." His cheeks heated up as his hackles were rising.

Dr. Liang chortled, as if this was expected. "Did the herbs work?" he asked. "Didn't they make you feel younger and more vigorous? I thought your young missus would enjoy that too."

"Good heavens, you thought she was my wife?"

"The two of you make a lovely couple."

"She's not my wife, she's my manager!"

"Well, it couldn't have hurt as long as you had a great time in bed. I meant to help you."

"But you messed me up. I'm a family man with a child—" He caught himself, realizing he had said too much.

Dr. Liang laughed and said, "All I knew was that you needed to have wholesome sex to keep your kidneys functioning normally."

Tian wanted to slap him but checked himself. The old fart's words only verified Shuna's accusation that he had appeared horny and lustful. He must also have shown some level of affection for Freda in front of Dr. Liang, who had then taken it upon himself to harmonize their supposed conjugal life. However, that could just be the herbalist's pretext—more likely, he only wanted to get them hooked on to his service. Yet those were merely Tian's conjectures, and all he could do now was shun Dr. Liang.

18

P EI PA KOA, the cough syrup Mrs. Siu had given Tian, was quite effective in soothing his windpipe and cleansing his lungs. It mainly consisted of honey, mixed with more than a dozen herbs. He took a teaspoon every morning, holding the morsel in his mouth and letting it drip slowly down his throat. He found that it was helping reduce phlegm and the heat in his lungs, and his voice was getting clearer, even stronger. He decided to take this medicinal syrup regularly from now on, though he was still angry at Dr. Liang. He stopped by the herbal pharmacy twice during the following month, but the old man was no longer there. Mrs. Siu grimaced and said Liang had quit and they'd have to find a new herbal physician, but so far without success.

He decided to speak with Yabin about what had happened with Freda. It was embarrassing to broach the subject, but he needed his friend's advice. He told Yabin about the one-night stand over the phone, mumbling, "I was drugged or wouldn't have lost self-control like that. You know I wasn't that fond of Freda."

Yabin chuckled. "I can understand, Tian. You hadn't been intimate with a woman for such a long time that she must have looked like a goddess to you."

"That was not it. I was given some powerful herbs to strengthen my kidneys, but they just turned me on and I couldn't contain myself."

"Don't worry about it, Tian. I should've told you the nickname I had for Freda."

"What's that?"

"Superglue." Yabin snickered.

That was a little mean, but Tian could see how it fit. Then the thought came to him again, and he asked Yabin, "Do you think Freda might be working for the Chinese government?"

"That's unlikely. She's absolutely unpredictable and vacuous. How could they possibly use someone like her? Besides, her college major was public relations, not related to espionage at all."

"I wish I had been more careful with her."

"Tell me, Tian, are you really interested in her? Do you like her in bed?"

"Like I said, I was drugged that day. Otherwise I wouldn't have gotten close to her, because I cannot trust her. Now I'm in trouble and Shuna is furious."

"Remember, Freda still views you as a celebrity. She might not give you up so easily."

"By now she should be able to see what a loser I am here. I can't even afford a manager. She just makes peanuts by working for me."

"Believe me, she isn't working for money. She only wants to stick around."

"How can I make her stop?"

"Make it clear that you're not her boyfriend. And don't sleep with her again."

"Of course I won't."

Yabin didn't seem to be doing well in Boston—he was enjoying the quieter pace of life, but his cousin's construction project had run into a snare. The Chinese government had begun to enforce a restrictive policy for transferring funds—nobody was allowed to send abroad more than fifty thousand dollars a year, so Yabin's cousin couldn't find a way to get the full amount for the land over to the seller in America. As a result, the land purchase and the spadework were all stalled. But Yabin sounded in good spirits, confident he'd find something else to do in Boston. It looked like he might not come back to New York.

.　　.　　.

For days Freda had been calling Tian, wanting to meet again. He told her that he couldn't use her help anymore, but she insisted on coming over and sorting out their account. He thought of seeing her in a café, but, fearing she might make a scene that could call attention to him, he agreed to let her come to his place again. They made a plan to meet on Saturday morning, and he'd drink a mug of strong black tea to keep himself awake and vigilant.

She arrived at around ten, and they talked about the remaining three engagements she had helped him set up. He was generous and wrote her a check that included her commissions for all the jobs she had booked for him even though he hadn't received some of the payments yet. She seemed pleased about this, but she was also eager to continue to be his manager, saying she'd surely get more business for him and would be useful in many ways he couldn't foresee yet. He was irritated by her stubbornness and said, "Look—it's over between us. I'm a married man and I made an awful mistake. I'm sorry about that. Freda, I've appreciated your help, but I'm taking a different path and will strike out on my own. You have seen how little my business is. I really don't need a manager at all."

"I know your business will grow bigger." She smirked, then licked the corner of her mouth.

"But I don't see it that way. I hope we can part ways as friends."

"You can't get rid of me like this!" she said fiercely, her eyes ablaze.

"What do you want from me? You've tried to wreck my marriage—how much more damage are you going to do?"

"I want to be with you. You can't just fuck a girl and then dump her like a whore. You can't use me this way!"

"I didn't use you."

"Then what did you do to me the other night? Why did you keep me busy in bed like that for so many hours?"

"It was a mistake."

"That's easy for you to say, but I'm not buying any of that."

A flush of anger seized him. "Get out of here!" He pointed at the door. "Get out!"

"I won't! Damn it, you'll have to kick me out."

He was enraged and rushed to her and grabbed her by the arm.

Pulling her up from the chair, he dragged her to the door. She swung around and scratched him on the neck.

"Ouch!" He rubbed the side of his neck and saw a glistening strip of blood across his fingers.

The sight of blood inflamed him. Forcefully he shoved her at the door. She fell and her head knocked on the wall with a thud. She was stunned, then let out a cry. "You beat me! You beat a woman! What kind of man are you? I won't let you get away with this."

Seated on the floor with her legs stretched out, she began blubbering as a purple swelling like a large grape emerged on her forehead. One of her stiletto heels had fallen off her foot. He was transfixed, aghast at what he'd done, but unable to find words to pacify her.

She fished out her phone and dialed a number. As he was wondering what she was doing, she cried to the other end, "My boyfriend is beating me up. Please come and help me!"

He realized she was speaking to the police. "Stop it!" He yelled and struck her hand to knock off her phone.

"Ow! He's beating me again. Please come to my rescue!" In the same breath she spat out his address.

Now he was completely at a loss. He grabbed the phone from her and began to condemn her, calling her a spy, a toxin in his life, sticky like superglue. He yelled out whatever came to mind. But to any names he called her, she wouldn't respond. She was lying on her side, her face toward the baseboard of the wall as if she were sleeping, too soundly to hear his furious words.

In no time a siren blared from the street. Then his buzzer went off. He hesitated for a moment but pressed the button to let in her rescuers. The police, two men and one woman, stepped into his apartment, all bearing batons and firearms. At the sight of Freda on the floor, the female cop took three photos of her. Then they stepped over and raised Freda's upper body and asked her if she could understand them. She looked at them with a blank face, her eyes half closed. The camera flashed again.

"Miss, did he do this to you!" asked the black policewoman, pointing at the purple bump on Freda's forehead.

Wordlessly, Freda nodded. Tian protested, "I didn't beat her. She fell and knocked her head on the wall."

"That's not what she called us for," the white policeman told him.

"Well, Mr. Yao," said the black policeman, the older man among the trio, "you must come with us."

"Why?" Tian said loudly. "I didn't beat her." Then, taking a deep breath and lowering his voice. "She was my manager and we were just discussing our final business arrangements."

The policewoman interrupted him by asking Freda, "Is he your boyfriend?"

Freda nodded. "Yes, he is."

Tian jumped in, "Damn it, I'm not her boyfriend! I'm her boss."

"That makes no difference if you hit a woman," the white cop said. "You're under arrest." He brandished a pair of handcuffs and stepped up to him. "You have the right to remain silent. Hold out your hands!" he ordered.

"Why? I'm not a criminal!" Tian refused to move his hands while red splotches appeared on his lean face.

"That's something you should prove in court," said the black cop, who looked disgusted. "No man should raise his hand against women and children in this country. Do you understand? This is an American value."

Reluctantly Tian let them cuff him. They took him out and dragged him to their white cruiser with blue stripes. Freda looked stupefied and followed them out of the building, too shaken to say anything. "Do you need to be treated at a clinic?" the policewoman asked her.

"No, I'm okay. Thank you," said Freda.

They put Tian into the car while Freda only stared at him, her mouth agape as they pulled away with the strobe slashing daylight.

They took him to their precinct and told him that he'd have to stay in there for two nights because nobody could process his case on the weekend. They snapped mug shots of him, from his front and both sides, and also had his fingers and palms printed. Then they stripped him of his phone and wallet and his belt and shoes. They made him wear slippers, which were so big that he had to move around with stiff legs. He wanted to contact Yabin and Cindy Wong so as to get hold of a lawyer, uncertain how his immigrant attorney would respond to his arrest, but he could not remember his friends' phone numbers. A stalwart guard supervising the jail cells shouted at him, "Be quiet and just wait for your time to gripe to the judge!"

Before slamming him into a room, they ordered him to undress. They checked every part of his body and even poked his anus. He was angry and cried, "Why do this to me? This is harassment!"

The same guard said, "Matter of fact, we're trying to be responsible. What if you have medical conditions and croak in our hands? We have to make sure you're physically okay and capable of going through the confinement. You think I enjoyed poking your stinking ass?"

After the "checkup," they put him into a sizable room, and he gradually got used to the semidarkness in there. It had two rows of bunk beds along the walls. In a corner sat a toilet, beside which there was a small sink. A pair of folded beds leaned against the wall beyond the toilet. On the ceiling a terrain of damp patches spread in the plaster, reminding him of a landscape ravaged by a flood. A fluorescent tube went on blinking above the door. Tian realized this room must be a temporary cell for new arrivals. Fortunately there were only two other detainees in it. One was a middle-aged black man wearing a graying ponytail and the other a squat young Korean with a large square face. In Tian's heart he couldn't stop cursing Freda, the madwoman who must have meant to do him in.

A tiny window, narrow and rectangular, looked onto an enclosed yard and let in a slanting column of sunlight. When he was tired of dozing on the top bed of a bunk, he would stand behind the window and observe the small empty yard. The sense of the double enclosure, of the cell plus the yard, made him feel more desolate. He was afraid they might send him to a real prison. If that happened, his life would be ruined.

The black man harrumphed and Tian turned around. The man said in a smoky voice, "Hey, I'm Kevin. What's your name?"

"I'm Tian."

"What brought you in?"

"I fought with my manager," Tian told him, reluctant to elaborate.

"You beat him up? You have guts, man." Kevin batted his large eyes.

"No, I pushed her and she fell, so she called the cops."

"Your manager's a woman? You can't fight with a woman, you'll never win."

"That's right. How about you? Why are you here?"

"I drove away somebody's automobile. The guy owes me lots of dough."

So this man was a car thief, Tian thought. But Kevin didn't look wild or mean. In fact, if in a suit and tie, he might resemble an office worker. "How about him?" Tian asked about the Korean, who was sullen and reticent, probably unable to speak English.

"Bong? Oh, he's nuts." Kevin's chin pointed at the young man lying at the bottom bed of a bunk. "He beat up a guy who slept with his sister."

"His sister didn't like the guy?"

"Their parents wouldn't give their approval."

Tian wasn't sure how much Bong could follow their conversation, so he stopped chatting with Kevin lest the young fellow take offense. Tian reminded himself to keep quiet and try to relax, waiting for Monday.

Late in the afternoon, a guard shoved their dinner on plastic trays through the tiny opening in the door. Tian lost appetite at the sight of the meal: four slices of white bread, two franks, steamed broccoli, a small carton of milk. "Eat before it gets cold," the guard's gruff voice told him. "You Asians like hot food, don't you?"

At first, Tian didn't want to touch the meal, but then he forced himself to eat. The watery broccoli stuck in his throat and wouldn't go down. He wondered why they hadn't put some flavor to it. A pinch of salt and black pepper would do and wouldn't cost anything. He didn't touch the cold milk, which could upset his digestion, so he gave it to Bong, who took it and mumbled, "Thanks." Tian wished they'd given him a small tub of yogurt instead, which his stomach had learned to tolerate.

After dinner, he lay down again, pulled up a smelly blanket, and tried to sleep as much as he could, to save his energy and while away the time.

19

F INALLY IT WAS MONDAY. Unable to contact Yabin or Cindy, Tian begged a middle-aged officer to let him call his lawyer. The policeman, wearing a name tag that said PERRY, was kind enough to help him find his attorney's office number. Marge Johnson gasped on hearing where Tian was. But after he explained the situation, she said she must get him out of the police's hands without delay and have his arrest removed from the record, or this might jeopardize his application for immigration. She assured him that she would start working on this right away.

Fortunately Freda showed up at the precinct around midmorning. She changed her story, saying Tian hadn't beaten her and she had phoned to get help because she'd been beside herself with anger when he was trying to show her the door. She also clarified to the police that Tian was her employer, not her boyfriend, and that the bruise on her forehead was the result of an accidental fall. It took her nearly a whole hour to convince them that her call had been nothing but an outrageous threat. When Marge Johnson arrived, they were ready to let Tian go, though they said his attorney would have to file some paperwork to get him released.

Tian was worried about the additional lawyer fees. Johnson's rate was $350 an hour. She had already spent three or four hours on his case today, and his bill would be increased considerably. But he was glad to be free again. He ran into Freda on his way out. She looked shamefaced and said, "I'm sorry, Tian. I didn't expect the cops to arrest you. I locked your apartment when they took you away." She handed him the keys he'd left behind.

He accepted them without a word, glaring at her. Deep down, though, he kind of appreciated her effort to make amends.

Riding the subway back, he found some text messages on his phone, including those from Cindy Wong, Yabin, and some media reporters. He suspected that his arrest might have become news. Coming out of the Flushing subway station, he picked up *The China Dispatch*. As he had expected, the incident was on the second page with the headline "Famous Singer Arrested for Battery." The short article described Freda as a young mistress of Yao Tian's and claimed that the two of them had been cohabiting for an extended period of time. Owing to an intense quarrel, the cause of which was still unclear, he had attacked her in their home, and out of desperation she'd called 911. The police showed up and took him into custody. The article went on to condemn him as a married man who had abandoned his wife and child back in China. It also reminded readers never to raise their hands against women and children. It concluded, "It looks like Yao Tian will have to fight a courtroom battle soon. A grim lesson, indeed."

Unsettled, he went to the public library across the street. Looking through the other Chinese-language newspapers there, he found his story in every one of them, though they each worded the case differently. They all carried a file photo of him singing onstage with his arms open and his head tossed back—the exaggerated movement he hated and was even ashamed of. He wondered how the papers had come to know of his arrest. He didn't remember seeing anyone on the street when he was put into the police cruiser. To his mind, the only possible source of the news was Freda.

Tian called Yabin, who had texted that he was worried. His friend sounded relieved on hearing his voice. "Where are you now?" Yabin asked.

"Back in my apartment," Tian said. "How did you get to know of my trouble?"

"Freda phoned me. She was distraught and begging for help. She said she'd called many people and I was the first one to pick up. She said the cops wouldn't listen to her explain and just dragged you away."

"That's a lie. She called 911 and claimed I was her boyfriend and had beaten her up."

"She knew she'd made a terrible mistake. Your name's come up on all the Chinese news sites—it's a big story now."

Tian didn't comment, though he cursed Freda mentally for spreading the word of his detention, wittingly or unwittingly. Every effort she'd made to salvage the disaster only got him deeper into it. He just hoped she would disappear from his life from now on.

For the rest of the day he stayed in, afraid of being recognized if he went out. He cooked ramen noodles with poached eggs and canned french-cut green beans and sliced beets. The simple meal, with soy cheese, tasted wonderful, and he wolfed it down while reading news on a Canadian Chinese media site. It too reported his arrest, quoting *The China Dispatch* as the source. Below the article a commenter remarked that Yao Tian should be barred from access to guns, as domestic abuse was often the precursor of gun violence. The person added, "A wife-beater can easily turn into a random assaulter of others." The words spoiled Tian's appetite, and he put away the remaining noodles. For the whole day he sat on pins and needles, fearing that his wife would soon hear of this scandal.

Toward ten p.m. that night Shuna called. She'd seen the story online but sounded calm. She asked him about the jail cell and the food he'd eaten in there. He told her that the detention was a mistake by the police, and that his attorney would get the arrest removed from the police log so that the incident would not affect his application for immigration. Shuna sighed and said, "You didn't keep your word. You promised me you'd break up with that woman, but obviously you didn't."

"Listen, Shuna." He tried to sound clearheaded. "Freda and I were together for the last time to square our accounts. But afterward she wouldn't leave, so I showed her the door by force. She scratched my neck and I got mad and pushed her. She fell and knocked her head on the wall. That was why she called the police."

"Why did she come to your place for the final settlement?" Shuna pressed. "Why not do that somewhere else?"

"She's touch and go. I feared she might make a scene publicly."

"Does this mean it's finally over between you and her?"

"Absolutely. From now on, I'll handle all my engagements by myself, without a manager."

Although Shuna seemed to accept his explanation, he was still agitated. For days he didn't shave. He avoided downtown Flushing and public places. When he had to buy groceries, he went to the bodega down the street, run by a Pakistani family who didn't know who he was. He spent a lot of time reading. Some of the exiled writers he'd met had given him their books, mostly self-published in North America, and he'd never had time to read them. Now finally he could enjoy them. He particularly liked some of the poetry books and often stayed for hours on a single poem if he found it beautiful. He would think about how to set it to music, and found some short verses that might work well as songs. How he wished he could have written such poems himself.

A handful of reporters contacted him, requesting interviews, but he declined them all. Attorney Johnson had emphasized that he mustn't speak publicly. "For now, silence and a low profile would do you good," she told him.

He enjoyed the solitude, but Freda still called him every night. If he saw her number, he would shut off the phone. Once he picked up by accident and greeted her. She pleaded, "Are you still angry at me? Can't we remain friends?"

He kept silent, fearful of starting a conversation with her.

She went on, "Can I do something to make up for my mistake, Tian?"

"No, it's over between us," he said and hung up.

Still she would phone him from time to time. She always sounded guilty in her messages, though he couldn't relent yet.

PART THREE

20

I N THE FALL TIAN'S APPLICATION for immigration was approved, and he was given a paper green card for the time being. The laminated one would arrive in a month or so. He was thrilled, and relieved that his arrest had not affected USCIS's assessment of his case. Though he'd paid almost five thousand dollars for the attorney fees, he was grateful to Marge Johnson, who had worked diligently on his behalf. He was glad he'd followed Yabin's advice and had avoided lawyers who represented only Chinese applicants— attorneys who, most often from China themselves, took advantage of their clients' ignorance of English and American society. To thank Marge, Tian presented her with a large panda doll for her five-year-old daughter.

He expected to join the Divine Grace in December to perform during the holiday season, which now started two weeks before Christmas, but no invitation came. This made him anxious—winter had always been his busy season, a time when he could count on more income. When he called Cindy Wong, she wouldn't say anything explicitly on the phone. Instead, she wanted to meet for coffee.

They met at Starbucks on Main Street the next morning after he'd done his voice practice at Queens College. Cindy wore a green tunic and jeans, which set off her slender body. They sat at a corner table, she with her latte and he with his chai tea. She smiled, a dimple emerging on the left side of her chin.

He reiterated his concern: He hadn't been invited to join the Divine Grace for this coming season. "Do you know if they need me?" he asked her. "Aren't they going to start the tour soon?"

"They're going to kick off in two weeks. This year they'll be debuting some new acts in their program. There'll be more dancers and musicians."

"And singers?"

"Of course—two young singers from Hong Kong, a man and a woman, have just signed up with the Divine Grace."

"So I'm already passé?"

"No, it's not that." She sighed. "Some in the troupe were opposed to having you join them again because of the news reports that you had battered your girlfriend. They worried that your appearance could tarnish the troupe's image."

"That woman was not my girlfriend and I didn't really beat her. I pushed her and she fell."

"I believe you, but the public perception is different. This is something the troupe has to consider."

"So I'm a liability to them now?"

"Try to be patient, Tian. When this blows over, I'm sure they will have you back. Some of them even said they would invite you next year."

"I don't need to join them," he said, trying uselessly to hide his hurt. "I'm tired of singing those preachy songs anyway."

"I'm sorry, Tian." Cindy took a sip of her latte, a pearl ring on her finger. She went on, "Perhaps Freda Liu could make a public statement to correct the story reported in the newspapers."

"What kind of statement do you have in mind?"

"That the incident was an accident and that there was no assault. Once we have that in writing, we can get it printed in a newspaper. Or maybe we can have her interviewed—that way she won't have to write anything."

"I have no ties with her anymore."

"Then we can wait for next year. By then the public might have forgotten the whole thing."

Her round eyes looked at him sympathetically, and he was impressed by her poise. She seemed to still treat him as a friend. He was disappointed, however, by what she said, and realized that it was going to be hard for him to continue to perform in New York, given the cloud of the scandal hovering over his head now. It looked like he might not have many performing opportunities in the near future. Then how was he going to support himself and make enough for his monthly remittance? The more he brooded about this, the more hopeless and impossible New York seemed to him. He began to imagine some place where few people would recognize him and where life was less expensive and less hectic. These days whenever he went out, he wore sunglasses and a navy baseball cap to avoid being recognized.

Freda seemed aware of his plight and continued to call him two or three times a week. He thought of blocking her, but he needed to have some sense of what she was up to. If he didn't answer, she'd leave long voice messages, offering to work for him again, bragging about her new connection with a cultural forum and her ability to "get lots of gigs" for him. Though sometimes tempted by her offers, he never called back.

He discussed his situation with Shuna, who didn't seem as troubled by his work difficulties as he felt she should be. Filled with optimism from his immigration success, she urged him to be patient and try to tough it out. She even said, "There's no river we can't cross. The darkest hours are those before dawn." That made him flinch a little—she had no idea what things were like here. She also urged him not to remit money home so often, assuring him that she and Tingting could manage without his help. But he was determined to send the remittance every month, including the sum for his mother.

He talked with Yabin about his predicament. His friend believed that the Chinese officials had unleashed what amounted to a character assassination against him, though he felt it unlikely that Freda had deliberately played a hand. To him, she was simply a capricious woman without goals of her own—someone who could easily be used by others.

Then he made a bold suggestion. "Why don't you leave New York for a while? You'll still be able to travel and perform in different places even if you're based in another city."

"Where would I go?" He was intrigued by his idea.

"Why not join me here? I can find some work for you—I'm not well connected with the entertainment world here, but I might be able to get you a job in home repairs. You should be able to make enough to live on until you find something more suitable. Do you think you can work in home renovation? You don't have to answer now."

"I can learn how to do it," Tian said. "Actually, I once worked at a construction site for two months."

"Then consider my suggestion as a possible option."

To Tian, Yabin was a survivor, who could manage to get by wherever he landed. His cousin's real estate project hadn't panned out, but he'd found a niche in the Boston area's Chinese community and seemed to be flourishing there. For half a year he had helped his cousin organize a construction team of Chinese workers, most of whom lived in Quincy, just south of Boston. Though his cousin's project had become defunct, the team of workers had endured, and Yabin had become an advocate for them, often intervening on their behalf when they ran into language barriers with customers. By and by he became a contractor of sorts and began to book jobs for the workers, receiving payment through commissions.

Tian knew he wouldn't mind doing odd jobs in home renovation—he was strong and capable of hard work. New York was indeed becoming too difficult, since people knew that the Divine Grace had dropped him, his career in a cul-de-sac now. But he had to continue and find his way out. If Yabin could thrive elsewhere, so could he. Deep down, he longed to be with his friend, with whose help he might get back on his feet again. He was not afraid to leave New York and grapple with fortune in Massachusetts, so he agreed to join Yabin in Boston. He feared his landlady might not return his deposit if he broke the lease, but considering the opportunities Yabin had promised him in the Boston area, he decided to leave. He had spoken with Shuna about his plan to move; she'd thought it was a good idea, saying their daughter might go to Boston for college eventually. He forced himself to be cheerful while speaking with Tingting. He assured her that he was going to Massachusetts to open new turf for their family. The girl didn't seem to care and just said, "I have to go, Dad. Please come home soon."

21

T IAN WAS PLEASED THAT Mrs. Guzzo, his landlady, agreed to refund his $1,300 deposit, which, according to the lease, was the rent for the final month. She seemed glad to hear he was leaving, perhaps because some tenants had complained about his singing exercises. Tian also suspected she'd be able to raise the rent substantially after he left.

He asked Yabin to help him find an apartment in Quincy. Tian wanted a quiet and private place, close to public transportation. Yabin called back in two days and with a lead on a condo in Quincy Center, a short walk to the subway. But the rent was a little steep—$1,400 a month. It had just one bedroom, 670 square feet, though heat and water were included in the rent. There was also garage parking, which Tian didn't need. Yabin said that since heating bills could be high during the winter, Tian should probably take the place. Tian slept on it, then decided not to, realizing that his future earnings were uncertain and that he had to be frugal. He asked Yabin to look for a cheaper place, under $1,300 a month, no parking necessary. At the same time he emphasized that he'd like to live alone—as an artist he must have his own space and privacy. Yabin joked, "I admire your integrity, Tian. I'll see what I can do."

He found what Tian was looking for. It was also in Quincy Center and quite convenient, so after reviewing the photos, Tian signed a lease with the landlord and put down two months' rent. How fortunate he felt to have Yabin as a resourceful friend.

He left New York just before Christmas, taking an Amtrak express to Boston. He had shipped his keyboard and a few belongings by UPS, but was carrying his guitar with him. The four-hour train ride was comfortable and exhilarating. He loved the vast landscape, the tranquil coves and half-deserted docks along the coast, the misty ocean spreading to the end of the sky, the forests that looked wild but were actually young and largely cultivated. The small towns along the way seemed still wrapped in sleep, despite the sun already rising toward the mid-sky. Boston was chillier than New York, feeling at least five degrees colder. He was delighted to see Yabin again. The man hadn't changed a bit, still husky and cheerful and sartorially elegant, wearing leather boots and a black duckbill cap and a woolen coat. From the subway station he took Tian directly to his new apartment, just a few blocks away. Tian was pleased to find a bed and a mattress already there. An old chest of drawers stood against the wall next to the bed. Yabin had placed these bedroom items in for Tian the day before. There were also a small table and a pair of chairs in a corner of the living room. Yabin was so thoughtful that he'd even gotten some cookware and tableware for Tian: a pot with a glass lid, a kettle, some bowls and plates. Though they were secondhand and miscellaneous, Tian was touched and gave his friend a big hug. He hadn't brought along any kitchenware except for a cleaver. He pulled the knife out of his duffel bag and slashed the air right and left with it. That made both of them laugh.

After Tian had washed up, Yabin drove him to President Plaza, pointing out the Asian stores there, where he could do his shopping. Actually, Yabin said, in addition to the area's Chinese immigrants, many Koreans and people from South Asia and Latin America also came here for groceries; a handful of fine restaurants were at that marketplace too. Tian was amazed by the new turquoise Range Rover Yabin was driving. "You must have made lots of money here," Tian said.

Yabin smiled, shaking his head. "I'm doing all right—not as well as I expected. But my cousin has lost almost half a million dollars."

"So he managed to transfer his money to the States?"

"He got some of it out of China."

"He has given up his real estate development here?"

"He has moved to Las Vegas."

"Why there? He's interested in the gambling industry?"

"No—still real estate. Home prices have dropped considerably there, so there are more opportunities in Vegas."

"Will you go join him there eventually?"

"I don't think so—I'm doing fine here. You will love this place too. Life is quieter here than in Queens."

At the moment, Yabin said, he was working for a home renovation business owned by Frank Chu, a recent immigrant from Guangdong. He was the company's coordinator because he spoke English well and knew how to deal with American customers. Tian was impressed again.

Yabin parked in front of a seafood restaurant called Marine Garden and said that his girlfriend Laura would be waiting for them inside. Entering through the glass door, Tian could see that the place was formal, all tables covered with cloth. There were only a few customers, but Yabin didn't see Laura. Then he stepped farther into the dining hall and peeked behind a floral screen. "Here you are," he said loudly. He motioned for Tian to join him.

"I'm Laura Yang." She held out her hand the second Tian stepped behind the screen.

He shook her small hand, which was soft and plump. She looked quite young, in her early twenties, her face round and fleshy. She was vivacious and pleasant like a teenager. Yabin was already thirty-eight—why would he date such a young thing? Compared to his former girlfriends, Laura was plain and chubby, even homely in spite of her shoulder-length hair and her sweet voice. In every way she was not the type of woman who was attractive to Yabin. Then why was he with her?

As Tian lifted a cup of jasmine tea, Laura smiled and said to him, "I'm so happy to meet you in person, Mr. Yao. I'm a big fan, and so is my mom. She'll be jealous when I tell her about this dinner."

"Oh, please thank your mother for me. Where is she?" he asked.

"In Hainan."

"Aren't they in Beijing now?" Yabin joined in.

"Ah, yes." She nodded. "They usually live on Hainan Island in the winter, but their home is in Beijing."

Yabin opened a purple menu the size of a large magazine. "What would you like, Tian?" he asked. "They have some special dishes here."

Tian was unprepared for such a question. The two of them had eaten many meals together, and he knew that Yabin rarely ordered food without comparing prices first. This restaurant was clearly upscale, but now he didn't bother to examine the menu. "Anything is fine for me," Tian told him honestly.

Yabin went ahead and ordered stewed abalone, lobster, sautéed bean sprouts, and jumbo clams, plus a soup made of chicken and tofu and fresh enoki mushrooms. Tian wondered how they cooked the clams, which he hadn't seen on the menu. Yabin assured him that this was something they had just begun to offer, that the clams had no fishy taste at all, and that he would surely enjoy it.

As they were waiting for their orders, Yabin remarked that the Spring Festival was approaching, and offered to contact people to see if they might engage Tian for their holiday celebrations. The Chinese immigrant population here was quite large, he said, more than one hundred thousand, though you didn't see many Chinese faces in the city—most of the new arrivals were professionals and lived in the suburbs. Tian thanked his friend and hoped there could be opportunities for him to perform here. Now that he'd been dropped from the Divine Grace and had no idea how to continue in this place, he needed Yabin's help badly.

Dinner was excellent and they ate well. The jumbo clams were cooked in an unusual manner: Each plate held a single opened shell, filled with chopped vegetables and bacon and the minced clam's flesh. The sauce for the dish was Americanized in a rich way, with plenty of cream in it. The lobster and the abalone were excellently made too. Though he had grown up in a coastal city, Tian didn't have a discriminating taste for seafood. He enjoyed the company more than he did the dishes.

Laura told him she'd been here for more than three years, and currently was studying for an MBA at Bentley University. She planned to return to Sanya City, where her parents were at the moment, and work for her brother, who owned a boat rental business there. Alternatively, she might join her cousin, who ran an organic food farm outside Beijing—he might need her to manage their supply lines. But those plans were some ways off—after graduation, she wanted to work here for a year or two before she went back.

Tian was impressed by her plans, so he turned to Yabin and asked, "How about you? Will you go back to China with Laura?"

Yabin smiled without speaking. Tian realized he'd made a gaffe— their relationship was not that serious yet. By the time Laura headed home, he might have already moved on to a new girlfriend. Tian was somewhat confounded by his friend's dating habits, considering he also wanted to settle down and raise a family.

A waitress, a twig of a woman, came over and placed the bill sleeve on the table, near Yabin. Tian reached out for it, but Laura snatched it and said, "Let me take care of this."

Tian protested that he was grateful to Yabin for all the help he'd given him, so he should pick up the tab. But his friend smiled and told him, "Let Laura do it. She's very generous."

Tian didn't know what to make of that. The thought came to him that Yabin might be kept by Laura, who seemed sweet and tenderhearted and also, apparently, well-heeled.

Tian's apartment was on the first floor and had a low ceiling. Behind the building was a large parking lot, which was always half full. There was nobody living below Tian, and in the basement were a laundry room and a common lounge. Still, he couldn't do vocal exercises with abandon in the building in the mornings, because some of the tenants worked in labs at MIT and Harvard and Mass General Hospital and would sleep during the day. He scouted around the neighborhood and found several spots where he could sing at will. In the southwest there was a deserted quarry that opened like the wilderness and with no pedestrians in view. About half a mile to the northeast spread a vast sports ground, where he could practice his voice too. He also strolled farther north. There was Merrymount Cemetery, where he couldn't disturb a soul if he shouted at the top of his lungs. Beyond the slopes of graves, just a quarter of a mile farther north, stretched the beach and the ocean. In addition, Merrymount Park was also within walking distance in the northwest. Nevertheless, professionally speaking, he ought to do vocal exercises indoors and rent a studio for it, but he couldn't afford it anymore.

He called Shuna and told her about his apartment and the surroundings. She was pleased to hear his report and said he must be careful when he mixed with others, especially women. He knew she still had Freda on her mind, believing that the scandal had messed up his career badly. He also spoke briefly with his daughter. Tingting sounded more mature now, but also more distant. He tried to be cheerful and said, "I'm living close to Harvard and MIT now. You should study hard so you can join me here for college."

"All right, I'll think about it," she said halfheartedly.

22

T HE LOCAL COMMUNITIES quickly learned about Tian's move to Boston—in no small part because Yabin and Laura had spread the word. *Sampan,* a biweekly based in Boston's Chinatown, called and did a short interview with Tian. It was done in English, the only language Tian had in common with the Cantonese-speaking reporter. Tian had seen *Sampan* available at grocery stores for free. It was bilingual, the same articles printed in both languages. This format was intriguing to him—it enabled readers to compare the same news reported in both English and Chinese so as to learn either language.

When the reporter asked him why he had moved to Boston, he answered that he had a good friend here and liked this city a lot, which he had indeed visited five years before. To him, Boston was the most European city in the States and gave him a strong impression of culture and order. It also brought to mind a big village—it had a country ambience that he liked. After the interview ran, people began to ask him to sing at celebratory events and festive gatherings. Several universities' student associations approached him—Boston University, MIT, Brandeis. He accepted every offer, more eager to perform than ever before. He'd been practicing new ways of singing to make his voice warmer and more intimate. He wanted to do more than just belt out songs to demonstrate his range and stamina like most professional singers in mainland China—he wanted to sing as if speaking to a few people in a small room.

By the lunar calendar, the Spring Festival fell on January 23 this year, less than two weeks away. He went to see the venues at the universities that had hired him, and he rehearsed with their bands. Most of the musicians were students, all quite skilled, and the organizers were very enthusiastic about promoting the holiday events, posting flyers everywhere and putting ads in the campus newspapers. They'd be paying him five or six hundred dollars, but unlike regular professional performances, all the events were free to the public, so there'd be no income from the ticket sales. That was fine for Tian. He just wanted to sing.

The next Sunday evening, outside the Tsai Performance Center at Boston University, more than four hundred people gathered in the lobby, having drinks and chatting while waiting for the holiday celebration to start. Trays of appetizers, held by servers in black tie, floated through the chattering crowds. Tian wouldn't mix with them, needing to stay focused before he took the stage, but he saw the caterer's delivery van parked behind the colossal classroom building and people carrying food in foil pans and large cartons into the lobby for the reception. He wished he could join the party like a regular attendee, but he didn't want to be recognized. The event, he was told, was organized by various student associations with the support of the university's Asian studies program. The sight of the large gathering moved him; there were even small children running around among the adults.

The evening's entertainment program was quite unusual to Tian, and various groups of students went up to perform. He watched from the side of the stage. A team of young men from Chinatown did a lion dance—four dancers were to play two lions, imitating the animals' frisky movements. Two men formed a pair, acting together as one lion in a brightly-colored costume, one playing the animal's head and the other its rear end. One of the lions onstage was wearing red and the other yellow. They pranced and frolicked briskly. By accident the red lion fell on its side and brought out laughter from the audience. Following the dancing animals, there was a show performed by the Monkey King, who held a golden cudgel and somersaulted at will, as he is believed capable of flying through clouds like a god. The dapper performer seemed to have fans among some of the girls in the audience, who cried out and waved their arms as he danced and sprang around. Then a team of young women from Taiwan gave a fashion show, each raising a tiny umbrella. Tian enjoyed seeing them wearing the traditional cheongsams and various types of gowns. A few of them donned the small caps and dresses of colorful fabrics like the minority women in Taiwan. He imagined his daughter among them in a couple of years, and his eyes misted over briefly. Then eight young men and women in knee-high boots did a Mongolian dance, each brandishing a phantom whip as if riding a horse in the vast steppe.

Tian liked the relaxed atmosphere onstage. A real holiday celebration should be like this, fun and folksy and spontaneous, and he felt more confident about his new way of singing. When his turn came, he stepped on the stage and turned to the applause. He began to sing a movie song he had just learned, while keeping his voice relaxed so that it could become softer. It was a sort of love song, titled "So Many Things":

> So many things never go away
> From my memory. I want you to see
> How the past still flows in circles
> Around us. Now, tell me
> What is your new favorite—
> Cappuccino or a colored cloud? . . .

He had expected that the audience would respond to this song warmly—many of them had doubtless seen the movie *Let Me Catch Sight of You Again,* in which it was repeated twice. But when he was done, the applause went up halfheartedly. People seemed uneasy about his new way of singing.

A woman, a thirtysomething wearing a pink anorak, rose on the upper floor and cried in earnest, "Teacher Yao, please sing 'In Praise of Our Motherland.'"

That was a patriotic song immensely popular in China since the mid-1950s, and it expresses some anti-American sentiment. The demand threw Tian, but he managed to reply, "I only like the first half of the song's lyrics, but not the second half. Also, the sentiment of that song goes against this festive occasion, so I'm sorry I can't sing that song here. Besides, my feelings for our homeland have changed too—I love China, but not unconditionally. Let me sing a fishing song instead."

The song was one of his early hits, so it was enthusiastically received. He was relieved that the song helped him salvage the faux pas he'd made with the first piece, though he didn't respond to the calls for an encore—he simply bowed twice to the audience, then left the stage.

A movie, *The King of Masks,* made by the mainland director Wu Tianming but acceptable to the audience of different backgrounds, was shown after the performances. Tian slipped out halfway through, realizing he didn't have the energy to mingle afterward. He left the building and hopped on a Green Line train headed back toward Quincy. It was snowing, fat flakes swirling in the wind as lights on both sides of the railway track flitted by. After the train went underground, it moved with ease, clanking rhythmically. It stopped service at Park Street, where he switched to the Red Line. Five or six stops later, the train surfaced into the open air. The night was gray and shimmered dimly as the train ran slowly alongside I-95. On the highway, vehicles floated back and forth like small boats in a black channel on a white sea. Due to the snowstorm, lights along the track went haywire and flashed red randomly. Whenever the train stopped, the sounds of the traffic, muffled by the snow, droned faintly, and the night turned eerily serene.

When Tian opened the door to his apartment, a wave of warm air surged up to greet him, like tiny fingers stroking his face. The sensation was comfortable and familiar—he remembered that as a teenager, he'd been greeted by the same kind of warmth in the wintertime when he stepped into his family's home in Dalian. His parents' old apartment building had central heating, so it was kept very warm during the winter, at times even too hot. Some of their neighbors went to complain about the overheating, but the head super told them, "It's always better to keep you warm than let you freeze. You ought to appreciate that we can provide enough heat for you. Uniform heating is a virtue of our socialism, don't you see?" In fact, there was simply no way they could adjust the temperature in the individual units, so all the apartments in the four residential buildings had no choice but to receive the same amount of heat, though in reality some had too much and some too little.

Now it dawned on him that he'd forgotten to turn down the heat when he left for Boston University that afternoon. This meant there'd be extra dollars on the utility bill. He hurried over to turn the thermostat down to sixty degrees. His own negligence upset him.

He'd been mindful about budgeting so that he could send money to Shuna every month. The holiday season was a kind of boom time for him, although he also sang at the community center in Chinatown for free. They had approached him through Yabin but said they didn't have extra funds for this year to pay Tian. Tian accepted the invitation anyway because the center had welcomed his arrival in Boston and seemed ready to help him as best they could. Besides Sunday school at the community center, they provided other services for new immigrants and senior citizens—affordable housing, evening English classes, daycare, weekend Bible studies. When he went to sing for them, his performance—mostly folk songs—was better received there than it was at the colleges, where students were more interested in what was popular at the moment.

Toward the end of February, a Chinese cultural association in New Zealand invited him to participate in a series of three concerts in their country for a fee of fifteen thousand U.S. dollars. He was stunned by the sum, never having been paid so generously. Their letter stated that they had recently obtained substantial funding and were therefore able to organize international concerts. They didn't specify the kind of songs he should sing. What pleased him even more, as he scanned the tentative program they'd sent him, was that he was one of only two singers they had invited. They had also engaged some Chinese instrumentalists, including Tan Mai, the pi-pa player.

Tian took Yabin and Laura out for dinner to celebrate the offer. They ate at Quincy Dynasty, which had an excellent buffet. He liked the assorted seafood there, mostly fried, crispy and fresh. As they sat down to eat, Laura said, "If you can get three or four engagements like this a year, you won't need to do any other work."

Tian smiled and said, "Do wish me luck so that more offers like this one will come."

She went on, "Of course. Pretty soon you'll make money more easily than my dad."

"Come on, your father is an official. He must rake in bribes and kickbacks regularly," he joked.

That set them all laughing. She corrected him with blushing cheeks, saying, "Actually, my dad is not a high official. He's a middleman, an agent of sorts, in a state-owned bank."

"What does he do exactly?" Tian asked.

"He helps companies secure loans and land acquisitions."

"See," he said, "without a lot of pull, he couldn't possibly do that kind of work. Definitely he has been making tons of money."

Yabin, who had been smiling quietly, piped in at last, "To be honest, Tian, even though this is a great opportunity, I'm not entirely comfortable about you going to New Zealand. That country might not be safe."

"What do you mean?" he asked in perplexity.

"Do you know Hao Nian, the historian based in Chicago, who often appears on New Tang Dynasty Television?" Yabin said.

"Not personally, but I've seen him on TV. He's very smart and erudite, an eloquent speaker."

"He has made statements that the Chinese government often tried to lure him to Asia and Australia so they could nab or eliminate him there. That's why he has refused to go to those parts of the world. At most he'll go to Canada and to certain European countries."

That was news to Tian. Unsettled, he asked Yabin, "Do you think the Chinese government might hurt me if I go to New Zealand?"

"I'm not sure. Don't be too disconcerted. I'm just sharing my misgivings with you. But if you decide to go, you must be very careful when you are there and avoid going out alone. Is the mainland government involved in funding the concerts?"

"I don't think so," Tian said. "I'm told that the funds are from Hong Kong."

"That's good. It can be messy and nerve-racking if you make money from the mainland—at any moment you might run into difficulties."

"I'll avoid dealing with the mainland, of course," said Tian.

"As far as you can, never get close to it."

For days Tian thought about Yabin's warning, but believed it unlikely that the Chinese government would take him out now. There were so many more serious troublemakers for them to handle. In addition, fifteen grand was such a large sum to him that he was willing to run the risk, and he didn't think it so dangerous to go to New Zealand, a free country ruled by law. He mustn't be too timid.

23

With a green card in hand, Tian could return to the States without trouble when he traveled abroad, but as a Chinese passport holder, he had to obtain a visa in order to enter New Zealand. His host would help him expedite the process, though he had to file the application online, pay a two-hundred-forty-dollar fee, and wait three weeks for processing. It was expensive, but he viewed this trip as an avenue to more opportunities. If the concerts were successful, he believed that more international offers would come.

But half a month later he again heard from the New Zealand cultural association. In an email, they informed him that they were regretfully obliged to revoke their invitation: The Chinese government had been pressuring them to drop him from the program, or else the sponsor, a Hong Kong businessman, wouldn't deliver the remaining half of the promised funding. The woman in communication with Tian apologized, saying they had no option but to comply. He was outraged and devastated, having built so much hope on this trip and on the illusion that he would soon be able to sing internationally so that he could earn enough without worrying about his livelihood. Now he felt like a fool.

When he told Yabin what had happened, his friend said he should always shun any project involving the Chinese government, because the Party would try to control the source of your income once you entered their orbit. That's their way to run your life. In their words, "If you eat our rice, you can't smash our pot." So Tian had to avoid making money from any projects supported by them. He saw that more obstacles might lie ahead of him. He'd better stop dreaming of performing outside the States from now on.

Yet his prospects in America didn't look heartening either—it was time to consider finding other kinds of work. He spoke with Yabin about his construction connections. His friend smiled and said, "I'll speak with Frank. He and his wife are fans of yours and will be happy to help, I'm sure. Are you positive you can do manual labor, though? Home renovation takes a lot of muscle and sweat."

Tian reminded Yabin that he had done this type of work before and had truly enjoyed it. Before college, he had worked at a construction site for a distant uncle of his, carrying bricks up the scaffolding, transporting mortar in a wheelbarrow, tying up rebar with steel wire, digging holes in the front and the back yards for aspen and linden saplings, paving driveways with asphalt. Even though the work made his muscles sore at the end of the day, he relished it. It gave him a physical sense of how common laborers earned their livelihood: Every sack of rice and every piece of clothing came from sweating work. Before leaving for college in Beijing, he handed to his father the money he'd made. His grandmother had died before he left home, so his wages covered the expenses of her funeral—otherwise his parents would have had to borrow. His father was so pleased about Tian's "largesse" that he often mentioned his son's "filial disposition" to his colleagues and friends.

Tian was sure that home renovation in Quincy couldn't be as heavy and dangerous as the job in his uncle's construction team. As long as he was careful about exposure to fumes and particles that might harm his vocal cords, he should be up to the work.

As Yabin had promised, he spoke with Frank Chu about Tian's need for work. Frank was in his mid-forties, with bright eyes and a booming voice that was slightly nasal. His dark skin was reddish and exuded health. Yabin had been working for Frank's company, a small operation called Paramount Home Improvement. Through Yabin, Tian had met Frank and his wife, Sami, before, though briefly. By now he knew quite a bit about the couple. They had run a small Cantonese restaurant up in Maine for five years, cooking and waiting tables together. Once they had saved some money, they sold the restaurant, moved down to Quincy, and embarked on a business in home renovation, since Frank was very handy and hardworking. Several of the workers Yabin had originally recruited for his cousin had started to work for Frank after the real estate developer had left for Las Vegas. With these capable hands joining him, Frank's business kept booming. Many real-estate agents began to refer their customers to him when their homes needed repairing. But Frank knew very little English and couldn't communicate with Americans directly. That was where Yabin's service was needed. As Frank began to receive more job orders than he could handle, Yabin helped him farm work out to others: electricians, plumbers, carpenters, masons, roofers, painters, floor setters. Most of these workers were Chinese, and some Hispanic; Yabin helped facilitate their communication with their customers too. He had even learned a little rudimentary Spanish. Some workers simply called him "Second Boss."

Probably to avoid hurting Tian's feelings, Frank didn't assign him work directly and simply let Yabin find him suitable jobs on an ad hoc basis. It was still winter and only some small indoor projects were under way. Since Tian had no special skills, Yabin put him into a group of cleaners, who were charged with sprucing up the renovated homes. Tian began by washing carpets with a heavy-duty cleaning machine. He had never used such a thing before, and it took him several floors to master pushing and pulling the machine with some ease. He liked the work and was paid $9.50 an hour. Though Tian had a Social Security Number, Frank still gave him cash.

Yabin also assigned him to paint the interiors of houses. With a few exceptions, all walls were painted in a white called 7050, which Frank said was a universal color, suitable for nearly all interiors. Tian thought this was quite neat and saw how it made the work easier.

A cousin of Sami's, Yu Funi, was the most skilled among the six painters. Tian was added to this group. Usually a house needed only two painters at a time, so the seven of them would be assigned to different homes. Since Tian was new, Funi kept him with her so that she could train him. She showed him how to tape the edges of socket covers and the sides of window and door frames, how to caulk cracks and small holes in a wall, how to pour paint into a tray, and how to wash brushes in a toilet.

She was in her late twenties and sturdy with muscular arms and thick shoulders. In spite of the cold weather she wore only a thin sweater and a pink headscarf when she was painting indoors.

"Can you do this?" she asked Tian as she was roll-painting a ceiling, assuming that he hadn't tried a roller yet.

"Of course," he said with forced confidence. "I did this kind of work back in my hometown."

"Huh? I don't believe you. We didn't use a roller in China."

"Right," he acknowledged. "I only used a brush."

He found it hard to paint an even coat on a ceiling, and at first his work often appeared patchy with various shades. Funi had to touch it up to finish the job.

She was easy to be with—he could relax around her as if they'd known each other for a long time. When she needed something, she would tell him to get it for her because her hands were full. When they took a break, she'd throw on her peacoat and go out for a cigarette with the other smokers on the crew. He always stayed inside, lounging around or catnapping with his head pillowed on his crossed hands. In spite of their age difference—thirteen years—he enjoyed working with her. Her youthful energy made him feel more active and alive. During the first week he had sore shoulders, but soon his muscles adjusted, and he was able to run a roller with ease.

Sometimes he was assigned to help a plumber fix a leaking toilet or sink or replace a water heater. Tian didn't have a flair for plumbing at all, but Yabin wanted him to become familiar with the different trades, sometimes sending him off with a carpenter or even an electrician. In general, the work was light on these trips: He just stood at the ready, handing them a part or a tool when they needed it. At most they'd have him help them return or buy parts at Home Depot, loading and unloading their trucks. Yabin joked that in due time Tian might take his job, helping Frank facilitate business and communicate with English-speaking customers. Tian said he was merely a part-timer and there was no way he could step into Yabin's shoes.

Soon he found his specialty: making window and door screens. This work used to belong to Sami, but now she was too occupied with bookkeeping and the three children she and Frank had. Home Depot did sell ready-made screens, but they were pricey and didn't fit well, so Paramount always made their own. When Tian started a screen, he was careful about the measurements, down to the millimeter, and as a result his products always fitted doors or windows precisely. Tian was happy to find himself useful in this way.

Unlike the rest of them, Frank was a master craftsman. Besides his own home, a clapboard raised ranch he had restored himself, he owned two multi-unit houses, which, because he had renovated every part of the two properties and had done such an excellent job, he had become unwilling to sell. Tian admired Frank's pride in his work and even thought that if he was ever born again, he'd like to be a master home renovator, earning a living with his hands and skill and physical strength—each year he would rebuild two or three old houses and sell them at a profit. That would be a decent way to make a living. Yet he had noticed that Frank always avoided acquiring properties in slums because he wanted to ensure that the renovated houses could get taken off his hands easily. Frank seemed to have a kind of instinct for how to operate within this capitalist system. He eschewed risks and tried to acquire building materials only from a network of reliable friends.

Frank seldom joined his workers on-site. He spent his days in downtown Boston or Cambridge, doing high-end custom work for clients who were often demanding but paid well. Frank once told Tian that a graduate student at MIT, a son of some high-ranking official in China, had paid him five thousand dollars to build an exquisite wine rack in his kitchen. The young man owned the apartment and wanted it to be furnished to his satisfaction, so the wine rack was one of a kind, made of hardwood. Frank had since become his personal handyman, and he often raved about the extravagance and openhandedness of his rich clients.

24

Y OUR MOTHER IS IN THE HOSPITAL," Shuna told Tian on the phone.

"What happened to her?" he asked, stunned, though he knew her health had been faltering.

"I'm not sure. Her neighbor called last night and said she had blacked out in the doorway of her home and couldn't get up from the floor. Some members of the neighborhood committee happened to be passing by and saw her. They rushed her to the hospital."

"Did the police do something to her?"

"I don't think so—you know she has been unwell for some time. I urged her to have a checkup in our medical school here, but she wouldn't come to Beijing."

"Do you need me to come back and care for her?" A paroxysm of homesickness hit him. He knew his mother and his wife had never gotten along and it would be unlikely for them to live comfortably under the same roof.

"Don't rush," Shuna said. "I'm going to Dalian in two days, after I teach my graduate seminar, and I'll see what she's like."

"Please keep me updated. I'll be waiting for your call."

Dalian City was about six hundred miles east of Beijing, but by high-speed rail one could get there in five hours. Tian feared his mother might have had a stroke, or worse—if so, he must hurry back to take care of her. Since Anji's death he'd been his mother's only living kin and he should be at her side. But he couldn't say this to Shuna, who seemed determined to have him stay in America so that their daughter could attend college there. To people back home, including officials, Tian's lengthy stay in the States signified that he had settled down, so it would be natural for Tingting to come join him. With her father already in America, there might be fewer official obstacles to her coming here. Tian was sure that must be Shuna's reasoning, though he felt she had simplified too much. To him, it was money that was the determining factor—as long as you got admitted by a college and your family had the funds to pay, you should be able to come and study. Whenever he thought of his daughter coming to college in America, Tian got unnerved by the cost. There was no way he and Shuna could support Tingting's education here with their incomes. Yet they owned two apartments in Beijing, both shabby and small. Perhaps they could sell one of them for the girl's college, but still that might be far from enough. He couldn't explain the money worries to his wife, afraid she might blame him for not having taken the government's offer of four million dollars.

He also realized that his mother's illness could become an excuse for him to give up the difficult work of a free life and retreat back to a secure livelihood and the endless restrictions he abhorred, like a freed bird back in its former aviary. With that awareness he decided to wait for Shuna's report after her visit to his mother.

To his dismay, Shuna abandoned her plans to go to Dalian that weekend because Tingting had a dance test out of town that would determine whether she could advance to the next level of classes. Shuna feared that Tingting might have gotten lost on the way if she'd gone alone. Further, the girl wouldn't have known where to get lunch and clean drinking water, both of which Shuna carried for her. Tian was angry—his mother was lying in the hospital while Shuna was more worried about their daughter's dance class. He could tell that Tingting was an unremarkable dancer and always attended her classes half-heartedly. Perhaps the girl also knew she was on the verge of aging out of her dancer's body, her frame getting heavier and her limbs thicker. Besides, she should be able to get around and find suitable food on her own. Shuna shouldn't pamper her so much.

Tian and his wife argued on the phone. He told her she needed to go to Dalian as soon as possible. She sounded annoyed, but promised to go see her mother-in-law as soon as she could. "Wait until you hear from me," she said. "Then you can decide what to do."

He called the hospital several times, but couldn't get hold of the doctors who had been treating his mother. Only once a nurse answered his questions, telling him that his mom had just come out of the ICU and would be kept in a ward for further treatment. The nurse was busy and couldn't speak with him at length.

When Shuna returned from Dalian the next Sunday evening, she told Tian that his mother didn't seem to be recovering. Her stroke had also caused a heart attack. Her condition was dangerous, and the doctors only said they were doing their best. The local Falun Gong branch had assigned three caregivers for her, who rotated around the clock. But Shuna could see that her mother-in-law might not survive: She could no longer recognize her daughter-in-law and was also incontinent.

This made Tian decide to head back without further delay. His passport was due to expire in just a month, however, and he wanted to get it renewed here before he departed. He was unsure how this was done, but he was positive that in China he'd be classified as someone under "border control" and the renewal would be denied. He decided to go to the Chinese consulate in New York to see if the renewal could be expedited. He'd heard that such a service was available if you paid an extra thirty-dollar fee. The visa and passport office on 42nd Street was open weekdays from nine a.m. to two-thirty p.m., and the line was said to be so long that applicants had to get there early in the morning so as to get their visas and passport renewals before the closing time. Ideally he should arrive one or two hours before nine a.m., but no bus ran after midnight from Boston. The cheapest service was Fung Wah, the Chinatown bus, which cost ten dollars at night and fifteen during the day. Many commuters used this bus between New York and Boston, despite its poor safety records and the frequent breakdowns and accidents. The last bus left South Station at ten p.m. and arrived in New York around two a.m. This meant he'd have to wait seven hours for the visa and passport office to open. Of course he could get there the night before, but a hotel room would cost more than $180 in Manhattan. In a crisis like this, he had to save as much as he could, and he was certain that there'd be a lot of expenses for his mother, so he decided to take the last Fung Wah bus.

He arrived at Port Authority at one-fifty a.m. and went out to stretch his legs a little on Eighth Avenue. The street was still strewn with pedestrians in spite of the early hour. The misty, rust-colored nightglow enlivened the sky beyond the buildings. A rancid odor lingered in the air, reminding him of overused cooking oil and underground sewage. It was still chilly in mid-March, people on the street wrapped in long coats and some in scarves. Tian realized he'd better stay inside the bus station before daybreak, so he went back in. In a hall on the second floor he came upon some twenty men and women sleeping along the bases of walls, most of them homeless covered in blankets, though a few looked like passengers, accompanied by bags and parcels, waiting for the morning buses. They all seemed in heavy sleep despite the musty air in there. Fortunately Tian had on an overcoat and could keep warm even lying on the cold terrazzo floor. He picked a spot and lay down next to an old man who was holding an empty whiskey bottle on his abdomen with both hands. As Tian was dozing off with his knit hat pulled over his face, a rush of sadness filled his chest. If someone recognized him here and took a photo of him, he was sure that word could go viral, that many people would know via social media that Yao Tian was like "a homeless bum" now. Yet in spite of his misery, soon he fell asleep.

The next morning he was amazed by his ability to sleep well inside the bus station. This reminded him of a saying his mother had been fond of dropping: "Human beings can stand any suffering but not much happiness."

After an egg-and-cheese bagel and a cup of coffee, Tian started out for the visa and passport office behind the Chinese consulate, less than a ten-minute walk from Port Authority. More than a dozen applicants were already in line outside the building, waiting for the visa office to open; most of them were from out of state and had arrived in New York the day before. Young couples were with their infants, wives and husbands holding the children by turns. Tian stood at the end of the line, leaning against the wall of the building and waiting, his arms crossed on his chest. In no time the line had grown behind him. Traffic was surging on the street, and along the Hudson locals walked hurriedly through the mist. Tian put on his pair of powerless glasses so that he wouldn't be recognized. Then four black men in navy uniforms appeared, security guards employed by the Chinese consulate. One of them checked the relevant forms in visitors' hands, tossing out a phrase or a short sentence in Mandarin now and then.

The hall on the second floor was full of people waiting for their numbers to be called. All the seats were taken. Some families had come together and stayed in knots in the corners or by the street-facing windows. A woman in her forties passed by, holding a brand-new Prada bag in front of her as if allowing the orange purse to drag her around. Tian was amused. Then a girl shouted at her father, "Your number's up, Dad. Go now." She pointed at window 9.

To get his passport renewed, Tian didn't need to go to any of those busy visa windows. When window 11 flashed his number, he rose and walked over, taking off his glasses. The woman behind the glass had goldfish eyes and a pageboy thick like a black cap. She bit the corner of her mouth as she flipped through his paperwork, ending with his immigration certificate that proved his permanent residency.

"Where is your green card? Can I have a look?" she asked, smiling kindly—perhaps she knew he was the singer.

"I don't have it on me, but here's a photocopy." He had read on the consulate website that a Xeroxed copy of permanent residency papers would be sufficient, and feared that, if they got the originals, they might not give them back. He asked her, "Is there a way to get my passport renewed quickly? My mother is ill, hospitalized, and I have to go back to look after her. I don't know how long I will need to stay with her."

She shook her head. "Because of heightened security measures, we don't renew passports anymore. We now just reissue new passports to Chinese citizens when their old ones expire—and the new ones are good for ten years now instead of five. But today, I'm sorry, Mr. Yao, I can't help you get a new passport."

The renewal used to be done with an official seal on the same passport, which specified the length of the renewed time, usually five years, but now China had followed the U.S. way, just issuing you a new passport instead.

"What should I do, then?" Tian sounded desperate.

She offered, "How about this—you leave your passport here and also give me a check for fifty-five dollars? I will put a note to your application saying it needs expediting. Sometimes you might get a new passport within ten days if they rush it." She sounded professional and eager to help him.

He paid the fee, which included the cost for the expediting, and thanked her again. Before leaving, he even said he was his mother's only son—the only family she had now, so he must see her in case she couldn't survive this time. The woman nodded and told him that he should get his new passport soon.

It was not yet one o'clock, and he bought a hot dog and a bottle of grapefruit juice from a food cart on his way back to the bus station. Though exhausted, he was happy about this trip. Once he had his new passport, he'd fly back to China without delay.

25

D URING THE FOLLOWING WEEK he was restless and called his mother's hospital every night. The calls never lasted long, since the medical personnel were all busy. Sometimes he could get hold of one of the Falun Gong caregivers at his mother's bedside, but they sounded uninformed of her actual condition, able only to describe her symptoms and how poorly she ate and slept.

The official mail from the Chinese consulate came in the middle of the third week after his visit to New York. When he unsealed the envelope, he was surprised to find only his old passport with the top corner of its front cover cut off. For a while he stared at it dumbly; then he understood that his passport had been revoked. Panicking, he opened it and found at the bottom of the first page a scarlet rectangle in which was printed CANCELED in both Chinese and English.

He tried to get his head around the invalidation. This meant he couldn't go back to China at all—not until he had a U.S. passport and was granted a visa, as a foreigner. But green card holders had to wait five years to apply for U.S. citizenship. He still had four years to go.

He went out to walk in the cemetery in the north. He needed a quiet place to subdue the turmoil in him. There was no one around, and he sat down on a boulder on the side of a trail while tears trickled down his face, stinging his cheeks. The air smelled damp in spite of the strong sunlight. In the distance a large rust-colored tanker ship was emerging, breaking the line between sky and water.

He might be barred from seeing his homeland as long as the current Chinese government stood. What about his mother? Shuna had her hands full with her job and their daughter—she couldn't go to Dalian more than two or three times a month. The only solution Tian could think of was to hire two caregivers to look after his mother in the hospital. But that would cost a lot, at least thirteen hundred dollars a month. He thought of having his mother transferred to a hospital in Beijing, but that would be infeasible—impossible unless they could afford the astronomical costs, whereas in Dalian the municipal government was to pay her medical bills.

To his knowledge, his mother had no savings at all. All she had was a shabby two-bedroom apartment. Though Shuna was a professor at a top university in China, she could make only about twelve hundred dollars a month, so Tian would have to provide the funds for his mother's care. But he was hardly able to make his own ends meet these days and was not sure how he could come up with that kind of money.

When he told Shuna that his passport had been canceled, she was silent for a good while before she spoke again. As she was speaking, she seemed to be generating and organizing her thoughts. He was always amazed by her perceptive mind.

She said, "You won't be able to return to China anymore. Tingting and I will have to join you in America."

"It looks that way."

"I've just heard that they didn't give me the research grant I was supposed to get. Without the official funding, I can't have my passport back from the university, which controls all the professors' international travel now. Like you, I'm stuck."

"This is awful," he said. He didn't add that he now believed they might have to stay separated for a long time. The cancellation of his passport clearly indicated that the Chinese government viewed him as a dissident. The official hands had been working against them at every opportunity; they knew the most effective way to destroy a dissident was to break their family.

Shuna went on, "See, that was why I urged you to take the offer of four million dollars two years ago. We could have immigrated through investments. The money could have transformed our lives."

"But I couldn't sell my voice like that."

"Once we had the money and landed in America, you could have kept singing somehow."

"But that would be devious, wouldn't it? I couldn't live with myself."

"In this time and age honesty is synonymous with stupidity. This is an awful truth, isn't it?"

"If we'd deceived the government, there could have been terrible consequences."

"Once we were outside their borders, they wouldn't have been able to harm us."

"They can always pin a criminal name on you and get you repatriated. It's dangerous to play tricks on them."

He changed the topic, saying that he'd have to hire caregivers for his mother. In order to pay for her care, he might need to suspend for some time his monthly remittance to her and Tingting. Shuna, always reasonable, said they could manage. That was a relief for him.

But for days, even while at work with the painters and cleaners, he couldn't stop pondering whether, despite everything, there might be a way to get a new passport. He talked to Yabin about his predicament. His friend believed there might be a way for him to get another passport. He mentioned that Freda had a classmate at the Chinese consulate in San Francisco and that he, Yabin, had once asked the man to help a friend of his expedite a visa application.

Tian was hesitant to contact Freda, but what was there to lose? He had to follow any lead that presented itself. According to Yabin, Freda was going back to China soon, so there should be no harm for Tian to contact her. He emailed her and asked about the diplomat who'd been her classmate. To his relief, she replied on the same day, saying she would contact her friend right away. She sounded calm and reasonable and seemed to have changed some.

Two days later he heard from her again. Her friend had looked into his case and had learned that the decision to revoke his passport had been made in China, and that the Chinese diplomatic offices in the States could only carry out the orders from above. The only place he could even try to get the cancellation reversed was in Beijing, at the Ministry of State Security. Tian had landed on a blacklist, from which he'd have to get his name removed—only after that could the Chinese consulate issue him another passport. Tian could hardly fathom the bureaucratic labyrinth involved, just the thought of which gave him chills.

These days Freda phoned him quite often, and now he was obliged to answer her calls. She also texted him lengthy messages. In their communications, she told him that she needed to return to China because she couldn't find a full-time job here, unable to use the professional training period allowed by her visa. She'd look for work in Tianjin, where her parents now lived. If she couldn't find a position that she really liked, she might immigrate to North America eventually. "I might come back to look for you one of these days," she wrote. "Don't forget me."

She still made him nervous, but intuitively he felt he could use her help once she was back in China. So he tried to be friendly to Freda and even asked her, once she was back, if she could find a way for him to get a passport. She'd always said she knew people in high places in Beijing—he could tell that might be an empty boast, but out loud he only said that she was absolutely remarkable, her ability to get things done.

"Of course," she said to him on the phone. "You're my friend. Besides, spending a single passionate night as lovers can guarantee an everlasting affection, right?" She quoted the proverb, which gave him a jolt.

Before she left, they arranged for him to transfer funds to her each month so that she could help his mother. She then would convert the amount into yuan and use it for his mother's care. In fact, Freda promised to go to Dalian personally and hire the right people to look after her. Tianjin wasn't very far from his home city, just four hours by high-speed train. He was touched by her help and even wondered if he'd been too hard on her. Flighty though she was, Freda could be loving and devoted. He had to admit that at heart she was a good person. Her last message to him before leaving New York was: "Cherish your talent, Tian! Please quit home repairs soon! Your field of action is the stage."

He wondered whether he should let Shuna know his arrangement with Freda, but decided against it. That might complicate matters. He told her only that he'd found a way to hire two local women to tend to his mother. Shuna didn't press him about this. Fortunately, prior to retirement, his mother had been a clerk in the municipal tax department, so her medical costs were to be covered by the government.

26

PARAMOUNT HOME IMPROVEMENT had run into trouble. The company had just finished renovating an antique house on Riverside Street, but before it could be put on the market, it had to be inspected by the Quincy municipality. The workers had gutted the old house and replaced everything inside except for the floors, which they sanded and then varnished so that they appeared like cherrywood, shiny and vintage. Funi kept saying, "This looks like a luxury home." And, viewed from inside, with the new cabinets, new bathtubs, new toilets, and new ceilings, the house did indeed look gorgeous. Frank had skimped on nothing.

The official inspector came, a broad man with a brushy mustache and a sunburned-looking face and wearing a short-sleeve button-down. His belly was hanging over his belt and his arms were thick and hairy. He went through the rooms on both floors, checking the heating system, the windows, and the sinks. He also poked here and there as if to see whether everything was firmly set. Then he went down into the basement. He looked at the PVC pipes overhead and told Frank, "You guys know the requirements, but you didn't follow code."

None of them knew what to make of that, so no one responded. When they were back on the first floor, the inspector explained to Frank, "I looked through the whole house and checked all the pipes in both bathrooms and under the sinks. I didn't see a single purple mark. How can I say you guys are up to code?"

Tian translated those words for Frank, whose face contorted as if he was struggling to smile but produced only a grimace. The inspector added, "You have to use purple marks on the pipes and the other PVC parts, following the code, or else how the hell can I tell if you used the right primer or any primer at all?"

"What should we do about this?" asked Tian.

"Redo all the pipes."

Frank looked baffled—code seemed to be something new to him. He tugged at Tian's sleeve and told him to ask the inspector to step outside with them so that they could talk more about this. Once they were on the front porch, just the three of them, Frank pulled out a signed check for two thousand dollars with his name and home address printed at the top. He said, "Just let us pass, officer. We already have buyers lining up for a view of this house." His forced smile crinkled the corners of his eyes to form a pair of fishtails.

Tian translated his request. The man took the check and glanced at it, then told them, "Here's my card. Contact me after you redo the pipes." The card stated he was Thomas Glashen, construction inspector contracted with the city government.

Without further ado, he strode away to his Ford pickup. Frank looked crushed. He had put more than one hundred eighty thousand dollars into the renovation. He needed to get the capital back so that he could start another project. Spring was a busy time, the beginning of the year for the real estate business, and he couldn't afford to be stuck. He called their plumber and asked about the purple marks. The man told Frank that the code was outdated and few took the trouble to follow it nowadays, but if the inspector chose to throw the book at them, they might not be able to do anything about it.

Tian was amazed that even Frank, a master in home renovation, was ignorant of the old rule. Despite his superb skills, his boss wasn't completely respected in the home repair business. He looked slow, if not silly, when interacting with English-speaking customers.

Yabin was more experienced in dealing with Americans, so he began to communicate with the inspector on their company's behalf. The major concern was the check Frank had given the man, which could be evidence of bribery. Obviously someone like the inspector hated to see so many Asians entering home renovation in Quincy and was trying to suppress the trend. Tian had noticed many small companies owned by Chinese or Vietnamese immigrants specializing in a single area of home improvement—floor setting, countertops, roofing, fences, garage doors, window replacements, landscaping. The quality of their work tended to be substandard, but they charged considerably less.

Ultimately, they had no choice but to redo the pipes in the house. The job took three plumbers a full day, using a purple primer on all the joints of pipes. Glashen never mentioned the check, which was cashed two weeks later after he provided his approval of the house. Absurdly, the clearing of the check brought a kind of relief to Frank. He kept saying that some Americans were insatiable beasts that would eat you without spitting out your bones.

Laura, Yabin's girlfriend, was outraged, saying it was a racist act. She believed that if the purple-mark rule was already obsolete, no longer in the book, it should never have applied to Frank's renovation. The inspector had cheated them two times over—since he'd accepted the money, he should have let the house pass the initial inspection. But instead, they'd had to redo the pipes and still lost the two thousand dollars. Laura wanted to write to *The Boston Globe* to complain, but Frank stopped her because he might have to deal with Glashen again down the road. "It would be foolish to tear down our bridges," he told them.

Tian's mother took a turn for the worse. For days she remained unconscious and the caregivers could no longer feed her the liquid food they prepared for her. She had to be kept alive by IV drips. The hospital issued to Shuna a crisis notice—a form stating that her mother-in-law might die at any minute. Shuna emailed it to Tian and said she was leaving for Dalian without delay. She had to ask two colleagues to teach her classes for the rest of the week. During her absence, Tingting would eat at a neighbor's home.

Tian was desperate but unable to figure out a way to go back. Normally, if a dissident's parent was dying, the Chinese government provided a onetime visa for the person to join the family for a deathbed reunion and for the funeral. But his case was unique: His passport was canceled, and even if he managed to return, he'd be stranded in China. He was so devastated that the next day he stayed home from work, crying from time to time. If only he were able to do something for his dying mother!

Every night he spoke with Shuna on the phone. The more they talked, the more hopeless he felt. She was quite certain that his mother didn't have many days left—she was having her final clothes prepared for her and was planning the funeral service. All the arrangements she made were fine with Tian, but he was seriously considering attending the funeral, heedless of whether he could return to Boston afterward. Although his passport was canceled, legally it would expire in a week—he might seize the last few days to get back home. Shuna was adamantly against the idea, saying that even his mother would hate to see him there if it meant he'd run such a risk for her.

"Didn't she tell you never to return?" Shuna asked him.

"But I want to see her one last time—"

"She's already unconscious, not able to recognize anyone. Tian, I know you're heartbroken, but the only safe thing for you to do is remain in America. I believe that's also what your mother wants you to do."

Later Tian told Yabin what Shuna had said. Yabin shook his head and breathed a long sigh. "I didn't go back when my father died," he said, "because I had to take a big exam for my MBA at Fordham. I was told that for many days he wouldn't lie down at night—he feared he might not wake up in the morning and would die without seeing me back. In his final moments he kept murmuring my name as if to keep his heart beating until he could see me for the last time. Since he passed away, I've felt his eyes on me now and then, smoldering with pain. Sometimes I wonder whether our way of life is right and whether all our sacrifices were necessary and justified. Why do we Chinese face so many obstacles in life?"

Tian echoed, "And all of them are artificial besides."

"Exactly. Since birth, we have been caged by all sorts of rules, some of which we have adopted as our way of life and even as part of ourselves. I can't help wondering if they've been coded into our DNA."

"I hate that ruthless country!" Tian cried, suddenly possessed by a fit of anger.

Wordlessly Yabin nodded in agreement.

Two days later Tian's mother died. Her body was shipped to a local crematory, where the funeral was held in a little hall, attended mainly by members of Falun Gong. A few neighbors were there too, but they all kept a low profile, dodging cameras, afraid of being associated with the religious group. Tingting had been there for her grandmother's funeral too, and Tian felt relieved to know that. His mother's ashes were left at the crematory and would, by custom, be interred two months later. Shuna sent Tian photos of the funeral, which showed about a dozen or so wreaths standing beside his mother's portrait and every attendee wearing a black armband and a tiny white flower on the chest. Shuna arranged for a reception in the adjoining room so that the mourners could share a light repast.

Tian was grateful to her for all she'd done for his mother. Shuna was strong, full of fortitude and capable of meeting the task. She often said, "There's no river we can't cross."

Then she found out that his mother's will contained almost nothing. Falun Gong had sold her apartment to pay her medical bills—her status as a practitioner had disqualified her for the health coverage that a retiree was entitled to. Shuna was upset, having hoped that his mother had bequeathed something to Tingting, her only grandchild. Tian was unhappy too, but understood the sale of her home had been necessary. Her apartment was shabby and fetched only 600,000 yuan, barely enough to cover her medical bills. For their unfailing help, Tian felt beholden to the local Falun Gong.

Tian had noticed that there weren't many dissidents living in the Boston area, and even fewer political activities among the expats and immigrants. Still, when the twenty-third anniversary of the Tiananmen massacre was approaching, some dissidents, mainly in academia, were preparing memorial events. Tian had never volunteered to participate in this kind of activity unless he was invited, so he hadn't attended the memorials of the past two years. One local dissident, a professor at Boston College, approached Tian, inviting him to perform at a gathering in memory of the tragedy. Partly owing to his anger, Tian agreed to take part in the memorial. There'd also be a conference at Harvard, where a course on the Tiananmen movement had been offered by a young professor, Rowena He. Tian had read that she was determined to preserve this piece of history in part because she had seen that students from mainland China hardly knew anything about the tragedy. The Chinese government had done a thorough job in producing a collective amnesia, making most young people ignorant of the massacre. At most some of the students had vaguely heard of it. So Professor He embarked on teaching such a history seminar centered on the Tiananmen massacre, which was eventually fully attended. At first, many Chinese students, particularly those from the mainland, wouldn't believe there'd been such bloodshed, and even expressed their resolve not to be convinced by the instruction, but as the class proceeded, more and more of them began to see the truth, verified by evidence of many kinds: personal accounts, photographs, footage, bloody clothes worn by the victims, live eyewitnesses. Some students emotionally collapsed toward the end of the course, never having imagined that the government could be so brutal. They were reminded that the student demonstrators in 1989 must have been the same age as they themselves were now. The seminar was a great success, yet Professor He lamented that to her knowledge, Harvard was the only school that offered such a course. Tian remembered that his father-in-law, who'd passed away a decade before, had once said that courage manifested in the way one lived and worked every day. Yet when Tian expressed his admiration for the professor in front of Yabin and Laura, they seemed underwhelmed. Laura even said that the woman must have too much leisure and extra energy to spare. "In retrospect, I'd say it was necessary to suppress the rebellion," Laura said blandly. "The crackdown at Tiananmen Square led to China's miraculous economic development."

"It was not a rebellion!" Tian almost shouted.

That silenced her. Tian felt he might not be able to take them as real friends anymore—obviously, they and he had different world-views. He said calmly, "The Communist government wants people to forget, but I choose to remember and do something to make others remember. We mustn't let that part of history vanish like smoke."

They both smiled without speaking, shaking their heads. Tian wondered why Yabin, a longtime dissident, had changed his position on the Tiananmen massacre—perhaps he'd heard too many stories of corruption among the former student leaders who had fled to the West. Some of them had taken bribes, some pocketed funds raised in the name of supporting dissidents' families, and some even covertly worked for the Chinese government.

Tian went to Boston Common for the memorial on Sunday, June 3. The afternoon sun was mild after a light shower in the morning, and about two hundred people had gathered by the time he arrived. The modest number of attendees disappointed him, and he understood why Yabin wouldn't come this year. Yabin seemed to have sensed the public's loss of interest in democratic movements, and Laura, too, had influenced him for the worse.

A row of blown-up photographs of the Tiananmen massacre stretched along the front of the makeshift platform. Two former student leaders were present, including Chai Ling, who was a local now, living in Cambridge, and slightly plumper than she'd been three years prior. She spoke about the importance of the twenty-third anniversary of the democracy movement and demanded that the Chinese government admit its crime, publish the names of the dead, punish the murderers, and compensate parents for their killed children. The other speaker, an eloquent Harvard sociologist with a broad forehead and wide cheeks, repeated the same demands, but he added that in hindsight, the students had been too docile and should have rebelled with arms because their enemies were savage and brutal and never hesitated to kill.

A young student went up and spoke about how she and her peers had been brainwashed back in China and how their eyes had finally been opened in the course taught here. She went on to say, "My mother was Deng Xiaoping's English interpreter, but she never divulged a word to me about the bloodshed. After learning the truth at Professor He's seminar, I called home and asked my mother where she'd been on that bloody night. She said she was with Deng Xiaoping in an underground bunker, because the top Communist leaders feared that the government might be overthrown. She knew, everybody knew, the Communist Party had committed a horrible crime!" The girl grew so emotional that she wept.

What she said shocked Tian. He'd never thought the Communist regime could be that fragile. No wonder many of the top leaders had bank accounts in Switzerland—they were prepared to flee the country anytime.

"Fight for a free China!" a young man shouted.

Some of the audience repeated the slogan, raising their fists.

"Democracy will prevail!" he cried again.

More people shouted in one voice, a swarm of arms thrust up in the air.

Then an American journalist, a tall fiftysomething man wearing a brown jacket, went up and spoke about what he had witnessed on the night of June 3, 1989. He saw pedestrians hit by random bullets, two civilians run over by a combat personnel carrier, and a gruesome scene at the front of a hospital, where dozens of bodies were lined up, waiting to be identified and claimed. "That night destroyed my vision of China," he said. "I used to study Chinese history and literature passionately at the University of Washington, dreaming of becoming a scholar in Chinese culture. The gunshots and bloodshed at Tiananmen Square killed the imagined China in my head and shattered my youthful dream. I simply can't forget the brutal and grisly sights. I want to shout to the world: Don't forget Tiananmen!"

After his speech, the performances began. Tian was the first, and he sang soulfully, giving all he had. With his eyes half closed, he began the song "I Cannot Forget":

Mama, I still remember the lullaby you used to sing.
Nestling in your arms, I went to sleep
While your voice lingered in my ears.

Mama, your sweet songs gave me
Beautiful dreams and a lifelong blessing,
But now you are no longer here.

Mama, now I'm far away from home,
But I still hear you murmuring at night.
Whenever I think of you, I'm full of tears . . .

As he was singing, he saw his mother's lined face, mild and radiating love. She now smiled, now frowned, now glowed. Tears streamed down his cheeks. He could hardly hold himself together, but managed to finish the song.

Out of habit, he didn't stay for the rest of the program, afraid that people would accost him or take photos with him. He never felt comfortable among a crowd. His throat was still tight and his temples kept throbbing. He could see that this memorial gathering had fallen short of expectations. Indeed, over the years such efforts had shrunk more or less to mere academic affairs, and the public seemed to have grown less interested and more forgetful. Hurriedly he edged away and headed for the Park Street station to catch the train back to Quincy.

The local Chinese-language media reported on the memorial event in Boston Common. One article praised Tian's performance, saying that he had put all his heart into the song and that he was clearly a devout patriot. The writer went so far as to claim: "Yao Tian must see the mother in his song as the motherland that has abandoned him and her other children abroad, though all of them still love her wholeheartedly."

"What a stupid cliché!" he said to himself. In the context of the Tiananmen massacre, China seemed to him more like an old hag, so senile and so ailing that she had to eat the flesh and blood of her children to sustain herself. In the back of his mind lingered a question to which he didn't yet know the answer: If a country has betrayed a citizen, isn't the citizen entitled to betray the country?

The article made him reflect on his personal emotion in the context of historical memory. In his performance he'd been motivated mainly by his mourning for his mother, but the manifestation of his grief was interpreted as a collective emotion shaped by the memory of a historical event. Nobody could tell how personal his singing was—all took it as a show of his love for the motherland. This was a misinterpretation, but he couldn't say it was a mistake—it only showed how the personal and the historical had converged.

27

F ROM SHUNA, TIAN HAD LEARNED that his mother's caregivers had been paid. Freda had also shown him in an email how she'd spent the money he'd given her. After that, he'd lost touch with her for more than a month. Then he heard from Freda again. She wrote: "I am very sorry that your mother passed away. If I can be of help in another way, just let me know."

Tianjin hadn't worked out for her, so she was in Beijing now, at a private cultural association called Two-Way Street. She ran a lecture series there and was also in charge of its advertising program. She enjoyed living and working in the capital, though she wasn't yet earning enough to make ends meet. Rent was exorbitant and everything pricey except for foods sold at eateries and snack bars.

His mother's ashes were still at the crematory. It had been two months now since her death, and, having let her stay away long enough, it was time to take her home—to inter her. She should return to the countryside where his father and his sister had been laid to rest, and where Tian's grandparents were also buried. He hadn't yet asked Shuna to take his mother's ashes to their home village, because he'd been thinking about erecting a headstone. His family's grave had just a wooden plaque at its front, and he realized he needed to seize this opportunity to put up a stone. But it would be expensive—a decent one with engraving would cost at least fifteen hundred dollars.

He decided to inter his mother with his family first. Shuna agreed to take his mother's ashes to the countryside personally and ensure that her casket was buried alongside his father's and Anji's. His home village was about forty miles east of Dalian, and the trip to the countryside and back to Beijing took her two days. She went without sending word in advance, since there were no longer any living relatives in the countryside. Most of the Yaos had left for southern coastal areas, where jobs were better paid and life more colorful. Shuna located his family's grave and hired a villager to dig it open. His mother's tiny casket was placed next to his father's and his sister's, together with his grandparents', then the grave was closed. Shuna took photos of the site and sent them to Tian. The cemetery looked like a miniature village sprawling all over a sloping hill, some graves elaborate like tiny temples. His family's was shabby and inconspicuous. This made him more determined to put up a decent headstone for them.

But he was afraid to ask Shuna to pay for it. He hadn't sent her money in five months, and now that his mother was buried, he knew it was time to pick up the remittances once more. He was sure she would oppose the idea of acquiring a gravestone for his family now, no matter how hard he tried to convince her that this was the opportune time. She would say that the stone always could wait, but that their daughter's education was more important now. Shuna had hired two tutors for Tingting, one for English composition and the other for math. In addition, she had to pay for the weekend dance classes. From her point of view it was time for Tian to resume some financial responsibilities in their household. He couldn't argue with that. Nevertheless, he couldn't stop thinking about the headstone he owed his family.

He decided to ask Freda to help. She seemed resourceful and well connected in northeastern China; plus, she was already familiar with his mother's affairs. To his relief, she agreed to look into the possibility. Within two days she emailed back, saying she could find a good headstone and have it erected for his family. He was pleased and deposited twenty-five hundred dollars into her account at HSBC bank, considering the labor, shipping, and other costs. He praised her and promised to remain grateful.

She came back, "There's no need to sweet-talk me like that. But one of these days you'd better show, with an actual deed, how you appreciate my help."

He replied, "Of course I will. Thanks for being willing to give me a hand."

He had no idea what he could do for her. For now, his immediate goal was to carry out his duty to his family. "Rest assured," Freda said, "I am going to find a good headstone for your family. You will be impressed."

Her eagerness unnerved him a little, but he appreciated her ability and alacrity. Within a week she emailed him a photograph of a fine slab, a kind of marble—it looked smooth and pinkish and expensive. He was glad and told her to buy it. Then he gave her the names of his parents and sister and his grandparents, as well as the years of their births and deaths.

Soon another photograph came showing the words and numerals etched on the slab. Freda said she'd have it shipped to his home village and then drive there personally to supervise the raising of it. Tian was amazed—she was handling the matter as efficiently as if she'd been in the funeral business for years. Their communications grew more frequent and no longer made him anxious.

By the end of August, the headstone was in place. Freda even had two dwarf cypresses planted beside the slab, one on each side. One of the photos she had sent him showed a tiny brass pot placed in front of the stone, planted with smoking joss sticks. A small pile of ghost money was burning in front of the pot. The grave looked nice and well kept now. Freda had done such an exemplary job that if she were here, he'd have had to acknowledge it with a substantial gift—a cruise voyage or front-row opera tickets. Secretively he felt relieved that she was so far away, since he wasn't sure how to get along with her or reciprocate the favor properly. She might even assume he still viewed her as a girlfriend of sorts. So he tried to distance himself from her little by little, no longer answering her messages and calls as readily as before.

She seemed incensed by his distancing and warned him not to be ungrateful. The more she pressured him to pay attention to her, the more jittery and cautious he became. By no means should he give her any illusion that there was some kind of intimate relationship between them. On the other hand, he mustn't let her feel he had just used her. He was grateful and took her as a friend. If only he had known how to pay her back appropriately.

Soon Shuna came to know he was still in touch with Freda. She wrote, "What is your true relationship with this woman? Why is she still meddling with our life?"

He was taken aback but explained, "Freda and I are in touch indeed, but we are not close at all. When my mother was in the hospital I asked Freda to find caregivers for her, since I was too far away and you had your hands full. I sent her money for the caregivers' wages. That is the honest truth."

He thought his explanation would pacify Shuna, but when she wrote back she was even angrier: "Don't lie to me. Your mother passed away four months ago, but you're still sending Freda money, aren't you? What for? Are you screwing her again? She's shown me her ten-year U.S. visa—I know she can go and join you there any day."

This was insane. He'd had no idea Freda had acquired a ten-year visa, and it looked like she did plan to come back. After brooding about Shuna's accusation for a day, Tian realized that Freda must be feeding this information to Shuna directly—she seemed determined to meddle with his marriage.

Now he had to level with Shuna. More equivocation would only stir up more complications. He called to tell her about the headstone—how he had enlisted Freda's help and how much he'd paid for it. Shuna only grew more upset by his explanation and blustered, "The gravestone could have waited. Didn't I tell you that?"

"I don't see it that way," he said. "A stone was the final duty I owed to my family. I wanted to put them and myself at peace."

That made her furious. She cried, "Do you know how hard it's been for Tingting and me to manage this past year? When your mother died, I went to Dalian to take care of her funeral and then I took her ashes to the village to bury her with the others of your family. Did I ever ask you for a dime? Did you ever send me a dollar in spite of all the expenses? Let me tell you, I was totally broke and Tingting almost got expelled from prep school—I had to borrow from my brother for her tuition. I never troubled you with money difficulties, but then without breathing a word, you just went ahead and spent twenty-five hundred dollars for the gravestone. Let me repeat, the stone could have waited and any delay wouldn't have hurt the dead. But we have to support our child now and give her what she needs to go to college."

He kept silent, not knowing how to argue. He realized he'd been at fault and shouldn't have rushed to erect the headstone. At least he should have let Shuna know beforehand and discussed the matter with her.

Their exchange upset him. He was so miserable that he walked all the way to the beach to the north and lingered at the waterside for a long time. Daylight seeped away as the tide receded, the ocean spread flat without a wave. To the west pedestrians were strolling along the beach and on the concrete embankment alongside Quincy Shore Drive. It was quiet and muggy, and he began to sing, just to get the sadness off his chest. Walking back and forth on the beach and at times standing with arms akimbo, he let out one song after another, until the moon emerged above the water, casting down soft rays. A ferryboat blew its horn from the distance, chugging away, its lights wavering in the dark.

Standing in the cool breeze coming from the ocean, he went on singing for more than two hours until he was exhausted.

28

T HESE DAYS, he was working for Frank full-time. In the fall their company took on a project in downtown Waltham. A business-man in Guangdong province planned on opening a massage parlor there, converting a small run-down building he'd bought, which had once been a garment factory. Their job was to gut the two-story house and then build sixteen units, which would be massage suites. Tian had misgivings about this job—according to the floor plans there'd be a full bathroom in every unit, which didn't make sense for a massage parlor and sounded more like an underground brothel. He wondered why Frank would be involved in such a shady business, considering that the investor might immigrate eventually. On the other hand, this job would provide work for all of them for the rest of the winter. If Frank turned it down, there were always others to step in.

Waltham was fifteen miles west of Quincy, accessible mainly by car since the local train service ran just a few times a day. So every morning he'd leave with Funi. She had a small Toyota and drove like a professional—she'd formerly worked in food delivery. She came and picked him up on her way to work in the mornings and brought him back in the evenings. He wanted to cover the gas, but she wouldn't let him, saying she'd go to Waltham anyway, with or without him. She often boasted that she'd buy a BMW someday when her ship came in. She was a little wild, full of energy and nerve.

The dismantling work in Waltham was laborious, but Tian was

interested in seeing the innards of the building—how it was constructed and what materials were used and how the utility and sewage systems were put in. He was fascinated by old houses—they were, without exception, better built than new ones. The earlier builders hadn't skimped on wood or bricks and other materials. Everything was made to last. Inside the old factory house, even the walls in the basement were made of solid wood. Everything in there was hard to tear off, but they, a team of six, managed gradually to gut the house with axes and crowbars and bolt cutters. Frank would stop by to check on their progress and to make sure that new materials were delivered on time. Yabin also showed up once in a while, mainly to handle paperwork. By chance, he mentioned to Tian that he wanted to become a real-estate agent, believing he could make more by selling houses. "Won't you have to take a class and pass an exam for a license?" Tian asked. Yabin smiled and said that was a piece of cake and he could do it online.

Tian mixed well with his fellow workers, but he felt uneasy about having not sung publicly in recent months. Although he tried to do some vocal practice early in the mornings before leaving for work, he missed singing onstage. He became restless, as if his skin were too small and too tight and as if something in him were continually clawing, desperate to get out. Fortunately, he liked the work of home renovation and the labor at the old factory house easily exhausted him by the end of the day.

After dismantling the interior of the house, they began to partition the floors into small units. A lot of steel was used for the walls in place of wood. They joked that it was like building prison cells—every way you turned, you ran into steel studs. They often talked about why the Cantonese businessman wanted a steel structure for every massage room—it cost so much more than wood. "Maybe his mistress is an expensive woman and she's gonna be the madam of this place," a fellow worker said. That brought out laughter among them.

Still, most of them agreed this was a smart way for the proprietor to transfer his wealth to the States, a popular haven for corrupt officials and businesspeople to shelter their money and wealth. The dollar was strong and the legal system reliably protected private property. But Songbing, a spare, bespectacled man who had been a bridge engineer back in Hunan province, gave a brown-toothed grin and said he would rather acquire a liquor store or a gas station instead—a massage parlor was such a dubious business. Tian could see his point. Songbing was in his early sixties, smart and sophisticated, but he was in poor health, suffering from gout and high blood pressure, and spoke no English, so he was the only part-timer among them. He planned to work for half a year to make some money, then go back to Changsha to retire.

In spite of the hard work, Tian was pleased to have stable employment now. The winter holiday season had come again, but the Divine Grace had yet to contact him. He had phoned Cindy Wong to see if they might invite him again, but to date he hadn't heard back.

Ever since the fight with Shuna over the gravestone, Tian had resumed sending her one thousand dollars a month. This was more than he could spare, given that he made only $9.50 an hour. Frank didn't pay overtime—none of the Chinese construction companies did. There was no way Tian could earn more, and his savings were almost gone. His only option was to cut his living costs. He sometimes felt trapped by his situation—at times he even regretted having married and fathered a child. Now no matter what, he had to find a way to support his daughter. Finally he saw why so many young people preferred to remain single. Indeed, why should one worry about carrying on one's family line? Life must have things more meaningful and important than providing for a family and raising children.

In mid-December Funi's roommate moved away to Silicon Valley, and she was having trouble finding a replacement during the holiday season, when few people wanted to move. Funi knew that Tian's lease had expired long ago and that he was a tenant at will, so she tried to persuade him to take her old roommate's spot. She also said that since they were both working at the Waltham site now, such an arrangement could make it easier for them to travel together to and fro. At first he felt it would be ridiculous for a young woman to have a man as her roommate, but Yabin and Laura laughed at him, saying it was common for men and women to share an apartment, especially in expensive cities. Tian gave thought to this and came to see that it made sense. If he moved in with Funi, he could cut his rent by half, and his utility bills would be reduced greatly too. Better yet, her place was very close to the public library on Washington Street, which he often used. So he agreed to take the room. Funi was pleased, telling him, "Your life will be easier once we're living together." She was not yet twenty-nine but acted like an expert in homemaking.

Her words unnerved him a little, but he managed a smile and said he would appreciate any help she could give him. After he settled his last month's rent with his landlord, Funi drove over and helped him move. He had few things, just a pair of suitcases, some table-ware and utensils, about a hundred books and a few dozen albums. Funi's former roommate had left behind some furniture, including a mattress, so Tian needed to bring only his chest of drawers with him. Funi was strong enough to help him carry the chest to her car after he had removed the drawers.

Her apartment was much better than his. It was clean and bright, well kept in every way. Here he would have to take off his shoes and wear slippers whenever he came in. He reminded himself to be careful, not to place anything randomly, not to bring in any dirt with his shoes. To celebrate his arrival, Funi made beef wontons. He kneaded the dough but didn't offer to prepare the stuffing, unwilling to show he was a decent cook. Yet he took part in wrapping the wontons. Dinner was delicious—he hadn't eaten such a homey meal for a long time. Funi stopped him when he was about to wash the dishes, saying she could do it. He didn't want to overstep, so he retired to his room early, checking his emails and reading the news online. There was a Canadian Chinese-language site called Creaders.net that he liked very much—its news tended to be more objective, often reported from a third party's perspective.

Being Funi's roommate made his life easier indeed. Every morning he left for work with her, and sometimes she also prepared lunch for him, saying she had extra bread and meat to spare. At lunch breaks the two often shared the food they brought along. Their company was making progress with the massage parlor, but the work wasn't proceeding smoothly. They often had to stop and wait for other contractors to complete the jobs farmed out to them before they could continue. During the holiday season, which starts before Christmas and ends after the Spring Festival, roughly from late December to mid-February, some of the workers couldn't come every day, having to join their families far away, so Funi and Tian became the most regular hands on the site. Because the electricians hadn't yet installed wires and sockets for the lighting and heating systems, the rooms, still without walls, remained cold and drafty. On their breaks, the two of them often got into her car and set the engine running so that they could keep warm. Funi avoided smoking during those breaks to let Tian feel more comfortable. They also began to have lunch and tea in her car. She kept a thermos bottle for tea, strapped in a corner of the backseat.

The Spring Festival was close at hand. On the weekend before the holiday, Funi offered to do the shopping with him. They lived about a mile away from Kam Man Food, where many immigrants in South Boston got their groceries. Some Americans would go there for fresh vegetables and seafood too. Tian was about to go with her but changed his mind. He feared they might run into people who would recognize him and think that Funi was his new girlfriend or mistress. He couldn't afford another scandal. So he said he had to get to a rehearsal and asked her to pick him up two tins of luncheon loaf, a small jar of kimchi, and four bags of dumplings stuffed with pork and cabbage and chives.

He'd been invited to sing at only three local celebrations this year. Usually February was his busiest month. Perhaps his way of singing was no longer popular. Or perhaps, in the eyes of the public, he was still the man who had abandoned his family and battered his mistress, making groups like the Divine Grace reluctant to hire him. For a whole year he had worked hard in the home renovation business and hadn't done a lot of vocal exercises in his spare time, so he was worried that his voice might have suffered. He didn't share his concerns and conjectures with anyone, not even with Shuna. He reminded himself that once his life became stable again, he must spend more time improving his singing, to make it warmer and livelier. He mustn't remain in the home repair business for too long.

Frank threw a dinner party for the few workers who hadn't left for the holiday. One of his tenants was a chef at China Pearl, a newly opened restaurant at President Plaza, so they gathered there. The place was well known for its dim sum, and on weekends it had so many customers that parking was difficult despite the large lot in front of and beside the restaurant.

The dinner was a multicourse banquet, cooked specially for them. In spite of the delicious seafood and the excellent meat dishes, Tian couldn't work up any appetite or holiday cheer. He missed home, missed Shuna and Tingting. Yabin and Laura were in Toronto, visiting her cousin. The others at the table were loud and exultant, but Tian felt like sobbing. He tried to suppress his sadness and misgivings about his immigration. Rationally, he knew that he ought to feel fortunate—many people never had an opportunity to get out of the rut of their lives. Unlike them, he could turn a new page, but never had he expected it to be so hard and so precarious and so lonesome.

Funi picked fish and shrimp and duck for him, urging him to eat more. He accepted whatever toasts others proposed and downed one shot cup after another of Five-Grain Sap, a strong liquor. Soon he got tipsy and began to see double. A thin fog was rising before his eyes, and every face at the table was blurred. Then his stomach churned and convulsed and he threw up on the floor. He was too drunk to feel embarrassed. A waitress came over immediately with a broom and a dustpan, followed by a stocky waiter holding a mop, while two of Tian's coworkers helped him to a long bench in a corner and left him supine on it. He began dozing away as the people at the table continued regaling themselves noisily.

Afterward, Funi drove him back and supported him all the way upstairs to their apartment. She pulled off his boots, put him to bed, and threw a duvet over him. Before she stepped out of his room, she flipped off the lights and said, "Sleep well, Tian."

29

I CAN TEACH YOU HOW TO DRIVE," Funi told Tian one morning on their way to work.

"I don't have a car," he said, wondering whether to accept the offer.

"You can use this one." She patted the steering wheel. "Cars are cheap here. For two or three thousand dollars you can get a decent used car. Don't you feel hampered, unable to drive?"

She was right—he always felt incapable when he tried to go to a place inaccessible by public transportation. Back in China he had never owned a car, and neither had he learned how to drive. He realized he should accept her offer. "Sure," he said, "it would be great if you could teach me."

The highway ahead was dappled with salt, and a cluster of office buildings appeared on the right. One of them was under construction, its windows still without panes. Tian knew that down the road he might need to be the driver for his family after Shuna and Tingting came, since they couldn't drive either.

That weekend, Funi took him to the seaside cemetery to practice. She said Frank had taught her how to drive in this quiet place, where there was no traffic and no cops. Still, he had to take care not to hit a tombstone or a tree.

He liked driving in the cemetery, and, to his relief, it wasn't too hard to handle the car. He began to cruise slowly with ease along the narrow winding paths, but Funi insisted he take the practice as seriously as though he were driving on an actual road. This meant that at every crossroads he had to stop as if encountering a red light or a stop sign. He thought she was overreacting—they were in the territory of dead souls, after all. But Funi wouldn't relent, saying, "If you don't develop good habits, you'll cause an accident once you're on the road."

"I'll be more careful," he muttered.

She got surprisingly hot-tempered the moment she assumed the teaching role. She barked instructions at him and even yelled at him if he made a mistake. Even after he got his learner's permit, she still treated him as though he were ignorant of traffic rules, a complete newbie. This nettled him, but he tried to be patient and took her instructions without protest. He once talked to Yabin about Funi's temper. His friend smiled and said people were inclined to have a short fuse when teaching others how to drive. As a matter of fact, Yabin had lost a girlfriend when she took driving lessons from him. "A car can be like a gunpowder chamber if you're teaching someone to drive—you can get touchy and ready to erupt," he said, shaking his head of wavy hair. Hearing Yabin's words, Tian tried to be more tolerant with Funi when she was crying out orders at him from the passenger seat.

Another spot they often went to was the shopping plaza off Falls Boulevard. In the evenings, after nine o'clock, it was almost deserted, so it was safe to practice three-point turns and parallel parking there. Funi wanted to make sure he mastered all the skills required for the road test, and he practiced as much as he could. Once in a while, at dusk, he even drove alone in the cemetery. Since she didn't accompany him to that place nowadays, he went there and came back alone only by small traffic-less streets. He promised her that he wouldn't get on any busy road without her beside him, and he never broke his word.

Then one evening, as they were heading back to Quincy Center along Furnace Brook Parkway, for some reason he kept crossing the yellow line that divided the blacktop. There were no other vehicles in view, so he cruised between the lanes with ease. Suddenly Funi grabbed the steering wheel and swerved the car back into the right lane. He was irritated and demanded, "Why did you do that?"

"It's dangerous to drive like that."

"Don't be a smartass," he said.

"You think you're about to get your license and become a good driver? Let me tell you, if you're not careful, you might get others and yourself killed."

"I've been careful and will be more careful, all right?"

"Damn it, Tian, once you develop a bad habit, it will creep up on you."

"You always think so highly of yourself. Ever since I started taking driving lessons from you, you've been snapping at me. Enough is enough!"

"Such a dope!" she spat out.

He pulled up and got out of the car and slammed the door shut. "Good night—I don't want to see your face for now." He strode onto a side street that led to a shortcut to Quincy Center.

Without missing a beat, Funi slid into the driver's seat and drove away. "Fuck you, Yao Tian!" she shouted through the half-down window. He was shocked that she would leave like that.

It was warm, a stir of spring in the air, and the tree branches were furry with sprouting leaves, waving in the fitful breeze. As he was walking along, he felt like singing, so he swung south to the deserted quarry, where a chorus of frogs was rising and expanding from the water. A broad-winged hawk coasted away and faded into a bank of indigo clouds above the shadowy woods of junipers and tamaracks. He entered the dark ground and began to bellow a song, garbling the lyrics in places. He sang with gusto and at moments only scatted. Without an audience to watch him, he just chanted freely. Yet as he was doing this, all the frogs turned quiet as if to give him an ear. He went on singing for almost an hour.

It was nearly midnight when he returned to the apartment, and the lights were all out. Without washing up or brushing his teeth, he crawled into bed and slept soundly.

The next morning, while he was still in bed, Funi called to him from the living room: "Tian, time to go to work!"

He got out of bed and pulled on his jeans and rushed to the bathroom to brush his teeth. When he came out, rubbing his face with a towel, Funi said, "We're gonna be late. Hurry up."

The moment he got into her car, she took out an egg sandwich with bologna on a bagel and handed it to him. "Your breakfast," she said evenly.

"Thanks." He took a bite. It was delicious, the fried egg still warm and the smoked meat spiced just right. He munched on the sandwich ravenously.

"I'll tell you what, Tian," she went on. "You don't know what's good for you. Don't assume because you used to be a celebrity, you're entitled to favors from others. If I were teaching someone else to drive, they'd need to pay me at least twenty dollars an hour."

That was true—she had refused to take money from him even though he had offered. She was entrusting him with her car, and he ought to be grateful. A rush of shame came over him, keeping him silent all the way to the work site.

Starting the next day, she let him drive them to work and back. This meant that every day he drove at least thirty miles on the highway, and his confidence grew by the day. The road test was in late April, just two weeks away, so he had to practice more, especially parallel parking.

He passed the test without incident and Funi was impressed. She confessed it had taken her three tries to get her license. He treated her to dim sum at China Pearl. She loved chicken feet and steamed crayfish. He enjoyed the exquisite dumplings enfolded in semitransparent wrappings, stuffed with vegetables or shrimp. The dim sum at China Pearl was more traditional, more authentically Cantonese, than what he was used to, and some of the items were exotic and dainty to him. He and Funi sat at a window table. Whenever a food cart passed by, he stopped it and urged her to pick something more. They also had Budweiser and Pu'er tea.

As they were eating, Funi confessed this was the first time a man had taken her out to a restaurant. Her confession surprised Tian. True, she wasn't a stunning beauty, but she was capable and healthy, with a sunny face and bright eyes and abundant hair; her youthfulness and vivacious manner should have drawn some man's attention.

"Haven't you had a boyfriend?" he asked.

"I've had two, but we lived in the countryside. If we went out, we just ate at a food stand—a bowl of rice noodles or a few pork buns. Poor folks don't eat in real restaurants, you know."

He attempted to lighten the topic. "Now you're rich compared to the village folks back home."

"Actually, my family and relatives in China are doing fine now. I'm not that eager to make money here. No matter how hard I work, I can't possibly get rich. I used to deliver food to homes in Weston and Lincoln and saw how wealthy people lived in those towns. There's no way I can ever get rich like them. But I like the simple and peaceful life here, and the freedom. Nobody can kick you around as long as you don't break the law and pay taxes. But what I really want is to get married and raise kids. I often have dreams, and in them I have two babies, and my breasts always heavy with milk. Well, in a couple years, I guess I'll be too old to have any of that." There was some wistfulness in her voice.

For a moment Tian had no idea how to respond. Then he remembered Frank's wife, Sami. "Can't your cousin help you find someone?" he said. "I'm sure there're more Chinese men than Chinese women here."

"Sami once recommended a guy to me, but I didn't know what to make of him. He was an odd bird from Shandong province and wanted me to leave with him for Alaska."

"Interesting. Did he end up going there himself?"

"Probably. I stopped seeing him after the second date. There was something about him that made my flesh creep."

"Why would he want to move to Alaska?"

"He said he wanted to eat king crabs and big cabbages there."

Tian laughed, then said, "He was a character, wasn't he?"

"I think he had something he couldn't shake off. He had to go somewhere nobody could recognize him. Maybe he had trouble with officials, or maybe he was deep in debt."

"Or he hadn't paid taxes."

"He was like a delinquent. He was crazy, like a tramp with rotten teeth and a beard and long hair."

"We're all vagrants of a sort. I often feel that way too—I mean longing to go somewhere nobody knows me. To be left alone—that's the essence of freedom."

"That's a smart thing to say. You are an excellent teacher, you know." She wiped her fingers with a napkin.

Funi's account of the odd man made Tian pensive. He realized many immigrants were in varying degrees of the same situation: They were attempting to break loose from the grip of the past and to start over in a faraway place. But few of them could foresee the price for that new beginning, or the pain and the hardship that came after.

30

IT WAS ALREADY LATE MAY, and there was still a lot of pollen in the air. Tian wasn't bothered by it, but Funi had been miserable ever since mid-April. She sneezed continually, her nose red and swollen. Her face was puffy and made her appear older than she was. To give her more time to rest, Tian continued to drive both of them to work and back.

One evening, as he sat at the dining table talking with his wife on the phone, Funi was doing dishes at the sink. All of a sudden she sneezed loudly, then coughed twice.

Shuna heard the noise and paused on the other end. "Who's that?" she asked him.

"My roommate, Funi."

"You've never told me you have a woman roommate."

Shuna sounded doubtful, her voice edgy, so he stood and went into his room to speak more privately. "Yes," he resumed, "I'm Funi's roommate. I moved in to share this apartment with her so that I can save some money."

"But you've kept me in the dark about this. Why?"

"I told you I was moving to share an apartment with a coworker."

"But you didn't say your roommate was a woman."

"You were so happy when you heard I could save money that you supported the move. Look, I've been working myself half to death every day, leaving for work at daybreak and coming back when the moon is already up."

"Don't use that as an excuse! You and a woman have been living together. This isn't normal."

"Things are different here. It's common for people of the oppo-site sex to share an apartment, just as roommates."

"What else do you share with her? A cooking pot and a bed too?"

"Don't be absurd. We're just coworkers. Of course, she's been kind and drives me to work. You know I have no car."

"All those can't justify your living with a woman. A young woman, isn't she?"

"She's twenty-nine. There's almost a generation between her and me. Rest assured, nothing will happen."

The more he tried to convince Shuna that Funi and he were just coworkers and roommates, the more agitated his wife sounded, saying she felt betrayed because he'd kept her in the dark. She demanded that he move out of the apartment, or she would let Tingting know that her father was shacking up with a young woman in America. He was bewildered, unable to understand why Shuna, a professor, couldn't see his reasons. Frustrated, he gave up and told her he would explain clearly via email.

The next evening he wrote her a long message, telling her the truths she couldn't see from the other side of the world. He was nearly a generation older than Funi and there was no chemistry between them, so no intimacy would develop between them either. To convince Shuna, he attached a photo from Frank's Spring Fes-tival party. In it, Funi was smiling broadly, an unlit cigarillo in her left hand. Shuna could see how plain she was, and that by no means could such an unattractive woman pose any threat to her. By shar-ing an apartment with Funi, Tian was saving hundreds of dollars a month, which he could then send home—it was the only way he could have enough money for Shuna and Tingting. He made merely $9.50 an hour and had to pay many bills, among which the rent was the biggest, and he had to reduce it as much as possible. Above all, this was a way to survive in a strange land. Here immigrants often shared resources and lived together so that they could endure hard-ship and isolation and help each other.

By now Shuna had composed herself. She replied, "Be careful about Funi. She looks wild and she must smoke like a chimney." In fact, the cigarillo in the photo had been given to Funi by one of the carpenters, and she rarely smoked nowadays. Tian didn't like Shu-na's remarks but made no argument. He'd better keep the peace.

The massage parlor was nearly completed, but again Frank ran into trouble. Some residents of Waltham abhorred the idea of having such a shady business in the center of their town. In recent months there'd even been protests against the project. Then the matter was put to a vote, in which the anti-construction side won. The Cantonese businessman had no choice but to scrap the whole plan. For days the workers had been talking about the unexpected loss, against which they believed that the businessman must have some kind of insurance—otherwise he wouldn't have given up the enterprise so easily. But they were certain that Frank didn't have that kind of protection.

As they predicted, Frank had no cash flow now. He did his best to pay his workers, but all the money spent on the building materials was lost—the Cantonese businessman refused to pay back the costs. In fact, Frank lost all contact with the man, who vanished and let the home improvement company deal with the mess on their own. Frank and Sami were devastated and said they might have to put their home up for a bank loan if they were going to save their business. Yet the fiasco didn't at all affect Yabin, who had just passed the real estate exam and was about to start as a broker, making good use of his multilingual skills. He could speak a smattering of Vietnamese now, having mixed with the local Vietnamese immigrants for the past two years. Tian wondered whether Yabin had foreseen their company's disaster on the horizon—the man was a survivor and seemed to have a sixth sense for danger. These days he often advised Tian, "It's time to change. You belong to the stage, not to home repairs."

Frank also urged his employees to look for work elsewhere. He said he had no idea when he would get back on his feet again, but unlike the rest of them, he could always find work for himself. Tian suspected Frank might just let the company go down and strike out on his own. Indeed, as a master handyman he was in great demand,

and he collected decent rents from the two multiunit houses he owned. Still, he was apologetic to his workers, especially Tian. He said, "Mr. Yao, you speak English beautifully and should find a real job that pulls in a big salary or make a living by getting commissions. You don't have to sell your brawn like me."

Tian replied, "If I could choose, I would prefer to be a master craftsman like you." That was the truth, but Frank shook his heavy-boned face, saying Tian wasn't built for manual labor and mustn't think that the food in someone else's pot always tasted better than his own. They both laughed.

Funi began to look for work elsewhere too. She wanted to find something in the city of Boston—Quincy was becoming too small for her, she often claimed. Instead of searching the job listings, though, she just hopped on the Red Line to Chinatown. Once there, she went from door to door and asked whether they needed help. Tian joked with her, saying, "You must have a thick skin to do that, like a solicitor."

She shook her roundish chin and said, "What else can I do? I need a job, it's a matter of survival, and I can't afford to do nothing."

"Actually, I admire your guts," he said sincerely.

"I would never have done such a thing in China. I'd rather stay home and raise kids. But that's out of the question here."

"I will follow your example and never give up."

"Don't make fun of me. Do I have a choice?"

The next week she landed a job in the warehouse of a supermarket in Chinatown. They hired her mainly because she could speak some English and could drive a truck. Also, she was strong enough to lift packages and vegetable crates. She would need to learn how to operate a forklift, which she said wasn't hard to drive–she had given it a try on the spot. She was excited about this job and could make $11.25 an hour. Better still, it would pay overtime and also offered benefits, including health insurance and a retirement plan. In every way it looked like a real job.

Meanwhile Tian was at a loss about what to do. He had a driver's license and could do deliveries, but that kind of work didn't appeal to him. Nothing seemed as good as a job in home renovation, but he wasn't skilled in any craft save for making screens, nor did he know where to look for such work. Then one evening Funi suggested, "Why not sing at the casino? I saw some entertainers when I was there last time. They hire a lot of Chinese. Many waitresses are Chinese and even some of the card dealers are Chinese too." Funi sounded excited as she spoke.

"Which casino are you talking about?" he asked.

"Twin Waters in Connecticut. Lots of Chinese work there, commuting up from Queens. You should give it a try."

He dismissed the suggestion, feeling uncomfortable about it, but the idea kept coming back to him. He began to grapple with it, weighing the pros and cons. He had been to that casino before and liked the place—it had a fabulous buffet. In the mornings, a bus stopped at President Plaza in Quincy and picked up people going to the casino and brought them back at night. Most of the passengers were senior citizens, who headed for the casino in droves. On behalf of Twin Waters, the bus conductor, a young Chinese woman, gave each of them sixty dollars' worth of coupons to encourage them to gamble, but they could also use half the coupons to get dinner at the buffet for free. It was a good bargain for them, an easy way to spend a fun day with others. Most of the senior passengers were so appreciative that they added five dollars to the round-trip fare, which was ten dollars, as a tip for the conductor and the driver.

After thinking about it for a week, Tian decided to try his luck at the casino. He called Twin Waters, and the entertainment director, Jesse, spoke with him at length. He asked Tian to send him his résumé, which Tian did without delay. Three days later Jesse interviewed him on the phone, saying he had mentioned him to some Chinese employees there, who all said Tian was a top-notch singer in China. The interview went so well that Jesse invited him to visit Twin Waters for "a small audition." Tian was delighted to accept the invitation. Before going, he brushed up on his standard folk songs and even learned a few popular new ones.

31

W<small>E MIGHT HAVE ROOM</small> for an experienced singer on our roster," said Jesse. He was Native American, a burly man with melting brown eyes and high cheekbones, wearing a flat straw hat. Tian hadn't expected to find him such a youthful man. At the phone interview the previous Friday, Jesse had sounded much older, with a slightly raspy voice.

"Is Yao or Tian your last name?" Jesse asked.

"Tian is my first name. The Chinese way is to put the last name first, so formerly I'm Yao Tian."

"Can you show how well you can sing, Tian?"

"I can sing popular songs," Tian said. As he spoke, he noticed two young Asian musicians seated nearby. One was holding a clarinet and the other an electric guitar. They were in the casino's informal entertainment area, called the Atrium, which also had a bar lounge. Small armchairs and coffee tables were scattered throughout the spacious enclosure encircled by a balustrade.

"You can announce my name if you'd like," he told Jesse. "The Chinese customers will recognize it."

"All right, let's do that. If they like your singing, we might take you on."

While Jesse stepped away to make the announcement, Tian turned to chat with the musicians, who both spoke Chinese. One was from Fuzhou and the other was American-born, having grown up in Texas. They knew of him and seemed puzzled by his appearance here. He told them that he needed to make money for his daughter's education. They nodded understandingly. He asked them what songs they could play, and they told him about their repertoire, which included many popular songs and movie songs, both Chinese and American. That would do—he felt relieved.

About thirty people, mostly Asians, had left the barstools and armchairs to gather below the small stage. Some raised their phones to snap photos. "Please don't do that before I sing," he begged.

One fiftysomething woman laughed and teased, "Aiyah, you can't have stage fright, can you?"

Jesse came back and told Tian to run through a couple of songs. As the two of them headed backstage, Tian said he would prefer to sing in Chinese.

"That's all right, as long as the audience can understand you," Jesse said.

Tian walked onto the little stage, standing behind its short, curved apron, and announced to the audience, "I'm going to share a few songs with you. The first one is called 'Facing the Ocean.'"

The crowd moved closer. The musicians started the music of the movie song and he began to sing:

> I'm standing alone on the shore,
> Gazing at the end of the waves where
> You disappeared. I want to say
> Something but have no idea
> How to begin. All my words of love
> Are gone with the wind. . . .

When he finished, sparse applause went up from the crowd. He realized the song might have flopped. He told the audience, "Sorry about that sad song. Let me sing you a happy one. This song might be more interesting." He turned to the musicians and asked, "Can you play 'I Miss You Like Having Ants in My Heart'?" They both nodded, then launched into the lighthearted, frolicsome Taiwanese song.

He began to sing, rocking a little with the music:

> I miss you like having ants in me,
> Who creep and creep in my heart.

Especially on a lonesome night
They move around and around.
Ah, they make me miss you all the more. . . .

He was surprised that many in the audience knew the song, clapping their hands to the rhythm. He had always viewed this song as decadent, but recently he'd begun to see something honest and sincere in the lyrics and the music that showed a distinct sensibility, lively and earthy. Now it was a hit with this casino crowd. The instant he was done, applause broke out and voices shouted for more.

Inspired by the warm acceptance, he sang another song written in a similar style, "A Mouse Loves Rice." Fortunately the musicians were able to play along, and Tian did his best to make the song intimate and amusing while imparting real feeling to the lyrics. The audience went wild. As he reached the last lines, some of them began humming along:

I love you, love you
Like a mouse loves rice.
No matter what hardship is ahead,
I will forever stay by your side.
No matter how hard life is,
As long as you're happy,
I will do anything
To love you like this.

He was experiencing the kind of thrill he hadn't felt for years. His eyes were moist and shivers were running down his neck and spine. The long hallway on his left turned hazy and the faces in the crowd, some moving and wavering, blurred for a moment while his soul seemed to be soaring.

He sang two more songs, one from Taiwan and the other from Hong Kong. The moment he got off the stage, three middle-aged Chinese women, clearly tourists, came up and asked him to sign the brochures in their hands. He did carefully. Then Jesse turned up, smiling, and said, "Well, Tian, can you sing songs in English too?"

"I know some, and I can learn more. I have 'Country Road,' 'Pack Up Your Sorrows,' and 'My Heart Will Go On' all in my repertoire." To be honest, he didn't like the last one much, but it was the best he could think of in the moment.

Jesse nodded and said, "Can you come to my office for a minute?"

He led Tian to a room with a glass wall down the hallway. The second they stepped into his office, he flipped on the lights. One after another the fluorescent rings flared on with a *ping* and began to glow. Jesse drew up a folding chair for him and said, "Welcome to Twin Waters, Tian." Grinning, he held out his hand.

Tian shook it. Jesse's grip was firm, but he was amazed that his palm was quite small compared to his burly build. Jesse then explained that actually he'd have to talk with the marketing director, because he himself couldn't make such a hire. But he was greatly impressed by how enthusiastically the audience had responded to his performance, and he'd love to have him here. He would let Tian know the final decision within a week.

Tian returned to Quincy in a cheerful frame of mind and told Funi about his visit to Twin Waters. She believed they would offer him a job. "It'll be like a windfall to them," she said. "The Chinese employees there must've told them how famous you are. You can bring more visibility to the casino for sure."

"I don't know," he said and sighed.

Her reference to his former reputation only made him sad, but he told her that if he got the job, he would help her find a boyfriend. She swatted his shoulder and said she could live just fine without a man. Deep down, he was grateful to her and longed for an opportunity to sing every day.

Now that Funi was taking the subway to work, she let him use her car during the day. He felt exhilarated with a car at his disposal, able to go anywhere with ease. He told his wife about his audition at the casino, but she was unimpressed and said only that it would do as a temporary job. Obviously she still thought of him as a star. She couldn't see how hard it was to carry on here, how his career was in limbo.

He also told her that he already had a driver's license, which impressed her more than the audition. She told him to be careful when he drove, saying he was always clumsy with his hands and feet. If she were here, Tian thought, she would have seen he could be quite handy, able to install ceiling fans, change door locks, repair driveway cracks, set ceramic tiles and wood floors, and make window screens like a professional.

He remembered that Shuna used to say he could do only two things well: sing and cook. But surely there were other potentialities in him, which nobody, including himself, would find unless he was given the opportunity to tap and develop them. Emigration was surely a way of self-discovery.

"Do you have a car?" Shuna asked.

"No, but I can drive Funi's car. She takes the train to work now and doesn't need to drive during the day."

"Huh, you and Funi really share a lot of things."

"Come on, now, don't be so sarcastic. She's generous to me. Without a car, it would be hard for me to get around."

"I hope you won't take advantage of her generosity."

"Of course not."

He was reluctant to exchange words with her like this for much longer. Lately her barbed remarks had been putting him on edge, or on the defensive. "Tell Tingting I love her," he said, as a signal for ending their conversation for the day.

On Friday afternoon Jesse called and offered Tian a job. He was to work full-time, five days a week, and the hours would vary depending on their programming needs. On Thursday evenings he'd sing English songs with some professional singers and instrumentalists in Twin Waters Theater, the biggest venue at the casino. The other days he would perform at the Atrium, the bar lounge, and could sing whatever he chose. They'd pay him five hundred dollars a week, but he could eat at their buffet free of charge. There'd also be some benefits, including basic health insurance. Tian was pleased about the offer and accepted it on the phone. Jesse sounded pleased and then told him that initially they had intended to employ him gig by gig or part-time, but some Chinese employees at the casino had convinced them that Tian might bring visibility to Twin Waters, so they decided to hire him full-time instead. "I really appreciate this," Tian said. "This job means a lot to me."

Despite the casual work arrangement, Tian could tell he was a significant component in their daily entertainment program. He performed on the small stage in the bar lounge, except for Thursdays, when he sang in the casino's theater with some professional performers, even some pop stars. In the lounge there was always a crowd gathering to listen to him. Most of them were Asian tourists who were there to gamble only as a lark or just to accompany their gambling spouses and friends. Once an old Chinese woman told him, "I heard you sing red songs back in China, but I had no idea you could sing pop songs and English songs so beautifully and with such genuine feeling." He was touched by her compliment and realized he was a different singer now. His Chinese fans even responded warmly to the English songs he managed to deliver, though he was never sure how adequately he did them: "I Won't Last a Day Without You," "My Favorite Things," "My Own True Love." Jesse and the other American coworkers were encouraging and showered praises on him if they especially liked a song.

Tian loved Hank Williams and once sang "I'm So Lonesome I Could Cry," but the result was a minor fiasco—he couldn't reproduce Williams's deep guttural voice and his smooth performance of the country song only seemed to confuse his listeners. Jesse smiled and said, "I have to say it's too sweet." Tian was embarrassed and didn't attempt Hank Williams again.

Within two months after he'd started at Twin Waters, word spread that Yao Tian was working at a casino now. Heated discussions revolved around him. Some people argued that his employment at Twin Waters was a disgrace, while others said it was just a job he needed at the moment so that he could survive in America, where most immigrants must adapt to circumstances. A weekly newspaper in Guangzhou wrote about his presence at the casino. Attached to the article, "Yao Tian's Plight," were two photos of him singing, his figure superimposed over a stock image of a garish gambling hall. The article described Tian's work as a kind of self-degradation—performing purely to make money and to entertain gamblers. The writer also hinted that he'd brought this disgrace on himself, having abandoned an illustrious career in China to become a mere lowly entertainer in America. "Yao Tian has chosen capitalism over socialism," the article concluded. "We can see his tragedy and also learn a lesson from it: Nobody can thrive if he has deserted his motherland." Then *The Global Post,* an international branch of *The People's Daily,* published a similar article, singling him out as a warning to all Chinese: "Whoever doesn't serve our country or even works against her will come to grief sooner or later. Yao Tian illustrates how a small misstep can lead to a disaster."

The *Global Post* article was picked up by numerous other news sites and stirred some controversy among readers. Someone wrote an article, a rebuttal, on Creaders.net, addressing the author of the piece in *The Global Post:* "Yao Tian himself might not feel the same way you do. Maybe he enjoys living alone and honestly. Maybe he prefers the freedom of a pauper to the ill-gotten luxury of a prince. I can't see anything tragic in his effort to strike out on his own." A reader commented on the same site, "Instead of joining the chorus of condemnations, we ought to admire Yao Tian's personal choice and his courage, and we ought to wish him the best of luck." But another reader rejoined, "It serves Yao Tian right. Anyone who betrays our country will suffer similar humiliation in the end." Some pitied Tian for his loss and failure; some lamented how hard it was for any Chinese artist to survive once they wandered beyond the sphere of Chinese culture; some supported Tian's decision to leave China because they saw freedom as essential, like fresh air and clean water; some declared that nobody was qualified to judge Tian's situation—like how a foot fitted in a shoe, only the wearer alone could tell.

A reporter at *The Beijing News* phoned Tian and asked for his response to the article. He only said, "I'm still an artist. No matter where I am, I can still sing my heart out. I feel liberated because I am singing the songs I love. Back in China, I often sang propaganda that I hated. It made me miserable in spite of my cheerful appearance, in spite of my fame as a star. So I don't regret having immigrated. My current hardships are a necessary step for my future growth." He took the opportunity to add, "I've been separated from my family for four years. My wife is not allowed to come visit me. This is entirely arbitrary, gratuitous—we're suffering for no purpose. I appeal to those in power to show compassion to my family and allow my wife to come join me!" Of course the newspaper printed none of his words about his separation from his family, though the young reporter did tell him that she liked what he'd said.

Yabin did his part to defend Tian too. He wrote a long piece on the Literary City website, saying that Tian was simply making an honest living, and people ought to admire his ability to adapt to new circumstances and confront adversity. "You all must keep in mind," he went on, "that Yao Tian is a husband and a father. How many of you, given the same setback, could also continue doing everything to support your families? We should applaud his integrity and fortitude!"

After Yabin's piece was posted, most of the negative chatter faded off, though Tian suspected that people still whispered about his disgrace and downfall.

32

YABIN CAME TO SEE TIAN on the last Sunday of August. He was facing a crisis: Laura's father had been imprisoned in Beijing. The man had been in charge of foreign currencies in a state-owned bank. During the past decade he had received tens of millions of dollars in bribes—kickbacks from helping real estate companies and large corporations secure loans. He had also accepted more than a dozen apartments in major Chinese cities, given to him as gifts. Without an actual charge he was held in custody, but his family couldn't find out his whereabouts. Obviously his case involved some high-ranking officials who had also taken bribes, so they had kept him in total isolation for now. All his family had been told was that he was being detained by the Party's Central Commission for Discipline Inspection. They were sure he was being interrogated, if not physically tortured. Laura's mother begged the investigators to pass this message on to him: Whatever happened, his family would stick by him.

Tian found the wife's attitude was quite extraordinary, considering how many corrupt officials, once arrested for interrogation, were abandoned by their mistresses and families and friends. But Yabin corrected Tian when he praised Laura's mother. They were seated in the Starbucks near the train station, and Yabin said, "This isn't so simple. There are many ramifications we can't foresee."

"They won't execute him, will they?" Tian asked. "Laura's father committed an economic crime, not violence or treason—he might do some years in prison, or at most be sentenced to life."

"But Laura is facing the problem of where she should go."

"Obviously she can't go back," said Tian.

"Her family is urging her to stay in America and start to apply for immigration."

"You mean as an immigrant investor?"

"Correct."

"She'll have to plunk down half a million dollars for that, won't she?"

"That's not a problem. Tian, just between you and me, her family has transferred a substantial amount to her. I don't know how much, but it should be enough for the rest of her life. If her two siblings come to North America as well, they won't need to worry about money either. That's the impression I got from Laura."

"Then it shouldn't be difficult for her to decide."

"Indeed, she should do her best to immigrate, but she isn't sure if she'll be able to keep the money in the States. The Chinese government and the White House have been working on an agreement to get illicit wealth back to China. If this pact is made, it might not be safe for Laura to live here."

"Rest assured, the White House won't be that cooperative with the Chinese government."

"Of course it will, because the United States can dock thirty percent of the illegal funds before they are returned to China. Money can make the devil grind your grain, and the Americans can be very active in cooperating with the Chinese police."

"Does Laura have alternative plans?" Tian asked.

"Yes, she might go to a third country secretly, taking her money with her. In fact, I suspect she might already have bank accounts in other countries."

"In Switzerland?"

"Also Canada, the Virgin Islands, and elsewhere."

"Then she shouldn't need to worry too much."

Yabin sighed and took a large sip of his mocha. "She's all right indeed, but this puts me in a bind. She wants me to leave this country with her."

"Well, do you love her?" Tian felt silly raising such a question. It was already extraordinary that Yabin had been with her for as long as he had. In the back of Tian's mind lingered another issue: Laura's money hadn't been made honestly and should not belong to her. So he wasn't eager to help Yabin figure out what to do; he didn't want to see his friend involved with such a woman for much longer.

"I'm fond of her," Yabin said. "She's very generous to me and loves me. I am serious about her."

"Can you imagine living with her for the rest of your life?"

"Frankly speaking, I'm not sure." Yabin shook his head, batting his large eyes.

"Do you know where she'd like to take you?"

Yabin shook his square chin and grinned. Apparently he was reluctant to share the information. He said, "It's not Paris of course, otherwise I wouldn't feel so torn. I would head for Paris with her in a heartbeat."

"You have already taken root in America, haven't you? Your real estate business is picking up and I'm sure you'll become a successful real-estate agent in this area. Can you give up everything you already have here?"

"That's the question I've been wrestling with." He heaved a feeble sigh. "She promised me many things." Yabin ran his fingers through his thick hair, which had a sprinkling of gray.

Tian didn't press him for details. His friend had changed quite a bit, no longer a lighthearted ladies' man—perhaps because Laura had let him taste the luxuries money could buy, or because, pushing forty now, he felt tired and eager to settle down. Nevertheless, Tian was sure Laura wasn't someone who could possess Yabin emotionally, and it was hard for him to imagine the two loving each other devotedly. Tian felt it unlikely that Yabin would leave America with Laura.

Cindy Wong called one evening in late October. She wondered whether Tian could join the Divine Grace for the holiday season once more. There still lingered a trace of bitterness in him for the way they had dismissed him two years earlier, but he listened to her offer. Cindy said they'd heard about his singing at Twin Waters. People were praising his performances there, saying he sang even better than before. Some Chinese-language newspapers on the East Coast had written about his new style, characterizing it as his artistic development.

"I know you might still feel hurt, Tian," Cindy said calmly. "But my colleagues all respect you and know you were wronged, and that the ridiculous accusation two years ago was groundless. Our new accountant here knew the woman—what's her name?"

"Freda Liu," he said.

"Yes, our accountant said she was a bitch and would bring disaster to anyone who got close to her."

He couldn't bad-mouth Freda behind her back, so he only said, "I'll have to speak to my employer at the casino first. I have a full-time schedule at Twin Waters."

"Understood. You don't need to make a decision now. I'm just giving you a heads-up."

Her offer was good news to him. The troupe was better known now and even performed in foreign countries from time to time. Though without a passport it was inconvenient for him to travel outside North America, he could go to Canada and Mexico on refugee papers. No doubt Cindy's offer was an opportunity he should seize.

He spoke with Jesse about whether he could work part-time for Twin Waters. Jesse said the casino actually would prefer to have Tian as a part-timer—some of the musicians on their roster were part-time—but Tian should be sure that this was what he wanted. Jesse also added that if Tian worked part-time, they'd pay him by the hour, but Jesse would do his best to give him a good rate. If his hours were reduced, he would no longer be entitled to the health insurance and the other benefits. That made Tian hesitant to reduce his hours there. He was healthy and still vigorous, yet he needed some basic coverage.

After speaking with Shuna—who, still hurt by the Chinese media gossip on his employment at Twin Waters, urged Tian to quit the casino altogether, but he was unwilling to do that because it was yearlong work, whereas the Divine Grace performed only in winter—he spoke with Cindy and asked whether the troupe could cover his travel expenses if he didn't travel with them, and instead joined them only in the cities where they were to perform. To his delight, she said that was not a problem, since a few members had done that before. As long as he turned up before the show, it would be fine. So he decided to cut his weekly hours at Twin Waters to eighteen. Such arrangements would enable him to go on tours with the Divine Grace. Shuna was pleased to hear this. She always emphasized, "You must treat yourself as an artist. If you don't take yourself seriously, who will?" Unlike Tian, she usually could see things in a broader perspective and even several steps ahead, but she didn't really have a handle on his situation here.

He phoned Cindy and informed her of his decision to rejoin their troupe. She was elated and promised this would be a long-term job, which implied they would book him for every holiday season from now on, from mid-December to late February.

"The troupe will be thrilled to hear that you're joining them," Cindy told him.

He thought that must be true.

Finally Yabin made up his mind. He would leave with Laura for Canada before Thanksgiving and might settle there permanently. He wouldn't disclose his exact destination, which Tian suspected must be somewhere in Quebec, since in recent months Laura and Yabin had gone to Montreal several times. Tian knew Laura's money was tainted, but money was money and didn't smell and could help one live comfortably and even move ahead in the world. He wondered whether he'd have made the same decision if given Yabin's opportunity. Probably not. Didn't he turn down four million dollars three years ago?

Then he wondered what he would have done if they had offered him forty million instead of four. He had to admit that might have tipped the scale. He knew that his integrity wasn't limitless, so he mustn't feel morally superior to Yabin. Like everyone else, the man had been struggling with the same problem: how to achieve security.

Yet Tian remembered Yabin had told him long ago that the price for freedom was uncertainty. To that Tian had echoed, "Of course certainty isn't the human condition." Just three or four years back they both had seemed to possess the willpower and strength to find their way in America, to fulfill the promise of their lives, and to reach their destinations they had envisioned: Tian was to become a great singer and Yabin a self-made man, a reputable activist in fighting for human rights in their native land. Reflecting on those hopeful days, Tian felt saddened by his friend's change of direction.

Tian had always suspected that money was a corrosive force that could undermine one's resolve to pursue one's vision. Clearly Yabin had chosen money over struggle. He even told Tian that he'd have no use for his real estate license anymore. In his heart Tian knew that an effortless life would be a meaningless life, but he couldn't tell his friend this. He just reminded himself not to become lost in making money as Yabin had.

Still, Yabin and Laura's departure threw him into a mild depression. Yabin had been the only genuine friend he could turn to whenever he ran into trouble. Now he felt more lonesome, more isolated, and as if unready to face his future alone.

PART FOUR

33

L IFE HAD BECOME MORE STABLE since Tian restarted touring with the Divine Grace. When he wasn't traveling, he'd ride the bus from Quincy to Twin Waters two or three times a week. Usually he worked on Wednesdays and Saturdays. With two incomes now, he managed decently, sending a thousand dollars home every month. His bank account had grown considerably during the winter. He could afford to find an apartment for himself, something he'd wanted for a while, but these days he'd been having second thoughts. He liked sharing the place with Funi. Her presence gave him some feeling of companionship, however vague and illusory that might be. He was rather mystified by such an emotional change in himself—he had always enjoyed solitude and independence.

Despite moving in different circles, Funi and Tian got along well and had no major disagreements. He didn't use any of her things without telling her beforehand and paid his share of the rent and utility bills promptly. Sometimes they didn't see each other for three or four days in a row. On holidays, such as the New Year and the Moon Festival, they would share a simple meal, either cooked by both of them together or bought from an eatery or restaurant. Funi had plain tastes and liked to eat almost anything—"a typical Cantonese," as Tian often joked about her. She celebrated Christmas and the Spring Festival at Frank and Sami's home. Frank, Sami, and Funi were all Buddhists, and also observed Wesak and Kuan Yin's Birthday. But two months ago she had quarreled with Sami and stopped visiting. Tian had no idea what had happened between them.

One evening he asked Funi why she'd fallen out with her cousin. She said vehemently, "Sami's a greedy woman, a fake Buddhist. She's been playing stocks and lost tens of thousands of dollars. Frank tried to stop her, but she's gotten so addicted to day-trading that she won't quit. The more she loses, the nastier she gets. She even wanted Frank to sell their house in Watertown so she could have more money to trade online. These days she's been talking about buying Bitcoin."

"That's awful. There's no way to stop her?" he asked.

"Don't even think about it. I once suggested to her that she go see a shrink, but she only blew up and lashed out at me. She accused me of making eyes at Frank and trying to flirt with him. She said he liked women who had more flesh. I told her that was bullshit. If I could seduce a man like Frank, I'd have married long ago." Funi laughed. "She ought to cherish what she has—a home with a husband and three fine kids."

In recent weeks Funi wouldn't even answer the phone when Sami called. Once Tian picked up, but Funi made him say she wasn't in. According to her, the less involved she was with Sami, the better it would be for everyone. "I just hope she wouldn't trade away their home and marriage," Funi said and sighed.

That seemed unlikely, though. Tian knew that Frank was strong-willed and wouldn't cave to Sami in business matters. Perhaps Frank had already managed to take their bank account and trading funds from her.

One night in May Tian came back late, around eleven. The light in the living room was still on, but Funi was already in bed, her room completely dark, no slit of light under the door. As he was pouring boiled water to make licorice tea for his throat, he heard her moaning. At first he thought she was suffering from her pollen allergies. Then she moaned again, her voice low and smothered.

He knocked on her door and asked, "Are you all right, Funi?"

"No," she gasped. "Come in, I need your help."

He entered her room and flipped on the light. She was lying on her bed, her face buried in a pillow. He froze in his tracks, seeing her body writhing a little. Then he stepped over and patted her neck. She lifted her head, her face sweaty and pale.

"What happened?" he asked. "Where do you hurt?"

"My belly," she said weakly. "I peed blood. Go to the bathroom and take a look. My belly was burning inside and it hurts like hell."

He rushed into the bathroom and saw the bloody liquid in the toilet. Good heavens, she was bleeding! He ran back into her room and said, "We must go to the hospital at once—to get you treated."

He returned to the kitchen and brought the licorice tea to Funi. He knew that licorice was anti-inflammatory and might reduce her pain a bit.

"All right, let's go now," he said firmly.

"Are you sure they're open at this hour?" she said, and sipped the tea.

"Positive. Every hospital here has an urgent-care center. Can you walk?" he asked as he helped her get out of bed.

"I can." She put her feet into her sneakers and stepped gingerly to the door. On the stairs he supported her, holding her left arm and elbow with both hands. She was bent a little due to the abdominal pain.

He parked at the side of the hospital and helped her toward the colossal brick building. A receptionist greeted them the moment they entered the automatic doors and reached the counter. Funi couldn't completely understand the questions the woman asked, so Tian translated for her. She produced her health insurance card, then was given a plastic bracelet with her name and birthday on it. In the waiting room there were four others, and the sight of them calmed Funi and Tian down some.

In no time a copper-haired nurse came and led Funi into an exam room. Tian went with her so that he could interpret. After getting her vitals, the nurse gave her a small plastic cup and asked her to provide a urine sample. The woman said to her, "Sweetheart, we have a special suite for you here." She pointed at the restroom within the exam room.

Funi went in with a folded patient gown under her arm. A few moments later she came out with half a cup of pink urine, wearing the light blue gown tied in the back. She looked pleased about the lighter color of her pee and said to Tian, "I feel better now. I should be all right."

Within ten minutes the test results came back. Funi had a common urinary tract infection. Tian was impressed by the speed of the work. Dr. Kim, a man in his late thirties with a swarthy and energetic face, said they shouldn't be too concerned and he'd soon have Funi's condition under control. Tian translated for Funi. As the doctor was palpating her abdomen with his hand, he asked if she'd ever had such a problem before. She shook her head no.

"I'm going to prescribe for you Keflex, a very good antibiotic drug," the doctor said. "You take it three times a day. Usually in four days the symptoms go away, but I want you to take it for a whole week. This is to prevent the infection from spreading to your other organs, like the kidneys. For the first time you take two pills, a double dose. Afterward one pill at a time."

Able to understand some basic English, Funi nodded gratefully, and Tian felt relieved.

"Are you Chinese or Korean?" Dr. Kim asked Funi.

"Chinese," she said.

"Some Koreans also have 'Yu' as their family name."

The doctor turned toward Tian a bit, but spoke to both of them. "You mustn't have sex during the next week," he said earnestly. "Urinary tract infections are sometimes caused by sexual activity, so abstain until the antibiotic is finished."

Tian grew embarrassed and Funi blushed, turning her face to the wall. Evidently she caught the drift of Dr. Kim's instructions.

The nurse with copper hair gave Funi a cup of water and two Keflex pills, each half turquoise and half apple-green. Funi tipped her head and swallowed the medicine. The woman told Tian, "Pick up the prescription at your pharmacy tomorrow morning and have her take one pill at a time, three times a day."

They thanked her and headed out toward the parking lot. The traffic on I-95 was droning faintly. The moon was like a giant banana. In the distance a helicopter bobbed through the starry sky, thumping *yak-yak-yak-yak* and setting the air pulsing.

The next morning Funi called in sick, but her abdominal pain was already nearly gone. Her urine looked clear and normal too. Tian went to the pharmacy next to Shaw's supermarket and got the

Keflex pills for her. She told him she felt fine now, already on the mend, so he shouldn't worry.

On his way to the casino, he went on thinking about their hospital visit. Dr. Kim had assumed that he was Funi's partner and obviously thought he'd had a hand in making her sick. Such a realization made Tian uneasy and he wondered whether he should talk with Funi.

The next evening, the two of them had tea in their kitchen. Tian asked her, "Do you have a boyfriend now?"

She shook her head. "No, I don't. Why do you ask?"

"Dr. Kim thought I'd made you sick and that your urinary tract infection must have been caused by sexual activity. I hope he was wrong of course."

She lowered her head and said, "I heard him urge you to abstain from sex for some time. You must've felt embarrassed. I'm sorry."

"Don't feel bad about it—I just don't want to be mistaken for your man."

She grimaced and asked, "Am I that awful, an embarrassment to you?"

"Of course not. I have a family and don't want to be misunderstood by others." He paused. "Did you have sex with someone recently?"

"Are you interrogating me now?" she cried. "Get out of here!"

"If you don't want to tell me, then don't. It's all right with me. Just don't tell anyone that you peed blood. People can stretch it wildly."

She sighed, then said almost tearfully, "I was sleeping with someone for a while. Do you want to know more about him?"

"No need for me to know, but I wish you good luck," Tian said sincerely. "I hope your boyfriend loves you."

"He's not my boyfriend. Dennis is just someone I met and liked. He used to work for Frank and then left for a job in Chinatown. He's married and has a baby."

"That's dangerous, Funi. You shouldn't be a man's mistress. Does he have some power over you? Do you work with him?"

"No, he's a cop, and his beat is in Chinatown. That's why he and

I often ran into each other. I know I shouldn't be with a family man like him. But I just can't help myself. Whenever he came to the warehouse and invited me out, I just went with him. He made me feel so cheap. Every time afterward I would blame myself, but then I just couldn't break up with him. I know he's been using me."

"But such a relationship can never go anywhere. You must get out of it soon."

"I wish I could, but I'm sort of desperate."

"Desperate about what?" Tian was flummoxed by her confession. She had always given him the impression of being carefree and at peace. When she was at home, she hardly made any noise, and sometimes he didn't even realize he wasn't alone.

"Honestly, I want to find a man," she told him. "I feel I'm getting old and soon will become an old maid nobody wants. I've just been trying to grab whatever I might get."

"You're still young and mustn't rush to have such a relationship."

"You're so kind, Tian. You understand how a woman like me feels. Can you keep my secret?"

"Of course, I won't breathe a word to anyone."

"Not even to Shuna."

"It will stay with me only."

"Thank you for all the help and for your kindness. I felt like I was dying the other night."

"We're friends and ought to help each other."

Her confession made him a little wary afterward. When he came back from work at night or from a long trip, he would check his room and other areas of their apartment, searching for traces of Dennis. But he never found anything. Probably they had a room that they went to in downtown Boston. Funi seemed as unflappable and vivacious as before. However, Tian noticed she was friendlier to him now. She began to keep his mail in order when he was away, and would jot down messages from people who phoned him. She stacked his *Boston Globe* on the storage shelf in the kitchen after she read the news. She had been learning more English and could read the paper now. If he was away for longer than a week, Funi would keep his room clean.

Once she said that after his family arrived to join him, she'd be happy to serve as a maid, cooking and keeping house, if the Yaos ever hired one. Tian laughed, surprised, and said he was unlikely to get rich or famous again. The two of them should be friends and equals. He asked what made her have such an idea. She explained, "I feel safe when I'm with you. You put me at peace."

"But how can you tell I'd be a good boss?"

"I know you're a decent man."

What she said moved him in a peculiar way. There is a saying in China that goes: "No woman loves a man who isn't bad." It means that a man's goodness and honesty tend to be viewed as weakness and stupidity. At least Funi took him to be a fine man. That pleased him, though seldom did he show his appreciation. In spite of their friendship, he meant to keep some distance between them.

34

ALTHOUGH THE DIVINE GRACE didn't tour during the summer, Tian received invitations to sing in other cities. This pleased him and made him feel like a professional again. In recent months he had often run into Tan Mai, who also gave more public performances now. Once in a while the two of them even shared a stage. Her mastery of the pi-pa was universally praised—she was regarded as an artist who had expanded the range of the instrument, which in her hands had become more expressive and could even play contemporary music. Her performance was usually the headlining act. Sometimes she'd give double encores and often got standing ovations.

However, all of Tan Mai's success was beginning to make her a target. A newspaper based in Vancouver, funded by the Chinese government, revealed that Tan Mai had been "so outrageous and so arrogant" that she had refused to play at the White House the year before, when China's paramount leader Hu Jintao had visited President Obama. In response, many people voiced criticisms and condemnations of Tan Mai, both online and in letters printed in newspapers. Some said she had too high an opinion of herself. For all her success, she mustn't forget she was merely an entertainer, no different from the minstrels of old, or storytellers with their bamboo clappers in teahouses. Without the motherland's years of nurturing support, she would have been nothing. Yet there were others who applauded her for her artistic integrity and for her position against the Communist regime. Tan Mai seemed to be caught in the crossfire but never broke her silence. The state media's disclosure seemed intended to make an example of her to other Chinese artists in the diaspora, implying that they should serve China unconditionally no matter where they were. Such a demand was later expressed overtly by an editorial in *The Global Post,* which went so far as to claim, "You must remain filial children to your motherland."

Tian had read about Tan Mai's trouble in newspapers and online. What had happened with the White House performance was that a Chinese official had approached Tan Mai before President Hu's visit and invited her to perform at the state dinner, sharing the program with an American jazz band. Without thinking twice, Tan Mai, feeling honored, accepted the invitation. But when she saw the list of pieces, she was appalled to find she was to play "In Praise of Our Motherland." The song had originally appeared in a 1950s movie about the Battle of Triangle Hill in the Korean War, and its lyrics were embedded with anti-American sentiment: "If friends arrive, we have good wine. / If wolves come, we have hunting guns." Tan Mai asked if she could play another song in its place, but the Chinese official responded rudely, telling her that she was not in a position to choose. As a protest, she canceled her appearance. They then invited the pianist Lang Lang to play the song in the White House instead, and he was delighted to oblige. The Americans at the banquet were completely unaware of the song's connotations, and they applauded Lang Lang's virtuoso performance. President Hu was so pleased by the resounding success that he even hugged the pianist. Later a newspaper in Taipei reported China's hoodwinking of the Americans with the headline: "A Brief Communist Takeover of the White House."

Now that Tan Mai's refusal to play at the state banquet had been made public, she was being attacked online by a swarm of "fifty cents"—a moniker for Internet commenters hired by the Chinese government because they are paid fifty cents for each post. There are tens of thousands of them, plaguing the Internet like locusts. Many of them are recent college graduates who can't find full-time work; some are haters of Western values or nationalistic freaks.

Tian wanted to show his support for Tan Mai, so he wrote to the newspaper *The China Press,* which had been printing comments on Tan Mai's case. He spoke as a colleague of hers, saying: "Certainly, like others, artists should serve their country, but the service must never be unconditional. No responsible individual should serve a country blindly. What if your country is an evil power, a danger to humanity and to world peace? What if your country has been ruthless to you and your family, making your life intolerable? What if your country has oppressed and exploited its citizens mercilessly? What if your country intends to reduce you to an insect or a tool? In short, if I serve my country, I must serve on my own terms, because I am an individual, not an obedient servant of the state. No one should do anything against their conscience."

His letter triggered a barrage of flak. Some people claimed Tian was a traitor to China, unqualified to join the debate. Some said that an artist was merely an entertainer and whoever paid could call the tune. One man even insisted that Tian was already an American and mustn't meddle with China's affairs. He was outraged and at last confronted them openly online. He challenged them: "What if you are paid by your country to hurt or murder others? As a human being, one must have his or her own principles and there are lines one must never cross!"

To counter the lie about his American citizenship, he posted online his Chinese passport with the upper corner of its front cover cut off to show that it had been canceled by China. He wrote, "I have been here without a passport for almost three years. As a result, I cannot travel outside North America, and my singing career has been crippled. If you were in my shoes, what would you do? Wouldn't you try to become a U.S. citizen? My country should be where freedom is, where I can feel safe and at home. Truth be told, once I have held my green card for five years, I won't wait a second to become naturalized. You can call me a traitor to China, but China has betrayed me first."

To his amazement, the condemnations stopped and a good number of people supported his choice to become a U.S. citizen. One even quoted Marx, though somewhat jokingly: "Workers of the world have no homeland." Three people said that they too had had their passports confiscated when they'd gone to the Chinese consulate to renew them. The security guards there had thrown them out of the building. One person even announced, "Fuck China! If my country rejects me, I can reject it too." Another weighed in, "China is just a pair of shoes I used to wear and have outgrown now." A third declared, "China is a beast that eats you without blinking its eyes!" A fourth wrote, "Your country is not your mother like you are told. You are the parents of your country!" A fifth claimed, "To me, my country is somewhat like my condo association, to which I pay a fee regularly. If it does not respond to my needs, I can fire it. Freedom also means that you can dismiss your country like a service." These cutting remarks unsettled Tian so much that he held back from making more comments. Of course those radical commentators caught a good deal of fire from the fifty-cent party.

Tan Mai noticed the criticism Tian was receiving for her sake, and she thanked him when they ran into each other again in Chicago. They had coffee together in a hotel bar. She had aged somewhat, but she was still quick with her words, and her face was as lively as four years earlier when they'd first met. She told him she'd been having some family trouble in recent months, mainly with her older son. The teenager was refusing to go to Chinese school on Sundays, claiming that he hated copying out the characters. For some reason he was convinced that the written language had made the Chinese habitual imitators with little originality. By copying the characters for millennia, people had evolved into copycats, whose imitative genes had been passed from generation to generation. Tan Mai and her husband thought this argument was nonsense, but still they couldn't persuade him to go back to Chinese school.

Though unconvinced by the boy's argument, Tian felt sympathetic toward him. He told Tan Mai, "If he doesn't use the script, he'll lose it anyway. Maybe he should live in China or Taiwan for a few years—that will help him learn and retain the language."

"He won't leave home at all. Totally spoiled. I feel like I'm at the end of my rope and don't know how to deal with him anymore. We shouldn't have been so protective of him when he was little."

"Now he's old enough to follow his own heart," Tian said. "You should let him be."

"But we'll have to pay for his college and everything."

"This is the parents' dilemma, isn't it?"

Tan Mai's problem reminded Tian of his own family—Shuna was having trouble with Tingting too. Their daughter seemed to be slacking in most of her classes. She wouldn't finish her homework and had flunked her last math test. Fortunately she liked English and reading, and they didn't have to make her work hard on a foreign language like Tan Mai's son. She had quit dance school long ago. That didn't bother Shuna, who had realized Tingting would never become a great dancer anyway.

Tian was worried that his wife and daughter were in an emotional tug-of-war. They would quarrel whenever one of the private tutors reported to Shuna on the girl's laziness. Tingting would call her mother a control freak and refuse to do her homework. As a result, she couldn't make any real progress. The math tutor had told Shuna, "I don't want to just pocket the fee for a perfunctory job. Your daughter's resistance to the work makes me feel frustrated. A failed student can hurt my reputation besides."

But Tingting had her own views. As Tian spoke with her on the phone, trying to defend Shuna, the girl wouldn't budge. She said, "You know I'm going to college in America, so I have to get a good SAT score and do well in the TOEFL. I have to concentrate on English, especially the listening comprehension and the reading. These sections are the hardest ones for Chinese students. I've learned enough math for the SAT already. As long as I can read fast enough in English, I can handle the math."

He couldn't argue with her, unfamiliar as he was with the American pre-college tests. In China, college admissions depend on the result of a single national entrance exam, which consists of a series of tests and is given only once a year. The combined score of all the tests will determine what kind of college a student can attend. Cutoff scores are set each year, which eliminate some applicants automatically. Therefore, if a cutoff line is 600, there will be a vital difference between a 600 and 599—a student below the line will only be admitted to the lower tier of schools. The SAT was something beyond Tian and Shuna's experience. Still, Shuna was too anxious to let the girl go her own way—like most parents in China, she saw college admissions as a matter of life and death.

Shuna told Tian that a boy in Tingting's school was interested in their daughter and that they often spent time together. Shuna didn't think highly of the boy and felt that Tingting had been wasting her time and ought to concentrate more on her schoolwork, so she tried to intervene. But if Shuna attempted to stop their phone chats, they would switch to texting each other. One night, on her way to the bathroom, Shuna noticed their daughter's light still on, so she tiptoed into Tingting's room and saw her dozing away at her desk. It was almost two a.m. and her computer screen displayed a written story in progress. Shuna glanced at it and recognized it as a piece of fantasy, a parody of an episode from a chivalrous novel by Liang Yusheng, the Hong Kong novelist. She was puzzled—Tingting had never been interested in writing anything like that. At this point the girl woke with a jolt and demanded to know what her mother was doing in her room. Shuna countered by asking why she'd been composing such a silly tale. Tingting admitted that she was writing it for Jawei, her boyfriend, to cheer him up—he'd been upset by an exchange of words with their physics teacher the day before. Shuna exploded and lashed out at Tingting for wasting her time. Midterms were just a week away and she needed to concentrate on her schoolwork. Mother and daughter wrangled for more than two hours. Their downstairs neighbor had to come up to calm them down.

Tian was caught in between—he knew nothing about Jawei, but he couldn't criticize Tingting just for having a boyfriend. He was rather open about this. If Jawei was decent and good to Tingting, it wouldn't hurt for her to date him, just to see where such a relationship would lead. But Tian couldn't say this to Shuna, who was adamant about breaking them up, saying it was too early for the girl to have a boyfriend who could distract her mind from her studies.

"Neither of them are really serious about this crush," Shuna told Tian on the phone.

"You're right," he echoed. "We shouldn't encourage them."

But deep down he wasn't sure. He suggested she bring their daughter to America the next summer to do her college visits. Once Tingting had a concrete goal in mind, she might be more motivated. Shuna agreed to apply for passports for both of them for the sake of Tingting's going to college in America. Tian also spoke with their daughter, who liked the idea of a pre-college tour. Now he had to prepare for their visit, which would be expensive, but with his steady income, he could afford it.

Meanwhile, Shuna continued to press Tian to quit his job at the casino, insisting that he had to pull out of "the dump of Twin Waters" soon, but he was reluctant to give up the work. He told her in an email, "The casino has a decent backing band, which would be impossible for me to come by if I were on my own. As long as I still have the thrill of singing live, semi-obscurity suits me fine." Tian's fellow workers at Twin Waters were friendly, and the flexible hours allowed him to tour. More fundamentally, the job was something he could depend on to bring him a stable income, even though he made only $12.75 an hour, and even though he was no longer entitled to health insurance. Shuna must have felt embarrassed when others talked about his casino work, but they couldn't see what things were like here. They didn't know how precious a reliable job was for him.

In recent months Shuna had also complained about her difficulties in learning English, which was very hard going for her. She used to think it was just another foreign language, like Japanese, which she knew well. But she told Tian, "I never needed to memorize vocabulary when I studied Japanese, but with English it's like a labor of Sisyphus. Many words are so slippery that they are impossible for me to remember. Also, the words are so hard to pronounce, they give me a sore throat. Perhaps I'm too old to learn it." Hearing that, Tian chuckled, then urged her to persevere, saying her effort would pay off in the long run.

35

Funi saw Tian pouring boiled water on jasmine tea and said, "You should wash your tea with hot water before drinking it."

"What do you mean?" he asked, baffled.

"Let me show you." She picked up a small steel strainer, poured the tea through it to catch the leaves, gave them a rinse, then put the leaves back into his cup. "Teas from mainland China can be contaminated with insecticide, so you should rinse it with hot water before using it."

"No wonder my throat feels itchy these days. It must be due to the polluted tea," he half-joshed.

"I just learned about this from my boss. He prefers Taiwanese tea, but it's expensive." She poured the remaining boiled water into his cup. "Now you're all set."

He made a mental note that from now on, he'd buy only Taiwanese tea.

Sometimes, especially on weekends, Funi and he would sit over a pot of tea, chatting idly. They would talk about their past and their experiences in America. Because of Tian's former career, once in a while he turned soft and regretted having left China and wondered whether he might have been more successful if he had stayed. But most of the time he was more convinced that he'd made the right decision to immigrate and to leave behind all the petty worries and constant fears of crossing official lines. He understood that now he'd left China, there would be no return. The spot he'd once occupied there had by now been taken by someone else—there was no room for him anymore. It was silly for Tian to lament his loss, and he ought to feel grateful for the opportunity to start anew. Here he could have control over his life. Unlike back in China, here no one would look down on you because you made a small salary or didn't own a house or a fancy car. What's more, he could sing any songs he wanted to. He didn't talk to Funi about his thoughts on artistic freedom though—she was unfamiliar with his professional life and preoccupations. She had never regretted immigrating to America—she hadn't passed the college entrance exam, and even if she had, her family couldn't have afforded to send her. In her home county, Lianping, most young people left for coastal cities to find employment, so at best she would have ended up in a factory. "I have a decent job here and live comfortably," she said. "I'm not like you, Tian. I'm nobody and am easily satisfied. I'll be happy if I can have a family and two or three kids."

She said those words so earnestly that he just nodded without speaking. She was already thirty and still single, though she might still be carrying on with Dennis, the cop in Chinatown. If she didn't get married soon, it might not be so easy for her to raise the family she wanted. Lately she'd been looking unwell, her lower eyelids puffy and her cheeks gray. In the feeble light of their kitchen her pallor appeared more pronounced.

Then one day, as he was cooking breakfast, he heard her retching in the bathroom. Following the flushing of the toilet there came the running of water at the sink. When she stepped out, he joked, "Are you having morning sickness?"

She looked astonished. "Yes," she said, "I'm pregnant."

He didn't know how to answer her, and for a while they just stared at each other. He tried to smile, but his face felt rigid. He managed to say, "Funi, what happened? I mean, what are you going to do?"

"I'm going to keep the baby."

"How will you raise it? With Dennis?"

"Maybe not." She sat down and picked up a slice of toast from his plate, scooped a gob of strawberry jam on it, and took a bite. "I have to eat more from now on." She smiled, her face misshapen and her eyes watery.

They often shared food; he took more from her than she did from him. He went on, "What do you mean? He won't help you raise the child?"

"He wants me to terminate the pregnancy, but I don't want to. I'm already thirty, and it won't be easy for me to have a baby again."

"But have you thought of the difficulties in bringing up a child alone?"

"I won't mind being a single mother," she said, then collapsed into sobs, her face buried in her forearms on the table.

He patted her on the shoulder. "It's tough, I know, but try to be rational about this." He couldn't say any more.

Hurriedly he finished breakfast and headed for President Plaza to catch the bus to Twin Waters. He paid his ten dollars for the round trip and took a front seat. On the way he mulled over Funi's pregnancy. The more he thought about it, the more uneasy he felt. Dennis, whom he'd met twice in passing, didn't seem reliable. This would make Funi a single mother and the child fatherless. For now she could work at the warehouse, but how long could she continue that way? Would she be able to make enough to provide for the child? Perhaps she should seriously consider finding someone to marry so the child could have an intact family. With her green card in hand, she should be able to find a recent arrival who was willing to marry her.

He was afraid to share his thoughts with Funi, worried he would appear too nosy. She went to work every morning, as usual. After a couple of weeks he noticed that her morning sickness had subsided, and she began to look like she was feeling better. He wondered whether she was still determined to keep the baby, or whether she and Dennis had worked out some plan. He tried to distance himself from her troubles, though he mentioned her pregnancy to Shuna. His wife said Funi should abort if the child was out of wedlock. "Imagine how hard life will be for the child if it doesn't have a father," Shuna said. Hers was a typical response from a Chinese woman of their generation, few of whom viewed a fetus as a human life. The argument about whether life started at conception was alien to them. So Tian said nothing to Funi about what Shuna had said, and neither did he form his own opinion on abortion, aware of the enormity of such a topic in the American context.

Then one late afternoon Funi phoned him, even though they were both in the apartment, just with two walls between them. She panted, "Tian, can you come in here and help me? I'm bleeding."

He rushed into her room and saw her lounging on her loveseat, her face pallid and her lips blue. At the sight of him, she pointed at her bed, on which was a bloody patch. He asked, "What happened?"

"I must be miscarrying," she groaned, clutching her abdomen and biting her lower lip. "I must have lifted too many vegetable boxes in the warehouse today."

"We must go to the hospital, now! Can you move?"

He supported her and put a flannel jacket on her shoulder. She first needed to change her pad to stanch the bleeding and turned into the bathroom. From the shelf in the living room Tian pulled out a book, *The Best American Poetry 2012,* and waited.

They went out the back door of their building, and he let her lean against the wall while he went to bring the car. Her cream-colored parka was unbuttoned, the front of her jeans soaked with blood—even a fresh pad didn't hide the bleeding—but he didn't know how to help besides rushing her to the ER. It was Friday and traffic was thick. The blacktop was littered with leaves, which a crosswind tossed up now and again. On the fringe of a small playground a stand of birch trees glimmered. Most of their branches were already naked, motionless in the darkening twilight.

The moment they entered the doors of the hospital he grabbed a wheelchair. He pushed Funi to the front desk and spoke with a receptionist.

"Who's her obstetrician or maternity nurse?" the plump woman asked kindly.

He turned to Funi and translated the question. She shook her head. He told the woman, "She doesn't have a maternity doctor or nurse."

"She's not under maternity care?"

"She says she's not," he said.

The receptionist raised her stenciled brows. "Who are you? Not the father?"

"Oh, no, I'm her roommate."

"It's very nice of you to keep her company. She needs someone with her to go through this."

A young nurse with a round face, named Karen, led them into the interior of the emergency center. After two turns through the twisting halls, Tian pushed Funi into an exam room. The nurse helped her lie down on the bed, which was a large gurney, and put a tiny clasp on Funi's index finger to measure her oxygen level. She then placed a thermometer under her tongue. Having typed down the results, she wrapped a Velcro cuff around Funi's arm and pushed a button to get her blood pressure and pulse.

Done with the vitals, which were all normal, the nurse told Funi, "The doctor will be with you momentarily, sweetie. You'll be all right." She turned to Tian and said, "Keep her lying like this."

Hurriedly he was doing paperwork for Funi, answering one question after another. She was weaker now and the bleeding continued, but she looked calm and answered his questions clearly. Below her signature, he wrote down his own name as her proxy.

Dr. Higgins came, a flaxen-haired woman with a doughy face and black-framed glasses. Tian stood up, wondering whether he should step out of the room, but Funi told him to stay. So he stayed and served as the interpreter. After she examined Funi, the doctor said to her, "I'm going to contact an obstetrician now. It looks like you might have a procedure today. You're still bleeding."

Funi nodded when Tian had translated. He asked Dr. Higgins, "You mean she has lost her baby?"

"Probably. I'm sorry." She spoke to him as though he were the father, but he made no correction. At that, Funi moaned in English, "I wanta keep baby!"

The doctor touched Funi's shoulder and said, "We can't decide now. An obstetrician will check you over, and then we can decide what to do."

Tian translated for Funi, who nodded again and calmed down some.

A few minutes later a young Chinese woman turned up. She looked like a college student; she had neck-length hair and wore a brown woolen poncho coat. She told them she was a medical interpreter, called in to serve at Funi's side while she underwent treatment. She stepped over as Tian moved aside so she could translate for the doctor. He was impressed by the quick arrangement. He'd been nervous about what he would do if they sent Funi to the operating room. Now he was relieved that he wouldn't have to be around when they gave her a D and C, a term he didn't understand but felt self-conscious asking about. Later he learned that it meant "dilation and curettage."

He patted Funi on the head and said, "Be brave. I'll be outside waiting for you. Whenever you need me, just let them give me a ring."

Funi nodded. "Thank you, Tian."

Stepping out of the exam room, he caught sight of Karen and told her that he'd be in the waiting room. "Please let me know when Funi's released," he said. "I'll take her home."

"Definitely. She'll need your help," Karen said. "You must be a good friend of hers."

"We're roommates."

He picked a seat and sat down, facing the door through which they wheeled patients in and out. He felt sad for Funi and yet wondered whether the miscarriage might be better for her in the long run. It looked like Dennis had already abandoned her. What a despicable act! What a scoundrel! Tian couldn't stop sighing.

Funi used to say her biggest regret in America was not having met a good man willing to marry her. Then she would correct herself, adding, "Actually, even in China it would be difficult for me too. I had no means and my parents had no pull. I didn't have pretty looks or talent. All I had was my ability to work." Tian told her that what she had was more precious than anything else. He once told her that he knew a man, a recent immigrant, who had two small children and a sickly wife, who was often bedridden; the man joked that if he could start over, he would have married a woman who could eat twenty hard-boiled eggs at a single meal—a hardy wife who could help him pull the weight of his household and tussle with fortune in this country. Funi laughed and said that if the man were unmarried and decent, she would have given it a try. Tian said she wouldn't need to eat that many eggs, and she could just tell the man she worked in a warehouse, lifting heavy boxes and parcels every day, and then show him her brawny hands and arms.

The door opened and a gurney loaded with Funi came out, accompanied by Karen and the interpreter. Tian went over and walked beside them. The nurse told him that the baby was lost and they were heading for the operating room, where the obstetrician was preparing for the surgery. It might take about an hour, but the procedure wasn't complex, and Funi, young and healthy, would be all right.

Putting his hand on Funi's arm, he said, "Don't be scared. You're in good hands and everything will be fine."

Her face was tearstained and she held his hand tight without a word, her eyes fixed on him as though eager to pull him along with her. He accompanied her all the way to the operating room. When its door closed behind them, he turned back to the waiting area. The receptionist said they would call him when Funi was ready to be released. She also showed him the bill for copay, $110 for the emergency visit, which he settled with his credit card. Then he sat down in a corner seat and touched the pocket of his coat and realized he'd left the poetry book in the car. He closed his eyes and tried to get some sleep.

36

T HEY DIDN'T GET BACK HOME until ten p.m. Funi was groggy from the anesthesia, but after eating the beef noodles that Tian cooked for her, she recovered some. Tian urged her to go to bed, which she did. He was exhausted too, and fell asleep the moment he turned in. But he slept fitfully—he felt Funi might need his help at any minute.

Toward daybreak, he had a dream in which some creature was scratching at his door. When he opened it, a shih tzu with a thick beige coat trotted in, frolicking around him and licking his ankles affectionately. Tian woke up and brooded about the dream, whose mystery he couldn't unravel. Traditionally, a dream about congenial dogs signifies friendship or the arrival of friends, but he had few of them here in spite of many acquaintances.

Funi got up in the morning as usual, though still weak and pale. Tian made breakfast for both of them, scrambled eggs with ham and rice porridge. He told her that he could take a day off if she needed him to stay home with her, but she said she could manage by herself. If she needed help, she would certainly ask him. After breakfast, following the instructions of the obstetrician's nurse, he went to the pharmacy to pick up some Tylenol. Funi wasn't required to take it, but she should have it on hand in case of abdominal pain.

Back from the pharmacy, Tian overheard Funi calling in sick. She promised her supervisor that she would return to work on Monday. Tian gave her the Tylenol and said she should take a tablet only when her pain became severe. Then he set out for President Plaza to catch the bus to Twin Waters.

It was Saturday. Tian took a seat on the right-hand side of the bus so that he could stay out of the sun. He read the news on his phone and texted a few messages. Then he reviewed in his head two songs he had newly learned and planned to sing that day: "Where Has My Time Gone?" and "Why Am I Crying?" He also went over "Thinking of My Comrades-in-Arms," a great song written in the early 1960s by a master composer whose daughter, also a composer on her own merit, had been a friend of Tian's. The man had studied composition in Japan in the early 1940s and then returned to China and produced songs for a movie studio. He composed for musicals as well; whatever he took on became a classic. Some of the Chinese visitors at the casino, mostly mainlanders, had demanded that Tian sing red oldies, which he would refuse to do categorically, but now he tried to satisfy them by singing a few genuine songs written in the 1950s and '60s. There were only a handful of such pieces that transcended politics, and "Thinking of My Comrades-in-Arms" was one of them.

He nodded off now and then on the bus, still tired from the night before.

He thought about Funi's situation. Now that her hopes of having a child had been dashed, what would she do about her dream of becoming a mother? Would she try to resume her affair with Dennis? That man seemed unlikely to appear in her life again. The more Tian considered her trouble, the gloomier he felt, and the more uncertain he was about how to maintain an appropriate relationship with her. But he reminded himself just to be her friend, kind and considerate and always ready to help. Beyond that, there wasn't much he could do.

About a month later he ran into Dennis at Park Plaza in Chinatown, where the man, in uniform and on duty, was walking his beat. Tian went up to him and said hello. Dennis was surprised. As he recognized Tian, he cringed a little, his face pale and his thick lips parted.

"Do you know that Funi miscarried?" Tian asked.

"I . . . I heard about that. Thank you for helping her." The corner of Dennis's mouth tilted up as he wrinkled his nose.

"Did she tell you in person?"

"Sort of. She called and left a short message. I promised my wife that I would stop seeing Funi, so it's over between her and me. Mr. Yao, you're a good man, and I'm sure she'll be all right with you by her side."

Tian's anger welled up, and he said, "Listen, I'm just her roommate. At least you should pay me the one hundred and ten dollars I put down for her copay. You can't just wash your hands of her altogether."

Dennis looked astonished and was speechless for a moment. He touched his pockets, then pulled out a checkbook from inside his jacket. He wrote a check and said, "Here's six hundred and ten dollars, made out to your name. If I gave this to Funi, she might just tear it up. Please deduct your one hundred and ten and give her the rest. This will make me feel a little better."

Tian hesitated. It was so cheap of Dennis to give her only five hundred dollars. Still, Tian took the check and kept it in his wallet for a long time. Later, when Funi asked him about the copayment for her procedure, he said Dennis had reimbursed him. She was perplexed and wanted him to explain. He was in a hurry to catch a flight to Houston and said he would explain when he got back. Eventually he gave her the money from Dennis, but she wouldn't take it, saying she wanted nothing to do with that bastard anymore. Tian left the envelope with the five hundred dollars on the kitchen table for her.

At last Shuna and Tingting got their passports, and together Tian and his family started to plan on their college tours. Tingting's school let out in late June, so she and Shuna would come in early July. Though the visit was still three months away, Tian was excited and talked with Funi about their plans, often after the dinners that they shared from time to time. In the week after her miscarriage, she'd finally found out that Tian could cook like a chef, so now and then she asked him to make a meal for them both, especially seafood.

One evening as they were chatting, he wondered aloud whether he should find another apartment for his family, even just for a month.

"No need for that," Funi said. Her round eyes narrowed as she smiled.

"But I can't cram them both into my room," he said.

"How long are they going to stay here?"

"One month at the most. During the time we'll be traveling to the various campuses."

"In that case Tingting can camp out on that sofa." Funi giggled as if she had just cracked a joke. Seeing him bewildered and knowing he was nervous about the girl, Funi added, "Seriously, don't bother to look for another place. The three of you can use this apartment and I can stay with Sami."

"Are you sure Sami will take you in?" he asked.

"Frank and Sami respect you and would take your family into their own home if you asked them. Besides, my nephew and nieces will be thrilled to have me over."

He accepted her offer and was amazed, knowing she hadn't made up with Sami yet. By now Tian knew Funi well enough to intuit that she thought there'd be enough time for her to patch things up with her cousin. He patted her hand gratefully.

In many ways Funi and Tian depended on each other now, economically and emotionally. When she came back from work in the evenings, she expected to find him in their apartment. If he happened to cook something for both of them, she'd get excited like a young girl. She exclaimed that Shuna was lucky to be married to such an excellent chef. When Tian worked late at the casino and returned home toward midnight, he knew that Funi would have left a light on for him. Once in a while she would save something in a pot or bowl for him, a boiled sweet potato or a steamed crab or fried shrimp. There would be a note on the dining table saying he should eat the snack before it got cold. Yet, for all their new intimacy, he was not attracted to her and regarded her only as a steady friend. He guessed she must feel the same about him. Perhaps in her eyes he was just a washed-up celebrity.

TIAN'S EMAIL CONTACT with Tingting was erratic. She didn't always bother to respond to his messages, but he wrote back as soon as he heard from her. Unexpectedly, through his daughter, he heard about Freda. In passing Tingting mentioned to him her college application adviser, Freda Liu, saying she was very fond of the woman. Amazed, he searched for Freda on social media and found that she was now at an education agency in Beijing that helped students apply for colleges abroad, assisting with tests and application forms and other paperwork. With her experience in the States, Freda had become an expert at the education agency. He was baffled by the coincidence and asked Tingting to send him a photo of her counselor, saying that he might know her.

Two days later Tingting wrote back with a photo attached, which showed the very Freda he knew. His daughter explained: "There is no need to be so clandestine, Dad. Freda knows I am your daughter and says she will do her best to help me get into a good college. She admires you."

Stunned, he asked Tingting, "Has your mother met Freda?"

"Of course. We both like her," his daughter returned.

He grew more mystified but took the conversation no further. He feared the young woman had wormed into his life again. Yet he suppressed his misgivings, as he remembered that it was Freda who had helped him put up the gravestone for his family. For that he was still grateful.

Shuna herself never mentioned Freda to him. Perhaps she still bore a grudge, or felt that the topic was too awkward and embarrassing to both of them. Tian remained quiet about it too. As long as Freda could help Tingting through the applications smoothly, he shouldn't interfere. In fact, because of their "friendship," she might go the extra mile for his daughter. He should take heart and think more positive thoughts.

In early July, Tian's wife and daughter arrived in Boston, and he drove to Logan Airport to pick them up. Funi had offered him the use of her car when his family was here, so he vacuumed and washed the Toyota Corolla, thinking that his ability to drive might impress his wife and daughter. He met them at Terminal E. Shuna and Tingting looked spirited in spite of the eighteen-hour flight, both dressed in long-sleeve T-shirts and yoga pants and leather sandals. Mother and daughter each also wore a Tignanello purse, Tingting's smaller in size. As the three of them hugged, their heads touching each other for a good minute, his eyes filled. The girl was tall now, even taller than her mother, but much thinner than before. Shuna looked a little aged; two wrinkles like big brackets appeared around her nose when she smiled, and the bangs over her forehead had traces of gray.

They turned to the baggage carousel to pick up their things, two aquamarine suitcases and a canary-yellow backpack. These pieces, all wheeled and in bright colors, looked suitable for a vacation at a seaside resort. He joked that the two of them seemed to be heading for Venice.

They pulled the baggage out the automatic door and crossed the street to the garage. At the sight of the silver sedan, Tingting asked her father, "Is this our car?"

"No, it's my roommate's. She let me use it for your visit."

"She's so nice."

They all got in, Tingting in the back.

"What's the smell here?" Shuna asked as she buckled up.

"Funi smokes," he said.

Neither Shuna nor Tingting asked anything more about the car, which apparently didn't impress them. It was getting dark and the city grew more congested, streets flowing with traffic, buildings looming against the indigo sky. Still, there were clear stars and a blade of the crescent moon cleaving roofs and treetops as they headed south. Mother and daughter were both amazed by Tian's ability to navigate the jungles of roads. Once they got on I-95, the southbound traffic, though still heavy, flowed smoothly.

When they entered Quincy twenty minutes later, Tingting asked, "Is this a county town?"

"No, it's a small city," he told her. "A satellite city of Boston."

"It looks like a village."

He laughed. "Yes, you'll see how big the village is in broad daylight. It isn't that rural at all."

He pulled up in front of his building and they all got out of the car. Shuna said, as if to herself, "The air is clean and cool here. I haven't breathed such fresh air for ages."

"That's true," agreed Tingting.

He told them, "Quincy is on the ocean, so there's always a breeze that keeps the air circulating."

As they were unloading the baggage, a cicada began chirring from the top of a beech tree, the chirps thin and a little sluggish. Mother and daughter stopped to listen. "I haven't heard a cicada in years," Tingting said.

Another creature squawked from a distance, sending an urgent hooting call. "What's that?" the girl asked, cocking her head.

"Must be a tree frog," Tian told her.

"What does it look like?"

"Light green in color, about half the size of a regular frog in Beijing."

Funi had cleaned up the apartment before leaving for Frank and Sami's house, which was nearby, on a maple-lined backstreet. Tian had made dinner beforehand—rice porridge, salted duck eggs, kimchee, sautéed bamboo shoots. Now he opened a bag of scallion pancakes and put them in the microwave to heat up. His wife and daughter were surprised by the homey meal, everything genuinely Chinese; they'd thought he ate American food most of the time:

bread, ham, sausages, milk, cheese. He told them that he wanted to serve them a light dinner that would soothe their stomachs after the long trip. They both appreciated this, saying they hadn't had much of an appetite, but at the sight of the food, they had turned eager to dig in. Tingting ate lustily, which pleased Shuna and Tian.

After dinner, mother and daughter each took a shower and then went to bed, Tingting sleeping in Funi's room, Shuna in Tian's. He washed the dishes and sat down on the sofa and began to read a poetry book by Mark Strand, whose work he had become interested in lately. He liked his poems, particularly the zany collection *Darker*—Tian had very much taken to its surreal touches and light tones, to its playful images and incisive intelligence.

Then Shuna came out of his room. "I can't sleep," she said. "It's morning in Beijing now."

"I thought you were tired," he said.

"I am, but I'm wide awake." She held out her hand and pulled him. "Come, let's chat in bed."

The instant he stepped into his room, she kissed him on the neck, smiling, her roundish cheeks pink. She patted his crotch, then peeled away her shirt and pajamas and underthings. He took off his T-shirt and pants and briefs, then slid into bed after her.

They didn't talk much, of course, but touched and fondled each other heatedly. Both of them were driven by a rush of hunger, and couldn't wait to make love. Soon they got more active; one of her legs held his back as if afraid he might slip away while her other leg was trembling a little. Not having slept with a woman for more than three years, he was out of practice and couldn't hold himself long and properly, though her familiar scent and her panting spurred him to act forcibly. After three or four minutes he came. He gasped, about to apologize, but checked himself.

"What happened?" she asked him.

"I'm rusty—I'm sorry. I haven't touched a woman for more than three years."

"Don't feel bad, Tian—I appreciate your abstinence. Now, we should go to sleep."

They were quiet for a long while. He heard her sigh a few times.

She might have remembered what Freda had said about him, about his virility and stamina in bed. Though Shuna turned him on easily, he couldn't summon the intimate passion and aching love he'd had for her four years before. Now this strange diluted emotion had come over him vaguely at the airport, where he'd been so happy to see his daughter that he'd had to remind himself to address Shuna more often, lest she feel left out. He sensed some kind of invisible barrier between her and him. Now their brief lovemaking made him wonder what had happened between them. Perhaps the old heady passion would come back once they spent enough time together again.

Had she had an affair with Professor Bai, or other men, since he'd left home? Perhaps she did, but he would never ask. Shuna was attractive in her own way, quick-witted and with a penetrating intelligence. Whenever she stood at a lectern or on a podium, she would glow with a vivacious face and brilliant eyes; his colleagues remarked that she was a born teacher. She'd once told Tian that one of her graduate students, a man just over thirty, had developed a crush on her, so she had to avoid being alone with him. When she met him in her office, she left the door ajar. Now she was a full professor and had three PhD students to supervise. In addition to the textbook coauthored with Bai, she was about to publish a new monograph on the Ming Dynasty's monetary system. She'd been making progress in her career by leaps and bounds.

Even as his wife breathed evenly beside him, his heart was as weary as if he hadn't recovered from a long run yet. With entangled thoughts and memories, he fell asleep.

Funi came over with a yellow Labrador the next morning, saying she was walking him for Sami. The dog was called Larry and had a tearstained face and large flappy ears. He kept sniffing at Tian's feet, glad to meet him again; his tongue licked his black nostrils from time to time as his tail wagged nonstop. Seeing how fond the dog was of Tian, Tingting sat down on her heels and stroked Larry's back.

Shuna warmed to Funi and thanked her for helping Tian, as if he'd been his roommate's charge. She said to Funi, "I thought you were a rich girl like your name suggests. We're so beholden to you for helping Tian all these years, and for the use of your car."

The name "Funi" means "Blessed Girl" and is also a homophone of "Rich Girl." It sounds a bit rustic indeed. As Tian was wondering whether Shuna was making fun of his roommate's name, Funi looked embarrassed and said, "No, no, actually Tian has always been helpful to me. He's patient with me and I depend on him for many things. He takes out trash and the recycling bin every Thursday morning."

Her last sentence discomforted him, but Shuna didn't seem to pay close attention and made no response. She must have no idea how trash was collected here.

Tian was glad to see that the two women were on friendly terms, at least in appearance. Perhaps it was Funi's plain looks that put Shuna at ease. His wife could see clearly that he was unattracted to Funi and that the two of them were just friends. Shuna went into the closet and took out a small scarlet package and gave it to Funi. Funi unwrapped the tissue paper and lifted out a thick jade bracelet, holding it up to the sunshine as though to see whether it was genuine. Then, as if abashed, she told Shuna, "This is so nice, but I have no use for it—I drive a forklift every day. You should keep it for Tingting."

"She has hers," Shuna said. "We want you to have it. You've been kind and generous to Tian. We all appreciate that."

Later his wife remarked that Funi seemed trustworthy. Shuna was pleased that Tian hadn't stayed under the same roof with a coquette, or "a Fox Spirit," in her words. She was especially happy to know that Funi attended a Buddhist temple with Sami and Frank. Tian didn't say much about his roommate, neither her troubles nor her virtues. When Shuna wondered aloud why Funi was still single, he only joked, saying it took so much energy to put down roots here that many immigrants had become eunuchs and nuns. At this, Shuna smiled pensively, as if pondering his words.

38

B OTH SHUNA AND TINGTING mainly wanted to visit Ivy League schools, but Tian wasn't sure about that. He knew his daughter's grades and test scores, and she'd be lucky if she could get into one of the top fifty colleges. Nevertheless, he didn't object when they showed him the list of schools they planned to see; he ought to take them sightseeing anyway.

They went to Harvard, Yale, Columbia, Princeton. At most of the schools, he followed Tingting and Shuna on the guided tours. Mother and daughter were struck by the grand gothic-style buildings at Princeton and Yale, but those structures only looked expensive and imposing to Tian. Harvard was different and easy—they took the Red Line train there and strolled around on their own. Tian snapped photos of his daughter and wife in front of the redbrick buildings and the grand Widener Library. They also went to some schools that were less of a reach for Tingting, like Boston University, Tufts, Brandeis, UMass-Amherst, and Tian's favorite, Wellesley College. These days he didn't go to work at the casino, which worried him a bit, though Jesse had granted him a two-week break, but he didn't mention his concern to Shuna and Tingting. His main job at the moment was to make them happy.

Tingting was going to bed late every night, staying up to use Google, which was banned in China. Everyone there had no choice but to use Baidu, an awful search engine that automatically weeds out censored information. Her emails to her boyfriend, Jawei, were often blocked by the Chinese Internet system due to some sensitive

words she had used, so she phoned him in the mornings instead—
Shuna had set up an account for international calls, and Tingting
could use it unlimitedly.

Tian chatted with his daughter about colleges. She didn't want
to go to a women's college, claiming it would be boring without
boys in the school. He wondered whether she had misgivings about
Jawei and whether they would stay together. The girl shook her
chin-length bob and said, "I just love to have boys around. That
makes life more exciting."

He was bemused but didn't press her for more. Deep down, he
was glad she was candid about being fond of boys. He could see
that she'd set her heart on opposing Shuna and him, especially with
respect to her personal matters. She often condemned the Great
Firewall, China's Internet control apparatus, which had been rising higher by the year. On their way to Walden Pond, Tingting said
from the backseat, "If I was strong in science, I would apply to MIT
to learn how to knock down the Great Firewall."

"Good thing you're not that strong," her mother shot back.

Walden Pond was rather deserted that afternoon, the lakeside
dense with trees and foliage, small trails snaking along here and
there. The sun was throwing warm rays on the water, flat and
motionless, ringed by the pebbly white beach. The Yaos walked on
the trail along the shore, bumping into an angler now and then.
They lingered for a while at the naked site of Thoreau's cabin, a pile
of boulders and nine short stone pillars chained together around a
hearth. They read the inscriptions on the sign and imagined what
Thoreau's life might have been like at such a secluded place one
and a half centuries before. From this spot they could catch the
vista of the entire lake, but the scene must have been more tranquil,
or more lonesome, in Thoreau's time.

Tingting asked Tian, "Didn't he have a family?"

"No, he was a bachelor," he answered.

Her mother chimed in, "He wasn't interested in women for sure."

"I admire him," Tian said. "His ability to become so detached and
so focused on his inner life."

They continued along the waterside. Shuna was amazed there

were no mosquitos following them. As they were about to turn east, a commuter train passed, clanking rhythmically. The train thrilled Tingting, who had never seen such an old-fashioned model, slow and short, with only six cars. She jumped and waved at the passengers. In no time the train disappeared and the track turned quiet again, hardly visible in the forest. They continued east. A flock of geese emerged, flying across the lake to the north, and one of them honked, its wings flapping lazily. Then the others followed suit and let out guttural cries. The whole flock swung abruptly as one, as if hit by a sudden fear, then headed to the opposite hill, thick with foliage and glossy in the setting sun. This was real countryside, mother and daughter agreed, but if given the choice, they couldn't say whether they would enjoy a life in such a place. It was so isolated, and it must feel forlorn at night.

At the replica of Thoreau's cabin across Walden Street, Tian shot a few photos of Tingting and Shuna, both standing before the statue of the hermit and holding his bronze hand. The girl then turned to the cabin and pushed its door. It wasn't locked. She stepped in and lay down on the straw mattress on the narrow wood-framed bed so that Tian could snap a picture of her. A pungent scent of incense remained in the poky room, as if the occupant had just left and would return at any minute. Tian lifted his eyes to the ceiling, which had tree trunks as beams, each about four inches thick and still covered with scaly bark. Shuna sat down on the small lacquered rocking chair and closed her eyes.

Tian caught sight of a cracked chamber pot under Thoreau's bed. He asked his daughter, "Can we leave you here?"

"All right, I will live and die here alone," Tingting said with a straight face.

"Bye-bye, now." Shuna stood and waved at her and turned to the door. The girl got up and followed them out.

He wondered if what Tingting said—"I will live and die here alone"—was something that had crossed Thoreau's mind. The recluse must have brooded about how long he'd stay at this place and whether his life might eventually end here. On their way back, Tingting wondered aloud why Thoreau had lived on the pond by himself. Shuna said, "He wanted to stand apart from society. He must have loved life among nature."

"But why did he live away from others?" the girl persisted.

"His idea of freedom was pure and absolute," Tian said. "In fact, solitude is a path to freedom, for which you must accept everything that happens to you, including hunger, disease, and even death. You're supposed to be responsible for your own existence, body and soul."

"My, I'm impressed," Shuna said, then turned to Tingting. "See, your dad is a philosopher now."

"What else can you say about me?" he fired back. "You think I've lived in America for so long without figuring out a thing or two?"

They all laughed.

Shuna and Tian discussed how to pay for their daughter's college if she came to the States. Most of the schools they had visited didn't offer scholarships to international students. They might have to pay every penny of Tingting's tuition and living costs. Tian was nervous about this topic—he couldn't possibly make enough to fund her education here.

"We can sell an apartment," Shuna said matter-of-factly, taking a sip of coffee. She seemed to have already thought this out.

"Would that bring us enough cash?" Tian asked. They had two apartments, both rather shabby and small, and he wasn't sure what price either of them could bring.

"The one near the hospital would go for about two million yuan," she said. "Now is a good time to sell—the real estate market in Beijing is climbing again." Indeed, the apartment was so far from Shuna's university that they had hardly ever used it. It made sense to sell it before the housing market fell.

Yet Tian was amazed, never having thought the small apartment could be worth that much. Originally they'd paid only a tenth of the price Shuna had mentioned. Such an amount, the asking price, would be around three hundred thousand dollars, enough to cover Tingting's college education here. Although still unsure whether their old apartment could really fetch such a price, a sense of relief washed over him. He suggested putting it up for sale as soon as Shuna went back. She agreed to hire a good broker.

Shuna also talked about her impressions of America. She loved the universities they'd visited, particularly their research libraries, full of resources that were carefully archived and accessible for readers. In Yenching Library at Harvard she had seen many rare books, some of them hundreds of years old, available for any student and faculty member to use. Nonetheless, she couldn't see herself teaching at one of those schools—she'd have to be able to give lectures and write in English, and she felt too old to learn the language, which was simply beyond her ability. Moreover, she was already a full professor at Tsinghua University and a vice-president of China's Historical Studies of the Ming Dynasty. Such a brilliant career was more than most Chinese historians could dream of. But—granted there were no restrictions on scholarly research here; granted professors could speak their minds in class and at conferences with impunity; granted they were paid more and could live in the suburbs with their own houses and gardens; granted she was very fond of small college towns—Shuna believed she was too deeply rooted in China, and if she moved here, her career would be disrupted and even lost. For every reason she should continue her work at Tsinghua University.

Tian was disappointed to hear that. Since she was here, he had vaguely sensed her reservations about their immigration and wondered how many years it might take her to learn enough English to start a teaching career here. Still, her words alarmed him. He had thought that she would come join him sooner or later, and together they would rebuild their life and home. His being here had been meant to pave the way for his wife and daughter.

She suggested that he try to live in both cities, Boston and Beijing, so that he could resume his singing career inside and outside China. To him, the idea was insane—he wasn't even sure he could get a Chinese passport anymore. In fact, he would be applying for U.S. citizenship soon so that he could travel internationally.

"Then, after you become a U.S. citizen, you can commute between China and America like a world citizen," she said.

He told her the truth. "I'm not sure how it can be done." To his knowledge, once you were put on the Chinese government's black-list, you were permanently barred from entry unless there was a regime change in China. The idea of "a world citizen" was nothing but a self-deceiving illusion. Yet Tian was reluctant to say more on the subject and only told Shuna, "We should be able to figure out a way. Let's not worry ahead of time."

Despite his placating words, he felt upset and even betrayed. For years they had planned to immigrate so that they could start over, relying on their own strength and ability to build a new life in America. He'd been living here to set up a base for their family, but now Shuna had grown too attached to her old rut to make the leap to join him here. As a result, in between them stretched a country that would divide them further and further. Unlike his own belief in freedom as a necessary condition for his life, Shuna still defined her existence within the system of her work unit, her professorship, her WeChat coteries, the Chinese state, and she would remain fixed there. It was as if she and he had grown into different species—she was unwilling to pay the high price for a free and independent life. If only they had foreseen that such a gulf would emerge between them.

39

O N THE DAY that Tian's wife and daughter were to fly back to Beijing, Tian didn't drive them to the airport—Funi's car hadn't passed the annual inspection and its carburetor had to be cleaned and adjusted. Instead they took the subway. Waiting for the train at Quincy Center, Tian saw the busker who often sang on the platform with a guitar in his arms. He was a fiftysomething Irishman, bulky and slightly stooped, with a thick neck, and had short blond hair and shining eyes. What struck Tian most about this man was his gentle face. Whenever someone dropped a dollar or two into his guitar case opened on the ground, he would nod with appreciation, then go on singing. His voice wasn't great, but he was confident and sang with charm.

"Is he a beggar?" Tingting asked Tian.

"No, he just enjoys singing."

A young woman stepped over and put a dollar into the case on the ground, which contained a small heap of bills. Shuna said, "Obviously he's making money."

"Lots of artists perform on streets like him to make a living," Tian told them, pulling out his billfold. "I once saw a famous Chinese composer playing the violin on a square in New York. It's just a way of survival here. Some Chinese immigrants play the erhu in train stations. They always sit on a small stool and saw away. I don't like it—the instrument gets too loud and too jarring when played indoors." He took out a dollar and dropped it into the guitar case.

The man nodded at Tian and his amber eyes twinkled. Tapping

his foot, he went on singing, his voice suddenly charged with yearning, "Oh look at those mountains. How old and youthful they have always been. . . ."

At the airport Tian helped his wife and daughter get their boarding passes and paid eighty-six dollars for their excess baggage. Shuna had bought heaps of presents for her friends and colleagues, while Tingting had gotten only a pair of Nike sneakers for Jawei, who played basketball. Tian had taken them to the outlets in Wrentham, where they had seen many other Chinese tourists. He'd talked to two young Chinese men standing guard over a swarm of shopping bags stuffed with brand-name products—Burberry, Polo, Calvin Klein, Brooks Brothers. One of them told Tian that his fellow tourists had left their purchases with the two of them and gone to the stores for more shopping; they all belonged to a group from Jiangsu province and had come here on a large bus. Tian could see that the salespeople in the stores, waving discount coupons, were thrilled at the sight of the Chinese shoppers. Shuna bought some jewelry there and two handbags, a Coach and a Kate Spade, each one just above two hundred dollars. The bags were for her superiors at the university—they had asked Shuna to get them and had given her a budget of four hundred dollars each. She said her leaders would be delighted to get the genuine American products at half the price they'd been willing to pay.

At Terminal E for international flights, Shuna and Tingting were ready to check into the waiting area, which was for ticketed passengers only. Tian hugged his daughter tightly and said she must work hard to get a high SAT score and that he'd love to see her here the next year. He then embraced Shuna, who whispered, "Take good care. Think about what I said last night."

"I will." He nodded and stopped in his tracks to watch them moving through the check-in line. Now and again they turned and waved at him. Shuna mouthed, "Go back now. Bye."

In no time his wife and daughter had disappeared into the crowd, and he turned around and made for the Silver Line bus to get back to the train station. The night before, he and Shuna had talked about his life here. She suggested he have a woman at his side because she realized how hard life was for him here. Honestly, Tian told her, he felt fine and was relishing his new freedom from the endless political studies and the official lines he'd had to toe back home. "But you need someone who can help you," she said earnestly. "I wish I were a better wife to you, Tian."

Now, he began to have misgivings about the motivation of what Shuna had said. He could tell that this time she was serious about her suggestion, since she might not be able to come join him in the States eventually. Perhaps she already had another man in her life back in Beijing. They both knew something was amiss in their marriage. They'd made love every night since she had come, but the passion and the intensity were no longer there. Every time it was finished within a few minutes. She surely couldn't be happy about this, as he remembered how much she'd enjoyed sex when they had been back in Beijing. She'd often joked that he had better be careful about one-night stands because any woman who went to bed with him once would stick to him for a long time. Now, unable to make love to her as he used to, all he could do was mock himself, saying he would need to practice more in bed to get his sexual drive back and that immigration must have desexualized a lot of folks. Or maybe he was just getting old. Another truth he wouldn't disclose to anyone: Since his brief fling with Freda he had remained guarded, fearful of being embroiled with another woman who might disrupt his life.

Deep inside, he felt another kind of change that was unsettling to him. He used to be able to respond to Shuna's feelings instinctively: Whenever she was upset or hurt, he would hurt for her. He could feel her presence in a room even if she came in noiselessly, and if she let out a cry in the kitchen, he'd get jolted. They were truly together, physically and mentally. Now he could no longer hurt for Shuna, but he could for Tingting. This emotional change disturbed him. Worse yet, he and his wife would be separated for a long time once more, and there'd be no opportunity for them to regain their intimate connection, the feeling of hurting for each other.

·   ·   ·

Funi moved back in after his wife and daughter had left, resuming her quiet life as if his takeover of the apartment had caused her no disruption. When he thanked her again for being so accommodating to his family, she wondered aloud whether Shuna had been disapproving.

"Disapproving of what?" he asked.

"Of you staying with me under the same roof. I was afraid she might want you to move out of here."

"Oh, she didn't mind that at all. Actually she appreciates your helping me all these years."

"Come on, you helped me more." Funi looked embarrassed, twitching her pug nose.

He felt at peace and at ease in this apartment. He and Funi were just like two small boats moored by chance at the same dock. Ultimately they were each supposed to go their own way, but for now this was a sensible arrangement that he wouldn't upset.

Since her miscarriage, Funi seemed to be done with men, as she claimed. Tian knew that Sami had been trying to introduce her to some young men, but Funi wouldn't bother to meet any of them. He once reminded her of her dream of having a family, but she merely smiled and said she was already lucky enough to have a stable job and a roof over her head. He guessed that her positivity might have something to do with the Buddhist congregation she was a part of, whose members gathered to meditate and worship on weekends. He wished he could be as serene as she was.

For months he kept busy working, trying to make as much as possible so that he could contribute some to his daughter's education. Tingting had just taken the SAT and done decently, though her score, only 1340, made it unlikely that she'd be admitted by a top college. This saddened her mother, who had believed their daughter was destined to become an Ivy Leaguer. But for Tian, as long as Tingting got into a decent school where she could study what she liked, he'd be happy for her. He didn't argue the point with his wife, saying only that she should give the girl more room for self-development. As a result, Tingting began to communicate with him more often than before. She was using Hotmail, which allowed messages to reach him most of the time, though there were still emails expunged or blocked by the Internet policing.

Tingting disclosed to him, without letting her mother know, that her boyfriend was applying to American colleges too. Jawei wanted to double-major in economics and philosophy so that he could prepare for a leadership position of some kind—an official or a CEO. The boy's father ran a think tank, which seemed rather spurious to Tian—very few independent thinkers were able to exist in China, and such an institute might serve no purpose at all. Still, the boy's ambition pleased Tian. He'd hate to see his daughter marry a young man who avoided challenges or who was obsessed only with making money. Tingting also revealed that she and Jawei would like to attend schools close to each other, so for her, a top college didn't mean that much. She wanted to study art history, which sounded impractical, but Tian wouldn't oppose her. He believed that cultural pragmatism had been holding the Chinese back for millennia, limiting people's visions and pursuits—this must be a major reason why historically they'd been underdeveloped in science. As long as Tingting was happy, Tian would be happy too.

PART FIVE

40

T IAN JOINED THE DIVINE GRACE AGAIN during the next holiday season. Now he had learned many songs popular among young people, and his singing was well received. The troupe's reputation was continuing to rise. In addition to enlisting Tan Mai—who had become Tian's friend even though they never saw each other outside their professional engagements—the Divine Grace had also hired an accomplished zither player, and their shows were being praised as "genuine Chinese art." To an extent, he felt his career coming back. Perhaps in the near future he'd be able to sing full-time again, but in the meantime he wouldn't give up his part-time job at Twin Waters yet. He might need the money for his daughter if she came to America in the fall. He took the bus to the casino at least twice a week and cherished the flexible schedule that Jesse allowed him.

In March Shuna sold their second apartment for 1,890,000 yuan—almost three hundred thousand dollars. Tian felt good about this, finally certain that they had enough funds for Tingting's college education in America. But his daughter soon began to receive rejection letters from the schools she'd wanted to attend most. Tian regretted not having helped her with the college essays. He had seen the ones she'd written with Freda's assistance and thought they were decent, but now he came to realize that an applicant's essays should be as original as possible, the more unorthodox, the better. It was just reported that a high-schooler in Nanjing had been admitted by a top U.S. college on the strength of his essay on the brand of instant noodles he loved. If only Tian had been more involved with his daughter's applications! He'd been too nervous about Freda to interfere.

Compared to Tingting, Jawei was doing a little better. He'd been admitted by Dartmouth and Brandeis, which made Tingting more determined to come to Boston for college. But she had to wait to hear from the last batch of schools she had applied to.

Not until early April did she get admission letters from UMass-Boston and the University of Michigan. Originally she had applied to Michigan only because Jawei wanted to go there, but he hadn't gotten in, so Tingting decided to give up that school. Shuna was furious and tried to insist that she go to Michigan, but the girl accepted UMass-Boston's offer as soon as Jawei had chosen Brandeis over Dartmouth. About this mother and daughter quarreled. Tian took Tingting's side and told Shuna that UMass-Boston would save them considerable money because he'd be naturalized soon. Once he became a U.S. citizen living in Massachusetts, they could pay in-state tuition, which would be only a third of that for an international student. But at hearing this Shuna exploded at him on the phone: "Money, money, all you care about is money! Has America made you so materialistic? I want our daughter to go to the best school she can get into and I'll be happy to pay every penny for it."

Later Tingting wrote to Tian to complain about her mother, saying, "She acts like all the top colleges belong to our family. Unlike her, I know I'm a small potato and don't mind remaining one."

"Don't bad-mouth your mom," he typed back. "She only wants the best for you, and you should appreciate that."

"I know what's best for me. She's crazy, an old fuddy-duddy who worships only books."

He changed the topic, afraid that the girl might say something more outrageous. Unlike his wife, who'd gone to Peking University, Tian had gotten his BA from a small college, studying English. In China, it's a great privilege to graduate from a top university, like belonging to an exclusive club whose network spreads everywhere. He guessed it must be the same here. He'd never met a Harvard graduate or a Yalie or a Princetonian who didn't have a decent job.

But Tingting would need to settle for UMass-Boston. Shuna went so far as to claim that their daughter had broken her heart. Tian didn't counter her, though he thought she sounded ridiculous. Tingting didn't seem to be interested in science or scholarship. He'd feel fortunate if she could finish her undergraduate studies at UMass-Boston, given all the difficulties she'd have to overcome. English alone could drive some Chinese students to drop out of college. Two months earlier it was reported that a sophomore from Changsha had jumped out of an apartment building in Baltimore, driven to despair by frustration and anxiety. Tian remembered a poem by a young Chinese who had once been a college student on the West Coast, which ends with these lines: "I've landed in a place my ancestors had never heard of, / And I must cultivate a new kind of fortitude."

There was another way to counter Shuna's resistance. Just think how many Chinese students had had to cram for the national entrance exam! All because their parents couldn't afford to send them abroad for college for a genuine education. Tian and Shuna were lucky—they happened to live in Beijing, where real estate was many times more valuable than it was in other cities. Tian had once met a young man studying at Boston College whose parents were middle school teachers in Jilin City, and he'd told Tian that his family had had to sell four apartments to pay for his college here. He added, "My parents were lucky to have bought those properties many years ago when they were still cheap." How many lucky people can be out there? There are millions of children in China's countryside who can only go to schools where the windows and doors are just gaping holes in the walls. They have no books other than tattered textbooks, their classrooms are not heated in the winter, and their PE class offers just soccer because the only equipment needed for the game is a ball. Very few of those kids can even graduate high school, and to them, attending college is as unimaginable as growing wings and learning to fly. In every sense Tingting was fortunate, and Shuna shouldn't throw such a tantrum about her going to an unremarkable university in the States.

In his heart Tian had another motive that he wouldn't reveal to his wife: He'd wanted their daughter to be close to him, though he was almost certain that Shuna had intuited his secret wish. She seemed resolved to keep Tingting and Jawei apart and often referred to Jawei as "the dandy." Tian wasn't sure he trusted her judgment of the boy, but then he'd never met Jawei and couldn't form his own opinion.

This summer blisters were growing on Tian's fingers again. Back in China he'd seen several dermatologists, but none of them had been able to diagnose the problem. One thought he must be allergic to gluten. For a short period of time Tian tried a gluten-free diet, which was hard to maintain in China and didn't help with the blisters. This year he also had shoulder pain that bothered him more. Yet he had no medical insurance now and wasn't willing to see a doctor for these seemingly minor complaints. Besides, Tingting would arrive soon, and he had to make preparations for her.

In mid-August his daughter and her boyfriend came to Boston together to start college. Tian went to the airport to meet them. Jawei struck him as cheerful and congenial, a tall young man with a mop of thick hair and a straight nose and eyebrows slanting toward the temples. He wore a green T-shirt and black chinos and white sneakers. In spite of the long flight, he appeared lively and kept smiling with his mouth wide open. Jawei knew Tian on sight, probably from his albums and press photos. The boy seemed restless around Tingting, ready to attend to her. When her baggage came out on the carousel, he grabbed the two suitcases and lugged them up to her and Tian. Jawei seemed considerate of Tingting and acted like a man already. Tian offered to give him a ride to his university, but a van from Brandeis was already waiting at the front of the terminal to collect international students. Still, Jawei thanked him with a little bow before he left with the van. Tian loaded Tingting's baggage into his trunk and drove her to Quincy.

She stayed with him that night, sleeping in his bed while he slept on an air mattress on the floor. Originally he had offered to rent an apartment for both of them so that she could stay with him, but the girl wanted to live on campus, especially for her freshman year. He didn't insist, since her mother would pay for her rent. Unlike Shuna, he wanted to let Tingting manage her own life.

Funi cooked a big breakfast the next morning—omelets, bacon, toast, rice porridge, sautéed slivers of pickled mustard tubers with lean pork. She even served them the food herself. Tian was moved. When he thanked her, she whispered to him, "I like your daughter."

But the girl didn't seem to know how to appreciate Funi's generosity—or maybe she was still suspicious of her. With chopsticks she picked up a glistening rasher and asked Funi, "I love this pork. What's it called?"

"Bacon," his roommate said.

"I mean what it's called in Chinese."

"Bacon," Funi repeated.

Tian stepped in, "We don't have a word for it in Chinese because there's no pork prepared this way. Maybe you could say 'smoked side meat.'"

"Then I'll just call it 'bacon' in Chinese," the girl said. "I remember seeing it written like that in a hotel restaurant."

Tingting loved the omelet, filled with dried baby shrimp and diced cayenne pepper. She asked her father whether Funi cooked for him like this every morning.

"No way," he told her. "She's treating you like a special guest."

After breakfast he was taking Tingting to her dorm on campus. Funi handed the girl a six-pack of orange soda and a small case of ramen noodles, saying Tingting should poach two eggs in the soup when she cooked the noodles. For a moment the girl looked uncertain whether to accept the items, but Tian told her to take them. Her school's board plan provided fourteen meals a week, so from time to time she would want to be able to cook something on her own.

Before they got on the highway, Tingting asked him, "Tell me, Dad, is Funi your girlfriend?"

"No, she's just a friend, a roommate. Why did you ask that?"

"Mom said Funi was very nice to you, and the two of you might grow close like a couple."

"That's absurd. What else did your mother say about Funi?"

"She just said you might need a woman who could take care of you."

"I can care for myself. Did she say anything critical about Funi?"

"Not really. She just said Funi's waters ran deep."

"You've seen what she's like. She is a simple woman with a good and reliable nature."

He wondered whether Shuna had assigned Tingting the task of reporting on Funi. Even if mother and daughter had made such an arrangement, he wasn't worried—the girl wouldn't find anything negative to report about his roommate. The most she could say was that Funi was an odd woman who was kind to him.

41

I N OCTOBER TIAN WAS NATURALIZED. At the ceremony about two hundred immigrants all swore their allegiance to their adopted homeland and vowed to defend the U.S. Constitution. If called upon, they must be willing to perform noncombatant service in the armed forces. The oath of allegiance bothered him a little. It took him some time to figure out the full meaning of the oath, after he had read the Constitution twice. He was struck by its concrete legal language, specifying the terms and rights that the American people give to the state or reserve for themselves. Tian saw that it was a contract between the citizens and the government. This new understanding threw him into a peculiar kind of excitement, because it indicated that the citizens and the country were equal partners in an agreement. Tian gathered that this equality must be the basis of democracy. Now he could see why the Constitution meant so much to the United States. It was the foundation of the nation. With such a realization he became willing to defend the Constitution, even to bear arms if he was called upon, simply because he believed in noble ideas and was willing to sacrifice for them.

With his new citizenship in hand he now could travel outside the States, so he began to accept international invitations. By and by more requests came from abroad. Many cultural associations were interested in him, mainly because his singing had changed and improved—he had enriched his repertoire with songs popular in mainland China and in the diaspora. He also could sing English songs, though his tongue still felt a little stiff when enunciating lyrics in English. Compared to Chinese, in which open-vowel words are common, English words often end with consonants—"students," "health," "desks." Such words are hard to pronounce for a foreigner, more so when they are sung. As more and more invitations came his way, he quit the casino so that he could travel more frequently. He felt like a professional singer again.

Yet he was aware that he was getting older, his voice no longer as youthful and energetic as before. In fact, lately he'd had trouble when performing onstage; sometimes he'd feel a sudden shortness of breath and would have to pause to inhale. So far he had managed to disguise such moments, but afterward he'd feel awful. At times there was even a dull pain in his chest. He became more careful about food and drink, not touching any hot spice or hard liquor. He did his voice exercises schematically every day and took the Pei Pa Koa cough syrup religiously.

Whenever he went to see Tingting, she would urge him to move out of Funi's apartment. He'd retort that the place was also now his—they had both signed the lease the summer before.

"Then find another place for yourself, Dad," Tingting said.

"Look, I lived alone in this country for years, and now I want a clean, comfortable place to return to, especially after a long trip."

"So the apartment feels like home to you."

"I suppose so."

"That might be what Funi wants. You'd better stop playing house with her."

He laughed. "You shouldn't worry about that. Nothing will happen between Funi and me. Remember that I love your mother."

In spite of his words, he could feel a fracture in their marriage. The distance between Shuna and him had only grown. Tormented as she was, it had become clear that she'd never give up her professorship at Tsinghua University. He had a presentiment that she would do something about their marriage soon. She wasn't someone who could remain passive for long.

To Tian's surprise, Yabin called one evening with the news that he had come back from Quebec—he was in New York now. Cheerfully, he told Tian he was a bachelor again.

Tian was mystified and asked, "Did Laura come back with you?"

"No, she's still in Canada."

"So the two of you are separated?"

"Divorced."

"When did you get married?"

"Last winter. But I'm finally free."

"What happened? Was Laura willing to give you up?"

Yabin sniggered and said, "It cost her quite a penny to let me go."

"Now you are rich?"

"You could say that. I'm thinking of doing something I've always wanted to do."

"Like what?"

"Travel around the world."

"So you won't be coming back to Boston?"

"No, I love New York—there are more opportunities here."

"Of course, if you're rich, New York can be a better place. But don't you want to settle down and raise kids? How old are you, forty-three?"

"Almost."

"If you don't start a family soon, it will be too late."

"Believe me, it's even harder for me to find a right woman now. By the way"—Yabin paused, then continued—"do you happen to have Freda Liu's contact information?"

Tian was surprised. "You want to reconnect with her?"

"Somehow I think of her often these days," he confessed.

"But she might not be available. You should find someone who's steadier, shouldn't you?"

"I might give her another try, but I'm interested in her mainly for business reasons. I've heard she's become quite successful in Beijing, and I've been looking for a representative there. The Chinese economy is booming, so I want to branch out to the mainland. Freda is experienced in the import-export business, and I might need her help, since I'm not allowed to go back to China."

"You still can't go back?"

"I was told I was an inveterate dissident. There's no way to convince the damned officials that I'm done with politics. Once an enemy, always an enemy. Of course, if they need you, they might treat you like a friend in appearance."

Tian joked, "As for Freda, are you not scared of her, the marks-woman? She might blow you to smithereens if you make her upset."

He chuckled. "She isn't really violent. She was just on a col-lege shooting team, you know that. Freda is a little wild, but I like wild women—they make life more exciting. I can handle her, be-lieve me."

Tian said, "I'll text you her phone number. She's working at an education agency in Beijing."

He also gave Yabin the name of her company so that he could find her on social media. Tian wasn't in direct contact with Freda these days, but she and Tingting seemed to have become friends and often exchanged messages. He remembered his daughter had once told him that Freda had a Russian boyfriend, who was in northern China, learning to cook like a chef. He had become a noted figure in the northeast—he carried a wok on his back when he walked the streets, as an advertisement, and his pork fried rice was quite popular.

When Tian told Funi about Yabin's return to the States, she shook her head and smiled knowingly, a shallow dimple on her right cheek. Two weeks back she'd been promoted to shift supervisor, leading a team of seven people at the warehouse. She got along with her fellow workers and was enjoying the job.

She and Tian were seated at their square dining table, which was cleared of the dishes after dinner. "That man was a gold digger, we all knew that," Funi said.

"That's too much," Tian objected. "He's a friend of mine and I know he's a ladies' man, but he's capable and makes decent money on his own."

Funi tittered, placing her palm on her glossy hair. "You're so naïve, Tian. Everybody knew Yabin couldn't get customers here. He was too glib to inspire trust."

"Really? I thought he was quite successful."

"He only appeared to be doing well. He could work with repair-men, but when it came to buying a home, not many people would use him as their agent. He often asked Frank and Sami to help him find a girlfriend."

"I don't believe you. He always had a woman with him. In his own way he's a lady killer."

"But he wanted more than female company. He told Sami he wanted a girlfriend who was rich and pretty."

"So Laura was rich but not pretty enough for him?"

"Obviously not."

"No wonder they're divorced."

"He must've got millions from her."

Tian couldn't summon much pity for Laura—she was an apologist for the Tiananmen suppression, and above all else her money was filthy to begin with. If Yabin shared some of it, that wasn't a great misfortune to her. Still, Tian asked Funi, "Do you think Yabin was planning this all along?" He was amazed by his own question. He couldn't believe that Yabin was that crafty.

"No doubt about it, but Laura must still have more than she'll ever need." Funi placed her hand on Tian's wrist, her palm warm and rough with calluses. "You're totally different from him."

"I'm not smooth like him. I don't have his kind of luck with women." He laughed, then added, "I also want a woman who's rich and pretty."

"You don't need that. I know you, Tian. You're a good man, a genuine artist at heart. You could have other women but you're loyal to Shuna. She's a lucky woman."

He wanted to move his hand away, but her words touched him and she kept caressing his wrist. He said, "You really know me."

"Tell me, what kind of women do you like?" She looked him in the face, her eyes bold, shining.

"Someone I can trust," he blurted out, then tried to laugh, but without success.

"You can trust me, you know," she whispered, and squeezed his wrist.

"I'm sure I can."

She moved closer and patted his upper arm, then leaned over and nestled her head in the crook of his shoulder, as if this were something she'd often done. "Tian, you don't know how attached I am to you. I think of you even when I'm at work."

He knew he should make some attempt at levity, but instead put his arm around her and pulled her closer. He breathed in her hair, which was musky. He noticed that her neck was flushed. She said, "I'm so fond of you, but I know I'm ugly and unworthy. You can do anything with me and I won't become a burden to you."

A fierce feeling, close to pain, seized his heart. He said, "I like you too. I know you are trustworthy, a good woman." As he was wondering what had gotten into her tonight, she kissed his cheek, then his mouth. Her kissing was hard and her tongue insistent.

Her persistence aroused his passion, suppressed for so long. He kissed her back. The more they touched each other, the more lustful he got. As he was stroking her chest, she kept moaning, panting a little. She murmured, "I've been thinking about this all the time. I'm yours, altogether. Just take from me whatever you want."

"I won't hurt you," he said.

"I know that. I'm so happy you want me."

They moved to her room, and they made love and slept in the same bed for the first time.

42

L IKE YABIN, TIAN TOO BECAME A BACHELOR. One day in the
spring Shuna asked him for a divorce. On some level he had
expected this, and so he wasn't upset or outraged. In a long email
to him, she listed the reasons she wished to end their marriage:
the absence of passion in their conjugal life, the distance that had
widened the gap between them—and, above all, she'd met someone else. He wondered if her lover was Professor Bai, but he didn't
press her for the truth. He couldn't blame her for the affair—he'd
been absent for six years. During such a long time anything could
happen. Had he met a woman he was really attracted to, he might
have fallen for her too.

Now, after reading Shuna's email again, he grew quiet. She was
offering to pay for their daughter's college, both tuition and living
expenses, but she'd like to keep their Beijing apartment because
she didn't have another place to live. He was reluctant to insist on
dividing their possessions, so without much thinking, he agreed to
sign the divorce papers.

He told her to get them prepared and sent to him and he would
sign as soon as he received them. After writing her back, he took
a long walk in the cemetery, strolling along the shaded trails. Two
young Mexican workers were trimming the flowers and ever-
green hedges. Beyond them, foxtails were rippling and dipping in
the breeze. The warm sun brightened the grass on the slope that
stretched all the way to the seaside. Oddly enough, the divorce
didn't trouble him too much. He felt calm, even at peace. He could

hardly remember the last time he'd felt tenderness toward Shuna, much less hurt for her. Their love had dwindled and mostly disappeared; the marriage had remained largely due to their daughter, whose existence had defined the boundaries of their happiness and distress for so many years.

When he broached the subject of their divorce with Tingting in her dorm, her thin eyes glinted and she twisted her lips. She blazed out, "I knew it wouldn't take long. My mother is a fast bitch and can't live without a man in her bed."

Swelling with sudden anger, he wanted to tell her to shut up, but he refrained. He knew that wasn't true of Shuna. He said to Tingting, "Don't ever talk like that about your mother! Even now she's paying for your college. She has been generous to both of us."

"I don't need her help."

"Don't act like a brat."

"You're no good either. You've been living under the same roof with that fool Funi. Maybe you're sleeping with her too."

"Are you out of your mind?"

Without waiting for her response and unwilling to continue in an argument that would only fluster him further, he stood and strode out of her room. He wanted her to cool off on her own. He went to the Red Line station, JFK/UMass, for the outbound train.

For all her anger, Tingting still came to see Tian on weekends, sometimes together with Jawei. Tian liked the young man more now and could see that, despite his bookish appearance, he was worldly in his own way. Jawei knew a lot about what was going on in the world and about how global events affected local economies and political activities. What pleased Tian most was his attitude toward the Western social system: He loved freedom and cherished the ideas of equality and justice. With disgust, Jawei would remark on some top Chinese leaders, "At best they're qualified to be a village head." For his irreverence Tian liked him more. He hoped Jawei loved Tingting devotedly.

When the two of them came to visit, Tian would cook a hearty meal. Naturally Funi would join them too. Jawei loved his cooking, saying it was better than most restaurants'. Tingting once asked Funi if Tian often cooked this way for her too. His roommate shook her head, saying, "What makes you think I'm so lucky? I often cook for him, but he only makes dinner for both of us once in a while, mainly when I buy seafood that I don't know how to cook properly."

At that, Tian noticed a shadow crossing his daughter's face. There was no need for her to be so nosy.

One Saturday afternoon in late April, Tingting came alone. It was unseasonably warm, in the mid-seventies, so she was wearing a floral halter. Before they sat down to a meal of braised rainbow trout and boiled jasmine rice, she went into Tian's room to get an orange soda from under his bed, where he kept it because the refrigerator was too full. She returned with a bottle for herself—her father and Funi didn't need one. As Tingting was twisting the cap of the bottle, Tian saw that her face was hardened, as if she was angry. She wouldn't raise her sullen eyes from her rice bowl or say a word to Funi. He didn't ask why. They went on eating cheerlessly, though the fish was well cooked.

After dinner he walked Tingting to the train station, where he wanted to pick up a jar of curry paste at a bodega. On the way she kept glaring sideways at Tian. He wondered what was wrong. She seemed to have swallowed gunpowder today. Finally, she asked him hotly, "Dad, are you sleeping with Funi?"

Aghast, he managed to reply, "What made you say that?"

"I saw her red slippers in your bedroom. They were together with yours under your bed."

"All right—I was with her last night. You know I've been alone all these years. I need a woman in my life."

"That's not my point. I mean, did Mom know about this before she decided to divorce you?"

"That was not her reason."

"I don't believe you. Mom often said you always had lots of women around you."

"But that doesn't mean I go to bed with them. That's not what I'm interested in."

"You made Mom worry about losing you all the time."

"You mean she didn't have other men with her after I left home?"

"I can't say that—but you're responsible for your divorce. Last summer Mom and I saw how close you were to that woman."

"That's completely groundless."

"I just don't believe you anymore!"

With those words, she swung away, swiped her train card at the entrance, and ran down the stairs toward the platform. He stood at the outside of the entrance, watching her recede among others. Her tall figure was slim, highlighted by the halter she was wearing; on her right shoulder was a giant ladybug and on her left shoulder was a dragonfly. He disliked her tattoos, which gave the impression that she was careless about her body, though he'd never told her what he thought. In a flash she was gone.

Later he called her, but for three days she wouldn't answer the phone. Then she sent him an email. She wrote:

Mom and I talked about your relationship with Funi. She doesn't care, since you're no longer her husband. She begged me to be understanding and said you needed a woman who could take care of you and Funi might be suitable. At least she seems humble and honest and reliable. But even if Mom forgives you, I do not. I also told Freda what you've been doing. She laughed and said that you could have picked a woman who looked less rustic and was better educated, and you had no taste. Actually, few women I know are as hard on the eyes as Funi. And she's got no figure to speak of and can eat a whole chicken in one sitting. To be honest, if you were with someone who was smart and attractive, I wouldn't object, because she would deserve you. But look at Funi—don't you feel ashamed of yourself? If you married her, I would feel humiliated to have an ugly stepmother like her!

Her message set Tian's blood boiling, but soon he composed himself and began to feel amused instead. Who was she to tell him about the kind of woman he should have in his life? He trusted Funi and the trust put him at ease and gave him peace when he was with her. He needed somebody he could always return to. Tingting was still too young to understand this, but she might one day.

In recent months Tian had been contacted separately by three men, all of whom represented the Chinese government. They were attempting to persuade him to go back to China and resume his career there. Now that he was traveling and performing internationally, his reputation had been restored and transformed. Across the Chinese diaspora he was regarded as a top singer with a large repertoire, which included the best songs from Taiwan, Hong Kong, even some popular new hits from the mainland. He attributed this success to his living away from China—the immigrant experience had opened his mind and expanded his ability. Lately he had been learning some American songs that were in a style that spoke to him—they had a psalmlike quality and a simple melody. He had translated the lyrics into Chinese, and since he could strum the guitar, he'd sing and accompany himself onstage. He liked songs full of poetry and religious longing, ecstatic and mysterious and solitary—for instance, some of Lady Lamb's songs. (Of course, he had to pick those no longer covered by copyright for his shows.) This kind of experiment was well received on the whole and set him apart. Among the singers of his generation, he outstripped those who were still in China, although he didn't have their kind of glamour and privileges and his life was much harder. Unlike most of them, he earned his living by honest work and had managed to reinvent himself. So he could feel at peace and wouldn't want more than this feeling of confidence and pride.

One of the government men approached him, serving as a broker of sorts. He had a military background. He offered Tian, together with his rancid breath, "If you join the Central Troupe of the Liberation Army, I'm sure they will let you start with the rank of one-star general. It's a tremendous deal, isn't it?" He gave a croaking laugh. One of his molars had a new crown, whiter than the others.

Tian shook his head and replied, "Look at me—am I martial material? The army would be too restrictive to me, like I'm a wild animal in a cage."

There were four or five acquaintances of his who had become "artist generals"—they were sometimes accompanied by bodyguards, even when they went out to eat at streetside food stalls. None of them had made real progress in their art, and they just went on rehashing their old work. Tian might have become one of them if he hadn't left China.

In his conversations with these government middlemen, he made no mention of his naturalization and got the impression that they didn't know he was already a U.S. citizen. Or maybe they were actually clear about his naturalization but just pretended ignorance—their task was only to bring him back. As for the opportunities and privileges that they dangled in his face, he'd say, "No, I love freedom more than anything else, even though freedom can be frightening and paralyzing, even though it takes a long time for me to get used to it."

Yet the men's persistence amazed Tian. No matter what he said, they kept their composure and always appeared congenial. They must have been routinely approaching people like him for many years to have developed such patience. They insisted that their motherland needed a talent like him, but he knew the truth: His stage appearances outside China threatened to tarnish the mainland government's image in the eyes of the public, so the authorities wanted to rope him in. Once he was back, it would be easy for them to control or destroy him. By now he had become a symbol, someone who showed that an artist from China could exist freely and meaningfully outside the sphere of the Chinese state. The middlemen always left him with their cards, saying if he changed his mind, he could simply get in touch and he'd be welcome to come back. Some of them even said, "Our country's arms will remain open to you." Others urged him, "Please seize such a precious opportunity. After this village there won't be the same inn." Tian was irritated by their platitudes—they assumed that patriotism was their common denominator. The truth was that much evil had been done in the name of the country and so many talents been ruined by it too. Tian was too afraid to get close to it now.

In his mind lingered the sentence "I'm not your homecoming prodigal son!" But he never let the words out.

43

T HAT SUMMER Tingting and Jawei went to New York. They planned to make some money there and also travel to see more of the country. They stayed in Flushing and worked at a restaurant, Tingting waitressing and Jawei busing tables. It was Yabin who had helped them find the jobs—the shifts were long, from ten a.m. to eleven p.m., but they were happy to be able to work. Their student visas didn't allow them to work off campus, but the restaurant used them anyway. Yabin said to Tian on the phone, "You're lucky to have such a grown-up daughter. You're only one year older than me."

Tian said, "That's the advantage of getting married early."

But Yabin didn't like Jawei, saying the young man was too aggressive, too full of himself. He even wondered how Tingting, lovely and smart, could fall for such a braggart. "It's like a fresh flower planted on a pile of cowpats," he told Tian.

He wasn't troubled by Yabin's negative view of Jawei, who in Tian's eyes was fine and decent in spite of his loose tongue and insouciance. As long as the young man and Tingting loved each other, Tian could accept and appreciate him.

In mid-September, he went to Portland, Oregon, to sing for a concert at an Asian culture fair. Onstage he felt something wrong with his throat and was able to sing with only half his usual energy. Afterward he began coughing continually. It was a kind of hacking cough he'd never had before, and there was a ferocious pain in his chest that wouldn't go away, no matter how many spoons of Pei Pa Koa syrup he took after he returned to Boston. He was sick, all energy drained out of him. Funi was worried and felt his forehead with her hand. "Gosh, you have no temperature—your forehead is so cold! You must go to the hospital."

He had been without medical insurance for two years, so he was reluctant to go. Instead he went to the herbal pharmacy at President Plaza. The place was run by Mrs. Kuo, who, with a slight underbite that gave her a longish chin, had once been a doctor back in Fuzhou City but couldn't practice here because of her poor English. In her shop she always wore an immaculate white coat as if she were still a physician. She prescribed a cocktail of herbs for Tian and said he should get well if he'd caught the flu, which she thought he must have. She also told him to come back if he still felt sick after taking the six packets of herbal extracts.

The herbs didn't help him. Every day he still coughed incessantly and his chest pain persisted. He was so weak that he had to cancel some engagements, unable to travel. Before leaving for work in the mornings, Funi would prepare lunch for him, and she would cook for him in the evenings. He could hardly do anything and had to carry a foam cup stuffed with a Kleenex wherever he went so that he could spit into it. As a result, he couldn't even go shopping anymore; in grocery stores people would turn to look at him, wondering about his cough, surely thinking he was a heavy smoker. At home alone, he tried to do his vocal exercises, but he couldn't manage it, interrupted by coughs. Again Funi urged him to go see a real doctor, yet he wanted to wait a little more.

A week later he returned to the herbal pharmacy to see if Mrs. Kuo could help him with another remedy. She looked at his tongue and felt his pulse, then said he should have a regular checkup in the hospital. She told him, "Herbal medicine is basically to nurture your body but can hardly treat emergency cases. When it comes to acute illness, Western medicine is much more effective. You should go to the hospital without delay, Mr. Yao."

"That can be expensive," he said. "I have no medical insurance."

"You haven't applied for the Massachusetts healthcare plan?"

"No, I haven't."

"You should apply for it right away. Haven't you heard of Romneycare?"

"What is it?"

"It's the universal healthcare plan for Massachusetts."

"You mean anyone can get insurance?"

"Right. How much do you make a year?" She smiled, as if this were a normal question from a doctor.

"Less than twenty thousand?" He told her his official income, which was lower because he was paid cash half the time, especially for local events.

"Then you are qualified for the low-income medical care. Go to the community health center on Hancock Street and fill out the form. As soon as you have the insurance, go to the hospital for a checkup."

Following her advice, he went to the small medical center and filed an application, which was accepted on the spot. The laminated insurance card would come to him in the mail, and in the meantime they gave him a temporary paper card he could use. He was thrilled by the simple application procedure and kept saying to himself, "This is like Canada and this is what a good country does for its citizens." Then he remembered that only Massachusetts had such universal coverage.

He went to Quincy Medical Center the next afternoon, where immediately they gave him a chest X-ray. Dr. Sabatino, his head bald with a shiny crown, frowned at the imaging and said, "This doesn't look good. You should get a scan first thing tomorrow morning."

"Is it very serious?" Tian asked, then coughed hard and spat into the foam cup in his hand.

"It's hard to say. There are two spots in the X-ray that look moist and blurry. We should have a CT scan to make sure."

"I have TB or pneumonia, right?"

"We need to have a scan to find out."

He was depressed after the visit and told Funi about the ominous diagnosis, uncertain though it was. She tried to comfort him, saying he'd get well soon and mustn't worry ahead of time. She cooked noodles with shredded chicken breast in the soup. He could eat only a small bowl in spite of the sesame oil she added for him. Even at dinner he couldn't stop coughing. Afterward she urged him to go to bed early, but she kept his door ajar and hers too, so that she could hear him when he needed help. He couldn't fully lie down because of the cough, so his back was rested on two folded blankets when he tried to sleep. In such a cumbersome position, he could only doze. His chest felt pressed hard, like a thick plate of iron was set upon it. His mind wandered through memories of his life in China and of his family, some of them sad and some pleasant. He felt awful about his predicament: At the time when his career was rising again, he'd suddenly fallen ill. He hoped he could be treated effectively and recuperate soon.

He went to the CT scan alone the next morning. He was the first patient of the day, so he was admitted into the scanning room without waiting. A slight young woman told him to lie on a blue narrow bed, then she pushed a button to slide him into a large tube. The bed stopped when his chest reached the middle of the tube, in which cameras began taking images of his lungs.

The whole process was painless and took just a few minutes. He was told to go home and wait to hear from the doctor. He was glad he was living within walking distance of the hospital. Holding the foam cup, he headed back along Whitwell Street. On the way back, he picked up a carton of eggs and a tin of Spam and a pack of twenty foam cups at Dollar Tree. He would force himself to eat more so as to recover soon.

Around midafternoon a nurse called and asked Tian to come to the hospital as soon as possible. She told him to bring someone with him. He thought that perhaps she assumed he was living far away. Funi happened to be back early, so he asked her to accompany him. Together they walked west to the hospital. It was a gorgeous day, the sky clear and cloudless, and Tian was amazed to see a pair of jet fighters soaring soundlessly in the distant sky, drawing two looping ribbons of contrails.

"Mr. Yao, we have bad news for you," Dr. Sabatino said. Another man, whiskered and with yellow eyes, was seated next to him. He introduced himself as Dr. Markson, an oncologist.

Dr. Sabatino explained to Tian that he had lung cancer, already at stage three at least. He went on to say that the final stage was four, so his case was not terminal. Tian was stunned, just staring at the two doctors, from one face to the other.

"Can you treat him?" Funi asked them. By now she could speak some English, as she used it at work.

Dr. Markson joined in, "I'm sorry to say that your two tumors are big—one is 5.7 centimeters in diameter and the other 2.4 centimeters. In fact, your cancer is quite advanced. You should see a surgeon. We have spoken to Dr. Hartley and you should make an appointment with his assistant right away."

For a while Tian was too shaken to say a word, his mind in turmoil. He coughed and spat into his foam cup. Dr. Sabatino patted Tian's knee with his hairy hand and said, "I'm so sorry about this, Mr. Yao. You should have come to us long ago. It must have taken some years for the tumors to grow so big."

Funi began sobbing quietly. Tian managed to ask, "What's your prognosis? What kind of chance do I have for recovery?"

The two doctors looked at each other, Sabatino's wide, heavy-boned face glum, while the oncologist shook his small head a bit. Then Dr. Markson swallowed, and, eyes lowered, he said to Tian, "Advanced lung cancer can be fatal, but there are treatments and a small percentage of patients have survived."

Tian knew his condition might be too advanced for them to treat. His uncle had died of lung cancer two decades before. The old man's tumor, a single one, was under an inch in diameter, but he couldn't go through the chemotherapy and had died at the last stage of the treatment due to his destroyed immune system. Tian's cancer was far more advanced, probably already terminal. He was in such a daze that his mind turned blank and he couldn't ask the doctors another question.

Funi called Tingting to inform her of Tian's condition. His daughter came straightaway and went about taking care of him, making tea and doing his laundry and cooking dinner, noodles with spaghetti sauce mixed with ground beef. Before they could eat, she slipped into the bathroom, crying. He heard her and knocked on the door, then stepped in. She was doubled over, clutching her stomach, so he patted her head while assuring her he'd be all right. "It's so unfair, unfair!" she moaned.

"Misfortune always strikes unexpectedly," he murmured. "It's life. Now come and eat."

"Let me wash my face. I'll be out in a moment."

She stayed with him that night, sleeping on the sofa, because she wanted to accompany him to see the surgeon the next morning. Throughout the night he coughed persistently, and Tingting got up time and again to make sure he had what he needed.

Dr. Hartley was a thickset man with a bulky face, his protruding eyes glinting with such coldness that Tian was reminded of a butcher. He didn't seem to be part of the full-time staff. More likely, he operated at various hospitals and got paid by piece rate. As he looked at the scans he exclaimed, "Jesus, how come you found out so late?" He showed them the images on the monitor. "See, it's a mess in your chest. You cough so much because this bigger tumor has pressed your windpipe. We can remove the tumors, then you will be able to breathe more easily."

"Will that cure him?" Tingting asked.

"It will help him breathe better for some time," Dr. Hartley said. "To be frank, the cancer is already too advanced."

Tian asked him bluntly, "How long do you think I might live?"

His question surprised the doctor, who replied without lifting his eyes, "Maybe six or seven weeks."

Tingting gasped. Tian placed his hand on her arm and gave her a squeeze. He then told the surgeon that he'd consider the procedure as an option, but he hadn't made up his mind yet. "Let me have a day or two before I can come to a decision," Tian said.

In fact, the previous night he and Tingting and Funi had talked about his treatment options. Both women believed he should choose "the conservative treatment," a palliative approach that combined herbal medicine and hospice care. They wanted him to suffer as little as possible during his final days, but they hadn't convinced him yet.

44

Tingting discussed her father's condition with her mother, who also suggested Tian choose the conservative treatment. He hadn't talked to Shuna since their divorce. Unless she contacted him directly, he wouldn't bother her with his problem. Tingting had told him that her mother would be remarrying soon, though she didn't say who the man was. Perhaps he was Professor Bai, whose wife, Tian was told, had died the winter before.

His daughter couldn't stay with him every night—there were early-morning classes and tests that she needed to keep up with. When she wasn't there, Funi stepped in for her. One morning he found Funi sleeping on the sofa. Soon his cough woke her and she sat up, rubbing her eyes. Her lids puffy and her face tired and slightly swollen.

She went into the bathroom and brushed her teeth. When she came out, seeing Tian set breakfast on the table, she said, "Gosh, I'll be late for work again. I didn't fall asleep until three in the morning." She speared a potato puff he had just microwaved, dipped it into ketchup, and put it into her mouth.

"You shouldn't have stayed up so late," he told her.

"I couldn't sleep. Whenever you coughed, I was worried you might suffocate. Whenever you didn't cough, I feared you might have passed out and stopped breathing. I was all nerves."

What she said touched him. He put his hand on her strong arm, saying, "Sorry to make you feel that way."

"I'm fine now. I have to run to work."

"Come, have some breakfast."

"No, I can grab a bagel at the train station."

After she'd left for the day, as planned the night before, he began to call his friends, just to say goodbye. He spoke with Tan Mai and Cindy Wong, telling them that his days might be numbered, and he thanked them for their friendship and the help they had given him. Cindy broke into tears and wailed, "My dad died of pancreatic cancer. It's so awful, Tian! You're a good man but have such terrible luck. I will pray for you. But don't give up so easily and a miracle might happen." Unlike Cindy, Mai took the news calmly. She urged him not to surrender to the disease without a fight. Her aunt had had lung cancer for almost a decade but was still living now. She'd been treated at a hospital in Houston. "In fact, a good number of her fellow cancer patients are still alive and active," Mai told him. Her words made him rethink his situation.

Then he called Yabin, to whom he had more to say. He'd like to have him as the executor of his will, and he had to get his affairs in order quickly.

"Of course, Tian, I'll do everything you want me to," Yabin assured him. "But I don't agree about the conservative treatment. Chinese medicine just makes you feel better and can't cure the disease. Boston has the best hospitals in the world. Why not take advantage of the medical services there?"

"My cancer is almost stage four," he said.

"That shouldn't be your reason for giving up. Some Chinese cancer patients have flown to Boston for treatment and their conditions have been either cured or improved considerably. Without exception, they all said the trip was worth it and their money well spent. Imagine, they would pay out of their own pockets to get treated in Boston."

"They must be very rich," Tian said.

"They're well off, I'd say, but not super-rich. Many Chinese can afford such expenses nowadays."

"Do you know at which hospital they've been treated here?"

"Mass General, Dana-Farber, Brigham and Women's Hospital— just a minute, I remember someone who used to work at Mass General. I'm going to contact him and also see if we can find some connections. It shouldn't be difficult. You have health insurance, don't you?"

"I just got it, but I'm not sure if they will accept it. I'm covered by the Massachusetts universal care."

"By law they have to admit you first before they check if you're covered or not, especially in Massachusetts. Let me call around— I'll get back to you very soon."

Tian was moved by Yabin's readiness to help. He was unfailingly resourceful and seemed to have infinite connections. True, he had shortcomings, but he was like his guardian angel—whenever Tian ran into a quagmire or dead end, he would stretch out his hand to pull him out.

Funi had also begun to cough. She didn't need to hold a foam cup like Tian, but still from time to time a flush would rise to her face. He urged her to have a checkup right away. To his surprise, she said with a grin, "I don't care. If I have lung cancer too, let's die together. I'll be happy to die with you. We can take a bottle of sleeping pills together."

Astounded, he didn't know what to say, though he was touched to the brink of tears. Again he urged her to go see her doctor.

She went to a community clinic the next day. The results of the checkup were all normal, her lungs clear and her X-ray unremarkable. Her cough must be due to a nasty cold. When she told him the good news, somehow a peculiar sadness gripped his heart. This rush of emotion bewildered him, and it was something he had never experienced before. He realized he wished she'd had lung cancer so that she could have accompanied him all the way to the other world. Such a realization disturbed him. He wondered whether this was love, but couldn't answer the question. He knew he was deeply attached to Funi. For having such a woman in his life, he felt grateful. By contrast, his ex-wife still hadn't contacted him yet. He gathered that their relationship, the former passion and love, had evaporated altogether. "Oh love, everlasting love, / I shall follow you to the end of the world!" Those lines from a song echoed in his mind. He used to belt them out with so much gusto and conviction, but now they sounded silly and mawkish. So often love could be changed by circumstances.

He congratulated Funi on the excellent results of her checkup. Then he went out to walk in Merrymount Park to batter down the confusing emotion that kept surging in him.

Yabin called and told him to contact Dr. Rabb at Mass General without delay. Following the phone call, Yabin sent Tian his email exchanges with a friend of his, who was in a fishing group and told the other anglers about Tian's case. One of them happened to be a doctor, who in turn reached out to the medical professionals in his network. He described Tian as a famous singer and begged someone to take a look at him and see if his cancer could be treated. That was how Dr. Rabb got involved. He replied that he'd be happy to see Tian and take charge of his treatment.

Tian looked up Dr. Rabb and found he was also a professor at Harvard Medical School, an expert in thoracic cancer. He called his nurse Samantha on Friday morning and made an appointment for Monday afternoon. Meanwhile Samantha would have his file transferred from Quincy Medical Center to Mass General. Tian was impressed by the prompt response. Back in Beijing, he had known that even some high-ranking officials stood in the hallways of hospitals waiting to hand doctors envelopes stuffed with cash so that their family members could be seen. The officials themselves could receive special medical care in designated hospitals, but their families could not, so sometimes they had to resort to bribes. Funi said to Tian, "If you were in China, you'd have to spend tens of thousands of yuan, and even then you might not be able to have access to such an expert doctor."

Tingting accompanied him to Mass General on Monday afternoon. They were led into an exam room, which was almost identical to those in the Quincy hospital. A nurse with a triangular face came in to check his vitals. Except for a low oxygen level, his signs were normal. A few minutes after she left, Dr. Rabb and Samantha stepped in, both wearing white coats that already showed the wear of the day. Rabb was tall and bone-thin, with deep-set eyes and an urbane air. His handshake was rather limp in spite of his large physique. He sat down on a chair and crossed one leg over the other. Samantha stood with her back against the wall, holding a clipboard and a pen. Dr. Rabb said to Tian with a smile, "I reviewed your file and can see how serious your case is. But don't be scared. I will be seeing you for some years to come. This is our beginning."

Those words put Tian at ease instantly. He realized he might still have some years to live, not just "six or seven weeks," as Dr. Hartley had said. His eyes suddenly went hot and misted over. He turned his face aside for a moment, then said, "Thank you, Dr. Rabb! What you said means a lot to me."

After listening to his back and chest and palpating his abdomen, the doctor told him, "We are going to do a biopsy to see what type of lung cancer you have, and you'll also have a PET scan and an MRI that will show whether there is cancer elsewhere in your body or in your brain. Usually when lung cancer disseminates, it goes to the brain first. Samantha can help you set up appointments with the lab and the radiology department. You should have the biopsy and the scans as soon as possible."

"At this stage, how serious do you think my cancer is?" Tian asked, aware that his question might be pointless.

"Basically there are two types of lung cancer, the large-cell cancer and the small-cell cancer. For large-cell lung cancer we can operate, and the recovery rate is much higher than the small-cell."

"Can you see what type I might have?"

"You don't smoke and have kept a healthy lifestyle. You might have large-cell lung cancer, but we can't tell for sure until we have the results of the biopsy. Let's not worry about that yet. We should go ahead and complete the biopsy and the scans first."

His meeting with Dr. Rabb made him feel much better. He was no longer hopeless or worried about his affairs. In the hospital he ran into two lung cancer patients, both Asian immigrants: One was a Vietnamese woman in her seventies who had been under

Dr. Rabb's care for thirteen years, and the other a middle-aged man from Shanghai who had been with Mr. Rabb for nearly fifteen years. They were both there accompanied by their family members for routine checkups. These encounters made a world of difference to Tian. He realized that if kept under control, lung cancer could become a chronic illness. Compared to them, he was younger and in better health and should be able to live for some years. He ought to take heart.

45

T HE BIOPSY WAS AN EASY PROCEDURE, though after the anes-
thetic wore off, the pain of the incision between his ribs set
in. It made his coughing more painful. The PET scan wasn't hard
either, but the MRI turned out to be very difficult. He was supposed
to lie on his back with his head inside the scanning tube, under the
camera system, and remain motionless for ten minutes. Given his
nonstop coughing, he didn't see how he could do it.

After he handed his wristwatch and pen to Tingting, he was led
into the waiting area outside the MRI suite. While he was there, a
wizened old nurse said to him, "You might not be able to do this.
The way you cough and gag will make it hard for you to keep still
and could disrupt the procedure."

"I'll do my best," he told her.

"Good luck, then."

After he lay down on the bed, the MRI tech, a young, chubby
woman with a squarish face, made sure that his head was resting in
the groove at the end of the bed. She threw a blanket over him and
placed a blue rubber ball on his chest. "Try not to move," she said.
"If you really can't go on, squeeze the ball to let me know."

"If we stop, does that mean we'll have to start over?"

"Yep, and it's best to get it done on the first try. I'm gonna make
this shorter for you, only five minutes. Just do your best not to
move."

He nodded and closed his eyes, trying to relax in spite of the
whirring roar of the machine. Time and again his chest contracted

and pushed him to the verge of coughing, but he clenched his jaws and suppressed the urge. The harder he attempted to remain still, the more excruciating the urge became. Soon his esophagus was filled with phlegm, which he had no choice but to swallow. Still, the pressure to cough grew stronger by the second. It made him dizzy and short of breath. His mind raced: "You have to do this, have to make it!" He knew there was no other way to find out whether his cancer had metastasized to his brain. Every cell in him seemed to be quivering as he marshaled every ounce of his energy to keep still. Mucus was seeping out of the corners of his mouth and leaking from his nostrils.

Finally the machine stopped. "Bravo!" the technician cried.

He struggled to sit up and motioned for his foam cup. The instant he had it he broke out coughing convulsively and spitting out mouthfuls of mucus. What a relief! She handed him a tissue and he wiped his face.

The old nurse saw him step out of the MRI suite. She beamed with amazement and congratulated him; her round cheeks, which once must have been apple-shaped and -hued, were like a pair of dried potatoes.

In the days that followed, his cough became more hacking. It continued so violently that another scan showed that two of his ribs had cracked. This made even his breathing painful. Then, during a new appointment, a nurse found that his lungs' oxygen level was very low. This explained why he was coughing without cease—his lungs struggled hard, often in vain, to inhale oxygen, but his bigger tumor was squeezing his windpipe so much that not enough air could pass through. After getting him a small oxygen cylinder on wheels, Samantha told him that a company would deliver to him an oxygen machine that could help him breathe more efficiently. "Please wait at home for the delivery this evening," she said.

Around seven p.m., a yellow van pulled up in front of his building and two men hopped out. They brought in a bulky oxygen concentrator and a pair of steel cans, each about one and a half feet long, like a small drum. One of the men showed Funi how to operate the machine, how to connect the thin plastic line to the outlet and how to fill the can with oxygen so that it could be brought along when Tian went out. Within the apartment, he didn't need to carry a can and could simply wear the nasal cannula in order to breathe with ease. His oxygen generator rumbled as it worked, so Funi put it in the bathroom and let the plastic line go under the doors into his room. At night, with the machine on, he could breathe properly, though it was still hard for him to fall asleep. Funi still slept on the sofa on the nights when Tingting couldn't come. He urged Funi to sleep in her own bed so that she could get enough rest for work the next day, but she wouldn't, saying the noise didn't bother her and she must make sure he'd get help when he needed it. He could see that she was tired and thinner than she'd been before.

Funi had the afternoon off and accompanied Tian to the hospital to meet with a surgeon, Dr. Moorcraft. Dr. Rabb was there too and told him that since he and Dr. Moorcraft wanted to begin treatment as soon as possible, they needed to make sure Tian understood what it would entail. The surgeon was an older man, in his early sixties, with a domed forehead and curled sideburns and sparkling eyes. Although the biopsy results hadn't come in yet, Dr. Rabb thought Tian was likely to have large-cell lung cancer, for which surgery would be the most effective treatment. Dr. Moorcraft even said that such procedures had cured many of his lung cancer patients. Tian was pleased to hear this, knowing that small-cell lung cancer would not be operated on in America. In China, hospitals cut lung cancer patients irrespective of whether their cancer was large-cell or small-cell. Doctors there took advantage of their patients' desperate families, who were willing to spend their savings just to prolong their loved ones' lives.

The meeting was quite encouraging and even pleasant. Everything was moving rapidly, as though all the lights were turning green for him. He could see that they treated every patient the same way—all the medical personnel showed a deep respect for life. In spite of the uncertain outcome of his prospective treatment, Tian felt grateful and full of hope.

Dr. Rabb called the next afternoon, speaking in a guarded voice. He said he had both good news and bad news for him. He told Tian, "The MRI and the PET scan show your cancer has not spread, and we haven't found anything abnormal in your brain and other organs. But the biopsy results just came out and indicate you have small-cell lung cancer. This is something we didn't expect." He paused, as if to give him time to let the news sink in. Then he said, "I'm sorry about this."

"So there won't be an operation anymore?" Tian asked.

"No, but we should start treatment immediately. The sooner, the better."

Tian sensed some urgency in his voice and said, "I'm available anytime."

"In that case, I would recommend chemotherapy and radiation."

"I accept your recommendation."

A long pause ensued. The doctor seemed amazed by his prompt answer. Having met some of Dr. Rabb's patients, Tian was positive he was in the best hands and saw no need to hesitate. Then Dr. Rabb asked, "Are you sure?"

"Yes, I am."

"Then I'm going to ask Samantha to make an appointment with you, and I will see you soon so that we can discuss the details. In short, we must start the treatment without further delay."

Finally he heard from Shuna. She emailed, saying it would have been too emotional for them to talk about his condition on the phone, so she was writing instead. She urged him to adopt the conservative treatment, so as to minimize his suffering. "I am so sorry to hear about your lung cancer, Tian," she wrote. "I shouldn't have let you go to America alone in the first place. I failed to be a good wife to you." In spite of her consoling words, he resented her attitude—she was talking as though his life were about to end.

He wrote back to inform her that they—Tingting, Funi, Jawei, and he—had decided to put up a fight. "Miracles can happen," he concluded. "Do pray for me if you can."

He thought about defending his immigration but was unsure what he would even say. He might not be able to hold back his anger. Yet Shuna might be right from her perspective: Had he remained in China, his life might have differed greatly. But who could predict when and where cancer would strike?

He knew Tingting had quarreled with her mother. The girl was adamant that Shuna come to Boston and spend some time with him, to see him off on the last leg of his life journey. Her mother refused, saying she had classes to teach. Tingting blew up and shouted at her, "My dad was once your husband. Don't you have any feelings left for him?"

Tingting told him that Shuna hadn't answered her question and had instead hung up. "She's heartless!" she said.

"Don't talk about your mother like that," he warned her.

From time to time Jawei would call Tian or come to see him in person. The young man was dead set against the conservative treatment and actively helped him combat cancer. He did research online to find alternative remedies. He knew a lot about lung cancer because his aunt and cousin had both died of this disease, mainly due to the air pollution, he believed. In spite of his support for the treatment recommended by Dr. Rabb, Jawei said it wouldn't be easy to go through all the chemo sessions. His cousin hadn't survived the therapy and died during the third session because of her low white blood cell count. Jawei suggested to Tian two herbal supplements, which he'd found after several nights of research. One was turmeric, a widely used remedy for cancer. He told Tian, "A top cancer hospital in Houston has been giving this supplement to its patients for years now. It has proved very effective."

As for the other supplement, IP-6, Jawei said, "It's made from rice bran and has no side effects at all. According to the clinical statistics, patients who took it during chemotherapy ended up with white blood cell counts even higher than before they had started the treatment. Uncle Yao, from now on, you must take IP-6 every day."

"I will," Tian said. "I'm going to order turmeric and IP-6 tonight."

Jawei also told him that the drugs used in chemotherapy hadn't changed for half a century, but the methods of administering them had improved, especially in America. In other words, Tian's chemotherapy was conventional, but its effectiveness depended on the details. Tian was impressed by his knowledge of cancer. Jawei said he might study it eventually if he ended up doing graduate work in biochemistry. He'd taken two premed courses and enjoyed them a lot. He'd found medicine more interesting than economics. Tian told his daughter privately that he was very pleased with Jawei. He hoped that their relationship would develop steadily.

46

F UNI ALSO HAD A SUGGESTION about how to approach chemotherapy. One of her coworkers had received the same treatment
for bladder cancer. She told Tian, "The man said he was shaking
nonstop with chills because of the drugs they pumped into his
bloodstream. You should take some ginger powder before going to
chemo."

That was what he'd do, he agreed. Funi went with him to Mass
General for his next appointment. Somebody had to carry the oxygen can for him; otherwise he wouldn't be able to move about.

They met with Samantha and discussed the plan for the chemotherapy, which Dr. Rabb believed should begin within a week. The
schedule for the infusions was frightening. Tian looked through
the dates of the treatment, spread over a period of more than three
months. There were four sessions, each consisting of three daily
infusions of the drugs. After each session was a three-week hiatus
for his white blood cell count to recover. Once it resurged above
1,500, the chemo would resume. Samantha blinked her large hazel
eyes and said in a soothing voice, "Bear in mind that between the
second and the third sessions we'll start your chest radiation. That
may be the toughest period of your treatment. We'll work on the
schedule for that when we come to it."

She also prescribed two kinds of laxatives that he could get over
the counter, since one immediate side effect of the chemo was constipation. There'd be hair loss too, but he mustn't be scared by it,
because his hair would come back. "As a matter of fact, your hair

might grow back better than before," Samantha said. A smile, a touch studied, emerged on her pale face, sprinkled with a smattering of freckles. Oddly enough, he felt rather peaceful in her presence, as he came to be aware that there was still kindness and even beauty in the world. Without her freckles, he'd say Samantha, willowy and sturdy, could have been a beautiful Irish blonde. He reminded himself that no matter how hard and daunting, he'd have to make it through the chemo sessions—life was good and worth struggling for.

At the end of the meeting, Samantha gave him a tip. "Don't eat any of your favorite foods when you come for the infusion, because afterward you'll hate that food. Chemotherapy can ruin your appetite and your taste buds."

On the train back to Quincy, Funi said that the medical personnel at Mass General's Cancer Center, especially the nurses, were so kind that it must be hard for them to keep their composure up for their entire shift. With his head resting against her shoulder, he echoed, "They're very different from doctors and nurses in China, aren't they?"

"Forget about China. Some doctors there are like robbers. A coworker of mine in Dongguan once hurt her foot and went to the hospital to get treated. They sewed up her toe but charged her more than three thousand yuan. She didn't have that kind of cash in her bank account and couldn't pay. She said this was blackmail and argued with them. They wouldn't let her go without settling the bill. Then the doctor, who had just treated her, came and cut the stitches and left her wound open. Later she had to sew up the gash with cotton thread by herself. She was limping for months afterward because of it."

He sighed. "Common people there are just treated like insects."

"I wish I will become a doctor if I'm born again," she said earnestly.

In spite of Funi's rustic looks, she was perceptive and literate, mostly self-taught by reading newspapers and magazines in both Chinese and English. She could even converse with Americans in English now.

She and Tingting had been getting along well since he had become ill. They shared the duty of accompanying him to the chemo infusions, filling in for each other whenever one of them was not available. He was glad that his daughter stopped grouching about Funi, without whose help he could hardly function now.

Meanwhile, he was living with the constant, ferocious pain of cancer, a hundred times more intense than regular pain. Yet he tried not to take too many of the oxycodone pills that Dr. Rabb had prescribed, afraid of becoming addicted. In his case they weren't very effective anyway. He longed to get through the treatment as soon as possible, thinking he would either survive it or get killed by it. He often went online to read the literature about lung cancer. An article on lung cancer victims' mortality stated that one-third of patients died of fright, another third of the severe treatments, and only the final third were actually killed by the disease itself. He reminded himself that he mustn't be frightened. He did some soul-searching too. He was not afraid of death even though he was not yet forty-five. He was sure his music would survive him by a long time. What's more, he had managed to live for six and a half years as a free man, independent of an oppressive political system. Yet there was an acute feeling of an unfulfilled artistic life. At his age he ought to have had a long career ahead—he had aspired to develop his style into full maturity, unique and even majestic.

The next Tuesday, before setting out for his first chemotherapy session, he drank a mug of ginger powder in boiled water. With his daughter he rode the subway to the hospital. The infusion room was on the eighth floor, lovely and sunny, its windows overlooking the Charles and offering a view of the city, dappled with red and orange leaves. As the drugs, cisplatin mixed with etoposide, flowed through the IV into his forearm, he felt less agitated than he'd anticipated. The Zofran tablets he had taken seemed to be helping. He was cold, shaking with chills from time to time, but there were small heat packs available that could keep individual parts of his body warm. The disposable plastic packs resembled tiny rubber hot-water bottles, and they were activated by shaking. When they get cold, they could be reshaken to heat them up again. Tingting put them under his arms and on his chest and stomach, all under a thick preheated blanket.

During the three-hour infusion, the nurse came several times to check on him and the other patients. There were eight chemo recipients in the room that day, each in an easy chair, and some, like himself, wearing oxygen cannulas. The black man next to him, named David, had prostate cancer; he was accompanied by his son, a bespectacled graduate student studying foreign affairs at Tufts. All the patients were quiet in the infusion room except for David. He had a short, graying beard, was quite extroverted, and chatted with others whenever he could. He called the nurses "sweetie" and asked for a soft drink whenever the service cart came. Tian was amazed by his buoyancy and asked him why he didn't seem stressed. David said, "If you're a good man, you shouldn't fear death." Tian pressed him, "Why? Can you elaborate?" David went on to explain, "I'm a Christian. If God wants me back, I'll return to him. If he wants me to stay here, I will continue to live. Everything is in God's hands."

Tian wanted to ask why he was so sure he was a good man, but he checked himself. Nonetheless, David's words made Tian pensive, and he wished he too were a Christian who believed he was going to a better place when he left this world. Between chatting with David and with Tingting, the time passed quickly. Down the hallway there was a small lounge where free coffee, tea, fruit, and snacks were provided for the patients and their companions. There was a sign in the coffee area that thanked the donors who'd funded the space, a couple who had both died of cancer a decade before.

Around lunchtime, a woman wearing a burgundy apron came with a cart loaded with drinks, chips, fruits, and a variety of sandwiches: cheese, beef, chicken, turkey, tuna. Tian couldn't take any cold soft drinks, feeling a little nauseated, so he got a hot tea from the woman. He found out she was a volunteer. She said she had been treated here for breast cancer, and that after she had recovered and after her daughter had gone off to boarding school, she decided to donate her time at the hospital helping other patients. She also said that most of the foods and drinks and fruits were bought with the funds donated by former cancer patients. Tian was deeply impressed by how good deeds could perpetuate themselves. For lunch he could eat only a chicken sandwich since he didn't like cheese, or tuna, or even turkey. Tingting was hungry and had a vegetable soup and a beef sandwich from the food cart.

The infusion went smoothly overall. He was grateful that his daughter had kept him company.

The following two infusions also proceeded without a hitch. So the first session of chemotherapy concluded successfully—he now had a three-week break before the next one. A few days later his hair began falling out. When he woke up in the morning, he was horrified to find his pillow littered with wads of hair and his sheets with tiny flakes of skin. Even his pubic hair and some of his eyebrow hair were falling out too. Within two days he could see his scalp in the mirror. It was scattered with large pimples and sores, some of which were ruptured and dripping with pus. The ulcerous spots seemed to be exit sites of sorts for the cancerous stuff to leave his body. In Chinese medicine, this process is called "poison excretion," a positive sign despite the nasty appearance. So he wasn't terribly bothered by the dripping sores on his head.

Miraculously, soon after his first chemo session he began to breathe with less difficulty. He could move around without wearing the cannula and could sleep somewhat peacefully at night. Funi stopped camping out on the sofa. Tian no longer coughed as much as he had before and was able to drop the foam cup too. Everybody was impressed by the rapid improvement—a new scan showed the tumors had shrunk by more than eighty percent. Even Mrs. Kuo at the herbal pharmacy, where he'd still go to pick up some herbs, said she must give credit to Western medicine. "There's no way Chinese medicine could treat cancer with such quick results," she said.

Though also pleased about the outcome, he had read enough about small-cell lung cancer to be wary of optimism. In general, chemotherapy works more effectively on small-cell lung cancer, but in the long run the disease can resurge and even become drug-resistant. He knew his cancer was among the most vicious and he couldn't afford to be too confident.

47

T IAN'S WHITE BLOOD CELL COUNT was a little low, but it was still high enough for the infusion to continue, so the second session of chemo began. It went well on the whole, though by the end of it he was bald altogether, having lost even his eyebrows, and became so frail that he wobbled a little when he walked. When he shuffled around indoors, instinctively he'd reach out for something to support himself. In spite of the positive effect of the chemotherapy, he had more pain now in his chest and in his back. Sometimes his waist felt like it was broken, probably due to the burden on his kidneys, forced to excrete the poisonous drugs pumped into his bloodstream. The drugs were designed to kill the cancerous cells, but they also destroyed a lot of good cells. The damage to his organs must have been systemic.

Because of his low white blood cell count, his third session of chemo was postponed for another week. Near the end of the break, the radiotherapy began. He was to receive twenty chest radiations, twice every weekday. This was the toughest part of his treatment, in which the infusion and the radiation overlapped. To prepare for the latter, he was given several drugs to mitigate the pain in his esophagus so that he could swallow food afterward. Five target spots for the rays were tattooed onto his chest. The radiations were grueling, one at seven a.m. and the other at three p.m. Everybody was afraid he might not be able to take the infusion, scheduled for nine-thirty in the morning. There would be a period of three hours between the chemo and the second radiation, but it would be impossible for him to return home and then come back. The hospital offered free lodging, but only to the patients coming from more than thirty-five miles away, so he lived too close to qualify. A hotel room wouldn't be worth the expense, since he'd be able to use it for only a few hours, during the breaks between treatments. Fortunately a nurse allowed him to lie down in a curtained area where patients on gurneys waited for examinations or treatment. The nurses were like angels, wearing white coats in place of scrubs, and they were always kind and cheerful. One of them, Beverly, petite and with a son already in college, told Tian that she worked long shifts, twelve hours at a time, but she came only three days a week so that she could keep her focus. He could tell how exacting and fatiguing their job was, but they were attentive and composed at all times. They called every patient by the first name. More heartening, Beverly encouraged Tian to be upbeat despite his condition. She said to him, "Unlike most patients and in spite of your small-cell lung cancer, you're basically a healthy man. All your vitals were normal, some perfect. You should be able to recover fully."

He thanked her for those timely words, which meant the world to him and gave him more confidence.

Yet after the second infusion of the third session, he had to declare a self-imposed break. He was scheduled to have the infusion and two radiations on Friday, but he was sure that his life would be at risk if he proceeded according to plan. So he arrived at the hospital and told his doctors he was refusing to go through with the procedures that day. He would come back for them on Monday—the Cancer Center was closed on the weekend, and he would need to take those two days to recover. Dr. Rabb and Samantha and Dr. Kesuma, the woman in charge of the radiology department, pressed him to continue as planned, but he was adamant. He told them, "Look, I have been a good patient and have never complained about the pain and the fatigue. I feel it in my bones that if I have the infusion and radiations today, it might kill me. My body tells me that. Just give me two days' rest. I promise to come back on Monday and will be cooperative again."

No one could dissuade him. His daughter was mad at his stubbornness, saying he might ruin the treatment if he disrupted the schedule, yet she had no option but to yield to his resolve. Dr. Kesuma said to him, "You're like my dad. He's so strong-willed that once he decides to do something, nobody can make him change his mind." Her bony face crinkled as she grimaced. She was a second-generation Malaysian immigrant and had grown up on the West Coast.

But, as it turned out, the weekend wasn't restful for him at all, because he came across the news of his lung cancer online. *The Global Post* reported that Yao Tian was suffering stage-four lung cancer, struggling between life and death. The article implied that his days were numbered, and even expressed pity because his singing career had "ended so prematurely." Tian was outraged by the article, which was using his condition as an illustration of the heavy price that people had to pay if they set themselves against the powers that be, if they deserted their motherland, if they chased the phantom of freedom in total earnest. It summed up his case this way: "Yao Tian lost his stage, then his audience and prestige, and now is about to lose his life. His career is over and he has reduced himself to nothing. We can't help but feel sad for Yao Tian, the wonderful singer, who once enjoyed an illustrious career but is now falling into total silence."

In spite of the stress triggered by the article, he managed to regain his composure and went on to complete the third chemo session and the daily radiotherapy the following week. When the twenty radiations were finally done, he felt a huge relief—from now on he could focus on the final session of chemotherapy. The last three infusions took place twenty days later, and he managed to get through them without incident. But physically he had reached his limit—he was sure that one more infusion would have killed him. He felt as if all the destructive power of the drugs had become concentrated on his heart, which was so painful that he could hardly lift his arms or raise his voice. Fortunately Funi knew how to do cupping and cupped his chest and back extensively, which reduced his pain somewhat.

Then serious side effects began to set in—loss of appetite, bone-deep fatigue, severe constipation, leaking bladder, palpitations, dizzy spells, leg cramps, sore throat. Jawei told Tian to eat a piece of salted vegetable whenever he had a leg cramp—the sodium and potassium might help restore the balance in his body. He'd take a bit of pickled mustard green or turnip, which could stop the pain in his calves for a time. Occasionally, when he coughed hard, he wet his pants, which made him feel ridiculous and wretched. Funi would have him change, then wash his pajamas together with other dirty clothes, including her own. She gave him massages and continued the cupping. She did everything she could for him. Ever since he'd been diagnosed, they hadn't slept together. At most they kissed a little. He was grateful that she wasn't demanding and was always considerate. Whenever he could, he would cook dinner for both of them—she tried to stop him, but he felt compelled to do something to ease her burden. These days she never ate out and would always hurry home after work.

A new scan showed that his tumors had shrunken almost to scars. Dr. Rabb was thrilled. Because of the excellent outcome of the treatment, he recommended more radiotherapy. He explained to Tian, "We give brain radiation only to those patients who have responded to chemotherapy successfully. The lung cancer, if it spreads, will go to the brain first, so in your case the brain radiation will be a proactive treatment. I think you should take it."

"Okay, I will do that."

Dr. Rabb added, "Brain radiation might have side effects, like compromising your hearing and vision for a period of time. They might also bring on Alzheimer's. I'll prescribe a drug to prevent that."

"Okay, how many radiations will I have?"

"Ten."

Tian was relieved to hear that and agreed to proceed. This treatment was relatively easy, only once a day, and no tattooing required. A nurse covered his face with a metal mask full of tiny holes and with openings for his mouth and eyes; the gear helped prevent his head from moving under the machine. The procedure was brief, just a few minutes, and Tian hardly felt anything during the treatment.

In every sense, his cancer treatment was successful and the doctors and nurses were all happy about the results. Yet he couldn't
bring himself to be too optimistic. He knew that the survival rate—
those who were still living five years after the treatment—was less
than four percent among stage-three small-cell lung cancer patients.
It would be a miracle if he stayed alive.

For weeks he'd been depressed. His mind seemed scattered, especially when he felt physically feeble and unable to function normally. Sometimes, when he lay down, the whole bed would revolve
slowly, as if he were on a giant lily pad that wavered and trembled. His vision grew disordered too. At times when he was reading, an entire page would go blank or have only one or two big
misshapen words on it—all the other words disappeared. When
he walked around indoors, a wall would move toward him like a
colossal distorting mirror, full of bumps and bizarre patterns, or
a door would change shape, its frame twisted. Terrified, he called
Samantha to report his symptoms, but she said they often occurred
among brain radiation recipients. She assured him that gradually
the symptoms would go away, but he must keep taking Memantine,
the drug Dr. Rabb had prescribed to prevent Alzheimer's—one tablet a day for six months. Whenever a new symptom appeared he
felt crushed, fearing permanent damage. Yet amazingly, with the
help of Funi and Tingting, he managed to reduce or eliminate the
fearsome symptoms one after another.

These days he often remembered Mr. Bao, who had been treated
for liver cancer at Mass General. The two of them had met twice at
the Cancer Center while waiting for their appointments with supporting professionals—nutritionists, psychiatrists, social workers.
Mr. Bao said he had come from Beijing for the treatment and was
paying for it out of pocket. Despite the horrendous cost, he was
in high spirits and made lively conversation with Tian. He said
he felt lucky just to be able to get treated here. Back in China, his
liver cancer had been declared terminal. Fortunately his son was a
postdoctoral at MIT, and this enabled Mr. Bao to come to Boston.

He told Tian he felt much better now and that he was jogging two or three miles along the Charles every day. "I should have come earlier," he said. "My son wanted me to retire and then come to Boston. I couldn't leave my office back in Beijing, but my wife forced me to quit and come and live with our son's family."

"Didn't you have better medical care back home?" Tian asked Mr. Bao, who he suspected must have been a senior official.

"Not really," he said. "The air is bad there and the water is polluted. There're so many additives in the foods. The environment is so ruined that the whole country has been reduced to an immense junkyard."

Tian felt that his analogy might be an exaggeration, but he liked Mr. Bao's cheerfulness. He was in his mid-sixties but still looked energetic and vigorous, wearing jeans and a plaid blazer with elbow patches. Tian enjoyed his company so much that he proposed that they exchange phone numbers. Mr. Bao knew his work, having seen him on TV several times. They agreed to stay in touch.

Later Tian mentioned the man, Bao Peng, to Yabin. His friend recognized the name at once. "My goodness, that man has a very high rank, the same as a minister's," Yabin said. "He was in charge of China's energy, an engineer by profession originally."

The more Tian came to learn about Mr. Bao, the more eager he was to get in touch with him again.

48

M R. BAO SOUNDED DELIGHTED on the phone and invited Tian to lunch. He gave him his address, which was in Cambridge, just a few steps from the Central Square subway station. Tian agreed to come and see him—it would be good to walk and get some light exercise, and he ought to go out from time to time to keep from becoming too depressed. As the train passed over the Charles, the water glittered in the morning sunshine. Numerous small boats were moored in the river, some narrow sails bellying out in the spring breeze. Through them a yellow duck boat, half full of tourists, was crawling west. Five or six seagulls were bobbing in midair, their wings waving like sickles.

Mr. Bao and his wife were living with their son and daughter-in-law on the MIT campus. The apartment in the graduate student dorm wasn't spacious, but it was clean and bright. Mrs. Bao was much younger than Tian had expected, with high cheekbones and a slender figure. She looked to be in her mid-fifties with graying bangs, but she said she had retired and loved Boston and wouldn't mind living here for good, provided they had their own home. After pouring Tian a cup of Pu'er tea, which was more suitable for the wintertime, she sat down next to her husband, leaning against him, which amazed Tian. In the presence of a stranger, she didn't hesitate to show her affection for her husband, touching him time and again—they must love each other dearly. She said Mr. Bao had often mentioned him of late. Apparently she knew him as a singer too.

As they chatted, he noticed a couple of photographs on a shelf, in which Mr. Bao was posed with various dignitaries. Tian pointed at the one that showed him and President Obama in conversation, both in a suit and tie. "Is that you?" Tian asked.

"Yes, I used to represent China at energy conferences and negotiations with other countries," said Mr. Bao, whose face widened as he smiled.

There was also a photo in which he was shaking hands with Hilary Clinton, who was then secretary of state. Tian wondered how Mr. Bao felt about his situation now—his complete obscurity here—but he refrained from asking.

As planned, the two men went out for lunch at a diner on Massachusetts Avenue. Mr. Bao donned a felt porkpie hat, which covered his gray hair and made him appear younger and rather dashing. The chilly air smelled of auto exhaust and chemicals. Ever since going through chemotherapy, Tian's nose had become extraordinarily sharp and he could tell the quality of the air the instant he stepped into a new space. He guessed that from now on, it would be hard for him to live in a teeming city where he could smell significant pollution and would instinctively hold his breath. In the diner he ordered a spinach calzone and a bowl of clam chowder while Mr. Bao had fish and chips. Mr. Bao ate with relish and even licked the tartar sauce and ketchup off his fingers. Tian was amazed by his lusty appetite. Small wonder he was so energetic and jogged along the Charles a couple of miles every morning.

As Tian ate his chowder with oyster crackers, he asked the question that had been on his mind for a long time. He said, "Mr. Bao, you were once a high-ranking official and must have had a lot of privileges: special medical care, business-class flights, luxury housing, domestic staff, personal chauffeur and secretary. But now you live in a small apartment here and go to the hospital as a regular cancer patient like me. How can you keep the psychological balance, the equilibrium? Do you feel life has treated you fairly? In other words, don't you regret coming here?"

Mr. Bao smiled as if to himself, then said, "Indeed I used to have plenty of privileges, but they didn't make me happy. As an official in China, it's impossible to get by without taking bribes and kickbacks, because all your colleagues do that. If you were different, you would become their enemy, an obstacle on their path to wealth. They'd get rid of you sooner or later. Among wolves you have to behave and howl like a wolf regardless of your own feelings and sense of decency. What I hated most were meetings, especially those given by the top leaders. Sometimes we had to wear diapers to attend them because the speeches were long and people dared not leave their seats. Those meetings were sheer torture. Once in a while I forgot to put on a diaper and had to struggle so hard to hold my pee."

Tian laughed. A crumb from his calzone dropped onto the table.

Mr. Bao continued, "See my hair? It's gray, the true color I don't need to hide here. I used to be in trouble constantly because I didn't dye my hair raven black like my superiors and colleagues. Concealing the truth is the essence of the official culture there. To be honest, after I landed here, I felt that at long last I could live cleanly and decently as myself, so I have no regrets. Finally I can eat and sleep like a normal person."

His watery eyes fixed on Tian's face, he seemed moved by his own words. Tian could tell he spoke from his heart. But Tian went on, "How about your liver problem? Do you feel you have received better medical care here?"

"Absolutely. Believe me, given the opportunity, most high-ranking officials would come here for cancer treatment. If I had stayed any longer in China, I might be already dead."

"How long have you been here?"

"Fourteen months."

Now he realized why Mr. Bao so often used the word "fortunate" whenever he talked about his cancer treatment. So, like him, Tian ought to feel fortunate too. He confessed to the old man, "My uncle died of lung cancer twenty years ago in Shenyang. If I had had this disease in China, I might just have undergone the conservative treatment, which would have amounted to succumbing to the cancer."

"I know what you mean, Tian. I am of the same opinion." Mr. Bao put his hand on Tian's wrist and gave it a shake. "You're still young and will have a long life ahead. Don't you feel much better now?"

"I do."

"See, this is the difference. In China I never met a person with advanced lung cancer who had survived. To most people with internal cancer there, it's like a death sentence."

"That must be true," Tian agreed. "A friend of mine said the same thing: Lung cancer is a death sentence in China. His father was a general in the North Sea Fleet at Port Arthur and had lung cancer. When he put his old man in an ambulance so he could get treated in Beijing, he knew he'd never be able to bring him back."

"So we both ought to feel fortunate." Mr. Bao put a long french fry into his mouth, munching heartily.

Tian's meeting with Mr. Bao was mind-opening and reassuring, although he could see that the two of them were in different boats. Mr. Bao didn't have to struggle to get used to the conditions here— his livelihood was secured by his pension and perks, and likely also by his vast connections back in China. Like most officials, he must have accumulated a considerable amount of wealth over decades of taking bribes. He couldn't possibly feel the way Tian did—like a freshwater fish having to live in salt water while striving to grow into a euryhaline creature, eventually capable of swimming in both rivers and seas. What's more, Mr. Bao could always return to their native land, and that must give him a good deal of emotional security. The truth was that if Tian were not living in Massachusetts, he couldn't have had the universal healthcare that allowed him to be treated at a fine hospital. Mr. Bao and he were both fortunate, but in different ways.

Yet their meeting pacified Tian considerably. He felt much better and managed to suppress the question that had been tormenting him all along: whether his lung cancer had been caused by his frustrations and grief during his seven years here, or had it been hereditary and would have struck him no matter where he was. Now he could see there was no answer to such a conundrum. To appease himself, he repeated the American slang: "Shit happens." He began to think how to rebuild his life, however long it might be. Now every day unfolded like a gift for him.

Yet death was always on his mind—he even bought a plot for $850 in the cemetery owned by Funi's Buddhist temple. He loved that clean, tranquil spot on a hillside, shaded by large maples and firs and oaks. A clear creek flowed along its eastern edge. Funi said she'd like to be buried there too, perhaps together with him. Knowing where he would rest eased his mind considerably, helped him accept death as a natural scenario. Indeed, it was part of life.

Since he had been missing from the Divine Grace holiday tour, rumors had spread that he must have died. In early May, he was shocked to see his obituary in *The Global Post*. The notice said he had died of lung cancer and his funeral had been attended by just five or six people. "It's tragic that Yao Tian passed in total obscurity, notwithstanding his wide fame back in China. He was a lost soul and went astray from the broad road that most artists have chosen to travel. His is a negative example of willfulness and megalomania. Nonetheless, like many of his former fans, we mourn his passing."

He was outraged and cursed the author in his mind—Son of a turtle, damn your mother! For weeks his anger lingered, though his friends—Yabin, Tan Mai, and others—had written to the *Post* to condemn the misinformation. An editor of the newspaper had responded, stating: "Yao Tian is already dead as a singer, so the obituary is symbolic. We printed it to lament the loss of his melodic, heartwarming voice. We all wish him solace and peace."

It felt like a stab in the back, but it made him more determined to restart his singing career. Shaking with anger, he imagined storming back onstage with a vengeance. But try as he might, he could no longer sing through a complete song, his memory incoherent and the lyrics often garbled. Worse, his voice had lost most of its beauty and sheen, and he would crack trying to hit the high notes that he'd formerly been able to reach with ease. He no longer had the energy to project his voice. Often he broke down in tears, realizing he couldn't possibly sing as before. Perhaps intensive practice would help, but, given his condition, this seemed out of the question.

He hadn't worked now in seven months, and his savings were dwindling away. He had to make some money now, but how? He remembered the Irishman who often sang at the train station.

Maybe he could do that too? But he no longer had the memory or the voice needed for a decent performance. He had his guitar, which he often took out and strummed while humming aimlessly. He could improvise a line here or there to keep a song going. As long as the tune was coherent, he could make it work. This realization, plus some experimenting, gave him enough courage to perform to make a little money. Now you're going to become a true street artist, he told himself.

He wouldn't sing in the open air because his lungs were still weak and might not be able to take the gusty wind. He picked the train stations with roofed platforms, where the air was fresh but not windy. Quincy Center, with its fully sheltered platform and bustling crowds, seemed like the best spot. But when he got to the station, he saw the Irish busker leaning against a concrete column and singing happily, a small, brand-new hand truck and a music stand beside him. So Tian instead rode to JFK/UMass, where there was also a large flow of passengers and where the platform was roofed as well. He feared that Tingting might see him there, but he had no choice. Setting up in a spot not too far from the stairway, he adjusted his guitar and began to sing. He closed his eyes and let his voice wordlessly follow the chords he strummed out. People paused to listen or turned their heads in his direction. From time to time someone would come over and drop a dollar or two into the opened guitar case on the ground. In spite of his camouflaging shades and blue baseball cap, he felt that his face must be familiar to some of the Chinese students passing through; now and again one of them would pause to stare. They must be wondering if he was the singer Yao Tian. How could he have been reduced to a singing peddler here?

On the first day, for two and a half hours, he made fifty-six dollars, which pleased him. From then on, he continued to sing at various train stations. Some of the logistics were hard for him to manage. Above all, there was no restroom at most of the Red Line stations, and if he went out through the turnstiles to use a bathroom in a coffee shop or restaurant, he'd have to pay for the $2.50 entry fee again. So as long as he could, he would try to avoid drinking too much liquid once he got into the station and also to hold his pee as long as possible. This also meant he wouldn't perform longer than one and a half hours at a time. He had already developed a bladder problem from the chemotherapy, and was unable to hold his urine. One day, on his way back from the Quincy Center station to his apartment, he needed to pee so badly that he couldn't walk anymore, so he sat on a wrought-iron bench on the sidewalk for a few moments to ease his bladder, then continued to trudge home. Still, he couldn't hold it all the way and wet his pants when he got home. Seeing his wretched state, he couldn't suppress his sobbing. Luckily, Funi was not in and he could change alone. From that day on, he'd wear a diaper and carry a plastic bottle in his bag when he went out to sing. He'd also drink some liquid at work, having to stay hydrated. If he had to pee, he'd find a secluded spot and pee into the bottle. In spite of the difficulties, he could pick up some cash steadily, though he was anxious, unsure how long he could go on like this.

Then one late afternoon, as he was singing at Quincy Center station, Funi stepped out of the train, wearing duck boots, and began heading toward the escalator. At the sight of him scatting with abandon, she rushed up and embraced him and burst into tears.

"You mustn't do this!" she said and groaned. "I won't let you! Please don't debase yourself this way!"

People turned to look at them. He tried to smile but felt his face tighten. He managed to say to Funi, "It's all right. A singer must sing to make a dollar. Our profession has been like this since ancient times, and there's no shame in honest work."

"I won't let you, I won't let you!"

She pulled him along to the escalator so they could go home together. She kept wiping her tearstained face all the way.

That night she spoke with Tingting heatedly on the phone. From time to time he caught a phrase or two that Funi let out. He heard her repeat, "We must never let this happen again!"

49

Tingting stayed in Boston during the summer. She and Jawei both found part-time jobs on campus, he as a lab assistant and she as an intern at her school's gallery. Jawei often came to see Tian, and they would talk a lot about life, politics, sports. The young man enjoyed American football, which Tian somehow could never appreciate, but they both loved basketball and soccer. They also talked about Jawei's plans for the future. He liked biotech and wanted to do graduate work in it, but he wasn't sure whether to study in China or in the States. He preferred the American social environment and the political transparency, but, like Tingting, he was still attached to their native land. He hoped he could do something for its development. Tian was pleased to know he had some kind of vision beyond his own career. Young people of their generation, who mostly grew up as only children, tended to be self-centered, preoccupied with personal gain and growth. Jawei seemed to be an exception. To put Tian at ease, he assured him, "I'll go wherever Tingting goes."

Tian was delighted to hear that. Deep down he hoped they would stay in America after college. Tingting and Jawei were young and should be able to put down roots and build a bright future in America. Also, their settling down here would feel like an extension of his own immigrant life and would also demonstrate his good sense to his ex-wife.

One evening in mid-August, his daughter came and handed him a check for twenty-five thousand dollars. "This is from my mother," she told him.

"What for?"

"She wants you to have it. She said you needed it. It's your money now."

"I've never thought she could be generous," he said with some bitterness.

"Come on, now, Dad. She doesn't mean this as a gift. She said this money belonged to you because you owned a part of our old apartment too. She also said she had been spending the money she got from the sale for my tuition. Actually there isn't much left."

That couldn't be true, because Tingting had become an in-state student the year before, since her father was a U.S. citizen and Massachusetts resident—her tuition was now only a third of an international student's. But he didn't say anything about this; her mother had a lot of cash now, he was sure.

Later he talked to Funi about what to do with the money from Shuna. Funi was adamantly opposed to his singing in the train stations again. She said, "Imagine if someone snaps a photo of you singing at a train station and puts it online. The official media would take advantage of your suffering again, and that would bring about a media feeding frenzy. I won't be able to bear the humiliation for you."

"It wouldn't bother me that much."

"But it'll hurt me like hell."

"Well, then I won't do it anymore."

"You know what I like most about you, Tian?"

"What?" He was puzzled.

"Even though you're famous, you are down-to-earth. You talk straight and walk straight too. You always try to make an honest living."

"What flattery!" He laughed, and so did she.

They decided to start a small singing school. He was sure he could teach well, now that he didn't travel to perform anymore and would become a full-time teacher. As long as he could make enough to live on, he'd be satisfied.

He rented an office suite at the back of a shopping center; it was small, with a low ceiling, but it was quiet and secluded enough for students to sing without disturbing others. At a church sale he bought a used black Steinway and had it shipped to his office. Then he hired a tuner to have the keys and strings adjusted. In total, he spent $1,180. He was excited about the piano, never having dreamed of owning a baby grand. Soon after he put out an ad in two community newspapers, he began to take students. Most of them were children whose parents believed they had an exceptional voice. A few also came to enroll thanks to his former name. They had listened to his albums and watched him on YouTube and were eager to study with him. The work wasn't hard, and in spite of his frailness he could manage. He only hoped that the Chinese officials would leave him alone and not sabotage his business again.

Meanwhile his health had been improving. His hair had grown back, darker but thinner than before. Despite the harrowing side effects of the chemo and the radiation, he noticed that his old problems, such as blisters on his fingers and his sore shoulders and neck, were gone. The chemotherapy must incidentally have cured them, though it had also damaged his immune system. These days he'd take a long walk every afternoon. On weekends, Funi would join him, strolling on Wollaston Beach to see the splendid sunset and share a basket of seafood at a clam shack near the seaside. He had to eat as much as possible to maintain his weight—he needed the body mass to resist the cancer.

One evening in the fall, Funi said to him, "Have you heard that they might cancel the universal healthcare?"

"Who are 'they'?" he asked.

"Some politicians have been talking about it. I heard them on the radio. One of them said that Obamacare was insane, calling it a socialist scam. He said it must be revoked and replaced with something more reasonable and more affordable."

He was alarmed. If there were major changes in the universal care, he might be among the first to be dropped because of his preexisting conditions. Perhaps by law they couldn't do that openly, but as an American musician in New Hampshire had once told him, they could increase his premium and then tell him in their letter: "We encourage you to shop around for a policy that can suit your needs better." The musician said that for years he'd been made to hop from one insurance company to another. As a result, he'd begun wondering whether he should move to Northern Europe, to Denmark or Norway, where his girlfriend was from originally.

Funi and Tian were seated at the dining table, drinking green tea. His medical expenses could easily have bankrupted him if he had not been covered by the Massachusetts universal care. He had seen the horrendous cost of his treatment. One bill, which included the MRI, showed that for a single day in the hospital he had been charged more than twenty-three thousand dollars. Now, if he was no longer covered, who could tell what might happen when he had a relapse? In fact, just his regular checkups, once every three months now, would cost a fortune; a CT scan alone came to twenty-seven hundred dollars. What could he do to protect himself?

Funi seemed to have detected his worry, her eyes fixed on him. Then she smiled and said, "I have an idea, but don't get mad at me if you don't like it, all right?"

"Of course I won't. Let me hear it."

"Why don't we get married? As long as I work, I can have decent benefits that will cover you."

He was astonished, uncertain how to respond. "I'm a sick man," he managed to say. "I might die any day. You shouldn't have to carry around a heavy piece of baggage like me."

"If you died, I wouldn't mind being your widow for the rest of my life. You know how I love you. I'm happy to do whatever I can for you. If you think we should get married to preempt any insurance problems, let's do that."

"You want kids, but I might not be able to give you any. I'm too sick, if not too old."

"A big family is my dream, but I'll be happy to give up that for you. Besides, who knows, maybe you can have a long life and we may even raise a family. Anyways, I will accompany you from now on so we can grow old together."

He was touched. He paused for a moment to fight down the hot lump expanding in his throat. Then he said deliberately, in a solemn voice like a priest's, "Yu Funi, do you take this man, Yao Tian, to be your husband?"

"Yes, I do!" She tittered, then laughed.

He laughed too, though his eyes blurred, welling.

That night they went to bed together for the first time since he'd fallen ill. He found her body remarkably muscular, due to the physical work she did every day. Her firm flesh and smooth skin exuded health. They made love and slept soundly afterward.

He woke before her, and with her breathing softly beside him, he thought about their imminent marriage; they planned to file an application for the license at City Hall that morning. They wanted to make it as simple as possible and avoid drawing any attention. He was amazed by his eagerness to join Funi in holy matrimony. Emotionally he must have been stunted to some degree, fearful of getting deeply involved with anyone. With his heart closed, he couldn't trust any woman completely, always afraid of being used or misused. That might explain why he hadn't really loved anyone for a long time. Indeed, he had once loved Shuna enough to marry her, but their feelings had soon cooled and their individual pursuits took them further apart and eventually separated them altogether. Funi was different from others. He couldn't say he loved her passionately, but he trusted her unconditionally and cherished her as part of his life, which he could no longer imagine without her.

After they got the marriage license from City Hall, they gave a small wedding dinner at Marine Garden, mainly for Funi's relatives: Frank, Sami, and their children. Tingting and Jawei also came. Funi's boss, Hank, and his wife, Connie, were invited too. Hank, the owner of two supermarkets and well respected in the Chinese community, was happy to join them, and Connie kept remarking that she'd finally met Tian in person. She'd seen him on TV, but hadn't thought he was such a normal man. He guessed she meant he was unassuming, yet he was pleased by her candid words. At the end of the dinner, Funi's boss signed their marriage license.

They didn't invite any of his friends to their wedding dinner—Tian didn't have many in the Boston area. But he notified them of his marriage and received congratulations from Tan Mai and Cindy Wong. As he had expected, Yabin said he would come to join them for a day or two.

On the weekend after Thanksgiving, he drove all the way from

New York in a midnight-blue BMW. Tian and Funi were delighted to see him. To their surprise, he looked aged despite his bright and lively outfit; he was more middle-aged than the man Tian had last seen two years before. He even had incipient eye bags. In the back of Tian's mind echoed the common saying "a man is a flower in his forties," which means that most men reach their prime when they turn forty. Yabin was only forty-four, but already like a withered flower. "I didn't expect him to have aged so much," he said to Funi while Yabin was out to hang the parking permit in his car.

She giggled and said, "Even a playboy can get old quickly. He must've lived a fast life these past two years."

"Or maybe Laura squeezed a lot out of him."

"That was his own doing. He had to pay something for the money he got from her, I guess."

Since Yabin was fond of Tian's cooking, he made a seafood dinner. There were pan-seared scallops and a braised flounder and sautéed soft-shelled crabs. They also opened a bottle of chardonnay, which Yabin loved, but neither Funi nor Tian could drink much. He was the first guest they had invited to their place as a married couple. He was pleased to hear that.

Over oolong tea, he talked about his life in New York. Funi and Tian were surprised to hear that he was single now. "How about Freda?" Tian asked.

"Freda is a bitch," Yabin said. "She hates my guts, but she's my rep in China."

"She's very capable and can help you a lot in your business," Tian told him.

"Yes, she's capable all right, a hard-nosed businesswoman now."

"She won't come back to you?" Funi asked.

"She gives me a toothache."

Funi and Tian laughed uneasily. But what happened to his ladies' man's charm? they asked him teasingly.

"I'm tired of ladies," he said with a feeble sigh.

"You don't like women anymore?" Funi asked, perplexed.

He shook his head of wavy hair streaked with gray and said, "Here's the enigma of life. I used to believe that if I had enough money, I'd have a life full of leisure and without worries. Now I have enough money, but there're more worries than before."

"What are you worried about?" Funi asked.

"About losing money." He smirked with self-mockery. "A good number of women have been eager to move in with me and some want to marry me, but I can trust none of them. I'm never sure if they have an eye on my money."

Funi and Tian both laughed. He said to Yabin, "Can't you just date some new woman and see where things go with her?"

"I'm no longer a young man. I want to settle down and raise a family. But the young women I like don't have marriage in mind. I'm stuck in a way."

"It's a happy dilemma." Tian tried to console him.

"You can say that—you already have a grown daughter. In five or six years I'll be fifty. I really mustn't play the field any longer."

Funi said, "I'm sure you can find the right woman willing to start a family with you. Just keep your eyes open and be patient."

He nodded appreciatively. He was in an import-and-export business now, mostly wines and liquors. He had his own storehouse and a staff of eleven. Professionally speaking, he was a successful businessman, but he confessed that everything he'd done was just a job. He didn't have his own passion, not knowing what he really liked, though he knew it was no longer female charm and fancy cars. He drove a BMW only because most of his associates also owned luxury cars. He was just tired of everything.

He wanted to smoke, so Tian accompanied him out. Together they took a stroll toward the cemetery. Tian was wearing a green down jacket Funi had bought for him, and Yabin was in a light parka coat with a CANADA GOOSE label on the upper arm. A faint odor was in the air, left by a skunk. Clumps of leaves were gathered against the curbs of the sidewalk here and there, and Yabin's Italian brogues crunched on them softly. It was overcast, the breeze a little chilly. He took a drag on his Camel cigarette and said, "Tian, you're lucky, do you know that?"

"Lucky for what?"

"To marry a young wife you can completely trust. Lately I've come to understand why people say they prefer pets to humans. In this world what's the most difficult to come by is a human being you can absolutely trust. Do cherish Funi, even though she isn't beautiful like your ex-wife."

"I will of course," Tian said. "I can take her as part of myself."

"That's what I admire most in a genuine marriage, the mutual understanding and support. And of course the love."

Tian wasn't sure his friend really understood their marriage, but Yabin obviously spoke from his heart, which was rare for a man like him. Tian picked up the topic Yabin had dropped at dinner, and asked, "So you're having trouble with Freda now? Doesn't she already have a Russian boyfriend, a rookie chef who traveled around?"

"That's old news, Tian. She broke up with the Russian guy when he went back to Vladivostok. Now she's my rep in my beverage business on the mainland, where American wines and beers sell very well. Freda gets commissions from the sales there. I know she hates me at heart, and I wish I didn't have to use her, but she's indispensable for my business."

"I can't imagine how you two can work together if you don't get along."

"In the beginning I tried to be nice to her, but it was hard going, like a cracked bowl—no matter how well you mend it, the crack is always there. So far we have managed because there's money to make."

"Does that mean you two can't have a real relationship like before?"

"Well, like I said, she's difficult. But to be fair, she said you'd made the right decision to marry Funi."

"Really? My daughter told me she said I had no taste in women."

"That was what she thought in the beginning. She gradually came to see that you and Funi suited each other well. She also said even if she loved you, she couldn't have been as devoted as Funi, and she would have tried her best to bring you back to China. She believed your ex-wife had betrayed and ruined you."

That reminded Tian of the same headstrong Freda, who would

never change her conviction. He asked Yabin, "Will she come back to the States eventually?"

"I don't think so. She claims her roots are in China and she won't leave our motherland. She's the same crackpot and more of a braggart now, plus a little pinko," said Yabin, dropping the term for a young patriotic zealot.

Tian said, "As long as she's there, she can be more useful to you."

"She has become a first-rate businesswoman. But she's also an old maid now, a typical 'leftover lady,' and seems to hate men categorically."

Tian felt that was overstated, but he didn't counter his friend.

On the distant beach two teenagers, a boy and a girl, were flinging a scarlet Frisbee. Beyond them the bay was still and boatless. Thick cumulus clouds floated above, some gliding and some bouncing.

Before Yabin left the next morning, he gave Funi a small envelope containing twenty hundred-dollar bills as a wedding gift. He told her, "I have no idea what you and Tian really need, so let me leave you this as a present. Please take good care of Tian. He'll be a model husband for you and will make you proud."

She nodded and thanked him.

50

A s long as you have no regrets, you shouldn't be afraid of death. That was what Tian had learned in the period of struggling between life and death. But he did have his regret, a deep one. He still wanted to sing, but his voice was no longer strong enough. This often made him ponder what to do.

Teaching his young voice students was a different kind of work. There wasn't the transcendent feeling of performance; he sang only to demonstrate techniques to his students. It was just routine work, though he was glad he could make a living. He charged each of them seventy dollars an hour. Their parents were pleased about the price, especially after seeing the progress their children had made. Among his students there was a teenager named Walter Lucero, whose mother was Chinese and father Dominican. Walter had a big deep voice and sang in a church choir, but his mother insisted he study with Tian in hopes that he would become a professional. That was the boy's ambition too. Tian was fond of Walter and paid extra attention to teaching him, expanding the range of his voice and developing his ability to sing various styles. Walter came to his lessons punctually and prepared without fail.

Sometimes Tian felt restless with his yearning to sing at full pitch, but he dared not. Dr. Rabb had advised him not to strain his voice—if he had to sing, he should sing moderately to avoid hurting his lungs. Thanks partly to his itching desire to perform, he began to write song lyrics, which might be set to music if they were good enough. He didn't know much about composition but he knew enough songs to sense what might work well.

He was a novice in songwriting, but as an experienced singer, he could tell what words would sound best. Sometimes he could write two songs in a day. He wanted his songs to have an edge, with words that had teeth, socially resonant and relatable. One of them bore the very title "Edges." It went:

> How is even my last edge gone?
> I tighten my belt every day
> But my waistline keeps growing.
> My face has lost its youthful color.
> Heavens, why is it so pudgy
> With all the sharp angles dulled?
>
> Since when did I become a round man,
> Every part of me smooth like a ball,
> Even my tongue glib with words
> Of caution and rules?
>
> From today on I will master the art of hunger
> And let myself shrink to my original size.
> I will shed all the extra weight
> To make my limbs move with ease.
> All my edges will surface again.

He sent some of his lyrics to Yabin and Tan Mai. Mai was impressed by them and offered to set a few to music. This pleased him greatly—she was one of the best composers he had known. She loved his short song "The Ostrich Spirit," though he had misgivings about how to sing such a sardonic piece:

> When trouble is coming
> I turn around and bury my head in sand.
> My eyes cannot see in the dark,
> My ears hear only silence.

Let others run the danger
So I can survive unharmed.

Ow, don't kick my rump!
Don't cut my neck with your machete!
Good man, I am too thin for your plate,
Not enough for a hamburger.

He also wrote some lyrics with the current global situation in mind. China had grown so strong economically in recent years that Western democracies had begun retreating from their fundamental principles so that they could make more profits. Some Western dignitaries were now being paid a quarter of a million dollars to speak at Chinese conventions, and, as a result, personal interests undermined their moral integrity. It was time to remind people that democracy must not retreat any further, or the Chinese government would export its system of digital autocracy to control and dominate the world.

Another song he was proud of also had some social resonance. It was called "Wings of Butterflies" and Tan Mai found it quite evocative. It went like this:

In the eyes of the powerful
We are just a swarm of butterflies,
Feeble without a voice
And no harm to anyone.

Now is the time to flap our wings together.
From our tiny motions a storm is gathering
And it will cross the ocean to throw
A hurricane on another shore.

Oh butterflies, go on flapping your wings.
Your little motions will shake
Many evil kingdoms far away
And topple them one after another.

Tan Mai assured him that she'd do her best to create appropriate music for the lyrics, and she also encouraged him to work to gain his voice back. She hoped that eventually he could perform his own songs. But to his mind, his own performance was less important than the songs themselves. If made well enough, they would find singers on their own wings.

Tan Mai came to visit. She hadn't yet met Funi, and she wanted to come and show her friendship and support for Tian's new marriage. She and Tian also had some business to discuss—the music she'd composed for his lyrics. In her music she often drew on the traditional Chinese teahouses in the countryside of the Yangtze delta; at those small public gatherings, comedians and storytellers entertained a familiar audience. Mai wanted to convey the lively atmosphere in her music, to make it irreverent and funny. She put in a small gong that would produce a crisp, jolly rhythm. The playful elements she created suited his comic lyrics well. Hearing her hum the melodies and beat the gong she'd brought along, he could tell that the music would animate his lines, infusing them with more drama.

As he and Tan Mai were comparing notes in the living room, Funi brought in lunch in foam boxes, which contained crepes stuffed with various fillings: chicken, fish, beef, vegetables. She'd bought them from an eatery inside Kam Man Food. Funi very much liked Tan Mai, who had presented her with a set of stainless-steel pots, five pieces in total, as a wedding present. Tian was amused to sec such an accomplished artist concerned with cookware. Tan Mai must be a good mother and a devoted wife. He respected her all the more for those roles as well.

"You should eat while the food is still warm," Funi told Tan Mai and Tian. Then she took four cups out of the dishwasher and turned to the refrigerator for orange juice and cider.

His daughter happened to be in his room, so he called her out for lunch. Tingting came over and helped Funi place napkins and plates on the table. As they munched on the crepes, Tan Mai seemed to enjoy every bite, but Tian still couldn't eat chicken and was having fish instead. During his chemotherapy, he'd eaten only chicken sandwiches for lunch in the infusion room, and as a result, he couldn't tolerate the taste of chicken now.

Tan Mai and Tingting started chatting about American campus life. Tan Mai, looking like a typical auntie now, had two sons in college, the older one at Carnegie Mellon majoring in finance, and the younger one a freshman at UCLA. Tian was afraid Funi might feel left out, so from time to time he tried to bring her into their conversation, but his efforts only felt intrusive.

"How old are you?" Tan Mai asked Tingting.

"Almost twenty-one," his daughter replied, smiling.

"My older son is twenty-two, a senior. How about being my son's girlfriend? I'd love to have you as my daughter-in-law someday."

Tingting blushed and dropped her eyes. "Well, Mai," Funi said, joining in at last, "it's so nice of you to say that, but Tingting already has a boyfriend, an excellent guy."

"Oh, I didn't mean to put you on the spot, Tingting," Tan Mai said. "My son has a girlfriend actually, but I'm sure they won't be together for long. That girl is too pampered, like a princess. She won't lift a finger to help me in my home, and my son must dance to her whistle. Worst of all, she came here from Shanghai originally when she was seven, and now she only speaks English. I really hope my son marries someone who speaks Mandarin so he can learn it too. Right now, he can't even communicate with his grandparents!"

"You shouldn't interfere too much with your son's life," Tian said cautiously.

"I'm his mother and ought to be worried about him. If you come to New York, Tingting, please visit us."

"I will, Auntie," said the girl.

Tan Mai was staying with her uncle in Newton. She was even driving the old man's car. As Tian went down to see her out, she said to him, "I'm so happy for you, Tian. Undoubtedly Funi loves you and will make you a good wife. Don't you feel like you're getting a second life?"

"I do," he said. "It's also because of you, helping me as a composer."

"We're a team. I make music for your lyrics because I love them."

"Thank you!" He couldn't say more. Instead he placed his hand on his heart and let it remain there.

"I like your daughter. You're lucky to have two young women around you."

"Well, you could say that."

Tan Mai slid into her uncle's Lincoln and pulled away. It was good that she had driven over rather than taking the train, because lately a heavy snowstorm had partly disabled the train service. For almost a week the Red Line was replaced by buses from Quincy Center to downtown Boston. Every sidewalk was banked with snow, some places as high as seven feet. People, especially senior citizens, had been talking about moving south to escape the New England winter and ice.

Tian often reflected on his partnership with Tan Mai, feeling it might be something preordained by a mysterious power beyond his perception. Over the years he'd met numerous accomplished musicians and composers—how come Tan Mai was the only one who had become a close friend and collaborator? This was a great stroke of fortune for him, like a miracle. By any means he had to cherish and nurture their friendship, now so essential for his artistic survival and growth. He hoped he would be able to collaborate with her for a long time to come.

He'd been taking turmeric and vitamins and fish oil religiously every day. Whenever he had pain in his body, Funi would give him cupping to relieve it. They'd found a new way of doing this, after watching on YouTube a doctor of traditional Chinese medicine in Guangzhou. The woman pierced the skin of her patients' sore spots so that the cups could improve the blood circulation in those areas more effectively. Funi performed cupping on Tian in a similar fashion, which bit by bit drew the extravasated blood from his body. He believed that this also prevented excess fluid from building up inside him, which could be a fatal symptom for victims of internal cancer. He told Dr. Rabb and Samantha about his cupping treatment. They remarked that the great swimmer Michael Phelps, among other American athletes, had used cupping to relieve his muscle pain and fatigue, so they didn't disapprove, as long as it reduced Tian's symptoms.

His most recent checkup showed that his cancer was in remission. The tumors were dead, having left only scars, and there was no new growth. Dr. Rabb told him, "From now on, you will have a checkup every six months. Your condition is stabilized and I must say that your family has done a great job."

Indeed, without Funi and Tingting and Jawei, he couldn't possibly have survived the treatment. He asked Dr. Rabb, "Does this mean I'm cancer-free now?"

"You're on your way to that goal. We will keep a close eye on you. You will be all right."

Tian often traded information with Mr. Bao, whose liver cancer was completely under control; he was down to a single annual checkup now. He told Tian on the phone, "When they give you only an annual checkup, that means your cancer is basically cured. They call you someone 'with a history of cancer.'"

Tian asked, "Does that mean cancer-free?"

"Not really. It means you are no longer a cancer patient. Tian, you must take heart. I bet, now that you've looked death in the eye, you are a wiser man than two years ago, and you know how to live a better life."

That was true. The life-and-death experience had given him clarity, and finally he could see what was really valuable. He was no longer worried about small gains and losses and wanted to live a meaningful life on his own terms.

CODA

51

THE NEXT SPRING he and Funi bought a new apartment in Quincy Center. It was a renovated condo in a former nursing home that had fallen into disuse long before. They liked the brick exterior and the solid structure of the building, so they decided to buy the unit when it was up for sale. It was small, less than seven hundred square feet, but enough for the two of them. Funi and he had come up with the down payment together. In fact, they had a joint bank account now. Every time he got a paycheck, he would hand it to her. She handled their financial matters—compared to him, she was better at balancing books and making budgets work. In every way they lived like an established couple. Their life had become uneventful.

Meanwhile his songs had gained popularity—some were now widely performed in the Chinese diaspora. Both Tan Mai and he were listed as the songwriters, she the composer and he the lyricist. Thus far, they had been selling sheet music mainly. Recently a recording company had approached them and offered to produce an album of the songs, twelve in total. He agreed to sing just one of them, "Wings of Butterflies." He would keep writing to the very end of his life in hopes of making a few great songs.

What pleased him more was that Tingting and Jawei were no longer talking about going back to China—the young man's father had urged him to stay on after college. The old man had lost his think tank, disbanded by the government on the grounds that the institute had "harbored many pro-Western thinkers," some of whom even ran websites for foreign NGOs. Jawei would pursue graduate work in biochemistry in the States, probably toward a PhD. Tian told them that he hoped they would both immigrate. Since he was a U.S. citizen, Tingting was qualified for immigration as long as she was unmarried. She and Jawei agreed to start the process without delay. Once she had a green card, they'd marry so that he could apply for it too.

Tian continued to work on his singing. His memory was improving and he could sing an entire song without pausing to recall the lyrics. Yet he could see that he couldn't possibly become a professional singer again. This awareness made him more determined to write better songs. He translated some of his songs into English, hoping they'd reach a wider audience. His teaching was going well. There were more applicants than he could accept. Right now he had seven students and would maintain such a number. Walter Lucero had been with Tian for one and a half years now and had just formed a small band of his own—they mainly played rock. In addition to singing, he also strummed the guitar and piped the bamboo flute. Tian could tell he was a well-rounded talent. Sometimes his band performed at local bars and community gatherings.

One early summer day Walter invited Tian to attend the opening of a bar in the South End. His band was going to play there, and he said Tian's presence would mean a lot to him and his bandmates. Tian agreed to come and even sing for them. Usually he went out alone or with a friend or two in the evenings—Funi disliked mixing with others at bars and public gatherings. Probably she also meant to give him more freedom. He had once joked that he might hit on someone without her around, but Funi only said, "I wouldn't mind if you have another woman. As long as she's good to you I'd have no problem with that."

Her words shamed him. He said in earnest, "I was just joking. You're the only one who can share my pain, who suffers and hurts for me. You can trust me that I'll be with you forever."

"I've known that since day one."

He wasn't sure what she meant by "day one." Did she mean the night they'd gone to bed together for the first time? Or the day they had applied for the marriage license? Or even the day they'd first met? He didn't ask her, moved by her absolute trust in him.

The bar where Walter's band was playing was decked with colorful Christmas lights, as if a holiday celebration was under way. The atmosphere was convivial and exuberant. Walter and his friends were already performing in full swing when Tian arrived. He ordered a ginger ale and took a seat near the back of the bar, but Walter caught sight of him and waved. After finishing the music, he stood and announced: "Ladies and gentlemen, we are honored to have a distinguished guest among us tonight. Mr. Yao is a great singer and also my teacher. He has taught me not only how to sing professionally but also how to work and act like a good man. Tonight he's going to sing for us one of his own songs. Please welcome Mr. Yao Tian."

Amidst the scattered applause he went over and turned to the audience. More people were gathering around now. He said, "I'm going to sing a new song of mine, 'My Heart Will Not Be Tamed.' The music was written by my friend Tan Mai, who is a marvelous composer and a virtuoso pi-pa player. I wrote the lyrics in Chinese originally, but then translated it into English for this occasion. The band and I rehearsed it today, and I hope we can do it right for you."

The band began and he swallowed, then sang:

> Some say I'm too stubborn.
> Stubborn in my dreams and my goals
> But that won't change no matter what I face.
>
> I'm a man of bygone days,
> Already out of season,
> Out of place in this climate.
> Still I dream of blooming in winter—
> Even snow cannot freeze my heart.
>
> My heart will not be tamed.
> It will soar with my songs to the sky,
> Like a bird without bounds
> Treading only air and sun.

As he sang, he was touched to the verge of tears, more by his words than by his voice, which at times shook.

Walter and his bandmates cheered the instant he finished. Tian kept saying "Thank you" while stepping off the bandstand. He headed for the back of the room so that he could gather himself. But people wouldn't leave him alone. A potbellied gentleman holding a glass of red wine came up to him and said, "That was a wonderful song, Mr. Yao! One of the best I've heard in a long time. Can I buy you a drink?"

Walter stepped in, a smile lengthening his face a little, and he told the man, "My teacher has a lung problem and can't drink alcohol."

"I could have a nonalcoholic beer," Tian said.

The man ordered one for him. With its mouth foaming, the beer bottle touched the wineglass.

"Cheers!" Tian cried, and took a swallow.

ACKNOWLEDGMENTS

My heartfelt thanks to LuAnn Walther, Catherine Tung, Lane Zachary, and Ellie Pritchett for their generous support and steady effort in making this a better book.

Ha Jin left his native China in 1985 to attend Brandeis University. He is the author of eight novels, four story collections, four volumes of poetry, a biography of Li Bai entitled *The Banished Immortal,* and a book of essays. He has received the National Book Award, two PEN/Faulkner Awards, the PEN/Hemingway Foundation Award, the Asian American Literary Award, and the Flannery O'Connor Award for Short Fiction. In 2014 he was elected to the American Academy of Arts and Letters. He lives in the Boston area and is a professor in the creative writing program at Boston University.

A NOTE ON THE TYPE

This book was set in Celeste, a typeface created in 1994 by the designer Chris Burke (b. 1967). He describes it as a modern, humanistic face having less contrast between thick and thin strokes than other modern types such as Bodoni, Didot, and Walbaum. Tempered by some old-style traits and with a contemporary, slightly modular letterspacing, Celeste is highly readable and especially adapted for current digital printing processes which render an increasingly exacting letterform.

Typeset by Scribe, Philadelphia, Pennsylvania
Printed and bound by Berryville Graphics, Berryville, Virginia
Designed by Maggie Hinders